A Torch
AGAINST THE
Night

SABAA TAHIR

HARPER
Voyager

HarperVoyager
An imprint of HarperCollinsPublishers Ltd
1 London Bridge Street
London SE1 9GF

www.harpercollins.co.uk

This paperback edition 2018
10

First published by HarperCollinsPublishers 2016

Maps by Jonathan Roberts

Sabaa Tahir asserts the moral right to
be identified as the author of this work

A catalogue record for this book is available from the British Library

ISBN: 978-0-00-816037-1

Set in Electra by Palimpsest Book Production Limited, Falkirk, Stirlingshire

Printed and bound in the UK by CPI Group (UK) Ltd, Croydon CR0 4YY

MIX
Paper from
responsible sources
FSC™ C007454

A TORCH AGAINST THE NIGHT

Sabaa Tahir is the *New York Times* best-selling author of AN EMBER IN THE ASHES, which has been published in thirty-four languages.

She grew up in California's Mojave Desert at her family's eighteen-room motel. There, she spent her time devouring fantasy novels, raiding her brother's comic book stash, and playing guitar badly. She likes thunderous indie rock, garish socks, and all things nerd. Sabaa currently lives in the San Francisco Bay area with her family.

Visit her website at SabaaTahir.com and on Twitter @SabaaTahir

Also by Sabaa Tahir

An Ember in the Ashes
A Torch Against the Night
A Reaper at the Gates

For my mother, my father, Mer, and Boon
All that I am, I owe to you

1. Entry Gate
2. Amphitheatre
3. Armoury
4. Stables
5. Main Training Field
6. Training Field 2
7. Training Field 3
8. 2nd Armoury
9. Commandant's House
10. Cliff Path
11. Centurion Quarters
12. Infirmary
13. Classrooms
14. Storage
15. Main Courtyard
16. Bell Tower/Drum Tower
17. Mess Hall
18. Slaves' Quarters
19. Training Rooms
20. Senior Skull Barracks
21. Skull Barracks
22. Cadet Barracks
23. Yearling Barracks

BLACKCLIFF
ACADEMY

KAUF
PRISON

17

RIVER DUSK

THE EASTERN SEA

Adisa

MARINN

Ayo

DUSKAN
SEA

PART ONE
FLIGHT

CHAPTER ONE

Laia

How did they find us so fast?

Behind me, the catacombs echo with angry shouts and the screech of metal. My eyes dart to the grinning skulls lining the walls. I think I hear the voices of the dead.

Be swift, be fleet, they seem to hiss. *Unless you wish to join our ranks.*

'Faster, Laia,' my guide says. His armor flashes as he hastens ahead of me through the catacombs. 'We'll lose them if we're quick. I know an escape tunnel that leads out of the city. Once we're there, we're safe.'

We hear a scrape behind us, and my guide's pale eyes flick past my shoulder. His hand is a gold-brown blur as it flies to the hilt of a scim slung across his back.

A simple movement full of menace. A reminder that he is not just my guide. He is Elias Veturius, heir to one of the Empire's finest families. He is a former Mask – an elite soldier of the Martial Empire. And he is my ally – the only person who can help me save my brother, Darin, from a notorious Martial prison.

In one step, Elias is beside me. In another, he is in front, moving with unnatural grace for someone so big. Together, we peer down the tunnel we just passed through. My pulse thuds in my ears. Any elation I felt at destroying Blackcliff Academy or rescuing Elias from execution vanishes. The Empire hunts us. If it catches us, we die.

Sweat soaks through my shirt, but despite the rank heat of the tunnels, a chill runs across my skin and the hairs on the back of my neck rise. I think I hear a growl, like that of some sly, hungry creature.

Hurry, my instincts scream at me. *Get out of here.*

'Elias,' I whisper, but he brushes a finger against my lips – *shh* – and tugs a knife free from the half dozen strapped across his chest.

I pull a dagger from my belt and try to hear beyond the clicking of tunnel tarantulas and my own breathing. The prickling sense of being watched fades – replaced by something worse: the smell of pitch and flame; the rise and fall of voices drawing near.

Empire soldiers.

Elias touches my shoulder and points to his feet, then mine. *Step where I step.* So carefully that I fear to breathe, I mimic him as he turns and heads swiftly away from the voices.

We reach a fork in the tunnel and veer right. Elias nods to a deep, shoulder-high hole in the wall, hollow but for a stone coffin turned on its side.

'In,' he whispers, 'all the way to the back.'

I slide into the crypt, suppressing a shudder at the loud *crrrk* of a resident tarantula. A scim that Darin forged hangs across my back, and its hilt clanks loudly against the stone. *Stop fidgeting, Laia – no matter what's crawling around in here.*

Elias ducks into the crypt after me, his height forcing him into a half crouch. In the tight space, our arms brush, and he draws a sharp breath. But when I look up, his face is angled toward the tunnel.

Even in the dim light, the gray of his eyes and the sharp lines of his jaw are striking. I feel a jolt low in my stomach – I'm not used to his face. Only an hour ago, as we escaped the destruction I wrought at Blackcliff, his features were hidden by a silver mask.

He tilts his head, listening as the soldiers close in. They walk quickly, their voices echoing off the walls of the catacombs like the clipped calls of raptor birds.

'—probably went south. If he had half a brain, anyway.'

'If he had half a brain,' a second soldier says, 'he'd have passed the Fourth Trial, and we wouldn't be stuck with Plebeian scum as Emperor.'

The soldiers enter our tunnel, and one pokes his lantern into the crypt across from ours. 'Bleeding hells.' He recoils quickly at the sight of whatever lurks within.

Our crypt is next. My belly twists, my hand shakes on my dagger.

Beside me, Elias releases another blade from its sheath. His shoulders are relaxed, his hands loose around the knives. But when I catch sight of his face – brows furrowed, jaw tight – my heart clenches. He meets my gaze, and for a breath, I see his anguish. He does not wish to deliver death to these men.

But if they see us, they will alert the other guards down here, and we'll be neck-deep in Empire soldiers. I squeeze Elias's forearm. He slides his hood over his head and pulls a black kerchief up to hide his face.

The soldier approaches, his footsteps heavy. I can smell him – sweat and iron and dirt. Elias's grip on his knives tightens. His body is coiled like a wildcat waiting to strike. I clamp a hand onto my armlet – a gift from my mother. Beneath my fingers, the armlet's familiar pattern is a balm.

The soldier reaches the edge of the crypt. He lifts his lantern –

Suddenly, further down the tunnel, a thud echoes. The soldiers spin, draw steel, and hurry to investigate. In seconds, the light from their lantern fades, the sound of their footsteps fainter and fainter.

Elias releases a pent breath. 'Come on,' he says. 'If that patrol was sweeping the area, there will be more. We need to get to the escape passage.'

We emerge from the crypt, and a tremor rumbles through the tunnels, shaking dust loose and sending bones and skulls clattering to the ground. I stumble, and Elias grabs my shoulder, backing me into the wall and flattening himself beside me. The crypt remains intact, but the ceiling of the tunnel cracks ominously.

'What in the skies was that?'

'It felt like a land tremor.' Elias takes a step away from the wall and eyes the ceiling. 'Except Serra doesn't have land tremors.'

We cut through the catacombs with new urgency. With every step I expect to hear another patrol, to see torches in the distance.

When Elias stops, it is so sudden that I barrel into his broad back. We've entered a circular burial chamber with a low, domed ceiling. Two tunnels branch out ahead of us. Torches flicker in one, almost too far away to make out. Crypts pock the chamber walls, each guarded by a stone statue of an armored man. Beneath their helmets, skulls glare out at us. I shiver, stepping closer to Elias.

But he does not look at the crypts, or the tunnels, or the distant torches.

He stares at the little girl in the center of the chamber.

She wears tattered clothing and her hand is pressed to a leaking wound in her side. Her fine features mark her as a Scholar, but when I try to see her eyes, she drops her head, dark hair falling into her face. *Poor thing.* Tears mark a path down her dirt-streaked cheeks.

'Ten hells, it's getting crowded down here,' Elias mutters. He takes a step toward the girl, hands out, as if dealing with a scared animal. 'You shouldn't be here, love.' His voice is gentle. 'Are you alone?'

She lets out a tiny sob. 'Help me,' she whispers.

'Let me see that cut. I can bandage it.' Elias drops to one knee so he's at her level, the way my grandfather did with his youngest patients. She shies away from him and looks toward me.

I step forward, my instincts urging caution. The girl watches. 'Can you tell me your name, little one?' I ask.

'Help me,' she repeats. Something about the way she avoids my eyes makes my skin prickle. But then, she's been ill-treated – likely by the Empire – and now she faces a Martial who is armed to the roots of his hair. She must be terrified.

The girl inches back, and I glance at the torch-lit tunnel. Torches mean we're in Empire territory. It's only a matter of time before soldiers happen by.

'Elias.' I nod at the torches. 'We do not have time. The soldiers—'

'We can't just leave her.' His guilt is plain as day. The deaths of his friends days ago in the Third Trial weigh on him; he doesn't wish to cause another. And we will, if we leave the girl here alone to die of her wounds.

'Do you have family in the city?' Elias asks her. 'Do you need—'

'Silver.' She tilts her head. 'I need silver.'

Elias's eyebrows shoot up. I cannot blame him. It is not what I expected either.

'Silver?' I say. 'We don't—'

'Silver.' She shuffles sideways like a crab. I think I see the too-quick flash of an eye through her limp hair. *Strange.* 'Coins. A weapon. Jewelry.'

She glances at my neck, my ears, my wrists. With that look, she gives herself away.

I stare at the tar-black orbs where her eyes should be, and scrabble for my dagger. But Elias is already in front of me, scims glimmering in his hands.

'Back away,' he snarls at the girl, every inch a Mask.

'Help me.' The girl lets her hair fall into her face once more and puts her hands behind her back, a twisted caricature of a wheedling child. 'Help.'

At my clear disgust, her lips curl in a sneer that looks obscene on her otherwise sweet face. She growls – the guttural sound I heard earlier. *This* is what I sensed watching us. *This* is the presence I felt in the tunnels.

'I know you have silver.' A rabid hunger underlies the creature's little-girl voice. 'Give it to me. I *need* it.'

'Get away from us,' Elias says. 'Before I take off your head.'

The girl – or whatever it is – ignores Elias and fixes her eyes on me. 'You don't need it, little human. I'll give you something in return. Something wonderful.'

'What *are* you?' I whisper.

She whips her arms out, her hands gleaming with a strange viridescence. Elias flies toward her, but she evades him and fastens her fingers on my wrist. I scream, and my arm glows for less than a second before she is flung backward, howling, clutching her hand as if it is on fire. Elias pulls me to my feet from the dirt where I am sprawled, pitching a dagger at the girl at the same time. She dodges it, still shrieking.

'Tricky girl!' She darts away as Elias lunges for her again, her eyes only for me. 'Sly one! You ask what am I, but what are *you*?'

Elias swings at her, sliding one of his scims across her neck. He's not fast enough.

'Murderer!' She whirls on him. 'Killer! Death himself! Reaper walking! If your sins were blood, child, you would drown in a river of your own making.'

Elias reels back, shock etched into his eyes. Light flickers in the tunnel. Three torches bob swiftly toward us.

'Soldiers coming.' The creature whirls to face me. 'I'll kill them for you, honey-eyed girl. Lay their throats open. I already led away the others following you, back in the tunnel. I'll do it again. *If* you give me your silver. He wants it. He'll reward us if we bring it to him.'

Who in the skies is he? I don't ask, only bring up my dagger in response.

'Stupid human!' The girl clenches her fists. 'He'll get it from you. He'll find a way.' She turns toward the tunnel. 'Elias Veturius!' I flinch. Her scream is so loud they probably heard her in Antium. 'Elias Vetu—'

Her words die as Elias's scim rips through her heart. '*Efrit efrit of the cave,*' he says. Her body slides off the weapon and lands with a solid thump, like a boulder falling. '*Likes the dark but fears the blade.*'

'Old rhyme.' He sheathes his scim. 'Never realized how handy it was until recently.'

Elias grabs my hand, and we bolt into the unlit tunnel. Maybe through some miracle, the soldiers didn't hear the girl. Maybe they didn't see us. *Maybe, maybe* –

No such luck. I hear a shout and the thunder of bootsteps behind us.

CHAPTER TWO

Elias

Three auxes and four legionnaires, fifteen yards behind us. As I race ahead, I whip my head around to gauge their progress. Make that six auxes, five legionnaires, and twelve yards.

More of the Empire's soldiers will pour into the catacombs with every second that passes. By now, a runner has carried the message to neighboring patrols, and the drums will spread the alert throughout Serra: *Elias Veturius spotted in the tunnels. All squads respond.* The soldiers don't need to be sure of my identity; they will hunt us down regardless.

I take a sharp left down a side tunnel, pulling Laia with me, my mind careening from thought to thought. *Shake them off quickly, while you still can. Otherwise . . .*

No, the Mask within hisses. *Stop and kill them. Only eleven of them. Easy. Could do it with your eyes closed.*

I should have killed the efrit in the burial chamber straightaway. Helene would scoff if she knew I'd tried to help the creature instead of recognizing it for what it was.

Helene. I'd bet my blades she's in an interrogation room by

10

now. Marcus – or Emperor Marcus, as he's now called – ordered her to execute me. She failed. Worse, she was my closest confidante for fourteen years. Neither of those sins will come without cost – not now that Marcus possesses absolute power.

She will suffer at his hands. Because of me. I hear the efrit again. *Reaper walking!*

Memories of the Third Trial jolt through my head. Tristas dying upon Dex's sword. Demetrius falling. Leander falling.

A shout from ahead returns me to myself. *The field of battle is my temple.* My grandfather's old mantra comes back to me when I need it most. *The swordpoint is my priest. The dance of death is my prayer. The killing blow is my release.*

Beside me, Laia pants, her body dragging. She is slowing me down. *You could leave her*, an insidious voice whispers. *You'd move faster on your own.* I crush the voice. Besides the obvious fact that I promised to help her in exchange for my freedom, I know that she'll do anything to get to Kauf Prison – to her brother – including trying to make her way there alone.

In which case, she'd die.

'Faster, Laia,' I say. 'They're too close.' She surges forward. Walls of skulls, bones, crypts, and spiderwebs fade away on either side of us. We're far south of where we should be. We've long since passed the escape tunnel in which I hid weeks' worth of supplies.

The catacombs rumble and shake, knocking both of us down. The stench of fire and death filters through a sewer grate directly above us. Moments later, an explosion rips through the air. I don't bother considering what it could be. All that matters is that the soldiers behind us have slowed, as wary of the unstable tunnels as we are. I use the opportunity to put another few dozen yards between us. I cut right into a side tunnel and then retreat into the deep shadow of a half-crumbled alcove.

'Will they find us, do you think?' Laia whispers.

'Hopefully no—'

Light flares from the direction we were headed, and I hear the staccato clomp of boots. Two soldiers turn into the tunnel, their torches illuminating us clearly. They halt for a second, bewildered, perhaps, by the presence of Laia, by my lack of a mask. Then they spot my armor and scims, and one of them releases a piercing whistle that will draw in every soldier who can hear it.

My body takes over. Before either of the soldiers can unsheathe their swords, I've impaled throwing knives into the soft flesh of their throats. They drop silently, their torches sputtering on the damp catacomb floor.

Laia emerges from the alcove, her hand over her mouth. 'E-Elias—'

I lunge back to the alcove, pulling her with me and loosening my scims in their scabbards. I have four throwing knives left. *Not enough.*

'I'll take out as many as I can,' I say. 'Stay out of the way. No matter how bad it looks, don't interfere, don't try to help.'

The last word leaves my lips as the soldiers who were following us come into view from the tunnel to our left. Five yards away. Four. In my mind, the knives have already flown, already found their marks. I burst from the alcove and let them loose. The first four legionnaires go down quietly, one after the other, as easy as scything grain. The fifth drops with a sweep of my scim. Warm blood sprays, and I feel my bile rising. *Don't think. Don't dwell. Just clear the way.*

Six auxes appear behind the first five. One jumps onto my back, and I dispatch him with an elbow to his face. A moment later, another soldier rushes me. When he gets a knee to the teeth, he howls and claws at his broken nose and bloody mouth. *Spin, kick, sidestep, strike.*

Behind me, Laia screams. An aux hauls her out of the alcove by her neck and holds a knife to her throat. His leer turns into a howl. Laia's shoved a dagger into his side. She yanks it out, and he staggers away.

I turn on the last three soldiers. They flee.

In seconds, I collect my knives. Laia's whole body shakes as she takes in the carnage around us: Seven dead. Three injured, moaning and trying to rise.

When she looks at me, her eyes grow round in shock at my bloodied scims and armor. Shame floods me, so potent that I wish I could sink into the ground. She sees me now, down to the wretched truth at my core. *Murderer! Death himself!*

'Laia—' I begin, but a low groan rolls down the tunnel, and the ground trembles. Through the sewer grates I hear screams, shouts, and the deafening reverberation of an enormous explosion.

'What in the hells—'

'It's the Scholar Resistance,' Laia shouts over the noise. 'They're revolting!'

I don't get to ask how she happens to know this fascinating tidbit, because at that moment, telltale silver flashes from the tunnel to our left.

'Skies, Elias!' Laia's voice is choked, her eyes wide. One of the Masks approaching is enormous, older than me by a dozen years and unfamiliar. The other is a small, almost diminutive figure. The calmness of her masked face belies the chilling rage that emanates from her.

My mother. The Commandant.

Boots thunder from our right as whistles draw even more soldiers. *Trapped.*

The tunnel groans again.

'Get behind me,' I snap at Laia. She doesn't hear. 'Laia, damn it, get – *ooof*—'

Laia dives straight into my stomach, a graceless, desperate leap so unexpected that I topple back into one of the wall crypts. I punch straight through the thick cobwebbing over the crypt and land on my back atop a stone coffin. Laia's half on top of me, half wedged between the coffin and the crypt wall.

The combination of cobwebs, crypt, and warm girl throws me, and I'm barely even capable of stuttering, 'Are you cra—'

BOOM. The ceiling of the tunnel we were just standing in collapses all at once, a thunderous rumble intensified by the roar of explosions from the city. I flip Laia under me, my arms on either side of her head to shield her from the blast. But it is the crypt that saves us. We cough from the wave of dust unleashed by the explosions, and I'm keenly aware that if not for Laia's quick thinking, we'd both be dead.

The rumbling stops, and sunlight cuts through the dust. Screams echo from the city. Carefully, I lift myself away from Laia and turn toward the crypt entrance, which is half-blocked by chunks of rock. I peer out into what's left of the tunnel. Which isn't much. The cave-in is complete – not a Mask to be seen.

I scramble out of the crypt, half dragging, half carrying a still-coughing Laia over the debris. Dust and blood – not hers, I affirm – streak her face, and she paws at her canteen. I put it to her lips. After a few swallows, she pulls herself standing.

'I can – I can walk.'

Rocks obstruct the tunnel to our left, but a mailed hand shoves them away. The Commandant's gray eyes and blonde hair flash through the dust.

'Come on.' I pull up my collar to hide the Blackcliff diamond tattoo on the back of my neck. We clamber out of the ruined catacombs and into the cacophonous streets of Serra.

Ten bleeding hells.

No one appears to have noticed the collapse of the street into the crypts – everyone is too busy staring at a column of fire rising into the hot blue sky: the governor's mansion, lit up like a Barbarian funeral pyre. Around its blackening gates and in the immense square in front of it, dozens of Martial soldiers are locked in a pitched battle with hundreds of rebels dressed in black – Scholar Resistance fighters.

'This way!' I angle away from the governor's mansion, knocking down two approaching rebel fighters as I go, and aim for the next street over. But fire rages there, spreading rapidly, and bodies litter the ground. I grab Laia's hand and race toward another side street, only to find that it is as brutalized as the first.

Above the clang of weapons, the screams, and the roar of flames, Serra's drum towers beat frenziedly, demanding backup troops in the Illustrian Quarter, the Foreign Quarter, the Weapons Quarter. Another tower reports my location near the governor's mansion, ordering all available troops to join the hunt.

Just past the mansion, a pale blonde head emerges from the debris of the collapsed tunnel. *Damn it.* We stand near the middle of the square, beside an ash-coated fountain of a rearing horse. I back Laia against it and duck, desperately searching for an escape route before the Commandant or one of the Martials spots us. But it seems as if every building and every street adjoining the square is aflame.

Look harder! Any second now, the Commandant will dive into the fray in the square, using her terrifying skill to tear a path through the battle so she can find us.

I look back at her as she shakes the dust off her armor, unmoved by the chaos. Her serenity raises the hair on the back of my neck. Her school is destroyed, her son and foe escaped, the city an absolute disaster. And yet she is remarkably calm about it all.

'There!' Laia grabs my arm and points to an alley hidden behind an overturned vendor's cart. We crouch down and race toward it, and I thank the skies for the tumult that keeps Scholars and Martials alike from noticing us.

In minutes, we reach the alley, and as we're about to plunge into it, I chance a look back – once, just to make sure she hasn't seen us.

I search the chaos – through a knot of Resistance fighters descending on a pair of legionnaires, past a Mask fighting off ten rebels at once, to the rubble of the tunnel, where my mother stands. An old Scholar slave trying to escape the havoc makes the mistake of crossing her path. She plunges her scim into his heart with a casual brutality. When she yanks the blade out, she doesn't look at the slave. Instead, she stares at me. As if we are connected, as if she knows my every thought, her gaze slices across the square.

She smiles.

CHAPTER THREE

Laia

The Commandant's smile is a bloated, pale worm. Though I see her for only a moment before Elias urges me away from the bloodshed of the square, I find myself unable to speak.

I skid, my boots still coated in blood from the butchery in the tunnels. At the thought of Elias's face afterward – the loathing in his eyes – I shudder. I wanted to tell him that he did what he had to do to save us. But I couldn't get the words out. It was all I could do not to retch.

Sounds of suffering rend the air – Martial and Scholar, adult and child, mingled into one cacophonous scream. I hardly hear it, focused as I am on avoiding the broken glass and burning buildings collapsing into the streets. I look over my shoulder a dozen times, expecting to see the Commandant on our heels. Suddenly, I feel like the girl I was a month ago. The girl who abandoned her brother to Empire imprisonment, the girl who whimpered and sobbed after being whipped. The girl with no courage.

When the fear takes over, use the only thing more powerful, more indestructible, to fight it: your spirit. Your heart. I hear the words spoken to me yesterday by the blacksmith Spiro Teluman, my brother's friend and mentor.

I try to transform my fear into fuel. The Commandant is not infallible. She might not have even seen me – her attention was so fixed on her son. I escaped her once. I'll escape her again.

Adrenaline surges through me, but as we turn from one street to the next, I stumble over a small pyramid of masonry and sprawl onto the soot-blackened cobblestones.

Elias lifts me back to my feet as easily as if I'm made of feathers. He gazes ahead, behind, to the windows and rooftops nearby, as if he too expects his mother to appear at any second.

'We have to keep going.' I yank at his hand. 'We have to get out of the city.'

'I know.' Elias angles us into a dusty, dead orchard bound by a wall. 'But we can't do that if we're exhausted. It won't hurt to rest for a minute.'

He sits, and I kneel beside him unwillingly. The air of Serra feels strange and tainted, the tang of scorched wood mingling with something darker – blood, burning bodies, and unsheathed steel.

'How are we going to get to Kauf, Elias?' This is the question that's plagued me since the moment we slipped into the tunnels from his barracks at Blackcliff. My brother allowed himself to be taken by Martial soldiers so that I'd have a chance to escape. I will not let him die for his sacrifice – he's the only family I have left in this blasted Empire. If I don't save him, no one will. 'Will we hide out in the country? What's the plan?'

Elias regards me steadily, his gray eyes opaque.

'The escape tunnel would have put us west of the city,' he says. 'We'd have taken the mountain passes north, robbed a Tribal caravan, and posed as traders. The Martials wouldn't have been looking for both of us – and they wouldn't have been looking north. But now . . .' He shrugs.

'What's that supposed to mean? Do you even have a plan?'

'I do. We get out of the city. We escape the Commandant. That's the only plan that matters.'

'What about after?'

'One thing at a time, Laia. This is my mother we're dealing with.'

'I'm not afraid of her,' I say, lest he think that I'm the same mouse of a girl he met at Blackcliff weeks ago. 'Not anymore.'

'You should be,' Elias says dryly.

The drums boom out, a barrage of bone-shaking sound. My head pounds with their echo.

Elias cocks his head. 'They're relaying our descriptions,' he says. '*Elias Veturius: gray eyes, six foot four, fifteen stone, black hair. Last seen in tunnels south of Blackcliff. Armed and dangerous. Traveling with Scholar female: gold eyes, five foot six, nine stone, black hair—*' He stops. 'You get the point. They're hunting us, Laia. *She* is hunting us. We don't have a way out of the city. Fear is the wise course right now – it will keep us alive.'

'The walls—'

'Heavily guarded because of the Scholar revolt,' Elias says. 'Worse now, no doubt. She'll have sent messages across the city that we haven't yet cleared the walls. The gates will be doubly fortified.'

'Could we – you – fight our way through? Maybe at one of the smaller gates?'

'We could,' Elias says. 'But it would lead to a lot of killing.'

I understand why he looks away, though the hard, cold part of me born in Blackcliff wonders what difference a few more dead Martials make. Especially in the face of how many he has already killed, and especially when I think of what they're going to do to the Scholars when the rebel revolution is inevitably crushed.

But the better part of me recoils at such callousness. 'The tunnels then?' I say. 'The soldiers won't expect it.'

'We don't know which ones have collapsed, and there's no point going down there if we'll just hit a dead end. The docks, maybe. We could swim the river—'

'I can't swim.'

'Remind me to remedy that when we have a few days.' He shakes his head – we're running out of options. 'We could lie low until the revolution dies down. Then slip into the tunnels after the explosions have stopped. I know a safe house.'

'No,' I say quickly. 'The Empire shipped Darin to Kauf three weeks ago. And those prisoner frigates are fast, are they not?'

Elias nods. 'They'd reach Antium in less than a fortnight. From there, it's a ten-day journey overland to Kauf if they don't run into bad weather. He might already have reached the prison.'

'How long will it take us to get there?'

'We have to go overland *and* avoid detection,' Elias says. 'Three months, if we're swift. But only if we make it to the Nevennes Range before the winter snows. If we don't, we won't get through until spring.'

'Then we cannot delay,' I say. 'Not even by a day.'

I look over my shoulder again, trying to suppress a growing sense of dread. 'She didn't follow us.'

'Not obviously,' Elias says. 'She's too damned clever for that.'

He ponders the dead trees around us, turning a blade over and over in his hand.

'There's an abandoned storage building near the river, up against the city walls,' he finally says. 'Grandfather owns the building – showed it to me years ago. A door in the back courtyard leads out of the city. But I haven't been back in a while. It might not be there anymore.'

'Does the Commandant know of it?'

'Grandfather would never have told her.'

I think of Izzi, my fellow slave at Blackcliff, warning me about the Commandant when I first arrived at the school. *She knows things*, Izzi had said. *Things she shouldn't.*

But we have to get out of the city, and I have no better plan to offer.

We set out, passing swiftly through neighborhoods untouched by the revolution, sneaking painstakingly through those areas where fighting and fire rage. Hours pass, and the afternoon fades to evening. Elias is a calm presence beside me, seemingly unmoved by the sight of so much destruction.

Strange to think that a month ago, my grandparents were alive, my brother was free, and I'd never heard the name Veturius.

Everything that has happened since then is like a nightmare. Nan and Pop murdered. Darin dragged away by soldiers, screaming at me to run.

And the Scholar Resistance offering to help me save my brother, only to betray me.

Another face flashes in my mind, dark-eyed, handsome, and grim – always so grim. It made his smiles more precious. Keenan, the fire-haired rebel who defied the Resistance to secretly give me a way out of Serra. A way out that I, in turn, gave to Izzi.

I hope he's not angry. I hope he'll understand why I could not accept his help.

'Laia,' Elias says as we reach the eastern edge of the city. 'We're close.'

We emerge from the warren of Serra's streets near a Mercator depot. The lonely spire of a brick kiln casts the warehouses and storage yards into deep shadow. During the day, this place must bustle with wagons, merchants, and stevedores. But at this time of night, it's abandoned. An evening chill hints at the changing season, and a steady wind blows from the north. Nothing moves.

'There.' Elias points to a structure built into the walls of Serra, similar to those on either side but for a weed-choked courtyard visible behind it. 'That's the place.'

He observes the depot for long minutes. 'The Commandant wouldn't be able to hide a dozen Masks in there,' he says. 'But I doubt she'd come without them. She wouldn't want to risk me escaping.'

'Are you sure she wouldn't come alone?' The wind blows harder, and I cross my arms and shiver. The Commandant alone is terrifying enough. I'm not sure she needs soldiers to back her up.

'Not positive,' he admits. 'Wait here. I'll make sure it's clear.'

'I think I should come.' I am immediately nervous. 'If something happens—'

'Then you'll survive, even if I don't.'

'What? No!'

'If it's safe for you to join me, I'll whistle one note. If there are soldiers, two notes. If the Commandant is waiting, three notes repeated twice.'

'And if it *is* her? What then?'

'Then sit tight. If I survive, I'll come back for you,' Elias says. 'If not, you'll need to get out of here.'

'Elias, you idiot, I need *you* if I want to get Darin—'

He puts a finger on my lips, drawing my gaze to his.

Ahead of us, the depot is silent. Behind, the city burns. I remember the last time I looked at him like this – just before we kissed. From the taut breath that escapes him, I think he remembers too.

22

'There's hope in life,' he says. 'A brave girl once told me that. If something happens to me, don't fear. You'll find a way.'

Before my doubts creep up again, he drops his hand and flits across the depot as lightly as the dust clouds rising from the brick kiln.

I follow his movements, painfully aware of the flimsiness of this plan. Everything that has happened so far is the result of willpower or sheer, dumb luck. I have no idea how to get safely north, beyond trusting Elias to guide me. I have no sense of what it will take to break into Kauf, beyond hoping that Elias will know what to do. All I have is a voice inside telling me I must save my brother, and Elias's promise that he will help me do so. The rest is just wishes and hope, the most fragile of things.

Not enough. It's not enough. The wind whips my hair about, colder than it should be this late in the summer. Elias disappears into the courtyard of the storage building. My nerves crackle, and though I inhale deeply, I feel as if I cannot get enough air. *Come on. Come on.* The wait for his signal is excruciating.

Then I hear it. So quick that I think for a second that I'm mistaken. I *hope* that I am. But the sound comes again.

Three quick notes. Sharp, sudden, and filled with warning.

The Commandant has found us.

CHAPTER FOUR

Elias

My mother hides her anger with practiced cunning. She wraps it in calm and buries it deep. She tramples the soil on top, puts a gravestone on it, and pretends it's dead.

But I see it in her eyes. Smoldering at the fringes, like the corners of paper blackening just before they burst into flame.

I hate that I share her blood. Would that I could scrub it from my body.

She stands against the dark, high wall of the city, another shadow in the night but for the silver glint of her mask. Beside her is our escape route, a wooden door so covered in dried vines that it's impossible to see. Though she holds no weapons in her hands, her message is clear. *If you wish to leave, you go through me.*

Ten hells. I hope Laia heard my warning whistle. I hope she stays away.

'You took long enough,' the Commandant says. 'I've waited hours.'

She launches herself at me, a long knife appearing so swiftly in her palm that it's as if it popped out of her skin. I dodge her – barely – before lashing out at her with my scims. She dances away

24

from my attack without bothering to cross blades, then flings a throwing star. It misses me by a hair. Before she reaches for another, I rush her, landing a kick to her chest that sends her sprawling.

As she scrambles up, I scan the area for soldiers. The city walls are empty, the rooftops around us bare. Not a sound comes from Grandfather's storage building. Yet I cannot believe that she doesn't have assassins lurking close by.

I hear shuffling to my right, and I lift my scims, expecting an arrow or spear. But it's the Commandant's horse, tethered to a tree. I recognize the Gens Veturia saddle – one of Grandfather's stallions.

'Jumpy.' The Commandant raises a silver eyebrow as she scrambles back to her feet. 'Don't be. I came alone.'

'And why would you do that?'

The Commandant flings more throwing stars at me. As I duck, she darts around a tree and out of range of the knives I send hurtling back at her.

'If you think I need an army to destroy you, boy,' she says, 'you are mis*taken*.'

She flicks opens the neck of her uniform, and I grimace at the sight of the living metal shirt beneath, impenetrable to edged weapons.

Hel's shirt.

'I took it from Helene Aquilla.' The Commandant draws scims and engages my assault with graceful ease. 'Before I gave her to a Black Guard for interrogation.'

'She doesn't know anything.' I dodge my mother's blows while she dances around me. *Get her on the defensive. Then a quick blow to her head to knock her out. Steal the horse. Run.*

A bizarre noise comes from the Commandant as our scims clash, their strange music filling the silence of the depot. After a moment, I realize it is a laugh.

I've never heard my mother laugh. Never.

'I knew you'd come here.' She flies at me with her scims, and I drop beneath her, feeling the wind of her blades centimeters from my face. 'You'd have considered escaping through a city gate. Then the tunnels, the river, the docks. In the end, they were all too troublesome, especially with your little friend tagging along. You remembered this place and assumed I wouldn't know about it. Stupid.

'She's here, you know.' The Commandant hisses in irritation when I block her attack and nick her on the arm. 'The Scholar slave. Lurking in the building. Watching.' The Commandant snorts and raises her voice. 'Tenaciously clinging to life like the roach that you are. The Augurs saved you, I presume? I should have crushed you more thoroughly.'

Hide, Laia! I scream it in my head, but don't call out, lest she find one of my mother's stars embedded in her chest.

The storage building is at the Commandant's back now. She pants lightly, and murder glimmers in her eyes. She wants this finished.

The Commandant feints with her knife, but when I block, she swipes my feet out from under me, and her blade comes down. I roll away, narrowly avoiding death by impalement, but two more throwing stars whistle toward me, and though I deflect one, the other cuts into my bicep.

Gold skin flashes in the gloom behind my mother. *No, Laia. Stay away.*

My mother drops her scims and draws two daggers, determined to finish me. She vaults toward me with full force, using darting strokes to wound me so that I won't notice until I'm breathing my last.

I deflect her too slowly. A blade bites into my shoulder, and I rear back, but not fast enough to avoid a vicious kick to my face that drops me to my knees. Suddenly, there are two Commandants

26

and four blades. *You're dead, Elias.* Gasps echo in my head – my own breaths, shallow and pained. I hear her cold chuckle, like rocks breaking glass. She comes in for the kill. It is only Blackcliff's training, *her* training, that allows me to instinctively lift my scim and block her. But my strength is gone. She knocks my scims from my hands, one by one.

From the corner of my eye, I spot Laia approaching, dagger in hand. *Stop, damn it. She'll kill you in a second.*

But then I blink, and Laia is gone. I think I must have imagined her – that the kick has rattled my mind, but Laia appears again, sand flying from her hand and into my mother's eyes. The Commandant jerks her head away, and I scramble for my scims in the dirt. I bring one up as my mother meets my eyes.

I expect her gauntleted wrist to come up and block the sword. I expect to die bathed in her gloating triumph.

Instead, her eyes flash with an emotion I cannot identify.

Then the scim hits her temple with a blow that will have her sleeping for at least an hour. She drops to the ground like a sack of flour.

Rage and confusion grip me as Laia and I stare down at her. What crime has my mother *not* committed? She has whipped, killed, tortured, enslaved. Now she lies before us, helpless. It would be so easy to kill her. The Mask within urges me to do it. *Don't falter now, fool. You'll regret it.*

The thought repulses me. Not my own mother, not like this, no matter what kind of monster she is.

I see a flash of movement. A figure skulks in the shadows of the depot. A soldier? Perhaps – but one too cowardly to come out and fight. Maybe he has seen us, maybe not. I won't wait to find out.

'Laia.' I grab my mother by the legs and drag her into the house. She's so light. 'Get the horse.'

'Is – is she—' She looks down at the Commandant's body, and I shake my head.

'The horse,' I say. 'Untether him and take him to the door.' As she does so, I cut a length of rope from the coil in my pack and bind my mother, ankle and wrist. After she wakes it won't hold her long. But combined with the blow to her head, it should give us time to get well away from Serra before she sends soldiers after us.

'We have to kill her, Elias.' Laia's voice shakes. 'She'll come after us as soon as she wakes up. We'll never make it to Kauf.'

'I'm not going to kill her. If you want to, then hurry. We're out of time.'

I turn away from her to scan the gloom behind us again. Whoever was watching us is gone. We have to assume the worst: that it was a soldier and that he'll sound the alarm.

No troops patrol the top of Serra's ramparts. *Finally, some luck.* The vine-covered door opens after a few sturdy pulls, its hinges creaking loudly. In seconds, we are through the thick city wall. For a moment, my vision doubles. *That damned blow to the head.*

Laia and I creep through an immense apricot grove, the horse clopping beside us. She leads the beast, and I walk ahead of her, my scims out.

The Commandant chose to face me alone. Perhaps it was her pride – her desire to prove to herself and me that she could destroy me single-handedly. Whatever the reason, she'd station at least a few squads of soldiers out here to catch us if we broke through. If there's one thing I know about my mother, it's that she always has a backup plan.

I'm thankful for the inky night. If the moon were out, a skilled bowman could pick us off easily from the walls. As it is, we blend in with the trees. Still, I don't trust the darkness. I wait for the crickets and night creatures to go quiet, for my skin to go cold, for the scrape of boot or creak of leather.

But as we make our way through the orchard, there is no sign of the Empire.

I slow our pace as we approach the tree line. A tributary of the Rei rushes nearby. The only points of light in the desert are two garrisons, miles from us and from each other. Drum messages echo between them, referring to troop movements within Serra. Distantly, horses' hooves pound, and I tense – but the sound moves away from us.

'Something's not right,' I tell Laia. 'My mother should have put patrols out here.'

'Maybe she thought that she wouldn't need them.' Laia's whisper is uncertain. 'That she would kill us.'

'No,' I say. 'The Commandant always has a backup plan.' I wish, suddenly, that Helene were here. I can practically see her silver brows furrowed, her mind carefully, patiently untangling the facts.

Laia cocks her head at me. 'The Commandant makes mistakes, Elias,' she says. 'She underestimated both of us.'

True, and yet the niggling feeling in my gut won't go away. Hells, my head aches. I feel like retching. Like sleeping. *Think, Elias.* What was that in my mother's eyes just before I knocked her out? An emotion. Something she wouldn't normally express.

After a moment, it hits me. *Satisfaction.* The Commandant was pleased.

But why would she be satisfied that I'd knocked her senseless after she tried to kill me?

'She didn't make a mistake, Laia.' We step out into the open land beyond the orchard, and I survey the storm building over the Serran Mountain Range, a hundred miles away. 'She *let* us go.'

What I don't understand is why.

CHAPTER FIVE

Helene

Loyal to the end.

The motto of Gens Aquilla, whispered into my ear by my father moments after I was born. I've spoken those words a thousand times. I've never questioned. Never doubted.

I think of those words now, as I sag between two legionnaires in the dungeons below Blackcliff. *Loyal to the end.*

Loyal to whom? My family? The Empire? My own heart?

Damn my heart to the hells. My heart is what landed me here in the first place.

'How did Elias Veturius escape?'

My interrogator cuts through my thoughts. His voice is as unfeeling as it was hours ago, when the Commandant threw me into this pit with him. She cornered me outside Blackcliff's barracks, backed by a squad of Masks. I surrendered quietly; she knocked me unconscious anyway. And somehow between then and now, she stripped me of the silver shirt gifted to me by the Empire's holy men, the Augurs. A shirt that made me near invincible after it sunk into my skin.

Perhaps I should be surprised that she managed to get it off me. But I'm not. Unlike the rest of the bleeding Empire, I've never made the mistake of underestimating the Commandant.

'How did he escape?' The interrogator is back at it. I suppress a sigh. I've answered the question a hundred times.

'I don't know. One moment I was supposed to be chopping his head off, and the next, all I could hear was my ears ringing. When I looked on the execution dais, he was gone.'

The interrogator nods to the two legionnaires holding me. I gird myself.

Tell them nothing. No matter what. When Elias escaped, I promised I'd cover for him one last time. If the Empire learns that he got away through the tunnels, or that he's traveling with a Scholar, or that he gave me his mask, the soldiers will track him more easily. He'll never leave the city alive.

The legionnaires shove my head back into a bucket of foul water. I seal my lips, close my eyes, and keep my body loose, though every part of me wants to fight off my captors. I hold on to one image, the way the Commandant taught us during interrogation training.

Elias escaping. Smiling in some distant, sun-drenched land. Finding the freedom he'd sought for so long.

My lungs strain and burn. *Elias escaping. Elias free.* I drown, die. *Elias escaping. Elias free.*

The legionnaires yank my head from the bucket, and I draw a deep gulp of air.

The interrogator tips my face up with a firm hand, forcing me to look into green eyes that glimmer pale and unfeeling against the silver of his mask. I expect to see a hint of anger – frustration, at least, after hours of asking the same questions and hearing the same answers. But he is calm. Almost placid.

In my head, I call him the Northman for his brown skin, hollow cheeks, and angular eyes. He is a few years out of Blackcliff, young to be in the Black Guard, let alone as an interrogator.

'How did he escape?'

'I just told you—'

'Why were you in the Skulls' barracks after the explosion?'

'Thought I saw him. But I lost him.' A version of the truth. I did lose him, in the end.

'How did he set the charges in the explosives?' The Northman releases my face and paces around me slowly, blending into the shadows but for the red patch on his fatigues – a screaming bird. It is the symbol of the Black Guard, the Empire's internal enforcers. 'When did you help him?'

'I didn't help him.'

'He was your ally. Your friend.' The Northman pulls something from his pocket. It clinks, but I can't see what it is. 'The moment he was to be executed, a series of explosions nearly leveled the school. Do you expect anyone to believe that was a coincidence?'

At my silence, the Northman motions for the legionnaires to dunk me again. I breathe deep, locking everything else out of my mind but that image of *him* free.

And then, just as I go under, I think of *her*.

The Scholar girl. All that dark hair and those curves and her damned gold eyes. How he held her hand as they fled through the courtyard. The way she said his name and how, on her lips, it sounded like a song.

I swallow a mouthful of water. It tastes of death and piss. I kick out and fight the legionnaires holding me. *Calm down.* This is how interrogators destroy their prisoners. One crack, and he'll drive a wedge into it and hammer until I split open.

Elias escaping. Elias free. I try to see it in my mind, but the image is replaced by the two of them together, entwined.

Maybe drowning wouldn't be so horrible.

The legionnaires pull me up as my world goes dark. I spit out a mouthful of water. *Shore up, Aquilla. This is when he breaks you.*

'Who's the girl?'

The question is so unexpected that for one damning moment, I'm unable to wipe the shock – or the recognition – from my face.

Half of me curses Elias for being stupid enough to be seen with the girl. The other half tries to quash the dread blooming in my gut. The interrogator watches the emotions play out in my eyes.

'Very good, Aquilla.' His words are deadly quiet. Immediately, I think of the Commandant. The softer she spoke, Elias once said, the more dangerous she was. I can finally see what the Northman pulled from his fatigues. Two sets of joined, metal rings that he slips onto his fingers. Brass beaters. A brutal weapon that transforms a simple beating into a slow, bloody death.

'Why don't we begin there?'

'Begin?' I've been in this hellhole for hours. 'What do you mean, *begin?*'

'This' – he gestures to the bucket of water and my bruised face – 'was me getting to know you.'

Ten bleeding hells. He's been holding back. He's ratcheted up the pain little by little, weakening me, waiting for a way in, for me to give something up. *Elias escaping. Elias free. Elias escaping. Elias free.*

'But now, Blood Shrike.' The Northman's words, though quietly delivered, cut through the chant in my head. 'Now, we'll see what you're made of.'

*   *   *

Time blurs. Hours go by. Or is it days? Weeks? I can't tell. Down here, I don't see the sun. I can't hear the drums or the belltower.

A *little longer*, I tell myself after a particularly vicious beating. *Another hour. Hold out for another hour. Another half hour. Five minutes. One minute. Just one.*

But every second is pain. I'm losing this battle. I feel it in the blocks of time that disappear, in the way my words jumble and trip over one another.

The dungeon door opens, closes. Messengers arrive, confer. The Northman's questions change, but they never end.

'We know that he escaped with the girl through the tunnels.' One of my eyes is swollen shut, but as the Northman speaks, I glare at him through the other. 'Murdered half a platoon down there.'

Oh, Elias. He'll torment himself about those deaths, not seeing them as a necessity but as a choice – the wrong choice. He'll keep that blood on his hands long after it would have washed off mine.

But some part of me is relieved that the Northman knows how Elias escaped. At least I don't have to lie anymore. When the Northman asks me about Laia and Elias's relationship, I can honestly say that I know nothing.

I just have to survive long enough for the Northman to believe me.

'Tell me about them – it's not so hard, is it? We know the girl was affiliated with the Resistance. Had she turned Elias to their cause? Were they lovers?'

I want to laugh. *Your guess is as good as mine.*

I try to answer him, but I'm in too much pain to do more than moan. The legionnaires dump me on the floor. I lay curled in a ball, a pathetic attempt to protect my broken ribs. My breath escapes in a wheeze. I wonder if death is close.

I think of the Augurs. Do they know where I am? Do they care? They must know. And they've done nothing to help me.

But I'm not dead yet. And I haven't given the Northman what he wants. If he's still asking questions, then Elias is free, and the girl with him.

'Aquilla.' The Northman sounds . . . different. Tired. 'You're out of time. Tell me about the girl.'

'I don't—'

'Otherwise, I have orders to beat you to death.'

'Emperor's orders?' I wheeze. I'm surprised. I thought Marcus would visit all sorts of horrors upon me himself before killing me.

'Doesn't matter whom the orders come from,' the Northman says. He crouches down. His green eyes meet mine. For once, they are less than calm.

'He's not worth it, Aquilla,' he says. 'Tell me what I need to know.'

'I – I don't know anything.'

The Northman waits a moment. Watches. When I remain silent, he stands and pulls on the brass beaters.

I think of Elias, in this very dungeon not long ago. What went through his head as he faced death? He seemed so serene when he came to the execution podium. Like he'd made his peace as he faced his fate.

I wish I could borrow some of that peace now. *Goodbye, Elias. I hope you find your freedom. I hope you find joy. Skies know none of the rest of us will.*

Behind the Northman, the dungeon door clanks open. I hear a familiar, hated gait.

Emperor Marcus Farrar. Come to kill me himself.

'My lord Emperor.' The Northman salutes. The legionnaires

drag me to my knees and slant my head downward in a semblance of respect.

In the dim light of the dungeon – and with limited ability to see – I can't make out Marcus's expression. But I can make out the identity of the tall, pale-haired figure behind him.

'Father?' What in the bleeding hells is he doing here? Is Marcus using him as leverage? Planning to torture him until I give up information?

'Your Majesty.' My father's voice as he addresses Marcus is smooth as glass, so uninflected as to be uncaring. But his eyes flick to me, horror-filled. With the little strength I have left in me, I glare at him. *Don't let him see, Father. Don't let him know what you feel.*

'A moment, Pater Aquillus.' Marcus waves my father off and looks, instead, to the Northman. 'Lieutenant Harper,' he says. 'Anything?'

'She knows nothing about the girl, your Majesty. Nor did she assist in the destruction of Blackcliff.'

So he did believe me.

The Snake waves away the legionnaires holding me. I order myself not to collapse. Marcus takes me by my hair and jerks me to my feet. The Northman watches, stone-faced. I grit my teeth and square my shoulders. I push myself into the hurt, expecting – no, *hoping* – that Marcus's eyes will hold nothing but hate.

But he regards me with that eerie tranquility he sometimes has. Like he knows my fears as well as his own.

'Really, Aquilla?' Marcus says, and I look away from him. 'Elias Veturius, your one true love' – the words are filthy when he speaks them – 'escapes from under your nose with a Scholar wench, and you know nothing about her? Nothing about how she survived the Fourth Trial, for instance? Or her role in the

Resistance? Are Lieutenant Harper's threats ineffective? Maybe I can think of something better.'

Behind Marcus, Father's face pales further. 'Your Majesty, please—'

Marcus ignores him, shoves my back against the dank dungeon wall, and presses his body against mine. He dips his lips close to my ear, and I close my eyes, wishing more than anything that Father wasn't witnessing this.

'Shall I find someone for us to torment?' Marcus murmurs. 'Someone in whose blood we can bathe? Or shall I have you do other things? I do hope you paid attention to Harper's methods. You'll be using them frequently as Blood Shrike.'

My nightmares – the ones he somehow knows of – rear before me with terrifying clarity: broken children, hollowed-out mothers, houses crumbling to ash. Me at his side, his loyal commander, his supporter, his lover. Reveling in it. Wanting it. Wanting *him*.

Just nightmares.

'I know nothing,' I croak. 'I'm loyal to the Empire. I have always been loyal to the Empire.' *Don't torture my father*, I want to add, but I force myself not to beg.

'Your Majesty.' My father is more forceful this time. 'Our arrangement?'

Arrangement?

'A moment, Pater,' Marcus purrs. 'I'm still playing.' He presses closer before a strange look crosses his face – surprise, or perhaps irritation. He flicks his head, like a horse shaking off a fly, before stepping back.

'Unchain her,' he says to the legionnaires.

'What is this?' I try to stand. My legs fail. Father catches me before I fall, draping my arm across his wide shoulders.

'You're free to go.' Marcus keeps his gaze fixed on me. 'Pater

Aquillus, report to me tomorrow at tenth bell. You know where to find me. Blood Shrike, you will come with him.' He pauses before leaving, and slowly runs a finger across the blood coating my face. There's a hunger in his eyes as he brings it to his mouth, licks it off. 'I have a mission for you.'

Then he is gone, followed by the Northman and the legionnaires. It is only when their footsteps fade up the staircase leading out of the dungeon that I let my head drop. Exhaustion, pain, and disbelief rob me of my strength.

I didn't betray Elias. I survived the interrogation.

'Come, daughter.' My father holds me as gently as if I were a newborn. 'Let's get you home.'

'What did you trade for this?' I ask. 'What did you trade for me?'

'Nothing of consequence.' Father tries to take more of my weight. I do not let him. Instead, I bite my lip hard enough to draw blood. As we inch out of the cell, I hone in on that pain instead of the weakness in my legs and the burning in my bones. I am Blood Shrike of the Martial Empire. I will leave this dungeon on my own two feet.

'What did you give him, Father? Money? Land? Are we ruined?'

'Not money. Influence. He is Plebeian. He has no Gens, no family, to back him.'

'The Gens are all turning on him?'

My father nods. 'They call for his resignation – or assassination. He has too many enemies, and he cannot jail or kill them all. They are too powerful. He needs influence. I gave it to him. In exchange for your life.'

'But how? Will you advise him? Lend him men? I don't understand—'

'It doesn't matter right now.' Father's blue eyes are fierce, and

I find I cannot look into them without a lump rising in my throat. 'You are my daughter. I would have given him the skin off my back if he asked it of me. Lean on me now, my girl. Save your strength.'

Influence can't be all Marcus squeezed out of Father. I want to demand that he explain everything, but as we go up the stairs, dizziness surges through me. I'm too broken to challenge him. I let him help me out of the dungeon, unable to rid myself of the unsettling feeling that whatever price he paid for me, it was too high.

CHAPTER SIX

Laia

We should have killed the Commandant.

The desert beyond Serra's orchards is quiet. The only hint of the Scholar revolution is the orange glow of fire against the limpid night sky. A cool breeze carries the smell of rain from the east, where a storm flashes over the mountains.

Go back. Kill her. I am torn. If Keris Veturia let us go, she has some diabolical reason for it. Besides which, she murdered my parents and sister. She took Izzi's eye. Tortured Cook. Tortured me. She led a generation of the most lethal, ignoble monsters while they pummeled my people into servile ghosts of themselves. She deserves to die.

But we are well beyond Serra's walls now, and it is too late to turn back. Darin matters more than vengeance against that madwoman. And getting to Darin means getting far away from Serra, as swiftly as possible.

As soon as we clear the orchards, Elias vaults on to the horse's back. His gaze never rests, and wariness suffuses his every move.

He is, I sense, asking the same question I am. *Why would the Commandant let us go?*

I grasp his hand and pull myself up behind him, my face heating at the close fit. The saddle is enormous, but Elias is not a small man. Skies, where do I put my hands? His shoulders? His waist? I'm still deciding when he puts heels to flank and the horse leaps forward. I grab on to a strap of Elias's armor, and he reaches out to pull me flush against him. I wrap my arms around his waist and press into his broad back, my head spinning as the empty desert streams past.

'Stay down,' he says over his shoulder. 'The garrisons are close.' He wags his head, as if shaking something out of his eyes, and a shudder rolls through him. Years of watching my grandfather with his patients has me putting a hand to Elias's neck. He's warm, but that might be from the fight with the Commandant.

His shudder fades, and he urges the horse on. I look back at Serra, waiting for soldiers to come streaming from its gates, or for Elias to tense and say he's heard the drums sending out our location. But we pass the garrisons without incident, nothing but open desert around us. Ever so slowly, the panic that has gripped me since seeing the Commandant eases.

Elias navigates by starlight. After a quarter hour, he slows the horse to a canter.

'The dunes are to the north. They're hell on horseback.' I lift myself up to hear him over the hoofbeats of the horse. 'We'll head east.' He nods to the mountains. 'We should hit that storm in a few hours. It'll wash away our tracks. We'll aim for the foothills—'

Neither of us sees the shadow that hurtles out of the dark until it is already upon us. One second, Elias is in front of me, his face a few inches from mine as I lean in to listen. The next, I hear the thud of his body hitting the desert floor. The horse rears, and I grasp at the saddle, trying to stay on. But a hand latches on to my arm and yanks me off as well. I want to scream at the inhuman coldness of that grip, but I can only manage a yelp. It feels as if winter itself has taken hold of me.

'*Givvve.*' The thing speaks in a rasp. All I see are streamers of darkness fluttering from a vaguely human form. I gag as the stench of death wafts over me. A few feet away, Elias curses, battling more of the shadows.

'*Sssilver,*' the one holding me says. '*Give.*'

'Get off!' I land a punch to clammy skin that freezes me from fist to elbow. The shadow disappears, and I'm suddenly, ridiculously grappling with air. A second later though, a band of ice closes about my neck and squeezes.

'*Givvve!*'

I cannot breathe. Desperately, I kick my legs. My boot connects, the shadow releases me, and I'm left wheezing and gasping. A screech shatters the night as an unearthly head sails past, courtesy of Elias's scim. He makes for me, but two more creatures dart out of the desert, blocking his path.

'It's a wraith!' he bellows at me. 'The head! You have to take off its head!'

'I'm not a bleeding swordsman!' The wraith appears again, and I pull Darin's scim from across my back, halting its approach. The second it realizes I have no idea what I'm doing, it lunges and digs its fingers into my neck, drawing blood. I scream at the cold, the pain, dropping Darin's blade as my body goes numb and useless.

A flash of steel, a chilling screech, and the shadow drops, headless. The desert falls abruptly silent but for my and Elias's harsh breaths. He sweeps up Darin's blade and closes the distance between us, taking in the scratches on my neck. He lifts my chin, his fingers warm.

'You're hurt.'

'It's nothing.' His own face is cut, and he does not complain, so I pull away and take Darin's scim. Elias seems to notice it for the first time. His jaw drops. He holds it up, trying to see it in the starlight.

'Ten hells, is this a Teluman blade? How—' A patter in the desert behind him has us both reaching for our weapons. Nothing emerges from the dark, but Elias lopes toward the horse. 'Let's get out of here. You can tell me on the way.'

We race east. As we ride, I realize that, other than what I told Elias on the night the Augurs locked us in his room, he knows almost nothing about me.

That might be a good thing, the wary part of me says. *The less he knows, the better.*

As I consider how much to say about Darin's blade and Spiro Teluman, Elias half turns in the saddle. His lips curve into a wry smile, like he can feel my hesitation.

'We're in this together, Laia. Might as well give me the whole story. And' – he nods to my wounds – 'we've fought side by side. Bad luck to lie to a comrade-in-arms.'

We're in this together. Everything he's done since the moment I made him vow to help me has reinforced that truth. He deserves to know what he's fighting for. He deserves to know my truths, however strange and unexpected they are.

'My brother wasn't an ordinary Scholar,' I begin. 'And . . . well, I wasn't exactly an ordinary slave. . . .'

* * *

43

Fifteen miles and two hours later, Elias rides silently in front of me as the horse trudges on. He holds the reins in one hand, keeping the other on a dagger. Rain mists from low-bellied clouds, and I've pulled my cloak tight against the damp.

Everything there is to tell – the raid, my parents' legacy, Spiro's friendship, Mazen's betrayal, the Augurs' help – I've shared it all. The words liberate me. Perhaps I have become so accustomed to the burden of secrets that I do not notice its weight until I am free of it.

'Are you upset?' I finally ask.

'My mother.' His voice is low. 'She killed your parents. I'm sorry. I—'

'Your mother's crimes are not yours,' I say after a moment's surprise. Whatever I thought he would say, this was not it. 'Do not apologize for them. But . . .' I look out at the desert – empty, quiet. Deceptive. 'Do you understand why it is so important for me to save Darin? He's all I have. After what he did for me – and after what I did to him – *leaving* him—'

'You have to save him. I understand. But, Laia, he's more than just your brother. You must know that.' Elias looks back at me, gray eyes fierce. 'The Empire's steelcraft is the only reason no one has challenged the Martials. Every weapon from Marinn down to the Southern Lands breaks against our blades. Your brother could bring down the Empire with what he knows. No wonder the Resistance wanted him. No wonder the Empire sent him to Kauf instead of killing him. They'll want to know if he's shared his skills with anyone.'

'They don't know he was Spiro's apprentice,' I say. 'They think he was a spy.'

'If we can free him and get him to Marinn' – Elias stops the horse at a rain-swollen creek and motions for me to dismount –

44

'he could make weapons for the Mariners, the Scholars, the Tribes. He could change everything.'

Elias shakes his head and slides off the horse. As his boots hit the dirt, his legs buckle. He grabs the pommel of the saddle. His face blanches white as the moon, and he puts a hand to his temple.

'Elias?' Beneath my hand, his arm trembles. He shudders, just like he did when we first left Serra. 'Are you—'

'Commandant landed a nasty kick,' Elias says. 'Nothing serious. Just can't seem to get my feet.' The color returns to his face, and he plunges a hand into a saddlebag, handing me a palmful of apricots so fat they are splitting their skins. He must have taken them from the orchards.

When the sweet fruit bursts between my lips, my heart twinges. I cannot eat apricots without thinking of my bright-eyed Nan and her jams.

Elias opens his mouth as if to say something. But he changes his mind and turns to fill the canteens from the creek. Still, I sense he's working himself up to a question. I wonder if I'll be able to answer it. *What was that creature you saw in my mother's office? Why do you think the Augurs saved you?*

'In the shed, with Keenan,' he finally says. 'Did you kiss him? Or did he kiss you?'

I spit out my apricot, coughing, and Elias rises from the creek to pat me on the back. I had wondered if I should tell him about the kiss. In the end, I decided that with my life dependent on him, it was best to hold nothing back.

'I tell you my life story and *that's* your first question? Why—'

'Why do you think?' His tilts his head, lifts his brows, and my stomach flips. 'In any case,' he says, 'you – you—'

He pales again, a strange expression crossing his face. Sweat beads on his forehead. 'L-Laia, I don't feel—'

His words slur, and he staggers. I grip his shoulder, trying to keep him upright. My hand comes away soaked – and not from the rain.

'Skies, Elias, you're sweating – quite a lot.'

I grab his hand. It's cold, clammy. 'Look at me, Elias.' He stares down into my eyes, his pupils dilating wildly before a violent tremor shakes his body. He lurches toward the horse, but when he tries to take hold of the saddle, he misses and falls. I get under his arm before he cracks his head on the rocks of the creekside and lower him as gently as I'm able. His hands twitch.

This can't be from the blow to the head.

'Elias,' I say. 'Did you get cut anywhere? Did the Commandant use a blade on you?'

He grabs his bicep. 'Just a scratch. Nothing seriou—'

Understanding dawns in his eyes, and he turns to me, trying to form words. Before he can, he seizes once. Then he drops like a stone, unconscious. It doesn't matter – I already know what he's going to say.

The Commandant poisoned him.

His body is frighteningly still, and I grab his wrist, panicked at the erratic stutter of his pulse. Despite the sweat pouring off him, his body is cold, not fevered. Skies, is this why the Commandant let us go? *Of course it is, Laia, you fool. She didn't have to chase you or set an ambush. All she needed was to cut him – and the poison took care of the rest.*

But it didn't – at least not right away. My grandfather dealt with Scholars maimed by poisoned blades. Most died within an hour of being wounded. But it took several hours for Elias to even react to this poison.

She didn't use enough. Or the cut wasn't deep enough. It doesn't matter. All that matters is that he still lives.

'Sorry,' he moans. I think at first that he is speaking to me, but his eyes remain shut. He puts up his hands, as if warding something off. 'Didn't want to. My order – should have—'

I tear off a piece of my cloak and stuff it in Elias's mouth, lest he bite off his own tongue. The wound on his arm is shallow and hot. The moment I touch it, he thrashes, spooking the horse.

I dig through my pack with its vials of medicines and herbs, finally finding something with which to cleanse the wound. As soon as the cut is clean, Elias's body grows slack and his face, rigid with pain, relaxes.

His breathing is still shallow, but at least he is not convulsing. His lashes are dark crescents against the gold skin of his face. He looks younger in sleep. Like the boy I danced with on the night of the Moon Festival.

I reach out a hand and place it against his jaw, rough with stubble, warm with life. It pours from him, this vitality – when he fights, when he rides. Even now, with his body battling poison, he throbs with it.

'Come on, Elias.' I lean over him, speaking into his ear. 'Fight back. Wake up. *Wake up.*'

His eyes fly open, he spits out the gag, and I snatch my hand back from his face. Relief sweeps through me. Awake and injured is always better than unconscious and injured. Immediately, he lurches to his feet. Then he doubles over and dry-heaves.

'Lay down.' I push him to his knees and rub his broad back, the way Pop did with ill patients. *Touch can heal more than herbs and poultices.* 'We have to figure out the poison so we can find an antidote.'

'Too late.' Elias relaxes into my hands for a moment before reaching for his canteen and drinking the contents down. When he finishes, his eyes are clearer, and he tries to stand. 'Antidotes for most poisons need to be given within an hour. But if the poison were going to kill me, it would have already. Let's get moving.'

'To where, exactly?' I demand. 'The foothills? Where there are no cities or apothecaries? You're *poisoned*, Elias. If an antidote won't help, then you at least need medicine to treat the seizures, or you'll be blacking out from here to Kauf,' I say. 'Only you'll die before we get there, because no one can survive such convulsions for long. So sit down and let me think.'

He stares at me in surprise and sits.

I pore over the year I spent with Pop as an apprentice healer. The memory of a little girl pops into my head. She had convulsions and fainting spells.

'Tellis extract,' I say. Pop gave the girl a drachm of it. Within a day, the symptoms eased. In two days, they stopped. 'It will give your body a chance to fight the poison.'

Elias grimaces. 'We could find it in Serra or Navium.'

Only we can't go back to Serra, and Navium is in the opposite direction from Kauf.

'What about Raider's Roost?' My stomach twists in dread at the idea. The giant rock is a lawless cesspit of society's detritus – highwaymen, bounty hunters, and black market profiteers who know only the darkest corruption. Pop went there a few times to find rare herbs. Nan never slept while he was gone.

Elias nods. 'Dangerous as the ten hells, but filled with people who wish to go as unnoticed as we do.'

He rises again, and while I'm impressed by his strength, I'm also horrified by the callous way he treats his body. He fumbles at the reins of the horse.

'Another seizure soon, Laia.' He taps the horse behind its left front leg. It sits. 'Tie me on with rope. Head straight southeast.' He heaves himself into the saddle, listing dangerously to one side.

'I feel them coming,' he whispers.

I wheel about, expecting the hoofbeats of an Empire patrol, but all is silent. When I look back at Elias, his eyes are fixed on a point past my head. 'Voices. Calling me back.'

Hallucinations. Another effect of the poison. I bind Elias to the stallion with rope from his pack, fill the canteens, and mount up. Elias slumps against my back, blacked out again. His smell, rain and spice, washes over me, and I take a steadying breath.

My sweat-damp fingers slide along the horse's reins. As if the beast senses I know nothing about riding, it tosses its head and pulls at the bit. I wipe my hands on my shirt and tighten my grip.

'Don't you dare, you nag,' I say to its rebellious snort. 'It's you and me for the next few days, so you better listen to what I say.' I give the horse a light kick, and to my relief, it trots forward. We turn southeast, and I dig my heels deeper. Then we are away, into the night.

CHAPTER SEVEN

Elias

Voices surround me, quiet murmurs that remind me of a Tribal camp awakening: the whispers of men soothing horses and children kindling breakfast fires.

I open my eyes, expecting the sunshine of the Tribal desert, unabashedly bright, even at dawn. Instead, I stare up at a canopy of trees. The murmuring grows muted, and the air is weighty with the green scents of pine needles and moss-softened bark. It's dark, but I can make out the pitted trunks of great trees, some as wide as houses. Beyond the branches above, snatches of blue sky darken swiftly to gray, as if a storm approaches.

Something darts through the trees, disappearing when I turn. The leaves rustle, whispering like a battlefield of ghosts. The murmurs I heard rise and fade, rise and fade.

I stand. Though I expect pain to shoot through every limb, I feel nothing. The absence of pain is strange – and wrong.

Wherever I am, I shouldn't be here. I should be with Laia, headed toward Raider's Roost. I should be awake, fighting the

Commandant's poison. On instinct, I reach back for my scims. They aren't there.

'No heads to lop off in the ghost world, you murdering bastard.'

I know that voice, though I've rarely heard it so heavily laced with vitriol.

'Tristas?'

My friend appears as he did in life, hair dark as pitch, the tattoo of his beloved's name standing out in sharp relief against his pale skin. *Aelia.* He looks nothing like a ghost. But he must be. I *saw* him die in the Third Trial, on the end of Dex's scim.

He doesn't feel like a ghost either – something I realize with abrupt violence when, after considering me for a moment, he slams his fist into my jaw.

The burst of pain that shoots through my skull is dulled to half what it should be. Still, I back away. The hatred behind the punch was more powerful than the blow itself.

'That was for letting Dex kill me in the Trial.'

'I'm sorry,' I say. 'I should have stopped him.'

'Doesn't matter, seeing as I'm still dead.'

'Where are we? What is this place?'

'The Waiting Place. It's for the dead who are not ready to move on, apparently. Leander and Demetrius left. Not me, though. I'm stuck listening to this bleating.'

Bleating? I assume he's referring to the murmur of the ghosts flitting through the trees, which to me is no more irritating than the swish of ocean tide.

'But I'm not dead.'

'Didn't *she* show up to give you her little speech?' Tristas asks. *'Welcome to the Waiting Place, the realm of ghosts. I am the Soul Catcher, and I am here to help you cross to the other side.'*

When I shake my head, mystified, Tristas flashes me a malevolent smile. 'Well, she'll be here soon enough, trying to bully you into moving on. All of this is hers.' He gestures to the Forest, to the spirits still murmuring beyond the tree line. Then his face changes – twists.

'It's her!' He disappears into the trees with unnatural speed. Alarmed, I spin around and see a shadow pull free from a nearby trunk.

I keep my hands loose at my sides – ready to grab, throttle, punch. The figure draws closer, moving not at all like a person. It is too fluid, too fast.

But when it's only a few feet away, it slows and resolves into a trim, dark-haired woman. Her face is unlined, but I cannot guess her age. Her black irises and ancient stare suggest something I can't fathom.

'Hello, Elias Veturius.' Her earthy voice is strangely accented, as if she's not used to speaking Serran. 'I am the Soul Catcher, and I am pleased to finally meet you. I've watched you now, for a time.'

Right. 'I need to get out of here.'

'Do you enjoy it?' Her voice is soft. 'The hurt you cause? The pain? I can see it.' Her eyes trace the air about my head, my shoulders. 'You carry it with you. Why? Does it bring you happiness?'

'No.' I recoil from the thought. 'I don't mean to – I don't want to hurt people.'

'Yet you destroy all those who get close to you. Your friends. Your grandfather. Helene Aquilla. You hurt them.' She pauses as the horrible truth of her words sinks in. 'I don't watch those on the other side,' she says. 'But you are different.'

'I'm not supposed to be here,' I say. 'I'm not dead.'

She regards me for a long time before cocking her head like a curious bird. 'But you are dead,' she says. 'You just don't know it yet.'

*   *   *

My eyes jolt open to a sky covered in clouds. It's mid-morning, and I'm slumped forward, my head jouncing in the space between Laia's neck and shoulder. Low hills rise and fall around us, dotted with Jack trees, tumbleweeds, and little else. Laia moves the horse southeast at a trot, straight toward Raider's Roost. At my movement, she twists around.

'Elias!' She slows the horse. 'You've been blacked out for hours. I – I thought you might not wake up.'

'Don't stop the horse.' I possess none of the strength I felt in my hallucination, but I force myself to sit up. Dizziness sweeps over me, and my tongue is heavy in my mouth. *Stay, Elias*, I tell myself. *Don't let the Soul Catcher pull you back.* 'Keep us moving – the soldiers—'

'We rode through the night. I saw soldiers, but they were far away and heading south.' Shadows have settled beneath her eyes, and her hands shake. She's exhausted. I take the reins from her, and she sags back against me, closing her eyes.

'Where did you go, Elias? Can you remember? Because I've seen seizures before. They can knock someone out for a few minutes, even an hour. But you were unconscious for far longer.'

'Strange place. A for-forest—'

'Don't you dare fade out on me again, Elias Veturius.' Laia spins and shakes my shoulders, and I snap my eyes open. 'I can't do this without you. Look at the horizon. What do you see?'

I force myself to look up. 'C-clouds. Storm coming. Big one. We need shelter.'

Laia nods. 'I could smell it. The storm.' She glances back. 'Reminds me of you.'

I try to work out whether this is a compliment or not but then give up. Ten hells, I'm so tired.

'Elias.' She puts a hand against my face and forces me to meet her gold eyes, as hypnotizing as a lioness's. 'Stay with me. You had a foster brother – tell me about him.'

Voices call me – the Waiting Place pulling me back with hungry claws.

'Shan,' I gasp out. 'His – his name is Shan. Bossy, just like Mamie Rila. He's nineteen – a year younger.' I blather on, trying to force away the cold grasp of the Waiting Place. As I speak, Laia shoves water into my hands, urging me to drink.

'Stay.' She keeps saying it, and I hold on to the word like it's driftwood in an open ocean. 'Don't go back. I need you.'

Hours later, the storm hits, and though riding in it is miserable, the wet forces me further awake. I guide the horse to a low-lying ravine littered with boulders. The storm is too heavy for us to see more than a few feet – which means that the Empire's men will be just as blind.

I dismount and spend long minutes trying to tend to the stallion, but my hands refuse to function properly. An unfamiliar emotion grips me: fear. I crush it. *You'll fight the poison, Elias. If it were going to kill you, you'd already be dead.*

'Elias?' Laia is beside me, concern etched on her face. She's strung a tarp between two boulders, and when I finish with the horse, she guides me there and makes me sit.

'She told me I hurt people,' I blurt out as we huddle together. 'I let them get hurt.'

'Who told you that?'

'I'm going to hurt you,' I say. 'I hurt everyone.'

'Stop, Elias.' Laia takes my hands. 'I freed you because you *didn't* hurt me.' She pauses, and the rain is a chilly curtain around us. 'Try to stay, Elias. You were gone for so long last time, and I need you to stay.'

We're so close that I can see the indent in the center of her lower lip. A ringlet of hair has come loose from her bun and spills down her long, golden neck. I'd give so much to be this close to her and not be poisoned or hunted, injured or haunted.

'Tell me another story,' she murmurs. 'I hear the Fivers see the southern islands. Are they beautiful?' At my nod, she prods me. 'What do they look like? Is the water clear?'

'Water's blue.' I try to fight the slur in my voice, because she's right: I need to stay. I need to get us to the Roost. I need to get the Tellis.

'But not – not dark blue. It's a thousand blues. And greens. Like – like someone took Hel's eyes and turned them into the ocean.'

My body trembles. *No – not again.* Laia takes my cheeks in her hands, her touch sending a bolt of desire through me.

'Stay with me,' she says. Her fingers are cool on my fevered skin. Lightning cracks, illuminating her face, making her gold eyes darker, giving her an otherworldly feel. 'Tell me another memory,' she demands. 'Something good.'

'You,' I say. 'The – the first time I saw you. You're beautiful, but there are lots of beautiful girls, and—' *Find the words. Make yourself stay.* 'That's not why you stood out. You're like me. . . .'

'Stay with me, Elias. Stay here.'

My mouth won't work. The blackness creeping at the edge of my vision draws closer.

'I can't stay. . . .'

'Try, Elias. Try!'

Her voice fades. The world goes dark.

* * *

This time, I find myself sitting on the Forest floor, warmth from a fire driving the chill from my bones. The Soul Catcher sits across from me, patiently feeding logs to the blaze.

'The wails of the dead don't bother you,' she says.

'I'll answer your questions if you answer mine,' I retort. When she nods, I continue.

'It doesn't sound like wailing to me. More like whispers.' I expect a response from her, but there is none. 'My turn. These seizures – they shouldn't be knocking me out for hours at a time. Are you doing this? Are you keeping me here?'

'I told you: I've been watching you. I wanted a chance to speak.'

'Let me go back.'

'Soon,' she says. 'You have more questions?'

My frustration rises, and I want to shout at her – but I need answers. 'What did you mean when you said I was dead? I know I'm not. I'm alive.'

'Not for much longer.'

'Can you see the future, like the Augurs?'

Her head comes up, and the feral snarl on her lips is unquestionably inhuman.

'Do not invoke those creatures here,' she says. 'This is a sacred world, a place the dead come to find peace. The Augurs are anathema to death.' She settles back. 'I'm the Soul Catcher, Elias. I deal with the dead. And death has claimed you – there.' She taps my arm, exactly where the Commandant's star cut me.

'The poison won't kill me,' I say. 'And if Laia and I get the Tellis extract, neither will the seizures.'

'Laia. The Scholar girl. Another ember waiting to burn the world down,' she says. 'Will you hurt her too?'

'Never.'

The Soul Catcher shakes her head. 'You grow close to her.

Don't you see what you are doing? The Commandant poisoned you. You, in turn, *are* a poison. You will poison Laia's joy, her hope, her life, like you have poisoned all the rest. If you care for her, then do not let her care for you. Like the poison that rages within you, you have no antidote.'

'I'm not going to die.'

'Willpower alone cannot change one's fate. Think on it, Elias, and you will see.' Her smile is sad as she pokes the fire. 'Perhaps I will call you here again. I have many questions. . . .'

I slam back into the real world with a harshness that makes my teeth ache. The night is cloaked in mist. I must have blacked out for hours. Our horse trots ahead steadily, but I feel its legs tremble. We'll need to stop soon.

Laia rides on, oblivious to the fact that I've woken. My mind isn't nearly as clear as it was in the Waiting Place, but I remember the Soul Catcher's words. *Think on it, Elias, and you will see.*

I sift through the poisons I know, cursing myself for not paying closer attention to the Blackcliff Centurion who instructed us on toxins.

Nightweed. Barely mentioned because it is illegal in the Empire, even for Masks. It was outlawed a century ago, after it was used to assassinate an Emperor. *Always deadly, though in higher doses, it kills swiftly. In lower doses, the only symptoms are severe seizures.*

Three to six months of seizures, I remember. Then death. There is no cure. No antidote.

Finally, I understand why the Commandant let us escape from Serra, why she didn't bother slitting my throat. She didn't have to.

Because she'd already killed me.

CHAPTER EIGHT

Helene

'Six broken ribs, twenty-eight lacerations, thirteen fractures, four torn tendons, and bruised kidneys.'

Morning sun pours through the windows of my childhood bedroom, glinting off my mother's silver-blonde hair as she relays the physician's assessment. I watch her in the ornate silver mirror in front of us – a gift she gave me when I was a girl. Its unmottled surface is the specialty of a city far to the south, an island of glassblowers my father once visited.

I shouldn't be here. I should be in the Black Guard barracks preparing for my audience with Emperor Marcus Farrar, to take place in less than an hour. Instead, I sit amid the silken rugs and lavender drapes of Villa Aquilla, with my mother and sisters tending to me instead of a military medic. *You were in interrogation for five days and they've been worried sick*, Father insisted. *They want to see you.* I didn't have the energy to refuse him.

'Thirteen fractures is nothing.' My voice is a rasp. I tried not to scream during the interrogation. My throat is raw with the times

I failed. Mother stitches a wound, and I hide a wince as she ties it off.

'She's right, Mother.' Livia, who at eighteen is the youngest Aquilla, gives me a dark smile. 'Could have been worse. They could have cut her hair.'

I snort – it hurts too much to laugh, and even Mother smiles as she dabs ointment onto one of my wounds. Only Hannah remains expressionless.

I glance at her, and she looks away, jaw clenched. She's never learned to quench her hatred for me, my middle sister. Though after the first time I pulled a scim on her, she at least learned to hide it.

'It's your own damned fault.' Hannah's voice is low, poisonous, and wholly expected. I'm surprised it took her this long. 'It's disgusting. They shouldn't have had to torture you for information about that – that monster.' *Elias.* I'm thankful she doesn't say his name. 'You should have given it to them—'

'Hannah!' Mother snaps. Livia, her back rigid, glares at our sister.

'My friend Aelia was to be married in a week,' Hannah snarls. 'Her fiancé is dead because of your *friend*. And you refuse to help find him.'

'I don't know where he—'

'Liar!' Hannah's voice trembles with more than a decade of rage. For fourteen years my schooling took precedence over anything she or Livvy did. Fourteen years where my father was more concerned with me than his other daughters. Her hate is as familiar as my own skin. That doesn't make it sting less. She looks at me and sees a rival. I look at her and see the wide-eyed, tow-headed sister who used to be my best friend.

Until Blackcliff, anyway.

Ignore her, I tell myself. I can't have her accusations ringing in my ears when I meet with the Snake.

'You should have stayed in prison,' Hannah says. 'You're not worth Father going to the Emperor and begging – *begging* on hands and knees.'

Bleeding skies, Father. No. He shouldn't have lowered himself – not on my behalf. I look down at my hands, enraged when I feel my eyes burn with tears. Bleeding hells, I'm about to face off with Marcus. I don't have time for guilt or tears.

'Hannah.' My mother's voice is steel, so unlike her usual gentle self. 'Leave.'

My sister lifts her chin in challenge before turning and ambling out, as if it's her idea to go. *You'd have made an excellent Mask, sister.*

'Livvy,' Mother says after a minute. 'Make sure she doesn't take her anger out on the slaves.'

'Probably too late for that,' Livvy mutters as she walks out. As I try to rise, Mother puts a hand on my shoulder and pushes me down into the seat with surprising force.

She dabs at a wicked, deep cut in my scalp with a stinging ointment. Her cool fingers turn my face one way and then another, her eyes sad mirrors of my own.

'Oh, my girl,' she whispers. I feel shaky, suddenly, like I want to collapse into her arms and never leave their safety.

Instead I push her hands away.

'Enough.' Better she think me impatient than too soft. I cannot show her the wounded parts of me. I cannot show anyone those parts. Not when my strength is the only thing that will serve me now. And not when I'm minutes away from meeting with the Snake.

I have a mission for you, he'd said. What will he have me do?

Quell the revolution? Punish the Scholars for their insurrection? *Too easy.* Worse possibilities come to mind. I try not to think about them.

Beside me, Mother sighs. Her eyes fill, and I stiffen. I'm about as good with tears as I am with declarations of love. But her tears don't spill over. She hardens herself – something she has been forced to learn as the mother of a Mask – and reaches for my armor. Silently, she helps me pull it on.

'Blood Shrike.' Father appears in the doorway a few minutes later. 'It's time.'

*　　*　　*

Emperor Marcus has taken up residence in Villa Veturia.

In Elias's home.

'At the Commandant's urging, no doubt,' my father says, as guards wearing Veturia colors open the villa's gate to us. 'She'll want to keep him close.'

I wish he'd picked anywhere else. Memory assails me as we pass through the courtyard. Elias is everywhere, his presence so strong that I know if I just turn my head, he'll be inches away, shoulders thrown back in careless grace, a quip on his lips.

But of course he's not here, and neither is his grandfather, Quin. In their places are dozens of Gens Veturia soldiers watching the walls and roofs. The pride and disdain that were the Veturia hallmark under Quin are gone. Instead, an undercurrent of sullen fear ripples through the courtyard. A whipping post is haphazardly erected in one corner. Fresh blood spatters the cobblestones around it.

I wonder where Quin is now. Somewhere safe, I hope. Before I helped him escape into the desert north of Serra, he gave me a warning. *You watch your back, girl. You're strong, and she'll kill you for it. Not outright. Your family is too important for that. But she'll find a way.* I didn't have to ask him whom he was talking about.

My father and I enter the villa. Here's the foyer where Elias greeted me after our graduation. The marble staircase we raced down as children, the drawing room where Quin entertained, the butler's pantry at its back, where Elias and I spied on him.

By the time Father and I are escorted to Quin's library, I am scrambling for control over my thoughts. It's bad enough that Marcus, as Emperor, can order me to do his bidding. I cannot also allow him to see me mourning Elias. He'll use such weakness to his advantage – I know it.

You're a Mask, Aquilla. Act like one.

'Blood Shrike.' Marcus looks up at my entry, my title somehow insulting on his lips. 'Pater Aquillus. Welcome.'

I'm not sure what to expect when we enter. Marcus lounging among a harem of bruised and beaten women, perhaps.

Instead, he's in full battle armor, his cape and weapons bloodied, as if he's been in the midst of the fighting. Of course. He's always loved the gore and adrenaline of battle.

Two Veturia soldiers stand at the window. The Commandant is at Marcus's side, pointing to a map on the desk before them. As she leans forward, I catch a glimmer of silver beneath her uniform.

The bitch is wearing the shirt she stole from me.

'As I was saying, my lord.' The Commandant nods in greeting, before picking up the thread of the conversation. 'Warden Sisellius of Kauf must be dealt with. He was cousin to the old Shrike and shared intelligence from Kauf's prisoner interrogations with him. It was the reason the Shrike was able to keep such a tight rein on internal dissent.'

'I can't look for your traitorous son, fight the rats' revolution, bend the Illustrian Gens to my will, deal with border attacks, *and* take on one of the most powerful men in the Empire, Commandant.' Marcus has taken to his authority naturally. As if he's been waiting for it. 'Do you know how many secrets the Warden knows? He could raise an army with a few words. Until we have the rest of the Empire sorted, we leave the Warden be. You're dismissed. Pater Aquillus.' Marcus glances at my father. 'Go with the Commandant. She will handle the details of our . . . arrangement.'

Arrangement. The terms of my release. Father still has not told me what they were.

But I can't ask now. Father follows the Commandant and the two Veturia soldiers out. The study door slams behind them. Marcus and I are alone.

He turns to regard me. I can't meet his glance. Every time I stare into his yellow eyes, I see my nightmares. I expect him to revel in my weakness. To whisper in my ear about the dark things we both see, the way he's been doing for weeks. I wait for his approach, for his attack. I know what he is. I know what he's been threatening me with for months.

But he clenches his jaw and half lifts his hand, like he's about to wave away a mosquito. Then he exerts control over himself, a vein popping at his temple.

'It appears, Aquilla, that you and I are stuck with each other, as Emperor and Shrike.' He spits the words at me. 'Until one of us is dead, anyway.'

I am surprised at the bitterness in his voice. His cat eyes are fixed in the distance. Without Zak beside him, he doesn't seem fully present – half a person instead of a whole. He was . . . younger around Zak. Still cruel, still horrible, but relaxed. Now he seems older and harder and, perhaps most terrifyingly, wiser.

'Then why didn't you just kill me in the prison?' I say.

'Because I enjoyed watching your father beg.' Marcus grins, a flash of his old self. The smile fades. 'And because the Augurs seem to have a soft spot for you. Cain paid me a visit. Insisted that killing you would lead to my own doom.' The Snake shrugs. 'To be honest, I'm tempted to slit your throat just to see what happens. Perhaps I still will. But for now, I have a mission for you.'

Control, Aquilla. 'I'm yours to command, my lord.'

'The Black Guard – your men now – have thus far failed to locate and secure the rebel Elias Veturius.'

No.

'You know him. You know how he thinks. You will hunt him down and bring him back in chains. Then you will torture him and execute him. Publicly.'

Hunt. Torture. Execute.

'My lord.' *I can't do it. I can't.* 'I am Blood Shrike. I should be quelling the revolution—'

'The revolution is quelled,' Marcus says. 'Your assistance is unnecessary.'

I knew this would happen. I knew he'd send me after Elias. I knew it because I dreamt it. But I didn't think it would be so soon.

'I've just become leader of the Black Guard,' I say. 'I need to get to know my men. My duties.'

'But first you must be an example to them. What better example than catching the Empire's greatest traitor? Don't worry about the rest of the Black Guard. They'll take orders from me while you're on this mission.'

'Why not send the Commandant?' I try to suppress the desperation in my voice. The more it shows, the more he'll revel in it.

'Because I need someone ruthless to crush the revolution,' Marcus says.

'You mean you need an ally at your side.'

'Don't be stupid, Aquilla.' He shakes his head in disgust and begins pacing. 'I don't have allies. I have people who owe me things and people who want things and people who use me and people whom I use. In the Commandant's case, the wanting and the using is mutual, so she will remain. She suggested that you hunt down Elias as a test of loyalty. I agreed with her suggestion.'

The Snake stops his pacing.

'You swore to be my Shrike, the sword that executes my will. Now is your chance to prove your loyalty. The vultures circle, Aquilla. Don't make the mistake of thinking I'm too stupid to see it. Veturius's escape is my first failure as Emperor, and the Illustrians already use it against me. I need him dead.' He meets my eyes and leans forward, knuckles bloodless as he clenches the desk. 'And I want you to be the one who kills him. I want you to watch the light die in his eyes. I want him to know it's the person he cares for most in the world who shoved a blade through his heart. I want it to haunt you for all of your days.'

There is more than just hatred in Marcus's eyes. For a fleeting, indiscernible moment, there is guilt.

He wants me to be like him. He wants Elias to be like Zak.

The name of Marcus's twin hovers between us, a ghost that will come to life if we only say the word. We both know what happened on the battlefield of the Third Trial. Everyone does. Zacharias Farrar was killed – stabbed in the heart by the man standing before me.

'Very well, Your Majesty.' My voice comes out strong, smooth. My training kicks in. The surprise on Marcus's face makes it gratifying.

'You'll begin immediately. I'll be receiving daily reports – the Commandant has chosen a Black Guard to keep us appraised of your progress.'

Naturally. I turn to go, my stomach churning as I reach for the door handle.

'One more thing,' Marcus says, forcing me to turn, my teeth gritted, 'don't even think about telling me that you're unable to catch Veturius. He's sly enough to escape the bounty hunters quite easily. But you and I both know that he would never be able to escape you.' Marcus cocks his head, calm, collected, and full of hatred.

'Happy hunting, Blood Shrike.'

* * *

My feet carry me away from Marcus and his terrible command, out the door of Quin Veturius's study. Beneath my ceremonial armor, blood from a wound soaks through a dressing. I skim a finger over the wound, pressing lightly, then harder. Pain lances through my torso, narrowing my sight to what is before me.

I must track Elias. Catch him. Torture him. Kill him.

My hands curl into fists. *Why* did Elias have to break his oath to the Augurs, to the Empire? He's seen what life is like beyond these borders: In the Southern Lands, there are more monarchies than people, each kinglet scheming to conquer the rest. In the northwest, the Wildmen of the tundra trade babies and women for firepowder and liquor. And south of the Great Wastes, the Barbarians of Karkaus live to reave and rape.

The Empire is not perfect. But we have held strong against the backward traditions of the broken lands beyond our borders for five centuries now. Elias *knows* that. And still he turned his back on his people.

On me.

Doesn't make a difference. He's a threat to the Empire. A threat I must deal with.

But I love him. How do I kill the man I love?

The girl I was, the girl who hoped, the weak little bird – that girl beats her wings and tosses her head against the confusion of it. *What of the Augurs and their promises? You'd kill him, your friend, your comrade-in-arms, your everything, the only one you've ever –*

I silence that girl. *Focus.*

Veturius has been gone for six days now. If he were alone and anonymous, trapping him would be like trying to trap smoke. But the news of his escape – and the reward – will force him to be more careful. Will it be enough to give bounty hunters a shot at him? I scoff. I've seen Elias rob half a camp of such mercenaries without any of them the wiser. He'll run circles around them, even injured, even hunted.

But then there's the girl. Slower. Less experienced. A distraction.

Distractions. Him, distracted. By her. Distracted because he and she – because they –

None of that, Helene.

Raised voices pull my attention outward, away from the frailty within. I hear the Commandant speaking from the drawing room, and I tense. She just left with my father. Does she dare to raise her voice to the Pater of Gens Aquilla?

I stride forward to shove open the cracked door of the drawing room. One of the benefits of being Blood Shrike is that I outrank everyone but the Emperor. I can dress the Commandant down and she can do nothing about it if Marcus isn't there.

Then I stop. Because the voice that responds does *not* belong to my father.

'I told you that your desire to dominate her would be problematic.'

The voice makes me shudder. It also reminds me of something: the efrits in the Second Trial, the way their voices sounded like the wind. But the efrits were a summer storm. This voice is a winter gale.

'If the Cook offends you, you can kill her yourself.'

'I have limitations, Keris. She is your creation. See to it. She has already cost us. The Resistance leader was essential. And now he's dead.'

'He can be replaced.' The Commandant pauses, choosing her words carefully. 'And forgive me, my lord, but how can you speak to me of obsession? You did not tell me who the slave-girl was. Why are you so interested in her? What is she to you?'

A long, tense pause. I take a step back, wary now of whatever is in that room with the Commandant.

'Ah, Keris. Busy in your spare time, I see? Learning about her? Who she is . . . who her parents were . . .'

'It was easy enough to find out once I knew what to look for.'

'The girl is not your concern. I tire of your questioning. Small victories have made you daring, Commandant. Do not let them make you stupid. You have your orders. Carry them out.'

I step out of sight just as the Commandant leaves the room. She stalks down the hallway, and I wait until her footsteps fade before coming out from around the corner – and finding myself face to face with the other speaker.

'You were listening.'

My skin feels clammy, and I find I'm clutching the hilt of my scim. The figure before me appears to be a normal man in simple garb, his hands gloved, his hood low to shadow his face. I look away from him immediately. Some lizard instinct screams at me to walk on. But I find, to my alarm, that I can't move.

'I am Blood Shrike.' I take no strength from my rank but square my shoulders anyway. 'I can listen where I wish.'

The figure tilts its head and sniffs, as if scenting the air around me.

'You've been gifted.' The man sounds mildly surprised. I shudder at the raw darkness of his voice. 'A healing power. The efrits woke it. I smell it. The blue and white of winter, the green of first spring.'

Bleeding skies. I want to forget about the strange, life-draining power I used on Elias and Laia.

'I don't know what you're talking about.' The Mask within takes over.

'It will destroy you if you're not careful.'

'And how would you know?' Who *is* this man – if he's even a man?

The figure lifts a gloved hand to my shoulder and sings one note, high, like birdsong. So unexpected, considering the gravelly depths of his voice. Fire lances through my body, and I grit my teeth together to keep from screaming.

But when the pain fades, my body aches less, and the man gestures at the mirror on a far wall. The bruises on my face are not gone, but they are considerably lighter.

'I would know.' The creature ignores my slack-jawed shock. 'You should find a teacher.'

'Are you volunteering?' I must be insane to say it, but the thing makes a queer sound that might be a laugh.

'I am not.' He sniffs again, as if considering. 'Perhaps . . . one day.'

'What – who are you?'

'I'm the Reaper, girl. And I go to collect what is mine.'

At this, I dare to look into the man's face. A mistake, for in place of eyes he has stars blazing out like the fires of the hells. As he meets my gaze, a bolt of loneliness rolls through me. And yet to call it loneliness is not enough. I feel bereft. Destroyed. As if everyone and everything I care about has been ripped from my arms and cast into the ether.

The creature's gaze is a writhing abyss, and as my sight goes red and I stagger back into the wall, I realize I am not staring into his eyes. I am staring into my future.

I see it for a moment. Pain. Suffering. Horror. All that I love, all that matters to me, awash in blood.

CHAPTER NINE

Laia

Raider's Roost juts into the air like a colossal fist. It blots out the horizon, its shadow deepening the gloom of the mist-cloaked desert. From here, it looks still and abandoned. But the sun has long since set, and I cannot trust my eyes. Deep in the labyrinthine cracks of that great rock, the Roost teems with the dregs of the Empire.

I glance at Elias to see his hood has slipped back. When I pull it up, he does not stir, and worry twists in my belly. He has been in and out for the past three days, but his last seizure was especially violent. The bout of unconsciousness that followed lasted for more than a day – the longest stretch yet. I do not understand as much as Pop about healing, but even I know that this is bad.

Before, Elias at least muttered, as if he was fighting the poison. But he hasn't spoken a word for hours. I'd be happy if he said anything. Even if it was more about Helene Aquilla and her ocean-colored eyes – a comment I found unexpectedly irritating.

He's slipping away. And I cannot let it happen.

'Laia.' At Elias's voice, I nearly fall off the horse in surprise.

'Thank the skies.' I look back to find his warm skin is gray and drawn, his pale eyes burning with fever.

He looks up at the Roost and then at me. 'I knew you'd get us here.' For a moment, he's his old self: warm, full of life. He peers over my shoulder at my fingers – chafed from four days of clutching the reins – and takes the leather straps from me.

For an awkward few seconds, he holds his arms away from me, as if I might take umbrage at his closeness. So I lean back against his chest, feeling safer than I have in days, like I've suddenly acquired a layer of armor. He relaxes, dropping his forearms to my hips, and the weight of them sends a flutter up my spine.

'You must be exhausted,' he murmurs.

'I'm all right. Heavy as you are, dragging you on and off this horse was ten times easier than dealing with the Commandant.'

His chuckle is weak, but still, something inside me relaxes at the sound of it. He angles the horse north and kicks it into a canter until the trail ahead rises.

'We're close,' he says. 'We'll head for the rocks just north of the Roost – lots of places for you to hide while I go in for the Tellis.'

I frown at him over my shoulder. 'Elias, you could black out at any moment.'

'I can fight off the seizures. I only need a few minutes in the market,' he says. 'It's right in the heart of the Roost. Has everything. Should be able to find an apothecary.'

He grimaces, his arms going rigid. 'Go away,' he mutters – though clearly not at me. When I look askance at him, he pretends he's fine and starts asking me about the last few days.

But as the horse climbs the rocky terrain north of the Roost, Elias's body jerks, as if yanked by a puppeteer, and he pitches wildly to the left.

I grab the reins, thanking the skies that I've roped him on so that he can't fall. I wrap my arm around him awkwardly, twisting in the saddle, trying to keep him steady so he doesn't frighten the horse.

'It's all right.' My voice shakes. I can barely hold him, but I channel Pop's unflappable healer's calm as the convulsions grow worse. 'We'll get the extract, and everything will be fine.' His pulse skitters frantically, and I lay a hand against his heart, fearing it will burst. It cannot take much more of this.

'Laia.' He can barely speak, and his eyes are wild and unfocused. 'I have to get it. Don't go in there alone. Too dangerous. I'll do it myself. You'll get hurt – I always – hurt—'

He slumps over, his breath shallow. He's out. Who knows for how long this time? Panic rises like bile in my throat, but I force it down.

It does not matter that the Roost is dangerous. I must go in. Elias will not make it if I don't find a way to get the Tellis. Not with his pulse so irregular, not after four days of seizures.

'You can't die.' I shake him. 'Do you hear me? You can't die, or Darin dies too.'

The horse's hooves slip on the rocks, and it rears, nearly ripping the reins from my hands and throwing Elias. I dismount and croon at the beast, trying to temper my impatience, coaxing it along as the thick mist gives way to a wretched, bone-chilling drizzle.

I can barely see my own hand in front of my face. But I take heart from it. If I cannot see where I'm going, the raiders cannot see who is approaching. Still, I tread carefully, feeling the press of danger from every side. From the sparse dirt trail I've followed, I can see the Roost well enough to make out that it is not one rock but two, riven in half as if by a great ax. A narrow valley runs through the center, and torchlight flickers within. That must be the market.

East of the Roost yawns a no-man's-land where thin fingers of rock rise up out of plunging chasms, punching higher and higher until the rocks meld together to form the first low ridgelines of the Serran Mountain Range.

I search the gullies and ravines of the land around me until I spot a cave large enough to hide both Elias and the horse.

By the time I've tethered the beast to a knob of jutting rock and dragged Elias off its back, I'm panting. The rain has soaked him through, but there's no time to change him into dry clothes now. I tuck a cloak around him carefully, then rifle through his pack for coins, feeling like a thief.

When I find them, I give his hand a squeeze and pull out one of his kerchiefs to tie about my face as he did in Serra, inhaling the scent of spice and rain.

Then I pull up my hood and slip out of the cave, hoping he'll still be alive when I return.

If I return.

*   *   *

The market at the heart of the Roost teems with Tribesmen, Martials, Mariners, even the wild-eyed Barbarians that harass the Empire's borders. Southern traders move in and out of the crowd, their bright, cheerful clothing at odds with the weapons strapped across their backs, chests, and legs.

I don't see a single Scholar. Not even slaves. But I do see plenty of people acting as shifty as I feel, and so I slump down and slip into the masses, making sure the hilt of my knife is clearly visible.

Within seconds of joining the crowd, someone grabs my arm. Without looking, I lash out with the knife, hear a grunt, and wrench away. I pull my hood lower and hunch, the way I did at

Blackcliff. *That's all this place is. Another Blackcliff. Just smellier and with thieves and highwaymen, in addition to murderers.*

The place stinks of liquor and animal dung, and beneath that, the acrid bite of ghas, a hallucinogen outlawed in the Empire. Ramshackle dwellings squat along the defile, most tucked into the natural cracks in the rock, with canvas tarps as roofs and walls. Goats and chickens are nearly as abundant as the people.

The dwellings might be humble, but the goods within are anything but. A group of men a few yards from me haggle over a tray of sparkling, egg-sized rubies and sapphires. Some stalls are filled with slab after slab of crumbling, sticky ghas, while others have firepowder barrels packed together in a dangerously haphazard fashion.

An arrow zings by my ear, and I've bolted ten steps before I realize it isn't intended for me. A group of fur-clad Barbarians stand beside an arms dealer, testing out bows by casually firing arrows every which way. A fight breaks out and I try to shove past, but a crowd gathers, and it's impossible to move. At this rate, I'll never find an apothecary.

'—sixty-thousand-mark bounty, they say. Never heard of a mark that big—'

'Emperor doesn't want to look a fool. Veturius was his first execution, and he botched it. Who's the girl with him? Why would he travel with a Scholar?'

'Maybe he's joining the revolution. Scholars know the secret of Serric steel, I hear. Spiro Teluman himself taught a Scholar lad. Maybe Veturius is as sick of the Empire as Teluman is.'

Bleeding skies. I make myself walk on, though I desperately wish to keep listening. How did the information about Teluman and Darin get out? And what does it mean for my brother?

That he might have less time than you think. Move.

The drums have clearly carried my and Elias's descriptions far. I move swiftly now, scanning the myriad stalls for an apothecary. The longer I linger, the more danger we are in. The bounty on our heads is massive enough that I doubt there's a soul in this place who hasn't heard about it.

Finally, in an alley off the main thoroughfare, I spot a shack with a mortar and pestle carved into the door. As I turn toward it, I pass a group of Tribesmen sharing steaming cups of tea beneath a tarp with a pair of Mariners.

'—like monsters out of the hells.' One of the Tribesmen, a thin-lipped, scar-faced man, speaks in a low voice. 'Didn't matter how much we fought. Kept coming back. Wraiths. Bleeding wraiths.'

I nearly halt in my tracks, but continue on slowly at the last moment. So others have seen the fey creatures too. My curiosity gets the better of me, and I lean down to fiddle with my boot-laces, straining to hear the conversation.

'Another Ayanese frigate went down a week ago off Isle South,' one of the Mariners says. She takes a sip of tea and shivers. 'Thought it was corsairs, but the only survivor raved about sea efrits. I wouldn't have believed him, but now . . .'

'And ghuls here in the Roost,' the scar-faced Tribesman says. 'I'm not the only one who's seen them—'

I glance over, unable to help myself, and as if I've drawn him with my gaze, the Tribesman flicks his eyes toward me and away. Then he jerks them back again.

I step right into a puddle and slip. My hood falls from my head. *Damn it.* I scramble to my feet, yanking the hood over my eyes and glancing over my shoulder as I do. The Tribesman still watches, dark eyes narrowed.

Get out of here, Laia! I hurry away, turning down one alley and then another before chancing a look over my shoulder. No Tribesman. I sigh in relief.

The rain thickens, and I circle back to the apothecary. I peek out of the alley I'm in to see if the Tribesman and his friends are still at the tea stall. But they appear to have left. Before they can return – and before anyone else sees me – I duck into the shop.

The smell of herbs washes over me, tinged by something dark and bitter. The roof is so low I nearly hit my head. Traditional Tribal lamps hang from the ceiling, their intricate floral glow in sharp contrast to the earthy darkness of the shop.

'*Epkah kesiah meda karun?*'

A Tribal child of about ten years addresses me from behind the counter. Herbs hang in bunches over her head. The vials that line the walls behind her gleam. I eye them, searching for anything familiar. The girl clears her throat.

'*Epkah Keeya Necheya?*'

For all I know, she could be telling me I reek like a horse. But I do not have time to puzzle it out, so I pitch my voice low and hope she understands me.

'Tellis.'

The girl nods and rummages through a drawer or two before shaking her head, coming around the counter, and scanning the shelves. She scratches her chin, holds up a finger to me as if to tell me to wait, and slips through a back door. I glimpse a windowed storage room before the door swings shut.

A minute passes. Another. *Come on.* I've been away from Elias for at least an hour, and it will take me another half hour to get back to him. And that's if this girl even has the Tellis. What if he has another seizure? What if he shouts or yells and gives away his location to someone happening by?

The door opens, and the girl is back, this time with a squat jar of amber liquid: Tellis extract. From behind the counter, she painstakingly pulls out another, smaller vial and looks at me expectantly.

I hold up both hands once, twice. 'Twenty drachms.' That should be enough to last Elias a while. The child measures out the liquid with excruciating slowness, her eyes darting up at me every few seconds.

When she's finally sealed the vial with wax, I reach out to take it, but she jerks it away, wiggling four fingers at me. I drop four silvers into her hands. She shakes her head.

'Zaver!' She takes out a gold mark from a pouch and waves it in the air.

'Four marks?' I burst out. 'You might as well ask for the bleeding moon!' The girl just juts out her chin. I don't have time to haggle, so I dig the money out and slam it down, holding out my hand for the Tellis.

She hesitates, her eyes darting to the front door.

I draw my dagger with one hand and grab the vial with the other, shoving out of the shack with teeth bared. But the only movement in the dark lane is from a goat gnawing on some garbage. The beast bleats at me before turning back to his feast.

Still, I am uneasy. The Tribal girl was acting strange. I bolt, staying away from the main thoroughfare and sticking to the muddy, poorly lit back alleys of the market. I hurry to the western edge of the Roost, so focused on looking back that I don't see the dark, lean figure in front of me until I've run right into him.

'Pardon me,' a silky voice says. The stink of ghas and tea leaves overpowers me. 'I didn't see you there.'

My skin goes cold at the familiarity of the voice. The Tribesman. The one with the scar. His eyes lock with mine and narrow.

'And what's a gold-eyed Scholar girl doing in Raider's Roost? *Running* from something, perhaps?' *Skies.* He did recognize me.

I dart to his right, but he blocks me.

'Out of my way.' I flash my knife at him. He laughs and puts one hand on my shoulder, neatly disarming me with the other.

'You'll put out your own eye, little tigress.' He spins my dagger in one hand. 'I am Shikaat, of Tribe Gula. And you are . . . ?'

'None of your business.' I try to yank away from him, but his hand is like a vise.

'I just want to chat. Walk with me.' He tightens the hand on my shoulder.

'Get off me.' I kick at his ankle, and he winces and releases me. But when I dart toward the entrance to a side alley, he snatches my arm, and then grabs my other wrist, shoving up my sleeves.

'Slaves' cuffs.' He runs a finger along the still-chafed skin of my wrists. 'Recently removed. Interesting. Would you care to hear my theory?'

He leans close, black eyes sparkling, as if he's sharing a joke. 'I think there are very few Scholar girls with golden eyes wandering the wilderness, little tigress. Your injuries tell me you've seen battle. You smell of soot – perhaps from the fires in Serra? And the medicine – well, that's most interesting of all.'

Our exchange has drawn curious glances – more than curious. A Mariner and a Martial, both wearing leather armor that marks them as bounty hunters, watch with interest. One approaches, but the Tribesman marches me down the alley away from them. He barks a word into the shadows. A moment later, two men materialize – his toadies, no doubt – and turn to head off the bounty hunters.

'You're the Scholar girl the Martials are hunting.' Shikaat glances between the stalls, into the dark places where threats

79

might lurk. 'The one traveling with Elias Veturius. And there's something wrong with him, otherwise you wouldn't be here alone, so desperate for Tellis extract that you'd pay twenty times what you should for it.'

'How in the skies did you know?'

'Not many Scholars around here,' he says. 'When one shows up, we notice.'

Damn it. The girl in the apothecary must have tipped him off.

'Now.' His smile is all teeth. 'You're going to lead me to your unfortunate friend, or I'll stick a knife in your gut and drop you down a crevasse to die slowly.'

Behind us, the bounty hunters argue heatedly with Shikaat's men.

'He knows where Elias Veturius is!' I shout at the hunters. They reach for their weapons, and other heads in the market swing up.

The Tribesman sighs, giving me an almost rueful look. The second he turns his attention from me to the bounty hunters, I kick his ankle and twist free.

I dart beneath tarps, upsetting a basket of goods and nearly knocking an old Mariner woman onto her back. For a moment, I'm out of Shikaat's sight. A wall of rock rises ahead of me, and a row of tents sits to my right. To my left, a pyramid of crates leans precariously up against the side of a fur cart.

I rip a fur off the top of the stack and dive beneath the cart, covering myself and pulling my feet out of sight just before Shikaat bursts into the alley. Silence as he scans the area. Then footsteps coming closer . . . closer . . .

Disappear, Laia. I shrink back into the darkness, grabbing hold of my armlet for strength. *You can't see me. You see only shadows, only darkness.*

Shikaat kicks aside the crates, letting in a sliver of light beneath the cart. I hear him bend, hear his breathing as he peers under it.

I'm nothing, nothing but a pile of furs, nothing important. You don't see me. You don't see anything.

'Jitan!' He shouts to his men. 'Imir!'

The swift footsteps of two men approach, and a moment later, lamplight chases away the darkness beneath the cart. Shikaat rips the fur free, and I find myself staring into his triumphant face.

Except his triumph turns to bewilderment almost immediately. He gazes at the fur and then back at me. He holds up the lamp, illuminating me clearly.

But he doesn't look *at* me. Almost as if he can't see me. As if I'm invisible.

Which is impossible.

The second I think it, he blinks and grabs me.

'You disappeared,' he whispers. 'And now you're here. Did you magick me?' He shakes me hard, rattling my teeth in my head. 'How did you do it?'

'Piss off!' I claw at him, but he holds me at arm's distance.

'You were gone!' he hisses. 'And then you reappeared before my eyes.'

'You're insane!' I bite at his hand, and he drags me close, forcing my face toward him, glaring down into my eyes. 'You've been smoking too much ghas!'

'Say it again,' he says.

'You're *insane*. I was there the whole time.'

He shakes his head, as if he can tell I'm not lying but still doesn't believe me. When he releases my face, I try to twist away – to no avail.

'Enough,' he says as his henchmen bind my hands in front of me. 'Take me to the Mask, or you die.'

'I want a cut.' An idea blossoms in my head. 'Ten thousand marks. And we go alone I don't want your men following us.'

'No cut,' he says. 'My men stay at my side.'

'Then find him yourself! Stick a knife in me like you promised, and go.'

I hold his eyes, the way Nan used to when Tribal traders offered too low a price for her jams and she threatened to walk away. My heart thunders like the hooves of a horse.

'Five hundred marks,' the Tribesman says. As I open my mouth to protest, he holds up a hand. 'And safe passage to the Tribal lands. It's a good deal, girl. Take it.'

'Your men?'

'They stay.' He considers me. 'At a distance.'

The problem with greedy people, Pop once said to me, *is that they think everyone else is as greedy as they are.* Shikaat is no different.

'Give me your word as a Tribesman that you won't double-cross me.' Even I know how valuable such a vow is. 'I don't trust you otherwise.'

'You have my word.' He shoves me forward, and I stumble, just catching myself from falling. *Swine!* I bite my lip to keep from saying it.

Let him think he's cowed me. Let him think he's won. Soon, he'll realize his mistake: He vowed to play fair.

But I didn't.

CHAPTER TEN

Elias

The second that consciousness seeps into my mind, I know better than to open my eyes.

My hands and feet are bound with rope, and I lie on my side. My mouth tastes strange, like iron and herbs. Everything aches, but my mind feels more lucid than it has in days. Rain patters on rocks just a few feet away. I'm in a cave.

But the air feels wrong. I hear breathing, quick and nervous, and smell the wool robes and cured leather of Tribal traders.

'You can't kill him!' Laia is in front of me, her knee pressing into my forehead, her voice so close that I can feel her breath on my face. 'The Martials want him back alive. To – to face the Emperor.'

Someone kneeling at the crown of my head curses in Sadhese. Cold steel digs into my throat.

'Jitan – the message. Is the bounty only given if he's brought back alive?'

'I don't bleeding remember!' This voice comes from closer to my feet.

83

'If you're going to kill him, then at least wait a few days.' Laia's voice has a cold practicality to it, but the tension beneath is as taut as the string of an oud. 'In this weather his body would decompose fast. It will take at least five days to get him back to Serra. If the Martials can't identify him, then neither of us gets any money.'

'Kill him, Shikaat,' says a third Tribesman standing near my knees. 'If he wakes up, we're dead.'

'He's not going to wake up,' the man they call Shikaat says. 'Look at him – he's got an arm and a leg in the grave already.'

Laia slowly eases her body over my head. I feel glass between my lips. Liquid dribbles out – liquid that tastes of iron and herbs. *Tellis extract*. A second later the glass is gone, shoved back to where Laia must be hiding it.

'Shikaat, listen—' she begins, but the raider shoves her back.

'That's the second time you've leaned forward like that, girl. What are you up to?'

Time's up, Veturius.

'Nothing!' Laia says. 'I want the bounty as much as you do!'

One: I imagine the attack first – where I will strike, how I will move.

'Why did you lean forward?' Shikaat roars at Laia. 'And don't lie to me.'

Two: I flex the muscles of my left arm to prepare it, as the right is trapped beneath me. I inhale silently to get breath to every part of my body.

'Where's the Tellis extract?' Shikaat hisses, suddenly remembering. 'Give it to me!'

Three: Before Laia can respond to the Tribesman, I shove my right foot against the ground for leverage and spin backward on my hip, away from Shikaat's blade, taking out the Tribesman at my feet with my bound legs and rolling up as he slams to the ground. I lunge for the Tribesman at my knees next, head butting him before he can lift his blade. He drops it, and I turn to catch it, thankful that he at least kept it sharp. With two saws, I'm through the ropes on my wrists, and with two more, the one on my ankles. The first Tribesman I knocked over scrambles up and bolts out of the cave – no doubt to get backup.

'Stop!'

I wheel toward the last Tribesman – Shikaat – who holds Laia against his chest. He has her wrists squeezed in one hand, a blade to her throat, and murder in his eyes.

'Drop the blade. Put your hands in the air. Or I kill her.'

'Go on then,' I say in perfect Sadhese. His jaw tightens, but he doesn't move. A man not easily surprised. I consider my words carefully. 'A second after you kill her, I'll kill you. Then you'll be dead, and I'll be free.'

'Try me.' He digs the blade into Laia's neck, drawing blood. Her eyes dart around as she tries to spot something – anything – she can use against him. 'I have a hundred men outside this cave—'

'If you had a hundred men outside' – I keep my attention on Shikaat – 'you'd have called them in alre—'

I fly forward mid-word, one of Grandfather's favorite tricks. *Fools pay attention to words in a fight,* he said once. *Warriors take advantage of them.* I wrench the Tribesman's right hand away from Laia while shoving her out of the way with my body.

Which, at that exact moment, turns traitor on me.

The adrenaline rush of the attack drains out of me like water down a sewer, and I stagger back, my vision doubling. Laia grabs something off the ground and spins round to the Tribesman, who grins at her nastily.

'Your hero still has poison running through him, girl,' he hisses. 'He can't help you now.'

He lunges at her, lashing out with the knife, aiming to kill her. Laia flings dirt into his eyes, and he roars, turning his face away. But he cannot stop the momentum of his body. Laia lifts her blade, and with a sickening squelch, the Tribesman impales himself upon it.

Laia gasps and releases the blade, backing away. Shikaat reaches out, grabbing her by the hair, and her mouth opens in a silent scream, her eyes fixed on the blade in the raider's chest. She finds my face, terror in her own as with his last bit of life, Shikaat seeks to kill her.

Strength finally returns to my body, and I shove him away from her. He releases her, looking at his suddenly weak hand curiously, as if it doesn't belong to him. Then he thuds to the ground, dead.

'Laia?' I call to her, but she stares at the body as if in a trance. *Her first kill.* My stomach twists in remembrance of my own first kill – a Barbarian boy. I recall his blue-painted face, the deep gash in his stomach. I know what Laia feels in this moment all too well. Disgust. Horror. Fear.

My energy comes back to me now. Everything is pain – my chest, my arms, my legs. But I am not seizing, I am not hallucinating. I call to Laia again, and this time she looks up.

'I didn't want to do it,' she says. 'He – he just came at me. And the knife—'

'I know,' I say gently. She won't want to discuss it. Her mind is in survival mode – it won't let her. 'Tell me what happened in the Roost.' I can distract her, at least for a bit. 'Tell me how you got the Tellis.'

She relates the tale swiftly, helping me bind the unconscious

Tribesman as she does so. As I listen, I'm half in disbelief and half bursting with pride at her sheer nerve.

Outside the cave, I hear the hoot of an owl, a bird that has no business being out in weather like this. I edge to the entrance.

Nothing moves in the rocks beyond, but a gust of wind blows the stink of sweat and horse toward me. Apparently Shikaat *wasn't* lying about having a hundred men waiting beyond the cave.

To the south, at our backs, is solid rock. Serra lies to the west. The cave faces north, opening out onto a narrow trail that winds down into the desert and toward the passes that would take us safely through the Serran Range. To the east, the trail plunges into the Jutts, a half mile of sheer fingers of rock that are death in the best of weather, let alone when it's pissing rain. The eastern wall of the Serran Range rises beyond the Jutts. No trails, no passes, just wild mountains that eventually drop away into the Tribal desert.

Ten hells.

'Elias.' Laia is a nervous presence beside me. 'We should get out of here. Before the Tribesman wakes up.'

'One problem.' I nod out to the darkness. 'We're surrounded.'

Five minutes later, I've roped Laia to me and moved Shikaat's lackey, still bound, to the entrance of the cave. I secure Shikaat's body to the horse, removing his cloak so his men will recognize him. Laia pointedly doesn't look at the body.

'Goodbye, nag.' Laia rubs the horse between his ears. 'Thank you for carrying me. I'm sad to lose you.'

'I'll steal you another,' I say dryly. 'Ready?'

She nods, and I move to the back of the cave, laying flint to tinder. I nurse a flame, feeding it the few pieces of brush and wood I could find, much of it wet. Thick white smoke billows up, filling the cave quickly.

'Now, Laia.'

Laia slaps the horse's rump with all her might, sending him and Shikaat thundering out of the cave and toward the Tribesmen waiting to the north. The men hiding behind the freestanding rocks to the west emerge, bellowing at the sight of the smoke, at their dead leader.

Which means they're not looking at Laia and me. We slip out of the cave, hoods pulled low, masked by smoke and rain and darkness. I pull Laia onto my back, check the rope I've tied to an unobtrusive and half-hidden finger of rock, and then swing down into the Jutts silently, going hand below hand until I've reached a rain-slicked rock ten feet below. Laia hops down from my back with a slight scrape that I hope the Tribesmen won't hear. I tug on the rope to release it.

Above, the Tribesmen cough as they enter the smoky cave. I hear them curse as they pull their friend free.

Follow, I mouth to Laia. We move slowly, the sounds of our passage covered by the thudding boots and shouts of the Tribesmen. The rocks of the Jutts are sharp and slippery, the jagged edges digging into our boots, catching on our clothes.

My mind goes back six years, to when Helene and I camped out at the Roost for a season.

All Fivers come to the Roost to spy on the Raiders for a couple of months. The Raiders hated it; getting caught by them meant a long, slow death – one of the reasons the Commandant sent students here in the first place.

Helene and I were stationed together – the bastard and the girl, the two outcasts. The Commandant must have gloated at a pairing she thought would get one of us killed. But friendship made Hel and me stronger, not weaker.

We skipped over the Jutts as a game, light as gazelles, daring

88

each other to make crazier and crazier jumps. She matched my leaps with such ease that you'd never guess she feared heights. Ten hells, we were stupid. So certain we wouldn't fall. So sure death couldn't find us.

Now I know better.

You're dead. You just don't know it yet.

The rain thins as we move across the rock field. Laia remains silent, her lips pressed together. She's troubled. I feel it. Thinking of Shikaat, no doubt. Still, she keeps up with me, hesitating only once, when I leap across a gap five feet wide, with a two-hundred-foot chasm beneath.

I make the jump first, clearing the gap easily. When I look back, her face is blanched.

'I'll catch you,' I say.

She stares at me with her gold eyes, fear and determination warring. Without warning, she leaps, and the force of her body knocks me back. My hands are filled with her – waist, hips, that cloud of sugar-scented hair. Her full lips part like she's going to say something. Not that I'll respond intelligently. Not with so much of her pressing against so much of me.

I push her away. She stumbles, hurt flickering across her face. I don't even know why I do it, except that getting close to her feels wrong somehow. Unfair.

'Almost there,' I say to distract her. 'Stay with me now.'

As we get closer to the mountains and farther from the Roost, the rain thins out, replaced by thick mist.

The rock field levels and flattens into uneven terraces, the shelves interspersed with trees and scrub. I stop Laia and listen for sounds of pursuit. Nothing. The mist lays thick on the Jutts like a blanket, drifting through the trees around us and lending them an eeriness that makes Laia draw closer.

'Elias,' she whispers. 'Will we turn north from here? Or circle back to the foothills?'

'We don't have the gear to climb the mountains north of us,' I say. 'And Shikaat's men are probably crawling all over the foothills. They'll be looking for us.'

Laia's face pales. 'Then how do we get to Kauf? If we take a ship from the south, the delay—'

'We go east,' I say. 'Into the Tribal lands.'

Before she protests, I kneel and draw a rough map of the mountains and their surrounds in the dirt. 'It's about two weeks to the Tribal lands. A bit longer if we're delayed. In three weeks, the Fall Gathering begins in Nur. Every Tribe will be there – buying, selling, trading, arranging marriages, celebrating births. When it's over, more than two hundred caravans will make their way out of the city. And each caravan is made up of hundreds of people.'

Understanding dawns in Laia's eyes. 'We leave with them.'

I nod. 'Thousands of horses, wagons, and Tribesmen head out at once. In case anyone *does* track us to Nur, they'll lose our trail. Some of those caravans will head north. We find one willing to shelter us. We hide among them and make our way to Kauf before the winter snows. A Tribal trader and his sister.'

'Sister?' She crosses her arms. 'We look nothing alike.'

'Or wife, if you prefer.' I raise an eyebrow at her, unable to resist. A blush rises in her cheeks and blooms down her neck. I wonder if it goes any lower. *Stop, Elias.*

'How will we convince a Tribe not to turn us in for the bounty?'

I finger the wooden coin in my pocket, the favor owed me by a clever Tribeswoman named Afya Ara-Nur. 'Leave that to me.'

Laia considers what I've said and finally nods her agreement. I stand and listen, feeling out the land around us. It's too dark to continue on – we need a place to camp for the night. We pick our way up the terraces and into the dark forest beyond until I find a good spot: a clearing beneath a rock overhang, bordered by old-growth pines, their pitted trunks overgrown with moss. As I clear the rock and twigs from the dry earth beneath the overhang, I feel Laia's hand on my shoulder.

'I need to tell you something,' she says, and when I look into her face I lose my breath for a second. 'When I went into the Roost,' she goes on, 'I was afraid that the poison would . . .' She shakes her head, and her words rush out. 'I'm glad you're all right. And I know you're risking so much to do this for me. Thank you.'

'Laia—' *You kept me alive. You kept yourself alive. You're as brave as your mother. Don't ever let anyone tell you different.*

Perhaps I'd follow the words by easing her toward me, running a finger along the golden line of her collarbone and up her long neck. Gathering her hair into a knot and pulling her close slowly, so, so slowly –

Pain lances through my arm. A reminder. *You destroy all those who get close to you.*

I could hide the truth from Laia. Finish the mission before my time is up and disappear. But the Resistance kept secrets from her. Her brother kept his work with Spiro from her. The identity of her parents' killer was hidden from her.

Her life has been nothing but secrets. She deserves the truth.

'You should sit down.' I pull away from her. 'I have to tell you something too.' She is quiet as I speak, as I lay bare what the Commandant has done, as I tell her about the Waiting Place and the Soul Catcher.

When I finish, Laia's hands shake, and I can barely hear her voice.

'You – you're going to die? No. No.' She wipes her face and

takes a deep breath. 'There must be something, some cure, some way—'

'There isn't.' I keep my voice matter-of-fact. 'I'm certain. I have a few months, though. As many as six, I hope.'

'I have never hated anyone the way I hate the Commandant. Never.' She bites her lip. 'You said she let us go. Is this why? She wanted you to die slowly?'

'I think she wanted to guarantee my death,' I say. 'But for now, I'm more useful to her alive than dead. No idea why.'

'Elias.' Laia huddles into her cloak. After considering for a moment, I move closer to her, and we lean into each other's warmth. 'I can't ask you to spend the last few months of your life on a mad dash to Kauf Prison. You should find your Tribal family. . . .'

You hurt people, the Soul Catcher said. So many people: the men who died in the Third Trial either by my hand or because of my orders; Helene, left to Marcus's predations; Grandfather, fleeing from his home and into exile because of me; even Laia, forced to face the butchering block in the Fourth Trial.

'I can't help the people I've hurt,' I say. 'I can't change what I did to them.' I lean toward her. I need her to understand that I mean every word of what I say. 'Your brother is the only Scholar on this continent who knows how to make Serric steel. I don't know if Spiro Teluman will meet Darin in the Free Lands. I don't even know if Teluman is alive. But I do know that if I can get Darin out of prison, if saving his life means that he can give the Empire's foes a chance to fight for their freedom, then perhaps I'll make up for some of the evil I've brought into the world. His life – and all the lives he could save – to make up for those that I've taken.'

'What if he's dead, Elias?'

'You said you heard men in the Roost talking about him? About his connection to Teluman?' She tells me again what they said, and I consider. 'The Martials will need to make sure Darin hasn't shared his blacksmithing knowledge and that if he has, that knowledge doesn't spread. They'll keep him alive for questioning.' Though I don't know if he'll survive the interrogations. Especially when I consider the Warden of Kauf and the twisted ways he gets answers out of his prisoners.

Laia turns her face to mine. 'How sure are you?'

'If I wasn't sure, but you knew there was a chance – the slightest chance – that he still lived, would you try to save him?' I see the answer in her eyes. 'It doesn't matter if I'm sure, Laia,' I say. 'As long as you want to save him, then I will help you. I made a vow. I'm not going to break it.'

I take Laia's hands in mine. Cool. Strong. I would keep them here, kiss every callus on her palms, nibble the inside of her wrist so she gasped. I would pull her closer and see if she too wished to give in to the fire that burns between us.

But for what? So that she can grieve when I'm dead? It's wrong. It's selfish.

I pull away from her slowly, holding her eyes as I do it, so she knows it's the last thing I want. Hurt washes across her eyes. Confusion.

Acceptance.

I am glad she understands. I can't get close to her – not in that way. I can't let her get close to me. Doing so will only bring grief and pain.

And she's had enough of that.

CHAPTER ELEVEN

Helene

'Leave her be, Nightbringer.' I feel a strong hand beneath my arm, forcing me away from the wall and upright. *Cain?*

Pale wisps of hair snake out of the Augur's hood. His wasted features are shadowed by his black robes, and his blood-red eyes are grave as he regards the creature. *Nightbringer*, he called it, like the old stories Mamie Rila used to tell.

The Nightbringer hisses softly, and Cain's eyes narrow.

'Leave her, I say.' The Augur steps in front of me. 'She does not walk in the darkness.'

'Doesn't she?' The Nightbringer chuckles before disappearing in a whirl of his cloak, leaving the scent of fire trailing. Cain turns to me.

'Well met, Blood Shrike.'

'Well met? *Well met?*'

'Come. We do not wish for the Commandant or her lackeys to overhear us.'

My body still shakes from what I saw in the Nightbringer's eyes. As Cain and I leave Villa Veturia, I get hold of myself. The

94

second we clear the gates, I wheel on the Augur. Only a lifetime of veneration keeps me from grabbing desperately at his robes.

'You promised.' The Augur knows my every thought, so I don't hide the crack in my voice or fight the tears in my eyes. It is a relief not to, in a way. 'You swore he would be all right if I kept my vow.'

'No, Blood Shrike.' Cain leads me away from the villa and down a wide avenue of Illustrian homes. We approach one that must have once been beautiful but is now a burned-out shell – destroyed days ago during the worst of the Scholar revolution. Cain wanders into the smoking debris. 'We promised that if you held the oath, Elias would survive the Trials. And he did.'

'What was the point of him surviving the Trials if he's just going to die a few weeks from now by my hand anyway? I can't refuse Marcus's order, Cain. I swore fealty. You *made* me swear fealty.'

'Do you know who lived in this house, Helene Aquilla?'

Changing the subject, of course. No wonder Elias was always so irritated by the Augurs. I force myself to look around. The house is unfamiliar.

'Mask Laurent Marianus. His wife, Inah.' Cain nudges aside a charred beam with his foot and picks up a roughly carved wooden horse. 'Their children: Lucia, Amara, and Darien. Six Scholar slaves. One of those was Siyyad. He loved Darien like a son.'

Cain turns the horse over and gently sets it back down. 'Siyyad carved this for the boy two months ago, when Darien turned four.' My chest tightens. *What happened to him?*

'Five of the slaves tried to flee when the Scholars attacked with torches and pitch. Siyyad ran for Darien. He found him, holding his horse, hiding beneath his bed in terror. He pulled him out. But the fire was too swift. They died quickly. All of them. Even the slaves who tried to run.'

'Why are you telling me this?'

'Because the Empire is filled with homes like this. With lives like these. Do you think that Darien's or Siyyad's lives matter less, somehow, than Elias's? They do not.'

'I know that, Cain.' I feel chagrined that he would need to remind me of the value of my own people. 'But what was the point of everything I did in the First Trial if Elias is just going to die anyway?'

Cain turns the full force of his presence upon me. I shrink back.

'You will hunt Elias. You will find him. For what you learn on that journey – about yourself, your land, your enemies – that knowledge is essential to the Empire's survival. And to your destiny.'

I feel like retching at his feet. *I trusted you. I believed you. I did what you wanted.* And now my fears will come to life for my trouble. Hunting Elias – killing him – that's not even the worst part of the nightmares. It's the feeling inside as I do it. That's what makes the dreams so potent – the emotions that roll through me: satisfaction as I torment my friend, pleasure at the laughter of Marcus, who stands beside me, looking on in approval.

'Do not let despair take you.' Cain's voice softens. 'Hold true to your heart, and the Empire will be well served.'

'The Empire.' *Always the Empire.* 'What about Elias? What about me?'

'Elias's fate is in his own hands. Come now, Blood Shrike.' Cain lifts a hand to my head, as if offering a blessing. 'This is what it means to have faith, to believe in something greater than yourself.'

A sigh escapes me, and I wipe the tears from my face. *This is what it means to believe.* I wish it weren't so hard.

I watch as he drifts away from me, deeper into the ruins of the house, finally disappearing behind a scorched pillar. I don't bother following. I already know he's gone.

* * *

The Black Guard barracks stands in a Mercator section of the city. It is a long, stone building with no markings but a silver, open-winged shrike embossed on the door.

The second I enter, the half dozen Masks within stop what they are doing and salute.

'You.' I look to the closest Black Guard. 'Go and find Lieutenant Faris Candelan and Lieutenant Dex Atrius. When they arrive, assign them quarters and arms.' Before the guard can even acknowledge, I move on to the next. 'You,' I say. 'Get me every report from the night that Veturius escaped. Every attack, every explosion, every dead soldier, every looted store, every eyewitness account – all of it. Where are Shrike's quarters?'

'Through there, sir.' The soldier points at a black door at the end of the room. 'Lieutenant Avitas Harper is within. He arrived just before you.'

Avitas Harper. Lieutenant Harper. A chill rolls across my skin. My torturer. Of course. He too is a member of the Black Guard.

'What in the bleeding skies does he want?'

The Black Guard looks surprised for a moment. 'Orders, I believe. The Emperor assigned him to your task force.'

You mean the Commandant assigned him. Harper is her spy.

Harper waits at my desk in commander's quarters. He salutes with unsettling blankness, as if he didn't just spend five days in a dungeon tormenting me.

'Harper.' I sit down opposite him, the desk between us. 'Report.'

97

Harper says nothing for a moment. I sigh in open irritation.

'You've been assigned to this detail, yes? Tell me what we know about the whereabouts of the traitor Veturius, *Lieutenant*.' I put as much disdain in the word as possible. 'Or are you as ineffective a hunter as you are an interrogator?'

Harper doesn't react to the jibe. 'We have one lead: a dead Mask just beyond the city.' He pauses. 'Blood Shrike, have you chosen your force for this mission?'

'You and two others,' I say. 'Lieutenant Dex Atrius and Lieutenant Faris Candelan. They'll be inducted into the Black Guard today. We'll call in backup as needed.'

'I do not recognize the names. Generally, Shrike, inductees are chosen by—'

'Harper.' I lean forward. He will not have control over me. Never again. 'I know you're the Commandant's spy. The Emperor told me. I can't get rid of you. But that doesn't mean I have to listen to you. As your commander, I order you to shut up about Faris and Dex. Now take me through what we know of Veturius's escape.'

I expect a retort. Instead, I get a shrug, which is somehow more infuriating. Harper details Elias's escape – the soldiers he killed, sightings of him in the city.

A knock comes at the door mid-report, and to my relief, Dex and Faris enter. Faris's blond hair is a mess, and Dex's dark skin is ashen. Their singed capes and bloodied armor are evidence of their activities the past few days. Their eyes widen when they see me: cut, bruised, a mess. But then Dex steps forward.

'Blood Shrike.' He salutes, and despite myself, I smile. Trust Dex to remember protocol, even when faced with the shattered remnants of an old friend.

'Ten hells, Aquilla.' Faris is aghast. 'What did they do to you?'

'Welcome, Lieutenants,' I say. 'I assume the messenger told you of the mission?'

'You're to kill Elias,' Faris says. 'Hel—'

'Are you prepared to serve?'

'Of course,' Faris goes on. 'You need men you can trust, but Hel—'

'This' – I speak over him, lest he say something that Harper can report back to the Emperor and the Commandant – 'is Lieutenant Avitas Harper. My torturer and the Commandant's spy.' Immediately, Faris clamps his mouth shut. 'Harper is also assigned to this mission, so beware of what you say around him, as it will all be reported back to the Commandant and Emperor.' Harper shifts uncomfortably, and a bolt of triumph shoots through me.

'Dex,' I say. 'One of the men is bringing in the reports from the night Elias escaped. You were his lieutenant. Look for anything that might be relevant. Faris, you're with me. Harper and I have a lead outside the city.'

I am thankful that my friends accept my orders stoically, that their training keeps their faces blank. Dex excuses himself, and Faris follows to procure horses. Harper stands, his head tilted as he looks at me. I cannot read his expression – curiosity, perhaps. He reaches into his pocket, and I tense, remembering the the brass beaters he used on me during my interrogation.

But he only pulls out a man's ring. Heavy, silver, and embossed with a bird, wings spread, beak wide in a scream. The Blood Shrike's ring of office.

'Yours now.' He takes out a chain. 'In case it's too big.'

It is too big, but a jeweler can fix that. Perhaps he expects me to thank him. Instead, I take the ring, ignore the chain, and sweep past him.

*　　*　　*

The dead Mask in the dry flats beyond Serra sounds like a promising start. No tracks, no ambush. But the moment I see the body – hanging from a tree and bearing clear signs of torture – I know Elias didn't kill him.

'Veturius is a Mask, Blood Shrike. Trained by the Commandant,' Harper says as we head back to the city. 'Is he not a butcher like the rest of us?'

'Veturius wouldn't leave a body out in the open,' Faris says. 'Whoever did this wanted the body found. Why do that if he doesn't want us on his trail?'

'To throw us off,' Harper says. 'To send us west instead of south.'

As they argue, I mull it over. I know the Mask. He was one of four ordered to guard Elias at his execution. Lieutenant Cassius Pritorius, a vicious predator with a taste for young girls. He'd done a stint at Blackcliff as a Combat Centurion. I was fourteen then, but I kept one hand on a dagger when he was around.

Marcus sent the other three Masks guarding Elias to Kauf for six months as punishment for losing him. Why not Cassius? How did he end up like this?

My mind leaps to the Commandant, but it doesn't make sense. If Cassius angered her, she'd torment and kill him publicly – all the more to build her reputation.

I feel a prickling on my neck, as if I'm being watched.

'Little ssssinger . . .'

The voice is distant, carried on the wind. I whirl in my saddle. The desert is empty but for a tumbleweed rolling past. Faris and Harper slow their horses, staring back at me quizzically. *Walk on, Aquilla. It was nothing.*

The next day of the hunt is equally useless, as is the one after that. Dex finds nothing in the reports. Runners and drum messages bring false leads: Two men killed in Navium, and a witness swears Elias is the murderer. A Martial and a Scholar reportedly checking in to an inn – as if Elias would be fool enough check in to a bleeding inn.

By the end of the third day, I'm exhausted and frustrated. Marcus has sent two messages already, demanding to know if I've made any headway.

I should sleep in the Black Guard barracks, as I have the past two nights. But I am sick of the barracks and particularly sick of the feeling that Harper is reporting my every move back to Marcus and the Commandant.

It's nearly midnight when I arrive at Villa Aquilla, but the lights of the house blaze, and dozens of carriages line the road outside. I take the slaves' entrance in to avoid family, and run straight into Livvy, who is supervising a late dinner.

She sighs at my expression. 'Go in through your window. The uncles have taken over the bottom floor. They'll want to speak with you.'

The uncles – my father's brothers and cousins – lead the main families of Gens Aquilla. Good men, but long-winded.

'Where's Mother?'

'With the aunts, trying to keep a rein on their hysteria.' Livvy raises an eyebrow. 'They're not happy about the Aquilla-Farrar alliance. Father asked me to serve dinner.'

So she can listen and learn, no doubt. Livia, unlike Hannah, has an interest in the running of the Gens. Father is no fool; he knows what an asset that can be.

As I leave through the back door, Livvy calls, 'Watch out for Hannah. She's acting strange. Smug. Like she knows something we don't.'

I roll my eyes. As if Hannah could possibly know anything I would care about.

I leap into the trees that curl toward my window. Sneaking in and out – even injured – is nothing. I used to do it regularly during leave to meet Elias.

Though never for the reason I wanted.

As I swing into my room, I berate myself. *He's not Elias. He's the traitor Veturius, and you have to hunt him.* Maybe if I keep saying the words, they'll stop hurting.

'*Little singer.*'

My entire body goes numb at the voice – the same one I heard in the desert. That moment of shock is my undoing. A hand clamps over my mouth, and a whisper sounds in my ear.

'I have a story to tell. Listen carefully. You might learn something worthwhile.'

Female. Strong hands. Badly calloused. No accent. I move to throw her off, but the steel held steady against my throat stops me. I think of the body of the Mask out in the desert. Whoever this is, she's deadly, and she's not afraid to kill me.

'Once upon a time,' the strange voice says, 'a girl and a boy tried to escape a city of flame and terror. In this city, they found salvation half-touched by shadow. And there waited a silver-skinned she-demon with a heart as black as her home. They fought the demon beneath a sleepless spire of suffering. They brought the demon low and escaped victorious. A pretty tale, is it not?' My captor puts her face close to my ear. 'The story is in the city, little singer,' she says. 'Find the story, and you'll find Elias Veturius.'

The hand over my mouth drops away, as does the blade. I turn to see the figure darting across my room.

'Wait!' I turn and put my hands in the air. The figure halts. 'The dead Mask in the desert,' I say. 'You did that?'

'A message for you, little singer,' the woman rasps. 'So you wouldn't be stupid enough to fight me. Don't feel badly about it. He was a murderer and a rapist. He deserved to die. Which reminds me.' She tilts her head. 'The girl – Laia. Don't touch her. If any harm comes to her, no force in this land will stop me from gutting you. Slowly.'

With that, she is moving again. I leap up and unsheathe my blade. Too late. The woman is through the open window and scuttling away across the rooftops.

But not before I catch sight of her face – hardened by hatred, mangled beyond belief, and instantly recognizable.

The Commandant's slave. The one who is supposed to be dead. The one everyone called Cook.

CHAPTER TWELVE

Laia

When Elias wakes me the morning after leaving the Roost, my hands are wet. Even in the pre-dawn gloom, I see the Tribesman's blood running down my arms.

'Elias.' I frantically wipe my palms on my cloak. 'The blood, it won't come off.' It's all over him too. 'You're covered—'

'Laia.' He is by my side in an instant. 'It's just the mist.'

'No. It's – it's everywhere.' *Death, everywhere.*

Elias takes my hands in his own, holding them up to the dim starlight. 'Look. The mist beads on the skin.'

Reality finally takes hold as he pulls me slowly to my feet. *Just a nightmare.*

'We need to move.' He nods to the rock field, barely visible through the trees a hundred yards away. 'There's someone out there.'

I don't see anything out in the Jutts, nor do I hear anything beyond the creaking of branches in the wind and the chirping of early-rising birds. Still, my body aches with tension.

'Soldiers?' I whisper to Elias.

He shakes his head. 'Not sure. I saw a flash of metal – armor, or perhaps a weapon. It's definitely someone following us.' At my unease, he offers a quick smile. 'Don't look so worried. Most successful missions are just a series of barely averted disasters.'

If I thought Elias's pace out of the Roost was intense, I was mistaken. The Tellis has nearly restored him to his former strength. In minutes, we have left the rock field behind and are making our way through the mountains as if the Nightbringer himself is on our heels.

The terrain is treacherous, pocked with overflowing gulches and streams. Soon enough, I find that it takes all of my concentration just to keep up with Elias. Which isn't a bad thing. After what happened with Shikaat, after learning what the Commandant did to Elias, I want nothing more than to push my memories into a dark closet in my mind.

Over and over again, Elias eyes the trail at our backs.

'Either we lost them,' he says, 'or they're being very clever about keeping themselves hidden. I'm thinking the latter.'

Elias says little else. His attempt, I assume, to keep his distance. To protect me. Part of me understands his reasoning – respects it, even. But at the same time, I feel the loss of his company keenly. We escaped Serra together. We fought the wraiths together. I cared for him when he was poisoned.

Pop used to say that standing by someone during their darkest times creates a bond. A sense of obligation that is less a weight and more a gift. I feel tied to Elias now. I do not *want* him to shut me out.

Midway through the second day, the skies open up and we are deluged. The mountain air turns cold, and our pace slows until I want to scream. Every second seems like an eternity I must spend with thoughts I want desperately to suppress. The Commandant

105

poisoning Elias. Shikaat dying. Darin in Kauf, suffering at the hands of the prison's infamous Warden.

Death, everywhere.

A forced march in bone-numbing sleet simplifies life. After three weeks, my world has narrowed to sucking in the next breath, forcing myself to take the next step, finding the will to do it again. At nightfall, Elias and I collapse in exhaustion, soaked and shivering. In the morning, we shake the frost off our cloaks and begin again. We push harder now, trying to make up time.

When we finally wind down from the higher elevations, the rain lets up. A chilly mist descends over the trees, sticky as cobwebbing. My pants are torn at the knees, my tunic shredded.

'Strange,' Elias mutters. 'Never seen weather like this so close to the Tribal lands.'

Our pace eases to a crawl, and when sunset is still an hour away, he slows.

'There's no use going on in this muck,' he says. 'We should reach Nur tomorrow. Let's find a place to camp.'

No! Stopping will give me time to think – to remember.

'It's not even dark yet,' I say. 'What about whoever is following us? Surely we can—'

Elias gives me a level look. 'We're stopping,' he says. 'I haven't seen any sign of our tail in days. The rain's finally gone. We need rest and a hot meal.'

Minutes later, he spots a rise. I can just make out a cluster of monolithic boulders atop it. At Elias's request, I start a fire while he disappears behind one of the boulders. He is gone for a long time, and when he returns, he's clean-shaven. He's scrubbed off the dirt of the mountains and changed into clean clothes.

'Are you sure this is a good idea?' I've nursed the fire to a respectable little flame, but I peer into the woods nervously. If our tail is still out there – if they see the smoke –

'The fog masks the smoke.' He nods to one of the boulders and gives me a quick once-over. 'There's a spring there. You should clean up. I'll find dinner.'

My face heats – I know how I must look. Ripped fatigues, covered in mud up to my knees, scratches on my face, and wild, uncouth hair. Everything I own smells of sodden leaves and dirt.

At the spring I strip away my shredded, disgusting tunic, using the one clean corner to scrub myself off. I find a patch of dried blood. Shikaat's. Swiftly, I cast the tunic away.

Don't think about it, Laia.

I peer behind me, but Elias is gone. The part of me that can't forget the strength of his arms and the heat of his eyes during the dance at the Moon Festival wishes he had stayed. Looked. Offered the comfort of his touch. It would be a welcome distraction to feel the warmth of his hands on my skin, in my hair. It would be a gift.

An hour later, I'm scrubbed raw and dressed in clean, if damp, clothes. My mouth waters at the smell of roasting rabbit. I expect Elias to get up the second I appear. If we're not walking or eating, he leaves on patrol. But today, he nods at me, and I settle in beside him – as close to the fire as possible – and comb the snarls from my hair.

He points to my armlet. 'It's beautiful.'

'My mother gave it to me. Just before she died.'

'The pattern. I feel like I've seen it before.' Elias tilts his head. 'May I?'

I reach up to take off the armlet but stop, a peculiar reluctance coming over me. *Don't be ridiculous, Laia. He's going to give it right back.*

107

'Just . . . just for a minute, all right?' I hand the armlet over, edgy as he turns it in his hands, examining the pattern barely visible beneath the tarnish.

'Silver,' he says. 'Do you think the fey could sense it? The efrit and the wraiths kept asking for silver.'

'No idea.' I take it quickly when he hands it back, my whole body relaxing as I put it on. 'But I'd die before I gave this up. It was the last thing my mother gave me. Do—do you have anything of your father's?'

'Nothing.' Elias doesn't sound bitter. 'Not even a name. Just as well. Whoever he was, I don't think he was a good person.'

'Why? You're good. And you didn't get it from the Commandant.'

Elias's smile is sad. 'Just a hunch.' He pokes the fire with a stick. 'Laia,' he says gently. 'We should talk about it.'

Oh skies. 'Talk about what?'

'Whatever it is that's bothering you. I can take a guess, but it might be better if you tell me.'

'You want to talk *now*? After weeks of not even looking at me?'

'I look at you.' His response is swift, his voice low. 'Even when I shouldn't.'

'Then why won't you say anything? Do you think I'm – I'm horrible? For what happened with Shikaat? I didn't want to—' I choke back the rest of my words. Elias drops the stick and inches closer. I feel his fingers on my chin and make myself look at him.

'Laia, I am the last person who will judge you for killing in your own defense. Look at what I am. Look at my life. I left you alone because I thought you might find comfort in solitude. As for not . . . looking at you, I don't want to hurt you. I'm dead in a few months. About five, if I'm lucky. It's best if I keep my distance. We both know that.'

'So much death,' I say. 'It's everywhere. What's the point then of living? Will I ever escape it? In a few months you'll . . .' I can't say the words. 'And Shikaat. He was going to kill me – and then . . . then he was dead. His blood was so warm, and he *looked* alive, but—' I suppress a shudder and straighten my back. 'Never mind. I'm letting this get the best of me. I—'

'Your emotions make you human,' Elias says. 'Even the unpleasant ones have a purpose. Don't lock them away. If you ignore them, they just get louder and angrier.'

A lump rises in my throat, insistent and clawing, like a howl that's been trapped inside me.

Elias pulls me into a hug, and as I lean into his shoulder, the sound lurking within emerges, something between a scream and a sob. Something animal and strange. Frustration and fear at what is to come. Rage at how I always feel as if I'm thwarted. Terror that I will never see my brother again.

After a long time, I pull back. Elias's face is somber when I look up at him. He wipes my tears away. His scent rolls over me. I breathe it in.

The open expression on his face fades. I can practically see him fling up a wall. He drops his arms and moves back.

'Why do you do that?' I try to rein in my exasperation and fail. 'You close yourself up. You shut me out because you don't want me to get close. What about what *I* want? You won't hurt me, Elias.'

'I will,' he says. 'Trust me.'

'I don't trust you. Not about this.'

Defiantly, I edge closer to him. He clenches his jaw but doesn't move. Without looking away, I bring a tentative hand to his mouth. Those lips, curved like they're always smiling, even when his eyes are lit with desire, as they are now.

'This is a bad idea,' he murmurs. We're so close that I can see a long eyelash that's landed on his cheek. I can see the hints of blue in his hair.

'Then why aren't you stopping it?'

'Because I'm a fool.' We breathe each other's breath, and as his body relaxes, as his hands finally slide around my back, I close my eyes.

Then he freezes. My eyes snap open. Elias's attention is fixed on the tree line. A second later, he stands and draws his scims in one fluid motion. I scramble to my feet.

'Laia.' He steps around me. 'Our tail has caught up. Hide in the boulders. And' – his voice takes on a sudden note of command as he meets my eyes – 'if anyone gets near you, fight with all you've got.'

I draw my knife and dart behind him, trying to see what he sees, to hear what he hears. The forest around us is silent.

Zing.

An arrow flies through the trees, straight at Elias's heart. He blocks it with a twitch of a scim.

Another missile hurtles out. *Zing* – and another, and another. Elias blocks them all, until a small forest of broken arrows sits at his feet.

'I could do this all night,' he says, and I start, because his voice is devoid of emotion. The voice of a Mask.

'Let the girl go,' someone snarls from the trees, 'and be on your way.'

Elias glances over his shoulder at me, one eyebrow cocked.

'A friend of yours?'

I shake my head. 'I don't have any—'

A figure steps out of the trees – dressed in black, heavily hooded, an arrow nocked in his bow. In the heavy mist, I cannot make out his face. But something about him is familiar.

'If you're here for the bounty—' Elias begins, but the archer cuts him off.

'I'm not,' he snaps. 'I'm here for her.'

'Well, you can't have her,' Elias says. 'You can keep wasting arrows, or we can fight.' Fast as a whip, Elias flips one of his scims around and offers it to the man with such blatant and insulting arrogance that I grimace. If our attacker was angry before, he'll be furious now.

The man drops his bow, staring at us for a second before shaking his head.

'She was right,' he says, his voice hollow. 'He didn't take you. You went willingly.'

Oh skies, I know him now. Of course I know him. He pushes his hood back, hair pouring out like flame.

Keenan.

CHAPTER THIRTEEN

Elias

While I attempt to work out how – and why – the redhead from the Moon Festival has tracked us all the way through the mountains, another figure trudges out from the woods, her blonde hair pulled back in a messy braid, face and eyepatch smudged with dirt. She was already slender when living with the Commandant, but now she looks like she's on the edge of starvation.

'Izzi?'

'Elias.' She greets me with a wan smile. 'You're looking . . . ah . . . lean?' Her brow furrows as she takes in my poison-altered appearance.

Laia pushes past me, a shriek bursting from her throat. She flings one arm around Red, another around the Commandant's former slave, and takes them down in a heap, laughing and crying at the same time.

'Skies, Keenan, Izzi! You're all right – you're alive!'

'Alive, yes.' Izzi throws Red a look. 'I don't know about all right. Your friend here set a wicked pace.'

Red doesn't respond to her, his gaze fixed on me.

'Elias.' Laia catches the glare and stands, clearing her throat. 'You know Izzi. And this is Keenan, a – a friend.' She says *friend* like she's not sure if it's an accurate description. 'Keenan, this is—'

'I know who he is.' Red cuts her off, and I suppress the urge to punch him for doing so. *Knocking out her friend within five minutes of meeting him, Elias – bad way to keep the peace.*

'What I want to understand,' Red goes on, 'is how in the skies you ended up with him. How could you—'

'Why don't we sit down.' Izzi raises her voice and drops next to the fire. I sit beside her, keeping one eye on Keenan, who has taken Laia aside and now speaks to her urgently. I watch his lips; he's telling her that he's coming with her to Kauf.

It's a terrible idea. And one that I'll have to shoot down. Because if getting Laia and myself safely to Kauf is nearly impossible, hiding four people is insanity.

'Tell me you have something to eat, Elias,' Izzi says under her breath. 'Maybe Keenan can live on obsession, but I haven't had a proper meal in weeks.'

I offer her the remains of my hare. 'Sorry, there isn't much left,' I say. 'I can catch you another.' I keep my attention on Keenan, half drawing my scim as he gets more and more worked up.

'He's not going to hurt her,' Izzi says. 'You can relax.'

'How do you know?'

'You should have seen him when he found out she'd left with you.' Izzi takes a bite of the hare and shudders. 'I thought he was going to murder someone – me, actually. Laia gave me her berth on a barge and told me Keenan would find me after two weeks. But he got to me a day after I left Serra. Maybe he had a hunch. I don't know. He calmed down eventually, but I don't think he's even slept since then. Once, he hid me in a safe house in a village and was gone all day looking for information, for anything that could lead us to you. All he could think about was getting to her.'

So he's infatuated. Wonderful. I want to ask more questions, like whether Izzi thinks Laia feels the same. But I hold my tongue. Whatever lies between Laia and Keenan cannot matter to me.

As I hunt through my pack for more food for Izzi, Laia takes a seat by the fire. Keenan follows. He looks thunderously angry, which I take to be a good sign. Hopefully Laia told him that we're fine and that he can go back to being a rebel.

'Keenan will come with us,' Laia says. *Damn it.* 'And Izzi—'

'—is coming too,' the Scholar girl says. 'It's what a friend would do, Laia. Besides, it's not as if I have anyplace else to go.'

'I don't know if this is the best idea.' I temper my words – just because Keenan is getting hotheaded doesn't mean I have to act like an idiot. 'Getting four people to Kauf—'

Keenan snorts. Unsurprisingly, his fist is clenched on his bow, the desire to put an arrow through my throat written all over his face. 'Laia and I don't need you. You wanted freedom from the Empire, right? So take it. Get out of the Empire. Leave.'

'Can't.' I take out my throwing knives and begin sharpening them. 'I made Laia a promise.'

'A Mask who keeps his promises. That I'd like to see.'

'Then take a good long look.' *Calm, Elias.* 'Listen,' I say. 'I understand you want to help. But taking more people along just complicates—'

'I'm not some child you'll have to babysit, Martial,' Keenan snarls. 'I tracked you here, didn't I?'

Fair enough. 'How *did* you track us?' I keep my tone civil, but he acts as if I've just threatened devastation upon his unborn children.

'This isn't a Martial interrogation room,' he says. 'You can't force me to tell you anything.'

Laia sighs. 'Keenan . . .'

'Don't get your knickers in a bunch.' I grin at him. *Don't be an ass, Elias.* 'Just professional curiosity. If you tracked us, someone else might track you.'

'No one followed us,' Keenan says through clenched teeth. Skies, he'll grind them down to nubs if he keeps this up. 'And finding you was easy enough,' he continues. 'Rebel trackers are as good as any Mask. Better.'

My skin prickles. Rubbish. A Mask can track a lynx through the Jutts, and such skill is won through a decade of training. No rebel I've heard of can do the same.

'Forget all that.' Izzi cuts through the tension. 'What are we going to *do*?'

'We find a safe place for you,' Keenan says. 'Then Laia and I will go on to Kauf and get Darin out.'

I keep my eyes on the fire. 'How are you going to do that?'

'You don't have to be a murdering Mask to know how to break into a prison.'

'Considering you couldn't break Darin out of Central Prison when he was there,' I say, 'I beg to differ. Kauf is about a hundred times more difficult to break out of. And you don't know the Warden like I do.' I nearly say something about the old man's chilling experiments, but I stop myself. Darin is in that monster's hands, and I don't want to frighten Laia.

Keenan turns to Laia. 'How much does he know? About me? About the rebellion?'

Laia shifts uncomfortably. 'He knows everything,' she says, finally. 'And we're not leaving him.' Her face goes grim, and she meets Keenan's gaze. 'Elias knows the prison. He can help us get inside. He's done guard duty there.'

'He's a bleeding *Martial*, Laia,' Keenan says. 'Skies, do you know what they're doing to us right now? Rounding Scholars up by the thousands. *The thousands.* Some are enslaved, but most are killed. Because of one rebellion, the Martials are murdering every Scholar they can get their hands on.'

I feel sick. *Of course they are.* Marcus is in charge, and the Commandant hates Scholars. The revolution is the perfect excuse for her to exterminate them like she's always wanted.

Laia pales. She looks to Izzi.

'It's true,' Izzi whispers. 'We heard that the rebels told the Scholars who weren't planning on fighting to leave Serra. But so many didn't. The Martials came for them. They killed everyone. We almost got caught ourselves.'

Keenan turns to Laia. 'They've shown the Scholars no mercy. And you want to bring one with us? If I didn't know how to get into Kauf, it would be one thing. But I can do this, Laia. I swear it. We don't need a Mask.'

'He's not a Mask.' Izzi speaks up, and I hide my surprise. Considering the way my mother treated her, she's the last person I expect to defend me. Izzi shrugs at Keenan's incredulous look. 'Not anymore, anyway.'

She wilts a bit under the dirty look Keenan casts her, and my ire is ignited.

'Just because he's not wearing his mask,' Keenan says, 'doesn't mean he's left it behind.'

'True enough.' I find Red's eyes, meeting his fury with cold detachment – one of my mother's most galling tricks. 'It was the Mask in me who killed the soldiers in the tunnels and got us out of the city.' I lean forward. 'And it's the Mask in me who will get Laia to Kauf so we can get Darin out. She knows that. It's why she set me free instead of escaping with you.'

If Red's eyes could light a blaze, I'd be halfway to the tenth pit of the hells right now. Part of me is satisfied. Then I catch a glimpse of Laia's face and feel immediately ashamed. She glances between me and Red, uncertain and anguished.

'It's pointless to fight,' I make myself say. 'More importantly, it's not up to us. This isn't our mission, Red.' I turn to Laia. 'Tell me what you want.'

The grateful look that crosses her face is almost worth the fact that I'm probably going to have to put up with this idiot rebel until the poison kills me.

'Can we still make our way north with the help of the Tribes if there are four of us? Is it possible?'

I stare across the fire and into her dark gold eyes, the way I've tried not to for days. When I do, I remember why I haven't looked: The fire in her, the fervent determination – it speaks to something at my very core, something caged and desperate to be free. A visceral desire for her grips me, and I forget Izzi and Keenan.

My arm twinges, sudden and sharp. A reminder of the task at hand. Convincing Afya to hide Laia and me will be difficult enough. But a rebel, two runaway slaves, and the Empire's most wanted criminal?

I'd say it's impossible, but the Commandant trained the word out of me.

'You're *sure* this is what you want?' I search her eyes for doubt, fear, uncertainty. But all I see is that fire. *Ten hells*.

'I am sure.'

'Then I'll find a way.'

* * *

That night, I visit the Soul Catcher.

I find myself walking beside her on a scanty path through the woods of the Waiting Place. She wears a shift and sandals, and appears untouched by the bite of the autumn air. The trees around us are gnarled and ancient. Translucent figures flit between the trunks. Some are nothing but niveous wisps, while others are more fully formed. At one point, I'm certain I see Tristas, his features contorted in rage, but he's gone a moment later. The figures' whispers are soft, melding into one murmuring rush.

'Is this it?' I ask the Soul Catcher. I thought I had more time. 'Am I dead?'

'No.' Her ancient eyes take in my arm. In this world, it is unscarred, unblemished. 'The poison advances, but slowly.'

'Why am I back here?' I don't want the seizures to begin again – I don't want her controlling me. 'I can't stay.'

'Always so many questions with you, Elias.' She smiles. 'In sleep, humans skirt the Waiting Place and do not enter. But you have a foot in the worlds of the living and the dead. I used that to call you here. Don't worry, Elias. I won't keep you long.'

One of the figures in the trees flutters closer – a woman so faded I cannot see her face. She peers through the branches, looks under bushes. Her mouth moves as if she's speaking to herself.

'Can you hear her?' the Soul Catcher asks.

I try to listen beyond the other ghosts' whispers, but there are too many. I shake my head, and the Soul Catcher's face holds something I can't decipher. 'Try again.'

I close my eyes this time and focus on the woman – only the woman.

I can't find – where – don't hide, lovey –

'She's—' I open my eyes, and the murmurs of the others drown her out. 'She's looking for something.'

'Someone,' the Soul Catcher corrects me. 'She refuses to move on. It has been decades. She hurt someone too, long ago. Though she did not mean to, I think.'

A not-so-subtle reminder of the Soul Catcher's request the last time I saw her. 'I'm doing as you asked,' I say. 'I'm keeping my distance from Laia.'

'Very good, Veturius. I'd hate to have to harm you.'

A chill runs up my spine. 'You can do that?'

'I can do a great many things. Perhaps I shall show you, before your end.' She places her hand on my arm, and it burns like fire.

When I wake up, it's still dark out, and my arm aches. I roll up my sleeve, expecting to see the knotted, scarred flesh where my injury was.

But the wound, which healed days ago, is now raw and bleeding.

CHAPTER FOURTEEN

Helene

TWO WEEKS EARLIER

'You're insane,' Faris says as he, Dex, and I stare at the tracks in the dirt behind the storage building. I half believe him. But tracks don't lie, and these tracks tell quite a tale.

A battle. One large opponent. One small. The small one nearly got the better of the larger one until the small opponent was knocked out – at least that's what I assume, since there's no dead body around. The large opponent and a companion dragged the small opponent into the storage building and escaped on horseback, out a gate in the back wall. The horse had the Gens Veturia motto carved into its shoe: *Always victorious*. I think back to Cook's strange tale: *They brought the demon low and escaped victorious*.

Even days old, the tracks are clear. No one has disturbed this place.

'It's a trap.' Faris lifts his torch to illuminate the shadowy corners of the empty lot. 'That crackpot Cook was trying to get you to come here so she could ambush us.'

'It's a riddle,' I say. 'And I've always been good at riddles.' This one took me longer than most – days have passed since Cook's visit. 'Besides, an old crone against three Masks isn't really an ambush.'

'She got the jump on you, didn't she?' Faris's cowlick tufts out, as it always seems to when he's agitated. 'Why would she even help you? You're a Mask. She's an escaped slave.'

'She's got no love for the Commandant. And' – I gesture to the ground – 'it's clear the Commandant is hiding something.'

'Besides, there's no ambush to be seen.' Dex turns to a door in the wall behind us. 'But there is *salvation half-touched by shadow*. The door faces east. It's only in shadow for half the day.'

I nod to the kiln. 'And that's the *sleepless spire of suffering*. Most of the Scholars who work there are born and die in its shadow.'

'But these tracks—' Faris begins.

'There are only two *silver-skinned she-demons* in the Empire,' I say. 'And one of them was getting tortured by Avitas Harper that night.' Harper, suffice it to say, wasn't invited on this little outing.

I examine the tracks again. Why didn't the Commandant bring backup? Why didn't she tell anyone she saw Elias that night?

'I need to talk to Keris,' I say. 'Find out if—'

'That's a terrible idea,' a mild voice calls from the darkness behind me.

'Lieutenant Harper.' I greet the spy, glaring at Dex as I do so. He grimaces, handsome face uneasy. He was supposed to make sure Harper didn't follow us. 'Skulking in the shadows as usual. I suppose you'll tell her all about this?'

'I don't need to. You're going to give it away when you ask about it. If the Commandant tried to hide what happened here, there's a reason. We should learn what it is before revealing we're on to her.'

121

Faris snorts, and Dex rolls his eyes.

Obviously, idiot. That's what I'm going to do. But Harper doesn't need to know that. In fact, the stupider he thinks *I* am, the better. He can tell the Commandant that I'm no threat to her.

'There is no *we*, Harper.' I turn away from him. 'Dex, check the reports from that night – see if there's anyone around here who saw anything. Faris, you and Harper track the horse. It's probably black or chestnut and at least seventeen hands. Quin didn't like variety in his stables.'

'We'll track the horse,' Harper says. 'Leave the Commandant, Shrike.'

I ignore him, swing into my saddle, and make my way to Villa Veturia.

* * *

It's not yet midnight when I arrive at the Veturia mansion. There are far fewer soldiers here than when I visited a few days ago. Either the Emperor has found another residence or he's away. *Probably in a brothel. Or off murdering children for fun.*

As I'm escorted through the familiar halls, I wonder briefly about Marcus's parents. Neither he nor Zak ever spoke of them. His father is a farrier in a village north of Silas, and his mother is a baker. What must they feel, with one son murdered by the other and the living one now crowned emperor?

The Commandant meets me in Quin's study and offers me a seat. I don't take it.

I try not to stare as she sits at Quin's desk. She wears a black robe, and the blue swirls of her tattoo – oft theorized about at Blackcliff – are just visible at her neck. I've only ever seen her in uniform. Without it, she seems diminished.

As if sensing my thoughts, her eyes sharpen. 'I owe you thanks, Shrike,' she says. 'You saved my father's life. I didn't want to kill him, but he wouldn't have given up the rulership of Gens Veturia easily. Getting him out of the city allowed him his dignity – and a smoother transition of power.'

She isn't thanking me. She was enraged when she learned her father had escaped Serra. She's letting me know that she *knows* I was the one who helped him. How did she find out? Persuading Quin not to storm Blackcliff's dungeons to save Elias was practically impossible, and sneaking him out under the nose of his guards was one of the most difficult things I've ever done. We were careful – beyond careful.

'Have you seen Elias Veturius since the morning he escaped from Blackcliff?' I ask. She doesn't betray a flicker of emotion.

'No.'

'Have you seen the Scholar Laia, formerly your slave, since she escaped from Blackcliff the same day?'

'No.'

'You are the Commandant of Blackcliff and adviser to the Emperor, Keris,' I say. 'But as Blood Shrike, I outrank you. You do realize I could haul you into interrogation and have you purged.'

'Don't pull rank with me, little girl,' the Commandant says softly. 'The only reason you're not already dead is that I – not Marcus, *I* – still have use for you. But' – she shrugs – 'if you insist on a purging, I will, of course, submit.'

I still have use for you.

'Did you, on the night of Veturius's escape, see him at a storage building on the eastern wall of the city, fight him there, lose, and get knocked unconscious while he and the slave escaped on a horse?'

'I just answered that question,' she says. 'Was there anything else, Blood Shrike? The Scholar revolution has spread to Silas. At dawn, I'm to lead the force that will crush it.'

Her voice is as mild as ever. But for a moment, something flares in her eyes. A well-deep flicker of rage. It's gone as quickly as it appeared. I'll get nothing from her now.

'Good luck in Silas, Commandant.' As I turn to leave, she speaks.

'Before you go, Blood Shrike, congratulations are in order.' She allows herself a slight sneer. 'Marcus is finalizing the paperwork now. Your sister's betrothal to the Emperor does him great honor. Their heir will be legitimately Illustrian—'

I am out the door and across the courtyard, my head filled with a rushing that makes me sick. I hear my father when I asked him what he'd traded for my freedom. *Nothing important, daughter.* And Livia, a few nights ago, telling me Hannah was acting strange. *Like she knows something we don't.*

I tear past the guards and vault onto my horse. All I can think is: *Not Livvy. Not Livvy. Not Livvy.*

Hannah is strong. She's bitter. She's angry. But Livvy – Livvy is sweet and funny and curious. Marcus will see it, and he will crush her. He'll enjoy doing it.

I reach home, and before my horse has had a chance to stop, I'm sliding off and shoving through the front gates – straight into a courtyard packed full of Masks.

'Blood Shrike.' One of them steps forward. 'You are to wait here—'

'Let her through.'

Marcus saunters out the front door of my house, my mother and father flanking him. *Bleeding skies, no.* The sight is so wrong that I want to scrub it from my eyes with lye. Hannah follows, head held high. The shine in her eyes bewilders me. Is it her, then? If so, why does she look happy? I've never hid my contempt of Marcus from her.

As they enter the courtyard, Marcus bows and kisses Hannah's hand, the epitome of a well-behaved, highborn suitor.

Get the bleeding hells away from her, you pig. I want to scream it. I bite my tongue. *He's the Emperor. And you're his Shrike.*

When he rises, he inclines his head to my mother. 'Set a date, Mater Aquilla. Don't wait too long.'

'Will your family wish to attend, Your Imperial Majesty?' my mother asks.

'Why?' Marcus curls his lip. 'Too Plebeian to go to a wedding?'

'Of course not, Your Majesty,' my mother says. 'Only I have heard tell that your mother is a woman of great piousness. I expect that she would observe the Augurs' suggested mourning period of four months quite strictly.'

A shadow passes over Marcus's face. 'Of course,' he says. 'It will take as long for you to prove that Gens Aquilla is worthy.'

He approaches me, and at the horror in my eyes, he grins, all the more savage for the pain he's just felt in remembering Zak. 'Careful now, Shrike,' he says. 'Your sister is to be in my care. You wouldn't want anything to happen to her, would you?'

'She – you—' While I gibber, Marcus strides out, his guards trailing. When our slaves have closed the courtyard gates behind him, I hear Hannah's quiet laugh.

'Won't you congratulate me, Blood Shrike?' she says. 'I am to be Empress.'

She's a fool, but she's still my little sister, and I love her. I cannot let this stand.

'Father,' I say through gritted teeth. 'I would speak with you.'

'You should not be here, Shrike,' my father says. 'You have a mission to complete.'

'Can't you see, Father?' Hannah whirls on me. 'Ruining my marriage is more important to her than finding the traitor.'

My father looks a decade older than he did yesterday. 'The betrothal papers have been signed by the Gens,' he says. 'I had to save you, Helene. This was the only way.'

'Father, he is a murderer, a rapist—'

'Isn't that every Mask, Shrike?' Hannah's words are a slap in the face. 'I heard you and your *bastard* friend speaking ill of Marcus. I know what I'm getting into.'

She swoops toward me, and I realize she's as tall as I am, though I don't remember when that happened. 'I don't care. I will be Empress. Our son will be heir to the throne. And the fate of Gens Aquilla will forever be secure. Because of *me*.' Her eyes glow with triumph. 'Think on that as you hunt down the traitor you call friend.'

Don't punch her, Helene. Don't. My father takes my arm. 'Come, Shrike.'

'Where's Livvy?' I ask.

'Sequestered in her room with a *fever*,' Father says as we ensconce ourselves in his book-stuffed study. 'Your mother and I didn't want to risk Marcus picking her instead.'

'He did this to get at me.' I try to sit but just end up pacing. 'The Commandant probably put him up to it.'

'Do not underestimate our Emperor, Helene,' Father says. 'Keris wanted you dead. She tried to persuade Marcus to execute you. You know her. She refuses to negotiate. The Emperor came to me without her knowledge. The Illustrians have turned on him. They use the escape of Veturius and the slave-girl to question his legitimacy as Emperor. He knows he needs allies, so he offered your life for Hannah's hand in marriage – and the full support of Gens Aquilla.'

'Why not throw our weight behind another Gens?' I say. 'There must be some who covet the throne.'

'They all covet the throne. The infighting has already begun. Who would you choose? Gens Sissellia is brutal and manipulative. Gens Rufia would empty the Empire's coffers in a fortnight. All would object to any other Gens ruling. They will tear each other apart vying for the throne. Better a bad Emperor than a civil war.'

'But, Father, he's a—'

'Daughter.' Father raises his voice – a rare enough occurrence that I fall silent. 'Your loyalty is to the Empire. Marcus is Augur-chosen. He *is* the Empire. And he needs a victory badly.' My father leans across his desk. 'He needs Elias. He needs a public execution. He needs the Gens to see that he is strong and capable.

'You are Blood Shrike now, daughter. The Empire *must* come first – above your desires, your friendships, your wants. Above, even, your sister and your Gens. We are Aquilla, daughter. *Loyal to the end.* Say it.'

'Loyal,' I whisper. *Even if it means my sister's destruction. Even if it means a madman running the Empire. Even if it means I have to torture and kill my best friend.* 'To the end.'

* * *

When I arrive at the empty barracks the next morning, neither Dex nor Harper mentions Hannah's betrothal. They are also wise enough not to remark on my black mood.

'Faris is at the drum tower,' Dex says. 'He heard back about the horse. As for those reports you had me look through . . .' My friend fidgets, pale eyes on Harper.

Harper almost smiles. 'There was something off about the reports,' he says. 'The drums gave conflicting orders that night.

Martial troops were in disarray because the rebels cracked our codes and scrambled all the communiqués.'

Dex's mouth drops open. 'How did you know?'

'I noticed it a week ago,' Harper said. 'It wasn't relevant until today. Two orders given that night went unobserved in the chaos, Shrike. Both transferred men from the eastern part of the city elsewhere, thereby leaving that entire sector unpatrolled.'

I curse under my breath. 'Keris gave those orders,' I say. 'She let him go. She *wants* me tied up in the hunt for Veturius. With me gone, she can influence Marcus without interference. And' – I glance at Harper – 'you're going to tell her I figured it out. Aren't you?'

'She knew that the moment you walked into Villa Veturia with questions.' Harper fixes his cool gaze on me. 'She doesn't underestimate you, Shrike. Nor should she.'

The door bursts open, and Faris lumbers through, ducking his head to avoid the frame. He hands me a slip of paper. 'From a guard post just south of Raider's Roost.'

Black stallion, eighteen hands, Gens Veturia markings, found on routine camp raid four days ago. Blood on saddle. Beast in poor condition and showed signs of hard riding. Tribesman in possession was questioned but insists horse wandered into his camp.

'What in the bleeding skies was Veturius doing at Raider's Roost?' I say. 'Why go east? The fastest way to escape the Empire is south.'

'Could be a ploy,' Dex says. 'He could have traded the horse outside the city and turned south from there.'

Faris shakes his head. 'Then how do you explain the beast's condition and where it was found?'

I let them argue. A chill wind blows through the open barracks door, rifling the reports on the table, bringing in the smell of crushed leaves, cinnamon, and distant sands. A Tribal trader trundles past with his cart. He's the first Tribesman I've seen in Serra in days. The rest have left the city, in part because of the Scholar revolt and in part because of the Fall Gathering in Nur. No Tribesman would miss it.

It hits me like a lightning bolt. *The Fall Gathering*. Every Tribe attends, including Tribe Saif. In the middle of all those people, animals, wagons, and families, it would be child's play for Elias to slip past Martial spies and hide among his adoptive family.

'Dex.' I silence the discussion. 'Send a message to the garrison at Atella's Gap. I need a full legion mustered and ready to depart in three days. And saddle our horses.'

Dex lifts his silver brows. 'Where are we going?'

'Nur,' I say as I walk out the door for the stables. 'He's heading to Nur.'

CHAPTER FIFTEEN

Laia

Elias suggests we rest, but sleep won't find me this night. Keenan is equally agitated; an hour or so after we've all bedded down, he gets up and disappears into the woods. I sigh, knowing I owe him an explanation. Delaying it will make the road to Kauf more difficult than it already promises to be. I rise, shivering from the cold and pulling my cloak closer. Elias, on watch, speaks quietly as I pass.

'The poison,' he says. 'Don't tell him or Izzi. Please.'

'I won't.' I slow, thinking of our almost-kiss, wondering if I should say anything. But when I turn to look at him, he's studiously staring out at the forest, his broad shoulders taut.

I follow Keenan into the woods and run to catch his arm just as he's moving out of view.

'You're still upset,' I say. 'I'm sorry—'

He throws off my arm and spins about, his eyes flashing dark fire.

'You're sorry? Skies, Laia, do you have any idea what I thought when you weren't on that barge? You know what I've lost, and you did it anyway—'

'I had to, Keenan.' I didn't realize it would hurt him. I thought he would understand. 'I couldn't let Izzi face the Commandant's wrath. I couldn't let Elias die.'

'So he didn't make you do any of this? Izzi said it was your idea, but I didn't believe her. I assumed he'd – I don't know – used coercion. A trick. Now I find the two of you together. I thought you and I . . .'

He crosses his arms, his bright hair falling into his face, and looks away from me. *Skies.* He must have seen Elias and me by the fire. How to explain? *I never thought I'd see you again. I'm a mess. My heart is a mess.*

'Elias is my friend,' I say instead. Is it even true? Elias *was* my friend when we left Serra. Now I do not know what he is.

'You're trusting a Martial, Laia. Do you realize that? Ten bleeding hells, he's the son of the Commandant. The son of the woman who killed your family—'

'He's not like that.'

'Of course he's like that. They're all like that. You and me, Laia – we can do this without him. Look, I didn't want to say it in front of him because I don't trust him, but the Resistance has knowledge of Kauf. Men inside. I can get Darin out of there, alive.'

'Kauf isn't Central Prison, Keenan. It's not even Blackcliff. It's Kauf. No one has ever broken out of there. So please, stop. This is my choice. I choose to trust him. You can come with me if you wish. I would be lucky to have someone like you along. But I'm not leaving Elias. He's my best chance of saving Darin.'

Keenan looks for a moment as if he wants to say more but then simply nods.

'Your will, then,' he says.

'There's something else I need to tell you.' I never shared with

Keenan *why* my brother was taken. But if rumors of Darin and Teluman have already reached the Roost, then he's certain to hear about my brother's skills at some point. He might as well hear it from me.

'Izzi and I heard the rumors while we were traveling,' he says after I finish explaining. 'But I'm glad you told me. I'm – I'm glad you trust me.'

When he meets my eyes, a spark jumps between us, heady and powerful. In the mist, his eyes are dark, so dark. *I could disappear there.* The thought pops unbidden into my mind. *And not mind if I never found my way out.*

'You must be exhausted.' He lifts a palm to my face, hesitant. His touch is warm, and when his fingers fall away, I feel empty. I think of how he kissed me in Serra. 'I'll be there soon.'

In the clearing, Izzi sleeps. Elias ignores me, his hand laid casually across the scim in his lap. If he's heard Keenan and me talking, he gives no indication of it.

My bedroll is cold, and I huddle within, shivering. For a long time, I lay awake, waiting for Keenan to return. But the minutes pass, and he stays away.

*   *   *

We reach the border of the Serran Mountain Range mid-morning, with the sun high in the east. Elias takes point as we zigzag out of the mountains and down a switchbacking trail to the foothills. The dunes of the Tribal desert roll away beyond those foothills, a sea of molten gold with an island of green a dozen or so miles away: Nur.

Long wagon trains snake their way toward the city for the Fall Gathering. Miles of desert stretch past the oasis, littered with striated plateaus that rise into the sky like enormous rock sentinels. A wind races along the desert floor and up through the foothills, bringing with it the scents of oil and horse and roasting meat.

The air nips at us – autumn has come early to the mountains. But it might as well be the depths of a Serran summer, the way Elias sweats. This morning, he quietly told me that the Tellis extract ran out yesterday. His gold skin, so hale before, is worryingly pale.

Keenan, who has been frowning at Elias since the moment we set out, falls into stride with him now.

'Are you going to tell us how we're going to find a caravan that will take us to Kauf?'

Elias looks at the rebel askance but doesn't respond.

'Tribesmen aren't exactly known for being accepting to outsiders,' Keenan presses. 'Though your adopted family is Tribal, right? I hope you're not planning to seek their aid. The Martials will be watching them.'

Elias's expression transforms from *what do you want* to *go away*.

'No, I don't plan on seeing my family while I'm in Nur. As for getting north, I have a . . . friend who owes me a favor.'

'A friend,' Keenan says. 'Who—'

'Don't take offense, Red,' Elias says, 'but I don't know you. So you'll forgive me if I don't trust you.'

'I know the feeling.' Keenan clenches his jaw. 'I only wanted to suggest that instead of using Nur, we use Resistance safe houses. We could bypass Nur and the Martial soldiers who no doubt patrol it.'

'With the Scholar revolt, rebels are probably being rounded up and interrogated. Unless you're the only fighter who knew about the safe houses, they're compromised.'

Elias speeds his gait, and Keenan drops back, taking a position far enough behind me that I think it best to leave him be. I catch up with Izzi, and she leans toward me.

'They've avoided ripping each other's faces off,' she says. 'That's a start, right?'

I choke back a laugh. 'How long until they kill each other, d'you think? And who strikes first?'

'Two days before all-out war,' Izzi says. 'My money's on Keenan striking first. He's got a temper, that one. But Elias will win, being a Mask and all. Though' – she tilts her head – 'he doesn't look so good, Laia.'

Izzi always sees more than anyone gives her credit for. I'm certain she'll notice me dancing around the question, so I try to keep my response simple.

'We should reach Nur tonight,' I say. 'Once he rests, he'll be fine.'

But by late afternoon, a powerful wind blows in from the east, and our progress slows as we enter the foothills. By the time we reach the stretch of dunes that lead to Nur, the moon is high, the galaxy a blaze of silver above. But we are all exhausted from fighting the wind. Izzi's walk has deteriorated to a stumble, and both Keenan and I pant in tiredness. Even Elias struggles, stopping short enough times that I begin to worry for him.

'I don't like this wind,' he says. 'The desert sandstorms don't start until late fall. But the weather since Serra has been odd – rain instead of sun, fog instead of clear skies.' We exchange a glance. I wonder if he's thinking what I am: that it feels as if something doesn't *want* us to reach Nur . . . or Kauf or Darin.

The oil lamps of Nur glow like a beacon only a few miles to the east, and we head straight for them. But a mile or so into the dunes, a deep hum thrums out across the sands, echoing in our bones.

'What in the skies is that?' I ask.

'The sand is shifting,' Elias says. 'A lot of it. A sandstorm is coming. Quickly now!'

The sands swirl restlessly, rising in taunting clouds before gusting away. After another half mile, the wind grows so frenzied that we can hardly make out the lights of Nur.

'This is insane!' Keenan shouts. 'We should turn back for the foothills. Find shelter for the night.'

'Elias.' I raise my voice over the wind. 'How much would that delay us?'

'If we wait, we miss the gathering. We need those crowds if we want to pass unnoticed.' *And he needs the Tellis.* We cannot predict the Soul Catcher. If Elias starts convulsing again and loses consciousness, who knows how long that creature will keep him in the Waiting Place? Hours if he's lucky. Days if he's not.

A shudder rolls through Elias, sudden and violent, and his body jerks – too sharply for anyone with eyes to miss it. I am beside him instantly.

'Stay with me, Elias,' I whisper into his ear. 'The Soul Catcher's trying to call you back. Don't let her.'

Elias grits his teeth, and the convulsion passes. I'm well aware of Izzi's bewildered look, Keenan's suspicion.

The rebel steps closer. 'Laia, what's—'

'We keep going.' I raise my voice so he and Izzi can hear. 'A delay now could mean a difference of weeks later if the snows come early or the northern passes are closed.'

'Here.' Elias pulls a stack of kerchiefs from his pack and hands them to me. As I dole them out, he cuts a length of rope into ten-foot sections. Another shudder ripples across his shoulders, and he clenches his teeth, battling against it. *Don't give in.* I give him a pointed look as Izzi huddles closer. *Now is not the time.*

He binds Izzi to himself and is about to bind me to Izzi when she shakes her head.

'Laia on your other side.' Her gaze flits to Keenan so swiftly that I'm not sure I even saw it. I wonder if she heard Keenan imploring me to leave with him last night.

My body shakes with the effort of standing in one spot. The winds scream around us, as violent as a chorus of funeral shrieks. The sound makes me think of the wraiths in the desert outside Serra, and I wonder if fey creatures haunt this desert too.

'Keep the rope taut' – Elias's hands brush mine, and his skin is fevered – 'or I won't know if we've been separated.' Fear stabs at me, but he drops his face close to mine.

'Don't be afraid. I grew up in this desert. I'll get us to Nur.'

We move east, our heads bowed against the onslaught of the storm. The dust blots out the stars, and the dunes shift beneath us so fast that we're staggering, fighting for every step. There's sand in my teeth, my eyes, my nose – I can't breathe.

The rope between Elias and me tightens as he pulls me onward. On his other side, Izzi curves her reedlike body against the wind, clutching her scarf to her face. A scream echoes, and I falter – Izzi? *Just the wind.*

Then Keenan, who I thought was behind me, jerks on the rope from my left. The force of it pulls me down, and my body sinks into deep, soft sand. I fight to get back to my feet, but the wind is like a great, pressing fist.

I yank hard on the rope that I know connects me to Elias. He must realize I've fallen. Any second, I'll feel his hands pulling me closer, lifting me to my feet. I scream his name into the storm, my voice useless against its rage. The rope jerks between us once.

Then it goes horribly slack, and when I pull it in, there is nothing at the end of it.

CHAPTER SIXTEEN

Elias

One second, I am using every ounce of strength I have to battle the winds and pull Laia and Izzi forward.

The next, the rope between Laia and me falls limp. I pull it in, staggered when it ends after only three feet. No Laia.

I lunge back toward where I hope she'll be. Nothing. *Ten hells.* I tied the knots too quickly – one of them must have come undone. *Doesn't matter*, my mind howls. *Find her!*

The wind screams, and I remember the sand efrits I fought during the Trials. A manlike shape rears in front of me, its eyes glowing with unrestrained malice. I stagger back in surprise – *where the hells did it come from* – then reach into my memory. *Efrit, efrit of the sand, a song is more than he can stand.* The old rhyme comes back to me, and I sing it out. *Work, work, please work.* The eyes narrow, and for a second, I think the rhyme is useless. Then the eyes fade.

But Laia – and Keenan – are still out here, defenseless. We should have waited out the sandstorm. The damned rebel was right. If Laia is buried in the sands – if she dies out here because I needed that accursed Tellis . . .

She fell just before we were separated. I drop to my knees and sweep out with my arms. I catch a scrap of cloth, then a patch of warm skin. Relief washes over me, and I pull. It's her – I can tell from the shape and weight of her body. I draw her close and catch a flash of her face beneath the scarf, terrified as she wraps her arms around me.

'I've got you,' I say, though I don't think she hears me. On one side, I feel Izzi jostle me, and then a flare of red hair – Keenan, still roped to Laia, bent over as he coughs the sand from his lungs.

I refasten the rope, my hands shaking. In my head, I hear Izzi telling me to bind Laia to myself. The knots were tight. The rope was whole and unblemished. It *shouldn't* have come undone.

Forget that now. Move.

Soon, the ground hardens from treacherous sand to the dry cobbles of the oasis. I graze a tree with my shoulders, and light flickers dimly through the sand. At my side, Izzi falls, clawing at her good eye. I lift her into my arms and push forward. Her body shakes as she coughs uncontrollably.

One light turns to two and then a dozen – a street. My arms shake, and I nearly drop Izzi. *Not yet!*

The hulking shadow of a rounded Tribal wagon looms out of the darkness, and I fight my way toward it. I hope to the skies that it's empty, mostly because I don't think I have the energy to knock anyone senseless right now.

I wrench the door open, undo the knot binding me to Izzi, and push her inside. Keenan bounds up after her, and I half lift, half shove Laia in last. I swiftly untie the rope between us, but as I untangle the knot, I notice that the rope has no frayed ends. The place where it broke apart is smooth.

As if it were cut.

Izzi? No, she was next to me. And Laia wouldn't do it. Keenan?

Was he that desperate to get Laia away from me? My vision fades, and I wag my head. When I look back at the rope, it's as frayed as an aging trawler's hawser.

Hallucinations. Get to an apothecary, Elias. Now.

'Tend to Izzi,' I shout at Laia. 'Wash out her eye – she's sand blind. I'll bring something from the apothecary to help.'

I slam the wagon door shut and turn back into the storm. A tremor takes me. I can almost hear the Soul Catcher. *Come back, Elias.*

The thick-walled buildings of Nur block enough of the sand that I can make out the street signs. I move carefully, keeping an eye out for soldiers. Tribesmen aren't crazy enough to be out in such a storm, but Martials will patrol no matter what the weather.

As I turn a corner, I notice a poster on one of the walls. When I get closer, I curse.

BY ORDER OF HIS IMPERIAL MAJESTY
EMPEROR MARCUS FARRAR

WANTED ALIVE:

ELIAS VETURIUS
MURDERER, RESISTANCE COLLABORATOR,
TRAITOR TO THE EMPIRE
REWARD: 60,000 MARKS
LAST SEEN:
TRAVELING EAST THROUGH THE EMPIRE
IN THE COMPANY OF LAIA OF SERRA,
RESISTANCE REBEL AND SPY

I tear the sign down, crumple it, and release it into the wind – only to see another a few feet away – and another. I step back. The entire bleeding wall is papered with them, as is the wall at my back. They're everywhere.

Get the Tellis.

I stumble away like a Fiver after his first kill. It takes twenty minutes to find an apothecary, an agonizingly clumsy five minutes to pick the lock on the door. I light a lamp with shaking hands and thank the skies when I see that this particular apothecary has alphabetized his remedies. I'm panting like a water-starved animal by the time I find the Tellis extract, but as soon as I gulp it down, relief sweeps through me.

As does clarity. Everything rushes in – the storm, Izzi's sand blindness, the wagon where I left the others. And the posters. Bleeding hells, the 'wanted' posters. My face, Laia's face, everywhere. If there were dozens on one wall, then who knows how many there are throughout the city?

Their existence means one thing: The Empire suspects we're here. So the Martial presence in Nur will be far greater than what I expected. *Damn it all to the hells.*

By now Laia will be frantic, but she and the others will have to wait. I swipe the apothecary's entire stock of Tellis, along with an unguent that will ease Izzi's eye pain. In minutes I am back in Nur's sand-scoured streets, recalling the time I spent here as a Fiver, spying on the Tribesmen and reporting my findings at the Martial garrison.

I take to the roofs to get to the garrison, wincing against the onslaught of the storm. It is still powerful enough to keep sane people inside but not nearly as bad as when we arrived in the city.

The Martial stronghold, built of black stone, is horribly out of place among the sand-colored structures of Nur. As I approach, I slink along the edges of a rooftop balcony across the street from it.

It's clear from the blazing lights and the soldiers entering and leaving that the building is packed. And not just with auxes and legionnaires. In the hour that I spend watching, I count at least a dozen Masks, including one wearing pure black armor.

The Black Guard. Those are Helene's men, now that she's Blood Shrike. What are they doing here?

Another black-armored Mask emerges from the garrison. He is huge with pale, messy hair. Faris. I'd recognize that cowlick anywhere.

He calls out to a legionnaire saddling a horse.

'—runners to every single Tribe,' I overhear. 'Anyone who shelters him is dead. Make that very clear, soldier.'

Another Black Guard emerges. The skin of his hands and chin is darker, but I can make out nothing more than that from here. 'We need a cordon around Tribe Saif,' he says to Faris. 'In case he seeks them out.'

Faris shakes his head. 'That's the last place El – Veturius would go. He wouldn't put them at risk.'

Ten burning hells. They know I'm here. And I think I know how. A few minutes later, my suspicions are confirmed.

'Harper.' Helene's voice is steel, and I start at the sound of it. She strides out of the barracks, seemingly unaffected by the storm. Her armor gleams darkly, her pale hair a beacon in the night. *Of course.* If anyone could puzzle out what I'd do, where I'd go, it's her.

I sink a little lower, certain she'll sense me – that she'll know, in her bones, I'm nearby.

'Talk to the runners yourself. I want diplomatic men,' she says to the Black Guard named Harper. 'They should seek out the Tribal chiefs – the *Zaldars* or the *Kehannis*, the storytellers. Tell them not to talk to the children – the Tribes are protective of them. And for skies' sake, make sure none of them so much as think about looking at the women. I don't want a bleeding war on my hands because some idiot aux couldn't keep his hands to himself. Faris, get that cordon up around Tribe Saif. And keep a tail on Mamie Rila.'

Both Faris and Harper leave to carry out Hel's orders. I expect her to go back into the garrison, to get out of the wind. Instead she takes two steps out into the storm, one hand on her scim. Her eyes are hooded, her mouth an angry slash.

My chest aches when I look at Helene. Will I ever stop missing her? What is she thinking? Is she remembering when she and I were here together? And why in the hells is she hunting me in the first place? She must know the Commandant poisoned me. If I'm dead anyway, what's the point of capturing me?

I want to go down to her, to grab her in a bear hug and forget that we are enemies. I want to tell her about Soul Catcher and the Waiting Place and how, now that I've tasted freedom, I only wish I could find a way to keep it. I want to tell her that I miss Quin and that Demetrius, Leander, and Tristas haunt my nightmares.

I want. I want. I want.

I wrench myself halfway across the rooftop, then leap to the next, leaving before I do something stupid. I have a mission. So does Helene. I have to want mine more than she wants hers, or Darin is dead.

CHAPTER SEVENTEEN

Laia

Izzi tosses in her sleep, her breathing ragged and labored. She flings out an arm, and her hand knocks into the ornate wooden paneling of the wagon. I stroke her wrist, whispering soothing words. In the muted lamplight, she looks pale as death.

Keenan and I sit cross-legged beside her. I've propped her head up so she can breathe easier, and I've washed out her eye. She still cannot open it.

I release a breath, remembering the violence of the storm, how small I felt against its raking claws. I thought I'd lose purchase with the earth and be flung into darkness. Against the storm's violence, I was less than a mote of dust.

You should have waited, Laia. You should have listened to Keenan. What if the sand blindness is permanent? Izzi will lose her sight forever because of me.

Get a hold of yourself. Elias needed the Tellis. And you need Elias if you want to get to Darin. This is a mission. You are its leader. This is the cost.

Where *is* Elias? It's been ages since he left. Dawn is no more than an hour or two away. While it's still windy outside, it's not bad enough to keep people off the streets. Eventually, the owners of this wagon will return. We can't be here when they do.

'Elias is poisoned.' Keenan speaks softly. 'Isn't he?'

I try to keep my face blank, but Keenan sighs. The wind rises, rattling the wagon's high windows.

'He needed medicine. It's why you made for Raider's Roost instead of heading straight north,' he says. 'Skies. How bad is it?'

'It's bad.' Izzi's voice is a rasp. 'Very bad. Nightweed.'

I stare incredulously at Izzi. 'You're awake! Thank the skies. But how do you know—'

'Cook amused herself by telling me all the poisons she'd use on the Commandant if she could,' Izzi said. 'She was quite detailed in her description of their effects.'

'He's going to die, Laia,' Keenan says. 'Nightweed is a killer.'

'I know.' *I wish I didn't.* 'He knows too. It's why we had to get into Nur.'

'And you still want to do this with him?' If Keenan's brows went any higher, they'd disappear into his hairline. 'Forget the fact that just being in his presence is a risk, or that his mother killed your parents, or that he's a Mask, or that his people are currently wiping ours out of existence. He's *dead*, Laia. Who knows if he'll even live long enough to get to Kauf? And skies, why would he *want* to come?'

'He knows Darin could change everything for the Scholars,' I say. 'He doesn't believe in the Empire's evil any more than we do.'

Keenan scoffs. 'I doubt that—'

'Stop.' The word is a whisper. I clear my throat and reach for my mother's armlet. *Strength.* 'Please.'

Keenan hesitates, then takes my hands as I curl them into fists. 'I'm sorry.' For once, his gaze is unguarded. 'You've been through the hells, and I'm sitting here making you feel worse. I won't mention it again. If this is what you want, then this is what we'll do. I'm here for you. Whatever you need.'

A sigh of relief escapes me, and I nod. He traces the *K* on my chest – the mark the Commandant carved into me when I was her slave. It is a pale scar now. His fingers drift up to my collarbone, my face. 'I missed you,' he says. 'Isn't that strange? Three months ago, I'd never even met you.'

I study his strong jaw, the way his brilliant hair spills across his forehead, the muscles bunched in his arm. I sigh at his scent, lemon and woodsmoke, so familiar to me now. How did he come to mean so much to me? We hardly know each other, and yet at his proximity, my body goes still. I lean into his touch involuntarily, the warmth of his hand drawing me closer.

The door opens, and I jump back, reaching for my dagger. But it's Elias. He glances between Keenan and me. His skin, so sickly when he left us in the wagon, is back to its usual gold hue.

'We have a problem.' He climbs into the wagon and unfolds a sheet of paper: a 'wanted' poster with frighteningly accurate depictions of Elias and me.

'How in the skies did they know?' Izzi asks. 'Did they track us?'

Elias looks down at the wagon floor, swirling the dust there with his boot. 'Helene Aquilla is here.' His voice is oddly neutral. 'I saw her at the Martial garrison. She must have worked out where we were going. She's got a cordon around Tribe Saif, and hundreds of soldiers here to help search for us.'

I find Keenan's eyes. *Just being in his presence is a risk.* Maybe coming into Nur *was* a bad idea.

'We need to get to your friend,' I say, 'so we can leave with the rest of the Tribes. How do we do it?'

'I was going to suggest we wait for night again and then use disguises. But that's what Aquilla would expect. So we do the opposite. We hide in plain sight.'

'How are we supposed to hide a Scholar rebel, two former slaves, and a fugitive in plain sight?' Keenan asks.

Elias reaches into his bag and pulls out a set of manacles. 'I have an idea,' he says. 'But you're not going to like it.'

* * *

'Your ideas,' I hiss at Elias as I trail him through the stiflingly packed streets of Nur, 'are almost as deadly as mine.'

'Quiet, *slave*.' He nods at a squad of Martials marching lockstep through an adjacent street.

I press my lips together, and the manacles weighing down my ankles and wrists clink. Elias was wrong. I don't just dislike this plan. I *hate* it.

He wears a red slaver's shirt and holds a chain that connects to an iron collar around my neck. My hair hangs in my face, mussed and tangled. Izzi, her eye still bandaged, trails me. Three feet of chain stretch between us, and she relies on my whispered directions to keep from tripping. Keenan follows her, sweat beading on his face. I know how he feels: as if we're actually being led to auction.

We follow Elias in an obedient row, heads down, bodies defeated, as Scholar slaves are expected to look. Memories of the Commandant flood my head: her pale eyes as she carved her initial into my chest with such sadistic care; the blows she delivered as casually as if casting pennies to beggars.

'Keep it together.' Elias glances back at me, perhaps sensing my rising panic. 'We've still got to get across the city.'

Like the dozens of other slavers we've seen here in Nur, Elias leads us with a confident disdain, barking out the occasional order.

He mutters at the dust in the air and looks down on the Tribesmen as if they are cockroaches.

With a scarf covering the lower half of his face, I can see only his eyes, almost colorless in the morning light. His slaver's shirt fits more loosely than it would have a few weeks ago. The battle against the Commandant's poison has stripped him of his bulk, and he is all edges and angles now. The sharpness heightens his beauty, but it seems almost like I'm looking at his shadow instead of the real Elias.

Nur's dusty streets are packed with people going from encampment to encampment. Chaotic as it is, there is a strange order to it. Each camp flies its own Tribal colors, with tents to the left, merchant stalls to the right, and the traditional Tribal wagons forming a perimeter.

'Ugh, Laia,' Izzi whispers from behind me. 'I can smell the Martials. Steel and leather and horse. It feels like they are everywhere.'

'That's because they are,' I whisper through the side of my mouth.

Legionnaires search shops and wagons. Masks bark orders and enter houses with no warning. Our progress is slow, as Elias takes a circuitous route through the streets in an attempt to avoid the patrols. My heart is in my throat the entire time.

I search in vain for free Scholars, hoping that some have escaped the Empire's butchery. But the only Scholars I see are in chains. News of what's happening in the Empire is scarce, but finally amid the incomprehensible snatches of Sadhese, I hear two Mercators speaking in Serran.

'—not even sparing the children.' The Mercator trader looks over his shoulder as he speaks. 'I hear the streets of Silas and Serra run red with Scholar blood.'

'Tribesmen are next,' his companion, a leather-clad woman, says. 'Then they'll come for Marinn.'

'They'll try,' the man says. 'I'd like to see those pale-eyed bastards get through the Forest—'

Then we are past them, and their conversation fades, but I feel like retching. *The streets of Silas and Serra run red with Scholar blood.* Skies, how many of my old neighbors and acquaintances have died? How many of Pop's patients?

'That's why we're doing this.' Elias glances back at me, and I realize he heard the Mercators too. 'It's why we need your brother. So stay focused.'

As we make our way through a particularly crowded thorough-fare, a patrol led by a Mask in black armor turns into the street just yards ahead.

'Patrol,' I hiss at Izzi. 'Head down!' Immediately, she and Keenan stare at their feet. Elias's shoulders stiffen, but he ambles forward in an almost leisurely manner. A muscle in his jaw jumps.

The Mask is young, his skin is the same golden-brown as mine. He's as lean as Elias but shorter, with green eyes that angle up like a cat's and cheekbones that jut as sharply as the hard planes of his armor.

I've never seen him before, but it doesn't matter. He's a Mask, and as his eyes pass over me, I find that I cannot breathe. Fear pounds through me, and all I can see is the Commandant. All I can feel is the lash of her whip on my back and the cold grasp of her hand on my throat. I can't move.

Izzi runs into my back, and Keenan into hers.

'Go on!' Izzi says frantically. People nearby turn to watch. *Why now, Laia? For skies' sake, get hold of yourself.* But my body won't listen. The manacles, the collar around my neck, the sounds of the chains – they overwhelm me, and though my mind screams at me to keep moving, my body only remembers the Commandant.

The chain attached to my collar jerks, and Elias swears at me with an insouciant brutality that is uniquely Martial. I *know* he is playing a part. But I cringe anyway, reacting with a terror that I thought I had buried.

Elias wheels as if he's going to strike me and yanks my face toward his. To an outsider, it would just appear as if a slaver is disciplining his property. His voice is soft, audible only to me.

'Look at me.' I meet his gaze. *The Commandant's eyes.* No. Elias's. 'I'm not her.' He takes my chin, and while it must look threatening to those watching, his hand is light as a breeze. 'I won't hurt you. But you can't let the fear take you.'

I drop my head and breathe deeply. The Mask watches us now, his whole body still. We are a few yards from him. A few feet. I peek out at him through my hair. His attention passes quickly over Keenan, Izzi, and me. Then it lands on Elias.

He stares. *Skies.* My body threatens to freeze again, but I make myself move.

Elias nods at the Mask perfunctorily, unconcerned, and walks on. The Mask is behind us, but I still sense him watching, poised to strike.

Then I hear the boots marching away, and when I look back, he's moved on. I release a breath I didn't realize I was holding. *Safe. You're safe.*

For now.

It's only as we approach an encampment on the southeast side of Nur that Elias finally seems to relax.

'Head down, Laia,' Elias whispers. 'We're here.'

The encampment is enormous. Balconied, sand-colored houses

line its edges, and in the space before them sits a city of gold-and-green tents. The market is the size of any in Serra – perhaps even larger. All the stalls have the same emerald draping patterned with glinting fall leaves. Skies knows how much such brocade costs. Whatever Tribe this is, it is powerful.

Tribal men in green robes encircle the camp, funneling those entering through a makeshift gate made of two wagons. None approach until we enter the domicile area, swarming with men tending cook fires, women preparing goods, children chasing chickens and each other. Elias approaches the largest of the tents, bristling when two guards stop us.

'Slavers trade at night,' one of them says in accented Serran. 'Return later.'

'Afya Ara-Nur is expecting me,' Elias growls, and at the sound of the name I start, thinking back to weeks ago, to the small, dark-eyed woman in Spiro's shop – the same woman who danced so gracefully with Elias on the night of the Moon Festival. *This* is who he trusts to take us north? I remember what Spiro said. *One of the most dangerous women in the Empire.*

'She sees no slavers in the day.' The other Tribesman is emphatic. 'At night *only*.'

'If you don't let me in to see her,' Elias says, 'I'm happy to inform the Masks that Tribe Nur is backing out of trade agreements.'

The Tribesmen exchange an uneasy glance and one disappears into the tent. I want to warn Elias about Afya, about what Spiro said. But the other guard watches us so carefully that I cannot do it without him seeing.

After only a minute, the Tribesman waves us into the tent. Elias turns to me, as if he's adjusting my manacles, but instead he palms me the key. He strides through the tent flaps as if he owns the encampment. Izzi, Keenan, and I hurry to follow.

The inside of the tent is strewn with handwoven rugs. A dozen colored lamps cast geometric patterns over silk-encased pillows. Afya Ara-Nur, exquisite and dark-skinned, with black-and-red braids spilling down her shoulders, sits behind a rough-hewn desk. It is heavy and out of place amid the dazzling wealth around her. Her fingers click the beads of a counting frame, and she inks her findings into a book in front of her. A bored-looking boy about Izzi's age, and with Afya's same sharp beauty, sits beside her.

'I only allowed you inside, slaver,' Afya says without looking at us, 'so I could personally tell you that if you ever step foot in my camp again, I'll gut you myself.'

'I'm hurt, Afya,' Elias says as something small spins from his hand and into Afya's lap. 'You're not nearly as friendly as the first time we met.' Elias's voice is smooth, suggestive, and my face heats.

Afya snatches the coin. Her jaw drops when Elias removes his face scarf.

'Gibran—' she says to the boy, but quick as flame, Elias draws his scims from across his back and steps forward. He has a blade at each of their throats, his eyes calm and terrifyingly flat.

'You owe me a favor, Afya Ara-Nur,' he says. 'I'm here to collect.'

The boy – Gibran – looks uncertainly at Afya.

'Let Gibran sit outside.' Afya's tone is reasonable, even gentle. But her hands curl into fists atop her desk. 'He has nothing to do with this.'

'We need a witness from your Tribe when you grant my favor,' Elias says. 'Gibran will do nicely.' Afya opens her mouth but says nothing, apparently flabbergasted, and Elias goes on. 'You're honor bound to hear my request, Afya Ara-Nur. And honor bound to grant it.'

'Honor be damned—'

'Fascinating,' Elias says. 'How would your council of elders feel about that? The only *Zaldara* in the Tribal lands the youngest ever chosen – casting away her honor like bad grain.' He nods at the elaborate geometric tattoo peeking out of her sleeve – an indication of her rank, no doubt. 'A half hour in a tavern this morning told me all I needed to know about Tribe Nur, Afya. Your position isn't secure.' Afya's lips thin to a hard line. Elias has hit a nerve.

'The elders would understand that it was for the good of the Tribe.'

'No,' Elias says. 'They'd say you're not fit to lead if you make errors in judgment that threaten the Tribe. Errors like giving a favor coin to a Martial.'

'That favor was for the future Emperor!' Afya's anger propels her to her feet. Elias digs his blade deeper into her neck. The Tribeswoman doesn't appear to notice. 'Not a traitor fugitive who, apparently, has become a slaver.'

'They're not slaves.'

I take out the key and unlock my manacles, and then Izzi's and Keenan's, to drive home Elias's point. 'They're companions,' he says. 'They're part of my favor.'

'She won't agree,' Keenan whispers to me under his breath. 'She's going to sell us out to the bleeding Martials.'

I've never felt so exposed. Afya could shout a word, and within minutes there would be soldiers all over us.

Beside me, Izzi tenses. I grab her hand and squeeze. 'We have to trust Elias,' I whisper, trying to reassure her as much as myself. 'He knows what he's doing.' All the same, I feel for my dagger, hidden beneath my cloak. If Afya does betray us, I will not go down without a fight.

'Afya.' Gibran swallows nervously, eyeing the blade at his throat. 'Perhaps we should hear him out?'

'Perhaps,' Afya says through clenched teeth, 'you should keep your mouth shut about things you don't understand and stick to seducing *Zaldars'* daughters.' She turns to Elias. 'Drop your blades and tell me what you want – and why. No explanation from you means no favor from me. I don't care what you threaten me with.'

Elias ignores the first order. 'I want you to personally escort my companions and me safely out of Nur and to Kauf Prison before the winter snows and, once there, aid us in our attempt to break Laia's brother, Darin, out of the prison.'

What in the skies? Just days ago, he told Keenan we didn't need anyone else. Now he's trying to pull in Afya? Even if we did reach the prison intact, she'd turn us over the second we arrived, and we'd disappear into Kauf forever.

'That's about three hundred favors in one, you bastard.'

'A favor coin is whatever can be requested in a breath.'

'I know what a bleeding favor coin is.' Afya drums her fingers on her desk and turns to me, as if noticing me for the first time. 'Spiro Teluman's little friend,' she says. 'I know who your brother is, girl. Spiro told me – and a few others too, from the way the rumors have spread. Everyone whispers of the Scholar who knows the secrets of Serric steel.'

'*Spiro* started the rumors?'

Afya sighs and speaks slowly, as if dealing with a small, irritating child. 'Spiro wanted the Empire to believe your brother passed his knowledge to other Scholars. Until the Martials get names from Darin, they'll keep him alive. Besides, Spiro always was one for foolish tales of heroism. He's probably hoping that this stirs up the Scholars – gives them a bit of backbone.'

'Even your ally is helping us,' Elias says. 'More reason for you to do the same.'

'My *ally* has disappeared,' Afya says. 'No one's seen him for weeks.'

I'm certain the Martials have him – and I have no wish to share the same fate.' She lifts her chin to Elias. 'If I reject your offer?'

'You didn't get to where you are by breaking promises.' Elias drops his scims. 'Grant my favor, Afya. Fighting it is a waste of time.'

'I cannot decide this alone,' Afya says. 'I need to speak with some of my Tribe. We'd need at least a few others with us, for appearances' sake.'

'In that case, your brother stays here,' Elias says. 'As does the coin.'

Gibran opens his mouth to protest, but Afya just shakes her head. 'Get them food and drink, brother.' She sniffs. 'And baths. Don't take your eyes off them.' She glides past us and through the tent flaps, saying something in Sadhese to the guards outside, and we are left to wait.

CHAPTER EIGHTEEN

Elias

Hours later, with evening deepening into night, Afya finally pushes through the tent flaps. Gibran, his feet up on his sister's desk as he flirts shamelessly with both Izzi and Laia, jumps up when she enters, like a soldier frightened of a superior officer's censure.

Afya eyes Izzi and Laia, scrubbed clean and clad in flowing green Tribal dresses. They sit close to each other in a corner, Izzi's head on Laia's shoulder as they whisper back and forth. The blonde girl's bandage is gone, but she blinks gingerly, her eye still red from the scouring it got in the storm. Keenan and I wear the dark pants and sleeveless hooded vests common in the Tribal lands, and Afya nods approvingly.

'At least you don't look – or smell – like Barbarians anymore. You have been given food? Drink?'

'We got everything we needed, thank you,' I say. Other than the one thing we need most, of course, which is the reassurance that she won't turn us over to the Martials. *You're her guest, Elias. Don't irritate her.* 'Well,' I amend, 'almost everything.'

Afya's smile is a flash of light, blinding as the sun glinting off a cheaply gilded Tribal wagon.

'I grant your favor, Elias Veturius,' she says. 'I will escort you safely to Kauf Prison before the winter snows and, once there, aid you in your attempt to break Laia's brother Darin out of the prison in any way you require.'

I eye her warily. 'But . . .'

'But' – Afya's mouth hardens – 'I won't put the burden on my Tribe alone.

'Enter,' she calls in Sadhese, and another figure comes through the tent flaps. She is dark-skinned and plump, with full cheeks and long-lashed black eyes.

She speaks, her voice a song. *'We bid farewell, but 'twas not true, for when I think your name—'*

I know the poem well. She sang it sometimes when I was a boy and couldn't sleep.

'—you stand with me in memory,' I say, *'until I see you again.'*

The woman opens her hands outward, a tentative offering. 'Ilyaas,' she whispers. 'My son. It has been too long.'

For the first six years of my life, after Keris Veturia abandoned me in Mamie Rila's tent, the *Kehanni* raised me as her own son. My adoptive mother looks exactly as she did the last time I saw her, six and a half years ago, when I was a Fiver. Though she is shorter than me, her embrace is like a warm blanket, and I fall into it, a boy again, safe in the *Kehanni*'s arms.

Then I realize what her presence here means. And what Afya has done. I release Mamie and advance on the Tribeswoman, my rage building at the smug look on her face.

'How dare you bring Tribe Saif into this?'

'How dare you endanger Tribe Nur by foisting your favor upon me?'

'You're a smuggler. Getting us north doesn't endanger your Tribe. Not if you're careful.'

'You're a fugitive of the Empire. If my Tribe is caught helping you, the Martials will destroy us.' Afya's smile is gone now, and she is the shrewd woman who recognized me at the Moon Festival, the ruthless leader who has brought a once-forgotten Tribe to glory with remarkable swiftness.

'You put me in an impossible situation, Elias Veturius. I'm returning the favor. Besides, while I *might* be able to safely smuggle you north, I cannot get you out of a city with a full Martial cordon around it. *Kehanni* Rila has offered to help.'

Of course she has. Mamie would do anything for me if she thought I needed aid. But I won't see anyone else I care about hurt because of me.

I find that my face is inches from Afya's. I glare into her dark, steely eyes, my skin hot with wrath. At Mamie's hand on my arm, I step back. 'Tribe Saif is not helping us.' I wheel on Mamie. 'Because that would be idiotic and *dangerous*.'

'Afya *Jan*.' Mamie uses the Sadhese term of endearment. 'I would speak with my impertinent son alone. Why not prepare your other guests?'

Afya gives Mamie a respectful half bow – aware, at least, of my adoptive mother's stature among her people – before gesturing Gibran, Izzi, Laia, and Keenan out of the tent. Laia looks back at me, brow furrowed, before disappearing with Afya.

When I turn to Mamie Rila, she's eyeing Laia and grinning.

'Good hips,' Mamie says. 'You'll have many children. But can she make you laugh?' Mamie waggles her eyebrows. 'I know *plenty* of girls in the Tribe who—'

'Mamie.' I recognize an attempt at distraction when I see it.

'You shouldn't be here. You need to get back to the wagons as soon as you can. Were you followed? If—'

'Shush.' Mamie waves me quiet and settles onto one of Afya's divans, patting the seat next to her. When I don't join her, her nostrils flare. 'You might be bigger than you were, Ilyaas, but you are still my son, and when I tell you to sit, you sit.

'Skies, boy.' She pinches my arm when I comply. 'What have you been eating? Grass?' She shakes her head, her tone serious now. 'What happened to you in Serra these last weeks, my love? The things I've heard . . .'

I've locked the Trials deep within. I have not spoken of them since the night I spent with Laia in my quarters at Blackcliff.

'It doesn't matter—' I begin.

'It has changed you, Ilyaas. It does matter.'

Her round face is filled with love. It will be filled with horror if she knows what I did. This will hurt her far more than the Martials ever could.

'Always so afraid of the darkness within.' Mamie takes my hands. 'Don't you see? So long as you fight the darkness, you stand in the light.'

It's not that simple, I want to shout. *I'm not the boy I was. I'm something else. Something that will sicken you.*

'Do you think I don't know what they teach you at that school?' Mamie asks. 'You must believe I am a fool. Tell me. Unburden yourself.'

'I don't want to hurt you. I don't want anyone else hurt because of me.'

'Children are born to break their mothers' hearts, my boy. Tell me.'

My mind orders me to stay silent, but my heart screams to be heard. She is asking, after all. She wants to know. And I want to tell her. I want her to know what I am.

So I speak.

* * *

When I finish, Mamie is quiet. The only thing I haven't told her is the true nature of the Commandant's poison.

'What a fool I was,' Mamie whispers, 'to think that when your mother left you to die, you would be spared from the Martials' evil.'

But my mother didn't leave me to die, did she? I learned the truth from the Commandant the night before I was to be executed: She had not abandoned me to the vultures. Keris Veturia held me, fed me, and then carried me to Mamie's tent after I was born. It was my mother's last – her only – kindness to me.

I nearly say as much to Mamie, but the sorrow on her face stops me. It doesn't make a difference now anyway.

'Ah, my boy.' Mamie sighs, and I'm certain I've put more lines on her face. 'My Elias—'

'Ilyaas,' I say. 'For you, I'm Ilyaas.'

She shakes her head. 'Ilyaas is the boy you were,' she says. 'Elias is the man you have become. Tell me: Why must you help this girl? Why not let her go with the rebel, while you remain here, with your family? Do you think we cannot protect you from the Martials? None in our Tribe would dare betray you. You are my son, and your uncle is the *Zaldar*.'

'You've heard the rumors of a Scholar who can forge Serric steel?' Mamie nods warily. 'Those stories are true,' I say. 'The Scholar is Laia's brother. If I can break him out of Kauf, think of what it could mean for the Scholars – for Marinn, for the Tribes. Ten hells, you could finally *fight* the Empire—'

The tent flap bursts open, and Afya enters, Laia trailing and heavily hooded.

'Forgive me, *Kehanni*,' she says. 'But it's time to move. Someone told the Martials you entered the camp, and they wish to speak with you. They'll likely intercept you on the way out. I don't know if—'

'They will ask questions and release me.' Mamie Rila stands, shaking out her robes, her chin high. 'I will not allow a delay.' She closes on Afya until inches separate them. Afya rocks very slightly on her heels.

'Afya Ara-Nur,' Mamie says softly. 'You will hold your vow. Tribe Saif has promised to do its part in assisting you. But if you betray my son for the bounty, or if any of your people do, we will consider it an act of war, and we will curse the blood of seven generations before our vengeance is spent.'

Afya's eyes widen at the depth of the threat, but she merely nods. Mamie turns to me, rises on her tiptoes, and kisses my forehead. Will I see her again? Feel the warmth of her hands, find comfort I don't deserve in the forgiveness of her eyes? *I will*.

Though there won't be much to see if, in trying to save me, she incurs the Martials' wrath.

'Don't do this, Mamie,' I plead with her. 'Whatever it is you're planning, don't. Think of Shan and Tribe Saif. You are their *Kehanni*. They can't lose you. I don't want—'

'We had you for six years, Elias,' Mamie says. 'We played with you, held you, watched your first steps, and heard your first words. We loved you. And then they took you from us. They hurt you. Made you suffer. Made you kill. I don't care what your blood is. You were a boy of the Tribes – *and you were taken*. And we did *nothing*. Tribe Saif must do this. I *must* do this. I have waited fourteen years to do this. Neither you nor anyone else will take it from me.'

Mamie sweeps out, and as she does, Afya jerks her head toward the back of her tent. 'Move,' she says. 'And keep your faces hidden, even from my Tribe. Only Mamie, Gibran, and I know who you are, and that's how it needs to stay until we're out of the city. You and Laia will stay with me. Gibran has already taken Keenan and Izzi.'

'Where?' I say. 'Where are we going?'

'The storytellers' stage, Veturius.' Afya arches a brow at me. 'The *Kehanni* is going to save you with a story.'

CHAPTER NINETEEN

Helene

The city of Nur feels like a damned powder keg. It's as if every Martial soldier I've released into the streets is a charge waiting to be lit.

Despite threats to the men of public whippings and reductions in rank, they've had a dozen altercations with the Tribesmen already. No doubt more are coming.

The Tribesmen's objection to our presence is ridiculous. They were happy enough to have Empire support in battling Barbarian pirate frigates along the coast. But come into a Tribal city looking for a criminal and it's as if we've unleashed a jinn horde upon them.

I pace the rooftop balcony of the Martial garrison on the western side of the city, looking down at the teeming market below. Elias could be bleeding anywhere.

If he's here at all.

The possibility that I'm wrong – that Elias has slipped south while I've been wasting time in Nur – offers a strange sort of relief. If he's not here, I can't catch him or kill him.

He's here. And you must find him.

But since arriving at the garrison at Atella's Gap, everything has gone wrong. The outpost was undermanned. I had to scrape reserve soldiers from surrounding guard posts in order to muster a force large enough to search Nur. When I arrived at the oasis, I found the force here depleted as well, with no information about where the rest of the men were sent.

All told, I have a thousand men, mostly auxes, and a dozen Masks. It's not nearly enough to search a city swollen to a hundred thousand. It's all I can do to maintain a cordon around the oasis so no wagon leaves without a search.

'Blood Shrike.' Faris's blond head pops up from the stairwell leading into the garrison. 'We've got her. She's in a cell.'

I suppress my dread as Faris and I head down a narrow flight of stairs to the dungeon. When I last saw Mamie Rila, I was a gangly, maskless fourteen-year-old. Elias and I stayed with Tribe Saif for two weeks on our way back to Blackcliff after finishing out our years as Fivers. And though, as a Fiver, I was essentially a Martial spy, Mamie'd only ever treated me with kindness.

And I'm about to repay her with an interrogation.

'She entered the Nur encampment three hours ago,' Faris says. 'Dex nabbed her on the way out. The Fiver assigned to follow her says she visited a dozen Tribes today.'

'Get me intelligence on those Tribes,' I tell Faris. 'Sizes, alliances, trade routes – everything.'

'Harper is speaking to our Fiver spies now.'

Harper. I wonder what Elias would make of the Northman. *Eerie as the ten hells,* I imagine him saying. *Less chatty too.* I can hear my friend in my head – that familiar baritone that thrilled and calmed me at the same time. Would that Elias and I were here together, hunting some Mariner spy or Barbarian assassin.

His name is Veturius, I remind myself for the thousandth time. *And he is a traitor.*

In the dungeon, Dex stands with his back to the cell, his jaw tight. Since he too spent time with Tribe Saif as a Fiver, I'm surprised at the tension in his body.

'Watch it with her,' he says under his breath. 'She's up to something.'

Within the cell, Mamie sits on the lone, hard bunk as if it is a throne, her back rigid, chin up, one long-fingered hand holding her robes off the floor. She rises when I enter, but I wave her back down.

'Helene, my love—'

'You will address the commander as Blood Shrike, *Kehanni*,' Dex says quietly as he gives me a pointed look.

'*Kehanni*,' I say. 'Do you know the whereabouts of Elias Veturius?'

She looks me up and down, her disappointment obvious. This is the woman who gave me herbs to slow my moon cycle so it wasn't hell to deal with at Blackcliff. The woman who told me, without an ounce of irony, that on the day I married, she would slaughter a hundred goats in my honor and make a *Kehanni*'s tale of my life.

'I'd heard you were hunting him,' she says. 'I've seen your child spies. But I didn't believe it.'

'Answer the question.'

'How can you hunt a boy who was your closest companion only weeks ago? He is your friend, Hel – Blood Shrike. Your shield brother.'

'He is a fugitive and a criminal.' I pull my hands behind my back and knot my fingers together, twisting the Blood Shrike ring round and round. 'And he will face justice, like other criminals. Are you harboring him?'

164

'I am not.' When I don't break eye contact, she breathes in through her nostrils, hackles rising. 'You have taken salt and water at my table, Blood Shrike.' The muscles of her hands are rigid as she clenches the edge of the bunk. 'I would not insult you with a lie.'

'But you would hide the truth. There's a difference.'

'Even if I am harboring him, what can you do about it? Fight all of Tribe Saif? You'd have to kill every last one of us.'

'One man isn't worth a Tribe.'

'But he was worth an Empire?' Mamie leans forward, her dark eyes fierce, her braids falling into her face. 'He was worth your freedom?'

How in the bleeding skies would you know that I traded my freedom for Elias's life?

The retort hovers on my lips but retreats as my training kicks in. *Weaklings try to fill silence. A Mask uses it to his advantage.* I cross my arms, waiting for her to say more.

'You gave up much for Elias.' Mamie's nostrils flare, and she stands, smaller than me by a few inches but towering in her rage. 'Why should I not give up my life for his? He is my *son*. What claim do you have on him?'

Only fourteen years of friendship and a trampled heart.

But that doesn't matter. Because in her anger, Mamie has given me what I need.

For how could she know what I gave up for Elias? Even if she heard tales of the Trials, she couldn't know what I sacrificed for him.

Not unless he told her.

Which means she's seen him.

'Dex, escort her upstairs.' I signal to him behind her back. *Follow her.* He nods and escorts her out.

I trail him and find Harper and Faris awaiting me in the garrison's Black Guard barracks.

'That wasn't an interrogation,' Faris growls. 'It was a bleeding high tea. What in the hells could you have possibly gotten out of that?'

'You're supposed to be herding Fivers, Faris, not eavesdropping.'

'Harper is a corrupting influence.' Faris nods at the dark-haired man, who shrugs at my glare.

'Elias is here,' I say. 'Mamie let something slip.'

'The comment about your freedom,' Harper murmurs. His assertion unnerves me – I hate how he always seems to hit the nail on the head.

'The gathering is nearly over. The Tribes will begin leaving the city after dawn breaks. If Tribe Saif is going to get him out, that's when they'll do it. And he *has* to get out. He won't risk staying and being spotted – not with the bounty so high.'

A knock sounds on the door. Faris opens it to a Fiver dressed in Tribal clothes, his skin stained with sand.

'Fiver Melius reporting, sir,' he salutes smartly. 'Lieutenant Dex Atrius sent me, Blood Shrike. The *Kehanni* you interrogated is heading to the storytellers' stage on the eastern edge of the city. The rest of Tribe Saif are on their way there too. Lieutenant Atrius said to come quickly – and to bring backup.'

'The farewell tale.' Faris grabs my scims from the wall and hands them over. 'It's the last event before the Tribes leave.'

'And thousands come out for it,' Harper says. 'Good place to hide a fugitive.'

'Faris, reinforce the cordon.' We plunge into the packed streets outside the garrison. 'Call in all the squads on patrol. No one gets out of Nur without going through a Martial checkpoint. Harper – with me.'

We make our way east, following the crowd streaming toward the storytellers' stage. Our presence among the Tribesmen is noted – and not with the reluctant tolerance I'm accustomed to. As we pass, I hear more than one insult muttered. Harper and I exchange a glance, and he signals the squads we run into until we have two dozen auxiliary troops at our backs.

'Tell me, Blood Shrike,' Harper says as we near the stage. 'Do you really think you can take him?'

'I've beaten Veturius in combat a hundred times—'

'I don't mean can you take him down. I mean when the moment comes, will you be able to put him in chains and take him to the Emperor, knowing what will happen?'

No. Bleeding, burning skies, no. I've asked myself the same thing a hundred times. *Will I do right by the Empire? Will I do right by my people?* I cannot object to Harper asking the question. But my answer comes out as a snarl anyway.

'I suppose we'll find out, won't we?'

Ahead, the storytellers' theater sits at the bottom of a steep, terraced bowl, and it's aglow with hundreds of oil lamps. A thoroughfare runs behind the stage, and beyond that, a vast depot filled with the wagons of those who will leave directly after the farewell tale.

The air crackles with expectation, a sense of waiting that has me clutching my scim with a white-knuckled grip. What is going on?

By the time Harper and I arrive, thousands of people pack the theater. I see immediately why Dex needed backup. The bowl has more than two dozen entrances, with Tribesmen flowing in and out freely. I deploy the auxes I've gathered to each gateway. Moments later, Dex finds me. Sweat pours down his face and blood streaks the brown skin of his forearms.

'Mamie's got something up her sleeve,' he says. 'Every Tribe she met with is here. The auxes I brought with me have already gotten into a dozen fights.'

'Blood Shrike.' Harper points to the stage, which is surrounded by fifty fully armed men of Tribe Saif. 'Look.'

The Saif warriors shift to let a proud figure through. Mamie Rila. She takes the stage, and the crowd shushes each other. When she raises her hands, any lingering whispers are silenced – not even children make a sound. I can hear the wind blowing off the desert.

The Commandant's presence prompted a similar silence. Mamie, however, seems to elicit it out of respect instead of fear.

'Welcome, brothers and sisters.' Mamie's voice echoes up the terraced bowl. I silently thank the Language Centurion at Blackcliff, who spent six years teaching us Sadhese.

The *Kehanni* turns to the darkened desert behind her. 'The sun will soon rise on a new day, and we must bid each other farewell. But I offer you a tale to take with you into the sands on your next journey. A tale kept vaulted and locked. A tale that *you* will all be a part of. A tale still being told.'

'Let me tell you of Ilyaas An-Saif, my son, who was *stolen* from Tribe Saif by the dread Martials.'

Harper, Dex, and I haven't gone unnoticed. Nor have the Martials guarding the exits. Hisses and ululations erupt from the crowd, all directed at us. Some of the auxes move as if to draw their weapons, but Dex signals a halt. Three Masks and two squads of auxes against twenty thousand Tribesmen isn't a fight. It's a death sentence.

'What is she doing?' Dex says under his breath. 'Why would she tell Elias's story?'

'He was a quiet, gray-eyed infant,' Mamie says in Sadhese, 'left to die in the swelter of the Tribal desert. What travesty, to see such a beautiful, strong child abandoned by his depraved mother and exposed to the elements. I claimed him as my own, brothers and sisters, and took great pride in doing so, for he came to me in a time of great need, when my soul searched for meaning and found none. In the eyes of this child, I found solace, and in his laughter, I found joy. But it was not to last.'

I already see Mamie's *Kehanni* magic working on the crowd. She tells of a child beloved by the Tribe, a child *of* the Tribe, as if Elias's Martial blood is incidental. She tells of his youth and of the night he was taken.

For a moment, I too find myself riveted. My curiosity transforms into wariness when Mamie turns to the Trials. She tells of the Augurs and their predictions. She speaks of the violence the Empire perpetrated upon Elias's mind and body. The crowd listens, their emotions rising and falling with Mamie's – shock, sympathy, disgust, terror.

Anger.

And that is when I finally understand what Mamie Rila is doing. She is starting a riot.

CHAPTER TWENTY

Laia

Mamie's powerful voice echoes across the theater, mesmerizing all who hear it. Though I cannot understand Sadhese, the movements of her body and her hands – along with the way Elias's face pales – tell me that this tale is about him.

We have found seats about halfway up the terraces of the storytellers' theater. I sit between Elias and Afya amid a crowd of men and women from Tribe Nur. Keenan and Izzi wait with Gibran a dozen or so yards away. I catch Keenan craning his neck, trying to make sure I'm all right, and I wave to him. His dark eyes drift to Elias and back to me before Izzi whispers something to him and he looks away.

In the green-and-gold clothes Afya gave all of us, we are, at a distance, indistinguishable from the other members of the Tribe. I retreat further into my hood, thankful for the rising winds. Nearly everyone has their hoods up or cloth over their faces to protect themselves from the choking dust.

We can't take you directly to the wagons, Afya said as we joined her Tribe in walking to the theater. *There are soldiers patrolling the depot – and they're stopping everyone. So Mamie's going to create a little distraction.*

As Mamie's story takes a surprising turn, the crowd gasps, and Elias looks pained. To have one's life story told to so many would be strange enough, but a story with so much suffering, so much death? I take his hand, and he tenses, as if to pull away, but then relaxes.

'Don't listen,' I say. 'Look at me instead.'

Reluctantly, he lifts his eyes. The intensity of his pale gaze makes my heart stutter, but I don't let myself look away. There's a loneliness to him that makes me ache. He's dying. He knows it. Perhaps life does not get more lonely than that.

Right now, all I want is for that loneliness to fade – even if it's for a moment. So I do what Darin used to when he wanted to cheer me up, and I make an absurd face.

Elias stares at me in surprise before cracking a grin that lights him up – and then he makes a ridiculous face of his own. I snicker and am about to challenge him when I spot Keenan watching us, his eyes flat with suppressed fury.

Elias follows my gaze. 'I don't think he likes me.'

'He doesn't like anyone at first,' I say. 'When he met me, he threatened to kill me and stuff me in a crypt.'

'Charming.'

'He changed. Quite a lot, actually. I would have thought it impossible, but—' I wince as Afya elbows me.

'It's beginning.'

Elias's smile fades as, around us, the Tribesmen begin to whisper. He eyes the Martials stationed at the theater exits nearest us. Most have hands on their weapons, and they watch the crowd dubiously, as if it will rise up and devour them.

Mamie's gestures grow expansive and violent. The crowd bristles

171

and seems to expand, pushing against the walls of the theater. Tension fills the air, spreads, an invisible flame that transforms all who come into contact with it. In seconds, whispers become angry mutters.

Afya smiles.

Mamie points to the crowd, the conviction in her voice raising goose bumps on my arms.

'*Kisaneh kithiya ke jeehani deka?*'

Elias leans toward me, his words quiet in my ear. 'Who has suffered the tyranny of the Empire?' he translates.

'*Hama!*'

'We have.'

'*Kisaneh bichaya ke gima baza?*'

'Who has seen children torn from their parents' arms?'

'*Hama!*'

A few rows down from us, a man rises and gestures at a knot of Martials I didn't notice. One of them has pale skin and a crown of blonde braids: Helene Aquilla. The man bellows something at them.

'*Charra! Herrisada!*'

Across the bowl, a Tribeswoman stands and shouts those same words. Another woman rises to her feet at the base of the theater. She is soon joined by a deep voice yards away from us.

Suddenly, the two words echo back and forth from every mouth, and the crowd transforms from spellbound to violent as quick as a pitch-soaked torch catching flame.

'*Charra! Herrisada!*'

'Thieves,' Elias translates, his voice flat. 'Monsters.'

Tribe Nur rises to their feet around Elias and me, shouting abuse at the Martials, raising their voices to join thousands of other Tribesmen doing the same.

I think back to the Martials tearing through the Tribal market-

172

place yesterday. And I understand, finally, that this explosive rage is not just about Elias. It has been present in Nur all along. Mamie just harnessed it.

I always thought the Tribesmen were allied with the Martials, however reluctantly. Perhaps I was wrong.

'Stay with me now.' Afya rises, her eyes darting from entrance to entrance. We follow, straining to hear her voice above the baying crowd. 'When first blood is shed, we head for the nearest exit. Nur's wagons wait in the depot. A dozen other Tribes will leave at the same time, and that should trigger the rest of the Tribes into leaving too.'

'How will we know when—'

A bloodcurdling howl cracks the air. I stand on tiptoe to see that at one of the exits far below us, a Martial soldier has cut down a Tribesman who got too close. The Tribesman's blood seeps into the sands of the theater, and the shriek comes again, from an older woman kneeling over him, her body shuddering.

Afya wastes no time. As one, Tribe Nur rushes to the closest exit. Quite suddenly, I cannot breathe. The crowd presses in close – surging, pushing, going in too many directions. I lose sight of Afya and spin toward Elias. He grabs my hand and pulls me near, but there are too many people, and we are wrenched apart. I spot a gap in the crowd and try to elbow my way toward it, but I can't penetrate the mass of bodies around me.

Make yourself small. Tiny. Disappear. If you disappear, you can breathe. My skin prickles, and I push forward again. The Tribesmen I shove past look around, strangely bewildered. I'm able to get through them easily.

'Elias, come on!'

'Laia?' He swivels, staring into the crowd, pushing in the wrong direction.

'Here, Elias!'

He swings toward me but doesn't seem to see me, and he grabs his head. Skies – the poison again? He scrambles for his pocket and takes a swig of the Tellis.

I push back through the Tribesmen until I am right beside him. 'Elias, I'm right here,' I take his arm, and he practically jumps out of his skin.

He wags his head like he did when he was first poisoned and looks me over. 'Of course you are,' he says. 'Afya – where's Afya?' He cuts through the crowd, trying to catch up to the Tribeswoman, whom I can't see anywhere.

'What in the skies are you two doing?' Afya appears beside us and grabs my arm. 'I've been looking all over for you. *Stay* with me! We have to get out of here!'

I follow her, but Elias's attention jerks to something farther down in the bowl, and he stops short, staring over the surging crowd.

'Afya!' he says. 'Where's the Nur caravan?'

'North section of the depot,' she says. 'A couple of caravans over from Tribe Saif.'

'Laia, can you stay with Afya?'

'Of course but—'

'She's seen me.' He releases me, and as he pushes into the crowd, Aquilla's familiar silver-blonde crown braid flashes in the sun a few dozen yards away.

'I'll distract her,' Elias says. 'Get to the caravan. I'll meet you there.'

'Elias, damn it—'

But he's already gone.

CHAPTER TWENTY-ONE

Elias

When my eyes meet Helene's across the crowd – when I see the shock roll across her silver face as she recognizes me – I don't think, nor do I question. I just move, delivering Laia into Afya's arms and then cutting through the crowd, away from them and toward Hel. I need to draw her attention from Afya and Tribe Nur. If she identifies them as the Tribe that's taken Laia and me in, a thousand riots won't stop her from eventually hunting us down.

I'll distract her. Then I'll disappear into the crowd. I think of her face back in my quarters at Blackcliff, fighting to hold in her hurt as she met my eyes. *After this, I belong to him. Remember, Elias. After this, we're enemies.*

The chaos of the riot is deafening, but within that cacophony, I witness a strange, hidden order. For all the shouting, yelling, and screaming, I see no abandoned children, no trampled bodies, no quickly deserted belongings – none of the hallmarks of true chaos.

Mamie and Afya have this riot planned down to the minute.

Distantly, the drums of the Martial garrison thud, calling for backup. Hel must have sent a message to the drum tower. But if she wants soldiers here to quell the riot, then she can't maintain the cordon around the city.

Which was, I now understand, Afya and Mamie's plan all along.

Once the cordon around the wagons is lifted, Afya can get us safely hidden and out of the city. Our caravan will be one of hundreds leaving Nur.

Helene entered the theater near the stage and has now pressed halfway toward me. But she is alone, an armored, silver-faced island in a roiling sea of human rage. Dex has disappeared, and the other Mask who entered the amphitheater with her – Harper – heads out one of the exits.

The fact that she's alone doesn't deter Helene. She makes for me with a single-minded determination that is as familiar to me as my own skin. She shoves forward, her body gathering an inexorable force that propels her through the Tribesmen like a shark toward bloodied prey. But the crowd closes in. Fingers grasp at her cloak, her neck. Someone puts a hand on her shoulder, and she pivots, grabs it, and snaps it in one breath. I can almost hear her logic: *It's faster to to keep going than to fight them all.*

Her movement is hampered, slowed, stopped. It is only then that I hear the hiss of her scims whipping out of their scabbards. She is the Blood Shrike now, a grim-faced knight of the Empire, her blades carving a path forward in sprays of blood.

I glance over my shoulder and catch Laia and Afya pushing through one of the gates and out of the theater. When I look back at Helene, her scims fly – but not fast enough. Multiple Tribesmen attack – dozens – too many for her to counter at once. The crowd has taken on a life of its own and does not fear her blades. I see the moment she realizes it – the moment she knows that no matter how swift she is, there are too many for her to fight.

She meets my stare, her fury blazing. Then she drops, pulled down by those around her.

Again, my body moves before my mind knows what I am doing. I pull a cloak off a woman in the crowd – she doesn't even notice its absence – and muscle my way through, my only thought to get to Helene, to pull her out, to keep her from being beaten or trampled to death. *Why, Elias? She's your enemy now.*

The thought sickens me. She was my best friend. I can't just throw that away.

I drop, lunge forward through robes, legs, and weaponry, and pull the cloak around Helene. One arm goes around her waist, and I use the other to cut the straps on her scims and her brace of throwing knives. Her weapons drop, and when she coughs, blood spatters her armor. I bear her weight as her legs fight to find their strength. We are through one ring of Tribesmen, then another, until we are moving quickly away from where the rioters are still howling for her blood.

Leave her, Elias. Get her clear and leave her. Distraction complete. You're done.

But if I leave her now, and any other Tribesmen attack while she's hardly able to walk, then I might as well not have pulled her out.

I keep walking, holding her up until she gets her feet. She coughs and shakes, and I know that all of her instincts are ordering her to draw breath, to calm her heartbeat – to survive. Which is perhaps why she doesn't resist me until we are through one of the theater's gates and halfway down an empty, dusty alley beyond.

She finally shoves me away and rips the cloak off. A hundred emotions flash across her face as she casts the cloak on the ground, things no one else would ever see or know but me. That alone extinguishes the days and weeks and miles dividing us. Her hands shake, and I notice the ring on her finger.

'Blood Shrike.'

'Don't.' She shakes her head. 'Don't call me that. Everyone calls me that. But not you.' She looks me up and down. 'You – you look terrible.'

'Rough few weeks.' I spot the scars on her hands and arms, the faded bruises on her face. *I gave her to a Black Guard for interrogation,* the Commandant said.

And she survived, I think to myself. *Now get out of here, before she kills you.*

I step back, but her arm shoots out, her hand cool on my wrist, her grip like iron. I find her pale gaze, startled at the mess of emotions laid bare there. *Leave, Elias!*

I yank my arm away, and as I do, the doors in her eyes, open just a moment ago, slam shut. Her expression flattens. She reaches back for her weapons – nonexistent, since I relieved her of them. I see her soften her knees, preparing to lunge at me.

'You are under arrest' – she leaps, and I sidestep her – 'by order of the—'

'You're not going to arrest me.' I wrap an arm around her waist and try to fling her a few yards away.

'The hells I'm not.' She jabs her elbow deep into my stomach. I double over, and she spins out of my grasp. Her knee flies up toward my forehead.

I catch it, shove it back, and stun her with an elbow to the face. 'I just saved your life, Hel.'

'I would have gotten out of there without you – oof—' I bull rush her, and her breath huffs out when her back hits the wall. I pin her legs between my thighs to keep her from crippling me, and I put a blade to her throat before she can knock me senseless with a head butt.

'Damn you!' She tries to twist free, and I press the blade closer. Her eyes drop to my mouth, her breath coming short and fast. She looks away with a shudder.

'They were crushing you,' I say. 'You'd have been trampled.'

'That changes nothing. I have orders from Marcus to bring you to Antium for a public execution.'

Now it's my turn to snort. 'Why in the ten hells haven't you assassinated him yet? You'd be doing the world a favor.'

'Oh, piss off,' she spits at me. 'I wouldn't expect you to understand.'

A thudding rumbles the streets beyond the alley – the rhythmic footsteps of approaching Martial soldiers. Reinforcements to quell the riot.

Helene uses my moment of distraction to try to force her way out of my grip. I can't hold her for much longer. Not if I want to get the hell out of here without half a Martial legion on my tail. *Damn it.*

'I have to leave,' I say into her ear. 'But I don't want to hurt you. I'm so sick of hurting people.' I feel the soft flutter of her eyelashes against my cheek, the steady rise and fall of her breath against my chest.

'Elias.' She whispers my name, one word full of wanting.

I pull back. Her eyes, blue as smoke a second ago, darken to a stormy violet. *Loving you is the worst thing that's ever happened to me.* She said those words to me weeks ago. Witnessing the devastation in her now and knowing that, yet again, I'm the cause makes me hate myself.

'I'm going to let go of you,' I say. 'If you try to take me down, so be it. But before I do, I want to say something, because we both know I'm not long for this world, and I'd hate myself if I never told you.' Confusion flashes across her face, and I barrel on before she starts asking questions. 'I miss you.' I hope she hears what I'm truly saying. *I love you. I'm sorry. I wish I could fix it.* 'I'll always miss you. Even when I'm a ghost.'

I release her and take a step away. Then another. I turn my back on her, my heart clenching at the strangled sound she makes, and walk out of the alley.

The only footsteps I hear as I leave are my own.

*   *   *

The depot is pure pandemonium, with Tribesman throwing children and goods into wagons, animals rearing, women shouting. A thick dust cloud rises in the air, the result of hundreds of caravans rolling into the desert at once.

'Thank the skies!' Laia spots me the moment I appear beside Afya's high-sided wagon. 'Elias, *why*—'

'You *idiot.*' Afya grabs me by the scruff of the neck and hurls me up into the wagon beside Laia with remarkable strength, considering she's more than a foot shorter than me. 'What were you *thinking?*'

'We couldn't risk Aquilla seeing me surrounded by members of Tribe Nur. She's a Mask, Afya. She'd have figured out who you were. Your Tribe would have been at risk.'

'You're still an idiot.' Afya glares at me. 'Keep your head down. And *stay.*'

She vaults onto the driver's bench and grabs the reins. Seconds later, the four horses pulling the wagon jerk forward, and I turn to Laia.

'Izzi and Keenan?'

'With Gibran.' She nods to a bright green wagon a few dozen yards away. I recognize the sharp profile of Afya's little brother at the reins.

'Are you all right?' I ask her. Laia's cheeks are flushed, and her hand is white-knuckled on the hilt of her dagger.

'Just relieved that you're back,' she says. 'Did – did you talk to her? To Aquilla?'

I'm about to answer when something occurs to me. 'Tribe Saif.' I scan the dust-choked depot. 'Do you know if they got out? Did Mamie Rila escape the soldiers?'

'I didn't see.' She turns to Afya. 'Did you —'

The Tribeswoman fidgets, and I catch her glance. Across the depot, I see wagons draped in silver and green, as familiar as my own face. Tribe's Saif's colors. Tribe Saif's wagons.

Surrounded by Martials.

They drag members of the Tribe out of the wagons and force them to their knees. I recognize my family. Uncle Akbi. Aunt Hira. Bleeding hells, Shan, my foster brother.

'Afya,' I say. 'I have to do something. That's my Tribe.' I reach for my weapons and edge to the open door between the wagon and the driver's seat. *Jump. Run. Come at them from behind. Take the strongest first* –

'Stop.' Afya grabs my arm in a viselike grip. 'You can't save them. Not without giving yourself away.'

'Skies, Elias.' Laia's face is stricken. 'Torches.'

One of the wagons – the beautiful, mural-decorated *Kehanni* wagon that I grew up in – goes up in flame. It took Mamie months to paint the peacocks and fish and ice dragons that adorned it. I'd hold the jars for her sometimes and wash the brushes. Gone, so fast. One by one, the other wagons are put to the torch until the entire encampment is nothing but a black stain against the sky.

'Most of them got away,' Afya says quietly. 'Tribe Saif's caravan is nearly a thousand strong. A hundred and fifty wagons. Of those, only a dozen were caught. Even if you could get to them, Elias, there are at least a hundred soldiers out there.'

'Auxes,' I say through gritted teeth. 'Easy to beat. If I could get swords to my uncles and Shan—'

'Tribe Saif planned for this, Elias.' Afya refuses to back down. In that moment, I hate her. 'If the soldiers see that you came from Nur's wagons, my entire Tribe is dead. Everything Mamie and I planned for in the last two days – every favor *she* called in to get you out of here – it will all be for nothing. You traded in your favor, Elias. This was the price.'

I look back. My Tribal family huddles together, heads bowed. Defeated.

Except for one. She fights, shoving at the auxes who have grabbed her arms, fearless in her defiance. Mamie Rila.

Uselessly, I watch her struggle, watch a legionnaire bring the hilt of his scim down on the side of her head. The last thing I see before she disappears from sight is her hands fluttering for purchase as she falls to the sands.

CHAPTER TWENTY-TWO

Laia

The relief of escaping Nur does nothing to assuage my guilt at what happened to Elias's Tribe. I do not bother trying to talk to him. What could I say? *Sorry* is a callous inadequacy. He is silent in the back of Afya's wagon, staring out at the desert in the direction of Nur, as if he can use his willpower to change what happened to his family.

I give him his solitude. Few people want witnesses to their pain, and grief is the worst pain of all.

Besides which, the guilt I feel is almost crippling. Again and again, I see Mamie's proud form crumpling like a sack of grain emptied of its bounty. I know I should acknowledge to Elias what happened to her. But it seems cruel to do so now.

By nightfall, Nur is a distant cluster of light in the sweeping blackness of the desert behind us. Its lamps seem dimmer tonight.

Though we fled in a caravan of more than two hundred wagons, Afya has split her Tribe a dozen times since then. By the time the moon rises, we are down to five wagons and four other members of her Tribe, including Gibran.

'He didn't want to come.' Afya surveys her brother, perched atop the bench of his wagon a dozen yards away. It is covered with thousands of tiny mirrors that reflect the moonlight, a creeking, trundling galaxy. 'But I can't trust him not to get himself or Tribe Nur into trouble. Fool boy.'

'I can see that,' I murmur. Gibran has lured Izzi up into the seat beside him, and I've caught flashes of her shy smile all afternoon.

I glance back through the window into Afya's wagon. The burnished walls of its interior glow with muted lamplight. Elias sits on one of the velvet-clad benches and stares out the back window.

'Speaking of fools,' Afya says. 'What's between you and the redhead?'

Skies. The Tribeswoman misses nothing. I need to remember that. Keenan has ridden with Riz, a silver-haired, silent member of Afya's Tribe, since our last stop to water the horses. The rebel and I hardly had a chance to speak before Afya ordered him to help Riz with his supply wagon.

'I don't know what's between us.' I am wary of telling Afya the truth but suspect that she could pick out a lie a mile away. 'He kissed me once. In a shed. Right before he ran off to help start the Scholar revolution.'

'Must have been quite a kiss,' Afya mutters. 'What about Elias? You're always staring at him.'

'I am not—'

'Not that I blame you,' Afya continues as if I haven't spoken, casting an appraising eye back at Elias. 'Those cheekbones – skies.' My skin heats, and I cross my arms, frowning.

'Ah.' Afya flashes her wolfish smile. 'Possessive, are we?'

'I have nothing to be possessive of.' An icy wind blows down from the north, and I huddle into my thin Tribal dress. 'He's made it clear to me that he's my guide and nothing more.'

'His eyes say different,' Afya says. 'But who am I to get between a Martial and his misplaced nobility?' The Tribeswoman raises her hand and whistles, ordering the caravan to a halt beside a high plateau. A cluster of trees stands at its base, and I catch the shine of a spring and the scrape of an animal's claws as it patters away.

'Gibran, Izzi,' Afya calls across the camp. 'Get a fire going. Keenan' – the redhead drops down from Riz's wagon – 'help Riz and Vana with the animals.'

Riz calls out something in Sadhese to his daughter, Vana. She is whip-thin with deep brown skin, like her father, and braid tattoos that mark her as a young widow. The last member of Afya's Tribe is Zehr, a young man about Darin's age. Afya barks an order at him in Sadhese, and he gets to it without hesitation.

'Girl.' Afya is, I realize, speaking to me. 'Ask Riz for a goat, and tell Elias to slaughter it. I'll trade the meat tomorrow. And talk to him. Get him out of this funk he's in.'

'We should leave him be.'

'If you're going to drag Tribe Nur into this ill-advised attempt to save your brother, then Elias needs to come up with a fool-proof plan to do so. We have two months before we reach Kauf – that should be enough time. But he can't do it if he's moping. So fix it.'

As if it's that easy.

A few minutes later, Riz points me to a goat with an injured leg, and I lead it to Elias. He guides the limping animal to the trees, out of sight of the rest of the caravan.

He doesn't need help, but I follow anyway with a lantern. The goat bleats at me mournfully.

'Always hated butchering animals.' Elias sharpens a knife on a whetstone. 'It's like they know what's coming.'

'Nan used to do the butchering in our house,' I say. 'Some of Pop's patients paid in chickens. She had this saying: *Thank you for giving your life, that I may continue mine.*'

'Nice sentiment,' Elias kneels. 'Doesn't make it any easier to watch it die.'

'But it's lame – see?' I shine the lantern upon the goat's wounded hind leg. 'Riz said we'd have to leave it behind and it would die of thirst.' I shrug. 'If it's going to die anyway, it might as well be useful.'

Elias draws the blade across the animal's neck and it kicks. Blood pours onto the sand. I look away, thinking of the Tribesman Shikaat, of the hot stickiness of his blood. Of how it smelled – sharp, like the forges of Serra.

'You can go.' Elias uses a Mask's voice on me. It is colder than the wind at our backs.

I retreat quickly, mulling over what he said. *Doesn't make it any easier to watch it die.* Guilt sweeps through me again. He wasn't talking about the goat, I think.

I try to distract myself by finding Keenan, who has volunteered to make dinner.

'All right?' he asks when I appear beside him. He looks briefly toward Elias.

I nod, and Keenan opens his mouth as if to say something. But perhaps sensing I'd rather not talk, he just hands me a bowl of dough. 'Knead it, please?' he says. 'I'm terrible at making flatbread.'

Grateful to have a task, I get to it, taking comfort from its simplicity, from the ease of having only to roll out disks and cook them on a cast iron pan. Keenan hums as he adds red chilies and lentils to a pot, a sound so unexpected that I smile when I first hear it. It is as soothing as one of Pop's tonics, and after a time, he speaks of Adisa's Great Library, which I've always wanted to visit, and of the kite markets in Ayo that stretch for blocks. The time passes quickly, and I feel as if a bit of the weight on my heart has been lifted.

By the time Elias has finished butchering the goat, I flip the last pieces of charred, fluffy flatbread into a basket. Keenan ladles out bowls of spiced lentil stew. The first bite makes me sigh. Nan always made stew and flatbread on cold fall nights. Just the smell of it makes my sadness seem further away.

'This is incredible, Keenan.' Izzi holds out her bowl for a second helping before turning to me. 'Cook used to make it all the time. I wonder—' She shakes her head and for a time, she is quiet. 'I wish she had come,' my friend finally says. 'I miss her. I know it must sound strange to you, considering how she acted.'

'Not really,' I say. 'You loved each other. You were with her for years. She took care of you.'

'She did,' Izzi says softly. 'Her voice was the only sound in the ghost wagon that took us from Antium to Serra after the Commandant bought us. Cook gave me her rations. Held me in the freezing nights.' Izzi sighs. 'I hope I see her again. I left in such a hurry, Laia. I never told her . . .'

'We'll see her again,' I say. It's what Izzi needs to hear. And who knows, maybe we will. 'And Izzi' – I squeeze her hand – 'Cook knows whatever you didn't tell her. In her bones, I'm sure she knows.'

Keenan brings us mugs of tea, and I take a sip, closing my eyes at the sweetness, inhaling the aroma of cardamom. Across the fire, Afya lifts her mug to her lips and promptly spews out the tea.

'Bleeding, burning skies, Scholar. Did you waste my entire honey pot on this?' She tosses the liquid onto the ground in disgust, but I curl my fingers around the mug and take a deep sip.

'Good tea is sweet enough to choke a bear,' Keenan says. 'Everyone knows that.'

I chuckle and smile at him. 'My brother used to say that when he made it for me.' As I think of Darin – the old Darin – my smile fades. Who is my brother now? When did he transform from the boy who made me too-sweet tea to a man with secrets too heavy to share with his little sister?

Keenan settles in beside me. A wind howls out of the north, battling the flames of our fire. I lean close to the fighter, savoring his warmth.

'Are you all right?' Keenan dips his head toward me. He takes a lock of hair flying across my face and tucks it behind my ear. His fingers linger at my nape, and my breath catches. 'After . . .'

I look away, cold again, and reach for my armlet. 'Was it worth it, Keenan? Skies, Elias's mother, his brother, dozens of members of his Tribe.' I sigh. 'Will it even matter? What if we can't save Darin? Or if . . .' *He's dead.*

'Family is worthy dying for, killing for. Fighting for them is all that keeps us going when everything else is gone.' He nods at my armlet. There's a sad longing in his face. 'You touch it when you need strength,' he says. 'Because that's what family gives us.'

I drop my hand from the armlet. 'I don't even know I'm doing it sometimes,' I say. 'It's silly.'

'It's how you hold on to them. Nothing silly about that.' He tips his neck back and looks up at the moon. 'I don't have anything from my family. I wish I did.'

'Some days I don't remember Lis's face,' I say. 'Just that she had light hair like Mother.'

'She had your mother's temperament too.' Keenan smiles. 'Lis was four years older than me. Skies, she was bossy. She tricked me into doing her chores all the time. . . .'

The night is suddenly less lonely with memories of my long-dead sister dancing around me. On my other side, Izzi and Gibran lean toward each other, my friend giggling delightedly at something the Tribal boy says. Riz and Vana reach for their ouds. Their strumming is soon accompanied by Zehr's singing. The song is in Sadhese, but I think they must be remembering those they have loved and lost, because after only a few notes, it raises a lump in my throat.

Without thinking, I search the dark for Elias. He sits slightly away from the fire, his cloak pulled tight around him. His attention is fixed on me.

Afya clears her throat pointedly and then jerks her head at Elias. *Talk to him.*

I glance back at him, and that heady rush I always experience when I look into his eyes rolls through me.

'I'll be right back,' I say to Keenan. I put down my mug and pull my cloak close. As I do, Elias rises in one smooth motion and moves away from the fire. He disappears so swiftly that I don't even see which direction he's gone in the darkness beyond the circle of wagons. His message is clear: *Leave me alone.*

I pause, feeling like a fool. A moment later, Izzi appears beside me.

'Talk to him,' she says. 'He needs it. He just doesn't know it. And you do too.'

'He's angry,' I whisper.

My friend takes my hand and squeezes. 'He's hurt,' she says. 'And that's something you understand.'

I walk out past the wagons, scanning the desert until I spot the shine of one of his bracers near the base of the plateau. When

I'm still a few feet away from him, I hear him sigh and turn toward me. His face, blank with a sort of bland politeness, is lit by the moon.

Just get it over with, Laia.

'I'm sorry,' I say. 'For what happened. I – I don't know if it's right to trade the suffering of Tribe Saif for Darin's life. Especially when it doesn't even guarantee that Darin will live.' I was planning a few demure and carefully chosen words of sympathy, but now that I've started talking, I can't seem to stop. 'Thank you for what your family sacrificed. All I want is for nothing like that to happen again. But – but I can't guarantee it, and it makes me feel ill, because I *know* how it feels to lose family. Anyway, I'm sorry—'

Skies. Now I'm just babbling.

I take a breath. Words seem suddenly trite and useless, so I step forward and grab Elias's hands, remembering Pop. *Touch heals, Laia.* I hold fast to him, trying to put everything I feel into that touch. *I hope your Tribe is all right. I hope they survive the Martials. I'm truly, truly sorry. It's not enough. But it's all I have.*

After a moment, Elias lets out a breath and leans his forehead against mine.

'Tell me what you told me that night in my room at Blackcliff,' he murmurs. 'What your Nan used to say to you.'

'As long as there is life' – I can hear Nan's warm voice as I say it – 'there is hope.'

Elias lifts his head and looks down at me, the coolness in his eyes replaced by that raw, unquenchable fire. I forget to breathe.

'Don't you forget it,' he says. 'Ever.'

I nod. The minutes pass, and neither of us pull away, instead finding solace in the coolness of the night and the quiet company of the stars.

CHAPTER TWENTY-THREE

Elias

I enter the Waiting Place the moment I fall asleep. My breath clouds in front of my face, and I find myself lying on my back atop a thick carpet of fallen leaves. I stare at the web of tree branches above, their foliage the vibrant red of autumn, even in the half light.

'Like blood.' I recognize Tristas's voice immediately and scramble to my feet to find him leaning against one of the trees, glaring at me. I haven't seen him since the first time I entered the Waiting Place weeks ago. I'd hoped he'd moved on.

'Like *my* blood.' He stares up at the canopy, a bitter smile on his face. 'You know. The blood that poured out of me when Dex stabbed me.'

'I'm sorry, Tristas.' I might as well be a simpleminded sheep bleating the words. But the rage in his eyes is so unnatural that I would say anything to ease it.

'Aelia's getting better,' Tristas says. 'Traitorous girl. I thought she'd mourn for at least a few months. Instead, I visit her to find that she's eating again. *Eating.*' He paces, and his face darkens into an uglier, more violent version of the Tristas I knew. He hisses under his breath.

Ten hells. This is so far from who Tristas was in life that I wonder if he's possessed. Can a ghost be possessed? Isn't it ghosts that usually do the possessing?

For a moment, I'm angry at him. *You're dead. Aelia's not.* But the feeling passes quickly. Tristas will never see his fiancée again. Never hold his children or laugh with his friends. All he has now are memories and bitterness.

'Aelia loves you.' When Tristas spins toward me, his face twisted in rage, I hold up my hands. 'And you love her. Do you truly want her to starve herself to death? Would you want to see her here, knowing that it was your death that did it?'

The wildness in his eyes dims. I think of the old Tristas, the Tristas from life. *That's* the Tristas I need to appeal to. But I don't have the chance. As if he knows what I wish, he whirls and disappears into the trees.

'You can soothe the dead.' The Soul Catcher speaks from above me, and I look up to find her sitting upon one of the trees, cradled like a child in its enormous, gnarled branches. A wreath of red leaves encircles her head like a crown, and her black eyes shine darkly.

'He ran away,' I say. 'I wouldn't call that *soothing*.'

'He spoke to you.' The Soul Catcher drops down, the carpet of leaves muffling the sound of her landing. 'Most spirits hate the living.'

'Why do you keep bringing me back here?' I look down at her. 'Is it just for your amusement?'

She frowns. 'I didn't bring you this time, Elias,' she says. 'You brought yourself. Your death approaches swiftly. Perhaps your mind seeks to understand better what is to come.'

'I still have time,' I say. 'Four – maybe five months, if I'm lucky.'

The Soul Catcher looks at me pityingly. 'I cannot see the future the way some can.' She curls her lip, and I sense she's speaking of the Augurs. 'But my power is not insignificant. I sought your fate in the stars the night I first brought you here, Elias. You will not live past *Rathana*.'

Rathana – The Night – began as a Tribal holiday but has spread throughout the Empire. For Martials, it's a day of revelry. For the Tribes, it's a day to honor one's ancestors.

'That's two months away.' My mouth is dry, and even here, in the spirit world where all is dulled, dread grips me. 'We'll have just made it to Kauf by then – if we're lucky.'

The Soul Catcher shrugs. 'I know not the small tempests of your human world. If you are so distraught with your fate, make the best use of the time you do have. Go.' She flicks her hand, and I feel that jerk in my navel, as if I'm being pulled through a tunnel by a great hook.

I wake beside the dimly glowing embers of the fire, where I bedded down for the night. Riz paces outside the circle of wagons. Everyone else sleeps – Gibran and Keenan by the fire, like me, and Laia and Izzi in Gibran's wagon.

Two months. How do I get to Kauf and free Darin with so little time? I could urge Afya to go faster, but that would only lead to us getting there a few days earlier than planned, if that.

The watch changes. Keenan takes Riz's place. My eyes fall on a cold-box hanging from the bottom of Afya's wagon, where she had me pack the goat I butchered earlier.

If it's going to die anyway, might as well be useful. Laia's words. The same applies to me, I realize.

Kauf is more than a thousand miles away. By wagon, it will take two months, true enough. The Empire's couriers, on the other hand, regularly make the journey in two weeks.

I won't have access to fresh horses every dozen miles, the way the couriers do. I cannot use the main roads. I'll need to hide or fight at a moment's notice. I'll need to hunt or steal everything I consume.

Even knowing all of that, if I head to Kauf alone, I can make it in half the time that it would take the wagons. I don't wish to leave Laia – I will feel the absence of her voice, her face, every day. I already know it. But if I can make it to the prison in a month, I'll have enough time before *Rathana* to break Darin out. The Tellis extract will keep the seizures at bay until the wagons get close to the prison. I *will* see Laia again.

I rise, coil my bedroll, and make for Afya's wagon. When I knock on the back door, it takes her only a moment to answer, despite it being the dead of night.

She holds up a lamp, raising her eyebrows when she sees me.

'I usually prefer to get to know my midnight visitors a bit better before I invite them into my wagon, Elias,' she says. 'But for you . . .'

'That's not why I'm here,' I say. 'I need a horse, some parchment, and your discretion.'

'Escaping while you still can?' She gestures me inside. 'I'm glad you've come to your senses.'

'I'm getting Darin out alone.' I step in the wagon and drop my voice. 'Faster and safer for everyone that way.'

'Fool. How will you sneak north without my wagons? Have you forgotten that you're the Empire's most wanted criminal?'

'I'm a Mask, Afya. I'll manage.' I narrow my eyes at the Tribeswoman. 'Your vow to me still stands. You will get them to Kauf.'

'But you'll get him out yourself? There will be no need for Tribe Nur's assistance?'

'No,' I say. 'There's a cave in the hills south of the prison. It's about a day's hike from the main gate. I'll draw you a map. Get them there safely. If all goes well, Darin will be waiting there when you arrive in two months. If not—'

'I won't just abandon them in the mountains, Elias.' Afya bristles, offended. 'They have taken water and salt at my table, for skies' sake.' She gives me an appraising look, and I don't like the sharpness in her eyes, like she'll cut the truth of why I'm doing this out of me if she has to.

'Why the change of heart?'

'Laia wanted us to do this together. So it never occurred to me to do it alone.' That part, at least, is true, and I let Afya see that in my face. 'I'll need you to give Laia something from me. She'll put up a fight if I tell her.'

'She will indeed.' Afya hands me parchment and a quill. 'And not just because she wants to do this herself, though you both might tell yourselves that.'

I choose not to dwell on that particular comment. A few minutes later, I've finished the letter and drawn a detailed map of the prison and of the cave where I plan to stow Darin.

'You're sure about this?' Afya crosses her arms as she stands. 'You shouldn't just disappear, Elias. You should ask Laia what she wants. It's her brother, after all.' Her eyes narrow. 'You're not planning to leave the girl high and dry, are you? I'd hate if the man to whom I made my vow was without honor himself.'

'I wouldn't do that.'

'Then take Trera, Riz's bay. He's headstrong but swift and cunning as a north wind. And try not to fail, Elias. I have no desire to break into that prison myself.'

Silently, I make my way from her wagon to Riz's, whispering to Trera in soothing tones to keep him quiet. I snatch flatbread, fruit, nuts, and cheese from Vana's wagon and lead the horse well beyond the camp.

'You're trying to get him out on your own, then?'

Keenan materializes out of the darkness like a bleeding wraith, and I jump. I didn't hear him – didn't even sense him.

'I don't need to hear your reasons.' He keeps his distance, I notice. 'I know what it is to do things that you don't want to for a greater good.'

On the surface, the words are almost sympathetic. But his eyes are as flat as polished stones, and my neck prickles unpleasantly, as if the second I turn around, he'll stab me in the back.

'Good luck.' He offers a hand. Warily I shake it, my other hand drifting to my knives almost unconsciously.

Keenan sees, and his half smile doesn't reach his eyes. He lets go of my hand quickly and fades back into the dark. I shake off the uneasiness that has stolen over me. *You just don't like him, Elias.*

I glance up at the sky. The stars still sparkle above, but dawn approaches, and I need to be well away before then. But what about Laia? Am I really going to leave with only a note to say goodbye?

On cat feet, I make my way to Gibran's wagon and open the back door. Izzi snores on one bench, her hands folded beneath her cheek. Laia is curled in a ball on the other, one hand on her armlet, fast asleep.

'You are my temple,' I murmur as I kneel beside her. 'You are my priest. You are my prayer. You are my release.' Grandfather would scowl at me for sullying his beloved mantra so. But I prefer it this way.

I leave and head toward Trera, waiting at the edge of the camp. As I climb up into the saddle, he snorts.

'Ready to fly, boy?' He flicks his ears, and I take it as a yes. Without another look back at the camp, I turn toward the north.

CHAPTER TWENTY-FOUR

Helene

He *escaped. He escaped. He escaped.*

I pace a groove into the stone floor of the garrison's main room, trying to block out the rasp of Faris sharpening his scims, the low murmur of Dex giving orders to a group of legionnaires, the tapping of Harper's fingers on his armor as he watches me.

There must be some way to track Elias. *Think.* He's one man. I have the might of the entire Empire behind me. *Send out more soldiers. Call in more Masks. Members of the Black Guard – you're their commander. Send them out after the Tribes Mamie visited.*

It won't be enough. Thousands of wagons poured out of the city while I put down a staged riot after *letting* Elias walk away from me. He could be on any of those wagons.

I close my eyes, wanting desperately to break something. *You're such an idiot, Helene Aquilla.* Mamie Rila played a tune, and I tossed my arms up and danced to it like a mindless marionette. She *wanted* me at the storytelling theater. She *wanted* me to know Elias was there, to see the riot, to call for reinforcements, to weaken the cordon. I was too stupid to realize it until it was too late.

Harper, at least, kept his head. He ordered two squads of soldiers assigned to quell the riot to instead surround Tribe Saif's wagons. The prisoners he took – including Mamie Rila – are the only hope we have of finding Elias.

I had him. Damn it all. I had him. And then I let him go. Because I don't want him to die. Because he's my friend and I love him.

Because I am a damned fool.

All the times I lay awake at night, telling myself that when the time came, I *needed* to be strong. I *needed* to take him. It was nothing in the face of seeing him again. Of hearing his voice and feeling his hands on my skin.

He looked so different, all muscle and sinew, like one of his Teluman scims brought to life. But the greatest change was his eyes – the shadows beneath and the sadness within, like he knew something he couldn't bear to tell me. It gnaws at me, that look in his eyes. More than my failure to catch and kill him when I had the chance. It frightens me.

We both know I'm not long for this world. What did he mean by it? Since healing him in the Second Trial, I've felt a bond with Elias – a protectiveness I've tried not to think about. It's born of the healing magic, I'm certain. When Elias touched me, that bond told me that my friend was not well.

'*Don't forget about us,*' he said to me in Serra. I close my eyes and allow myself one moment to imagine a different world. In that world, Elias is a Tribal boy, and I am a jurist's daughter. We meet in a market, and our love isn't tainted by Blackcliff or by all the things he hates about himself. I hold myself in that world, just for a second.

Then I release it. Elias and I are finished. Now, there is only death.

'Harper,' I say. Dex dismisses the legionnaires, turning his attention to me, and Faris sheathes his scims. 'How many members of Tribe Saif did we capture?'

'Twenty-six men, fifteen women, and twelve children, Blood Shrike.'

'Execute them,' Dex says. 'Immediately. We need to show what happens when you harbor an Empire fugitive.'

'You can't kill them.' Faris glares at Dex. 'They're the only family Elias ever—'

'Those people aided and abetted an enemy of the Empire,' Dex snaps. 'We have orders—'

'We don't have to execute them,' Harper says. 'They have other uses.'

I catch Harper's intent. 'We should question them. We have Mamie Rila, yes?'

'Unconscious,' Harper says. 'The aux who took her was too enthusiastic with the hilt of his sword. She should come around in a day or two.'

'She'll know who got Veturius out of here,' I say. 'And where he's heading.'

I look at the three of them. Harper has orders to remain with me, so he cannot stay in Nur to question Mamie and her family. But Dex might kill off our prisoners. And more dead Tribesmen are the last thing the Empire needs while the Scholar revolution still rages.

'Faris,' I say. 'You'll handle the interrogations. I want to know how Elias got out and where he's going.'

'What of the children?' Faris says. 'Surely we can release them. They won't know anything.'

I know what the Commandant would say to Faris. *Mercy is weakness. Offer it to your enemies and you might as well fall upon your own sword.*

The children will be a powerful incentive for the Tribespeople to tell us the truth. I know this. Yet the idea of using them – hurting them – makes me uneasy. I think of the ravaged house in Serra that Cain showed me. The Scholar rebels who burned down that house showed no mercy to the Martial children who lived there.

Are these Tribal children so different? In the end, they are still children. They didn't ask to be a part of this.

I catch Faris's eye. 'The Tribesmen are already restless, and we don't have the men to put down another riot. We'll let the children go—'

'Are you insane?' Dex shoots a glare first at Faris then at me. 'Don't let them go. Threaten to throw them into ghost wagons and sell them into slavery unless you get some bleeding answers.'

'Lieutenant Atrius.' I flatten my voice as I address Dex. 'Your presence is no longer needed here. Go and divide the remaining men into three groups. One goes with you to search east, in case Veturius makes for the Free Lands. One with me to search south. One stays here to hold the city.'

Dex's jaw twitches, his anger at being dismissed warring with a lifetime of obeying the orders of a superior officer. Faris sighs, and Harper watches the exchange with interest. Finally, Dex stalks out, slamming the door behind him.

'Tribesmen value their children above all else,' I say to Faris. 'Use them as leverage. But don't hurt them. Keep Mamie and Shan alive. If we can't run Elias down, we might be able to use them to lure him in. If you learn *anything*, send me a message through the drums.'

When I leave the barracks to saddle my horse, I find Dex leaning against the stable wall. Before he can tear into me, I turn on him.

'What in the bleeding skies were you doing in there?' I say. 'It's not enough that I have one of the Commandant's spies questioning my every move? I need you plaguing me too?'

'He reports on everything you do,' Dex says. 'But he doesn't question you. Even when he should. You're not focused. You should have seen that riot coming.'

'You didn't see it coming.' Even to my own ears, I sound like a petulant child.

'I'm not the Blood Shrike. You are.' His voice rises, and he takes a level breath.

'You miss him.' The edge in his voice fades. 'I miss him too. I miss all of them. Tristas. Demetrius. Leander. But they're gone. And Elias is on the run. All we have now, Shrike, is the Empire. And we owe it to the Empire to catch this traitor and execute him.'

'I *know* that—'

'Do you? Then why did you disappear for a quarter hour in the middle of the riot? Where were you?'

I stare at him long enough to make sure my voice doesn't shake. Long enough for him to start thinking that he might have crossed a line.

'Begin your hunt,' I say quietly. 'Don't leave a single wagon unsearched. If you find him, bring him in.'

We are interrupted by a step behind us: Harper, holding two scrolls with broken seals.

'From your father and sister.' He doesn't apologize for the fact that he's clearly read the missives.

Blood Shrike,

We are well in Antium, though autumn's chill does not agree with your mother and sisters. I work to solidify the Emperor's alliances but find myself thwarted. Gens Sisellia and Gens

Rufia have put forth their own candidates for the throne. They attempt to rally other Gens to their banners. The infighting has killed fifty in the capital, and it's just begun. Wildmen and Barbarians have intensified their border attacks, and the generals on the front are in desperate need of more men.

At least the Commandant has dampened the fire of the Scholar revolution. When she was done, I am told, the River Rei ran red with Scholar blood. She continues the cleansing in the lands north of Silas. Her victories reflect well on our Emperor, but better still upon her own Gens.

I hope to hear news of your success in tracking down the traitor Veturius soon.

Loyal to the end,

Pater Aquillus

P.S. Your mother asks that I remind you to eat.

Livvy's note is shorter.

My dear Hel,

Antium is lonely, with you so far away. Hannah feels it too – though she'd never admit it. His Majesty visits her nearly every day. He also inquires after my welfare, as I am still in isolation with a fever. Once, he even attempted to bypass the guards and visit me. We are lucky our sister is marrying a man so dedicated to our family.

The uncles and Father try desperately to keep the old alliances strong. But the Illustrians do not fear His Majesty the way they should. I wish Father would look to the Plebeians for aid. I believe His Majesty's greatest supporters may lie there.

Father calls for me to hurry, or I'd write more. Be safe, sister.

With love,

Livia Aquilla

My hands shake as I roll the parchment up. Would that I'd received these messages a few days ago. Perhaps I would have realized the cost of failure and taken Elias into custody.

Now, what Father feared has begun. The Gens turn against each other. Hannah is that much closer to marrying the Snake. *And* Marcus is trying to get to Livia – she never would have mentioned it if she didn't think it was significant.

I crush the letters. Father's message is loud and clear. *Find Elias. Give Marcus a victory.*

Help us.

'Lieutenant Harper,' I say. 'Tell the men we move out in five minutes. Dex—'

I can see from the stiff way that he turns to me that he's still angry. He has a right to be.

'You'll handle the interrogations,' I say. 'Faris will search the desert to the east instead. Let him know. Get me answers, Dex. Keep Mamie and Shan alive in case we need them as bait. Otherwise, do what you must. Even . . . even in regard to the children.'

Dex nods, and I quash the sick feeling in the pit of my stomach at speaking the words. I'm Blood Shrike. It is time to show my strength.

* * *

'Nothing?' The three squad leaders fidget under my scrutiny. One stamps his foot in the sands, antsy as a penned stallion. Behind him, other soldiers in our encampment, some miles north of Nur, watch surreptitiously. 'We've searched this blasted desert for six days, and we *still* have nothing?'

Harper, the only one of the five of us not squinting from the punishing desert wind, clears his throat. 'The desert is vast, Blood Shrike,' he says, 'We need more men.'

He's right. We must search thousands of wagons, and I have only three hundred men to do it. I sent messages to Atella's Gap, as well as to the Taib and Sadh garrisons requesting backup – but none has soldiers to spare.

Strands of hair whip around my face as I pace before the soldiers. I want to send the men out once more before nightfall to search whatever wagons they find. But they are too exhausted.

'There's a garrison a half day's ride north in Gentrium,' I say. 'If we push hard, we'll make it by nightfall. We can get reinforcements there.'

Evening nears as we approach the garrison, poking up over the top of a hill a quarter mile to the north. The outpost is one of the largest in the area and straddles the forested lands of the Empire's interior and the Tribal desert.

'Blood Shrike.' Avitas shifts a hand to his bow and slows his horse when the garrison comes into view. 'Do you smell that?'

A western wind brings a whiff of something familiar and soursweet to my nose. Death. My hand goes to my scim. An attack on the garrison? Scholar rebels? Or a Barbarian sortie, slipping through the Empire unnoticed because of the chaos elsewhere?

I order the men forward, my body coiled, blood rising, yearning toward the battle. Perhaps I should have sent a scout ahead, but if the garrison needs our aid, there's no time for reconnaissance.

We clear the hill, and I slow the men. The road leading to the garrison is littered with the dead and dying. Scholars, not Martials.

Far ahead, beside the garrison's gate, I see a row of six Scholars kneeling. Before them paces a small figure, instantly recognizable, even at a distance.

Keris Veturia.

I nudge my horse forward. What in the bleeding hells is the Commandant doing all the way out here? Has the revolution spread so far?

My men and I pick our way carefully through the bodies left in haphazard piles. Some wear the black of Resistance fighters. But most do not.

So much death, all for a revolution that was doomed before it even began. Anger flares as I stare at the bodies. Didn't the Scholar rebels understand what they would unleash when they revolted? Didn't they realize the death and terror the Empire would rain down upon them?

I swing down from my horse at the garrison gate, a few yards from where the Commandant observes her prisoners. Keris Veturia, her armor splashed with blood, ignores me. So do her men, who flank the Scholar prisoners.

As I draw myself up to reprimand them, Keris plunges her scim into the first Scholar prisoner, a woman who crumples to the ground without so much as a whimper.

I force myself not to look away.

'Blood Shrike.' The Commandant turns and salutes. Immediately, her men follow suit. Her voice is soft, but as ever, she manages to mock my title while keeping her face and expression flat. She glances at Harper and he offers a bare nod in acknowledgement. Then she addresses me. 'Shouldn't you be scouring the lands to the south for Veturius?'

'Shouldn't you be hunting Scholar rebels along the River Rei?'

'The revolution along the Rei has been crushed,' the Commandant says. 'My men and I have been purging the countryside of the Scholar threat.'

I eye the prisoners shaking in terror before her. Three are twice my father's age. Two are children.

'These civilians do not look like rebel fighters to me.'

'It is such thinking, Shrike, that encourages revolts in the first place. These *civilians* harbored Resistance rebels. When brought to the garrison for questioning, they – along with the rebels – attempted to stage an escape. No doubt they were encouraged in their insurgency by rumors of a Martial rout in Nur.'

I flush at her pointed remark, seeking a retort and finding none. *Your failure has weakened the Empire.* The words are unspoken. And they are not wrong. The Commandant curls her lip and shifts her gaze over my shoulder, to my men.

'A ragged bunch,' she observes. 'Tired men make for failed missions, Blood Shrike. Did you not learn that lesson at Blackcliff?'

'I had to divide my forces to cover more ground.' Though I try to keep my voice as unfeeling as hers, I know I sound like a sullen Cadet defending an unsound battle strategy to a Centurion.

'So many men to hunt a traitor,' she says. 'Yet you've had no luck. One would think you do not truly wish to find Veturius.'

'One would be wrong,' I grind out from a clenched jaw.

'One would hope,' she says with a soft derision that brings an enraged flush to my cheeks. She turns back to her prisoners. One of the children is next, a dark-haired boy with freckles across his nose. The sharp tang of urine permeates the air, and the Commandant looks down at the boy and cocks her head.

'Afraid, little one?' Her voice is almost gentle. I want to retch at the lie in it. The boy trembles, staring at the blood-soaked dirt before him.

'Stop.' I step forward. *Bleeding skies, what are you doing, Helene?* The Commandant looks at me with a mild sort of curiosity.

'As Blood Shrike,' I say, 'I order—'

The Commandant's first scim whistles through the air, divesting the child of his head. At the same time, she draws her second scim, plunging it through the heart of the second child. Knives appear in her hands, and she flings them – *zing-zing-zing* – one by one into the throats of the last three prisoners.

In the space of two breaths, she has executed them all.

'Yes, Blood Shrike?' She turns back to me. On the surface, she is patient, attentive. No hint of the madness that I know roils deep within. I survey her men – well over a hundred of them watching the altercation with cold-eyed interest. If I challenge her now, there is no telling what she will do. Attack, possibly. Or try to butcher my men. She certainly won't submit to censure.

'Bury the bodies.' I suppress my emotions and flatten my voice. 'I don't want the garrison's water supply contaminated by corpses.'

The Commandant nods, her face still. The consummate Mask. 'Of course, Shrike.'

I order my men into the garrison and retire to the empty Black Guard barracks, dropping into one of the dozen hard bunks along the walls. I am filthy from a week on the road. I should bathe, eat, rest.

Instead, I find myself staring at the ceiling for a solid two hours. I keep thinking of the Commandant. Her insult to me was clear – and my inability to respond displayed my weakness. But though I'm upset by that, I'm more disturbed at what she did to the prisoners. At what she did to the children.

Is this what the Empire has become? *Or is this what it always was?* a quiet voice within asks.

'I brought you food.'

I jerk upright, hit my head on the bunk above me, and curse. Harper drops his pack on the floor and nods to a steaming plate of golden rice and spiced minced meat on a table by the door. It looks delicious, but I know that right now, anything I eat will taste of ashes.

'The Commandant left about an hour ago,' Harper says. 'She's headed north.'

Harper removes his armor, laying it neatly beside the door before digging around in the closet for fresh fatigues. He turns his back to me and changes. When he strips off his shirt, he steps into the shadows so I cannot see. I crack a smile at his modesty.

'The food won't jump down your throat on its own, Shrike.'

I look suspiciously at the plate, and Harper sighs, pads to the table in bare feet, and tastes the food before handing me the plate. 'Eat,' he says. 'Your mother asked you to. How would it look if the Empire's Blood Shrike fainted dead away from starvation in the middle of a fight?'

Reluctantly, I take the plate and force myself to chew a few morsels of it.

'The old Blood Shrike had tasters.' Harper sits on a bunk across from me and rolls his shoulders back. 'Usually an aux soldier from some nameless Plebeian family.'

'People tried to assassinate the Shrike?'

Harper looks at me like I'm an especially dim Yearling. 'Of course. He had the Emperor's ear and was first cousin to Kauf's Warden. There are probably only a handful of secrets in the Empire that he didn't know.'

I press my lips together to quell my shudder. I remember the Warden from my time as a Fiver. I remember how he got his secrets: through twisted experiments and mind games.

Harper's eyes cut to me and glitter like the pale jade of the Southern Lands. 'Will you tell me something?'

I swallow the bite I've only half chewed. That placidness in his tone – I've learned what it means. He's about to strike.

'Why did you let him go?'

Bleeding skies. 'Let who go?'

'I know when you're trying to mislead me, Shrike,' Harper says. 'Five days in an interrogation room with you, remember?' He leans forward on his bunk, tilting his head mildly, like a curious bird. I am not fooled; his eyes burn with intensity. 'You had Veturius in Nur. You let him go. Because you love him? Is he not a Mask, like any other?'

'How dare you!' I slam the plate down and stand. Harper grabs my arm, not releasing when I try to throw him off.

'Please,' he says. 'I mean no harm. I swear it. I too have loved, Shrike.' Old pain flickers and fades in his eyes. I see no lie there. Only curiosity.

I shove away his arm and, still assessing him, sit back down. I look out the open window of the barracks to the wide stretch of scrubby hills beyond. The moon barely lights the room, and the darkness is a comfort.

'Veturius is a Mask like the rest of us, yes,' I say. 'Bold, brave, strong, swift. But those were afterthoughts for him.' The Blood Shrike's ring of office feels heavy on my finger, and I spin it around. I have never spoken of Elias to anyone. Whom would I speak to? My comrades at Blackcliff would have mocked me. My sisters would not have understood.

I *want* to speak of him, I realize. I crave it.

'Elias sees people as they should be,' I say. 'Not as they are. He laughs at himself. He gives of himself – in everything he does.

'Like with the First Trial.' I shiver at the memory. 'The Augurs played with our minds. But Elias didn't falter. He looked death straight in the face and never considered leaving me behind. He didn't give up on me. He's the things that I can't be. He's good. He never would have let the Commandant kill those prisoners. Especially not the children.'

'The Commandant serves the Empire.'

I shake my head. 'What she did doesn't serve the Empire,' I say. 'Not the Empire I fight for, anyway.'

Harper watches me with an unsettling, fixed gaze. I wonder briefly if I've said too much. But then I realize that I don't care what he thinks. He is no friend of mine, and if he reports what I said to Marcus or the Commandant, it will change nothing.

'Blood Shrike!' The shout makes both Harper and me jump, and a moment later, the door bursts open to reveal an aux courier panting and coated in dirt from the road. 'The Emperor orders you to ride for Antium. Now.'

Bleeding skies. I'll never catch Elias if I detour to Antium. 'I'm in the middle of a mission, soldier,' I say. 'And I'm not inclined to leave it half-finished. What's so damned important?'

'War, Blood Shrike. The Illustrian Gens have declared war on each other.'

PART TWO

NORTH

CHAPTER TWENTY-FIVE

Elias

For two weeks, the hours pass in a blur of nighttime riding, thieving, and skulking. Martial soldiers swarm over the countryside like locusts, tearing through every village and farmstead, every bridge and shack, in their search for me.

But I am alone, and I am a Mask. I ride hard, and Trera, desert born and bred, eats up the miles.

After a fortnight, we reach the eastern branch of the River Taius, glimmering like the groove of a silver scim beneath the full moon. The night is quiet and bright, without a breath of wind, and I lead Trera up the riverbank until I find a place to cross.

He slows as he splashes through the shallows, and when his hooves hit the northern bank, he tosses his head wildly, his eyes rolling back.

'Whoa – whoa, boy.' I drop into the water and pull his bridle forward to get him up the bank. He whinnies and jerks his head. 'Did you get bitten? Let's see.'

I pull a blanket from one of the saddlebags and rub his legs gently, waiting for him to flinch when the blanket hits the bite. But he just lets me rub him down before turning south.

'This way.' I try to urge him north, but he's having none of it. Strange. Up until now, he and I have gotten along fine. He's far more intelligent than any of Grandfather's horses, and he has more stamina too. 'Don't worry, boy. Nothing to fear.'

'Are you certain of that, Elias Veturius?'

'Ten bleeding hells!' I don't believe it's the Soul Catcher until I see her sitting on a rock a few yards away.

'I'm not dead,' I say quickly, like a child denying a wrongdoing.

'Obviously.' The Soul Catcher stands and shakes back her dark hair, her black eyes fixed on me. Part of me wants to poke her to see how real she is. 'You are, however, in my territory now.' The Soul Catcher nods east, to a thick, dark line on the horizon. The Forest of Dusk.

'That's the Waiting Place?' I never linked the oppressive trees of the Soul Catcher's lair to anything in my world.

'Didn't you ever wonder where it was?'

'I mostly spent my time figuring out how to get out of it.' I try again to pull Trera from the river. He doesn't budge. 'What do you want, Soul Catcher?'

She pats Trera between his ears, and he relaxes. She takes his reins from me and leads him north as easily as if *she's* the one who's been with him for the past two weeks. I give the beast a dark look. *Traitor.*

'Who says I want anything, Elias?' the Soul Catcher says. 'I'm simply welcoming you to my lands.'

'Right.' What a load of dung. 'You won't need to worry about me lingering. I have someplace to be.'

'Ah.' I hear the smile in her voice. 'That might be a problem.

You see, when you stray so close to my realm, you disturb the spirits, Elias. For that you must pay a price.'

Welcoming me indeed. 'What price?'

'I'll show you. If you work quickly enough, I'll help you pass through these lands faster than you would have on horseback.'

I mount Trera reluctantly and offer her a hand, though the idea of her otherworldly body so close to mine makes my blood turn to ice. But she ignores me and breaks into a run, her feet fleet as she matches Trera's canter with ease. A wind blows in from the west, and she catches it like a kite, her body floating upon it as if she is made of fluff. Too soon for it to be natural, the trees of the Forest of Dusk rise like a wall before us.

Fiver missions never brought me this close to the Forest. Centurions warned us to keep a good distance from its borders. Since anyone who didn't listen tended to disappear, it was one of the few rules no Fiver was stupid enough to break.

'Leave the horse,' the Soul Catcher says. 'I'll make sure he's cared for.'

The moment I step into the Forest, the whispers begin. And now that my senses are not dulled by unconsciousness, I can make out the words more clearly. The red of the leaves is more vivid, the sweet scent of sap sharper.

'Elias.' The Soul Catcher's voice dulls the soughing of the ghosts, and she nods to a space in the trees where a spirit paces. Tristas.

'Why is he still here?'

'He won't listen to me,' the Soul Catcher says. 'Perhaps he will listen to you.'

'I'm the reason he's dead.'

'Exactly. Hatred anchors him here. I don't mind ghosts who wish to stay, Elias – but not when they upset the other spirits. You need to talk to him. You need to help him move on.'

'And if I can't?'

The Soul Catcher shrugs. 'You'll stay here until you can.'

'I need to get to Kauf.'

The Soul Catcher turns her back on me. 'Then you better get started.'

* * *

Tristas refuses to speak with me. He first tries to attack me, but unlike when I was unconscious, his fists fly through my corporeal body. When he realizes he cannot hurt me, he rushes away, cursing. I try to follow, calling his name. By evening, my voice is hoarse.

The Soul Catcher appears beside me when the Forest falls full dark. I wonder if she's been watching my ineptitude. 'Come,' she says tersely. 'If you do not eat, you will only weaken and fail again.'

We walk along a stream to a cabin filled with pale wooden furniture and handwoven rugs. Multifaceted Tribal lamps of a dozen colors light the space. A bowl of stew steams on the table. 'Cozy,' I say. 'You live here?'

The Soul Catcher turns to leave, but I step in front of her, and she collides with me. I expect cold to jolt through me, like when I touched the wraiths. But she's warm. Almost feverish.

The Soul Catcher jerks away, and I raise my eyebrows. 'You're a living thing?'

'I'm not human.'

'I gathered that,' I say dryly. 'But you're not a wraith, either. And you have needs, obviously.' I look at the house, the bed in the corner, the pot of stew bubbling over the fire. 'Food. Shelter.'

She glares and darts around me with unnatural swiftness. I'm reminded of the creature in Serra's catacombs. 'Are you an efrit?'

When she reaches for the door, I sigh in exasperation. 'What

216

harm is there in talking to me?' I say. 'You must be lonely out here, with only spirits to keep you company.'

I expect her to turn on me or run away. But her hand freezes on the door handle. I move aside and gesture to the table.

'Sit. Please.'

She eases back into the room, black eyes wary. I see a flash of curiosity deep within that opaque gaze. I wonder when she last spoke with someone who wasn't already dead.

'I am not an efrit,' she says after settling herself across from me. 'They are weaker creatures, born of the lower elements. Sand or shadow. Clay, wind, or water.'

'Then what are you?' I say. 'Or' – I take in her deceptively human form, save for those ageless eyes – 'what *were* you?'

'I was a girl, once.' The Soul Catcher looks down at the speckled pattern cast upon her hands by one of the Tribal lamps. She sounds almost thoughtful. 'A foolish girl who did one foolish thing. But that led to another foolish thing. Foolish became disastrous, disastrous became murderous, and murderous became damned.' She sighs. 'Now here I am, chained to this place, paying for my crimes by escorting ghosts from one realm to the next.'

'Quite a punishment.'

'It was quite a crime. But you know about crime. And repentance.' She stands, severe once more. 'Sleep where you wish. I will not disturb you. But remember, if you want your own chance at repentance, you must find a way to help Tristas.'

Days blur together – time feels different here. I sense Tristas but don't see him. As the days pass, I plunge deeper into the woods in my increasingly agitated attempts to find him. Finally, I discover a part of the Forest that looks as if it hasn't seen sunlight in years. A river rushes nearby, and I spot an angry red glow ahead. *Fire?*

The glow intensifies, and I consider calling out to the Soul

Catcher. But I smell no smoke, and when I get close, I realize it's not a fire I saw but a grove of trees – enormous, interconnected, and *wrong*. Their gnarled trunks glow as if consumed from within by the flames of the hells.

Help us, Shaeva. Voices within the trees cry out, the sound grating and harsh. *Don't leave us alone.*

A figure kneels at the base of the largest tree, hand stretched flat against the burning trunk. The Soul Catcher.

The fire from the trees trickles into her hands and spreads to her neck, her stomach. In the space of a breath, her body is ablaze, smokeless flames of red and black consuming her. I cry out, rushing toward her, but as suddenly as she is consumed, the flames die and she is whole again. The trees still glow, but their fire is muted. Tamed.

The Soul Catcher crumples, and I pick her up. She's as light as a child.

'You should not have seen that,' she whispers as I carry her from the grove. 'I did not know you would travel so deep into the Forest.'

'Was that the gateway to the hells? Is that where the evil spirits go?'

The Soul Catcher shakes her head. 'Good or evil, Elias, spirits simply move on. But it *is* a hell of sorts. At least for those trapped within it.'

She collapses on a chair inside her cabin, her face gray. I tuck a blanket around her shoulders, relieved when she doesn't protest.

'You told me efrits are made of the lesser elements.' I sit across from her. 'Are there higher elements?'

'Just one,' the Soul Catcher whispers. Her hostility is so diminished that she seems like a different creature. 'Fire.'

'You're a jinn.' It dawns on me suddenly, though I can hardly make sense of it. 'Aren't you? I thought some Scholar king tricked the other fey creatures into betraying and destroying your kind long ago.'

'The jinn weren't destroyed,' the Soul Catcher says. 'Only trapped. And it wasn't the fey who betrayed us. It was a young, prideful jinn girl.'

'You?'

She pushes the blanket away. 'I was wrong to bring you here,' she says. 'Wrong to take advantage of your seizures to speak with you. Forgive me.'

'Take me to Kauf then.' I seize upon her apology. I need to get out of here. 'Please. I should be there by now.'

The Soul Catcher regards me coldly. Damn it, she's going to keep me here. Skies know for how long. But then, to my relief, she nods once. 'In the morning then.' She hobbles to the door, waving me off when I try to help.

'Wait,' I say. 'Soul Catcher. Shaeva.'

Her body stiffens at the sound of her name.

'Why *did* you bring me here? Don't tell me it was just for Tristas, because that doesn't make any sense. It's your job to comfort souls, not mine.'

'I needed you to help your friend.' I can hear the lie in her voice. 'That is all.'

With that, she disappears out the door, and I curse, no closer to understanding her than the first time I met her. But Kauf – and Darin – await. All I can do is take my freedom and go.

As promised, Shaeva delivers me to Kauf in the morning – despite the impossibility of such a thing. We depart from her cabin at a stroll, and minutes later, the trees above are bare. A quarter hour after that, we are deep in the shadows of the Nevennes Range, crunching through a fresh layer of snow.

'This is my realm, Elias,' Shaeva says to my unspoken question. She is far less wary now, as if my use of her name has unlocked a long-buried civility. 'I can travel where and how I wish when I am within its boundaries.' She nods to a break in the trees ahead. 'Kauf is through there. If you wish to succeed, Elias, you must be swift. *Rathana* is a mere two weeks away.'

We walk to a high ridge that overlooks the long black ribbon of the River Dusk. But I hardly notice. The moment I am free of the trees I want nothing more than to turn back and lose myself among them.

The smell hits me first; it's what I imagine the hells must smell like. Then the despair, borne upon the wind in the hair-raising cries of men and women who know nothing but torment and suffering. The cries are so unlike the peaceful whispers of the dead that I wonder how they can exist in the same world.

I lift my eyes to the monstrosity of cold iron and carved stygian rock that erupts from the mountain at the north end of the valley. Kauf Prison.

'Do not go, Elias,' Shaeva whispers. 'Should you find yourself trapped behind those walls, your fate will be dark indeed.'

'My fate is dark anyway.' I reach back and loosen my scims in their sheathes, taking comfort from their weight. 'At least this way, it won't be for nothing.'

CHAPTER TWENTY-SIX

Helene

In the three weeks it takes Harper and me to reach Antium, deep fall arrives in the capital, a red-gold blanket edged with white frost. The smell of pumpkin and cinnamon fills the air, and thick wood smoke curls up into the sky.

But beneath the glowing foliage and behind heavy oaken doors, an Illustrian rebellion brews.

'Blood Shrike.' Harper emerges from the Martial garrison perched just outside the city. 'The Black Guard escort is on its way from the barracks,' he says. 'The garrison sergeant says the streets are dangerous – particularly for you.'

'All the more reason to get in quickly.' I squeeze my hand over dozens of messages in my pocket – all from Father, each more urgent than the next. 'We can't afford to wait.'

'We also can't afford to lose the Empire's highest internal enforcer on the eve of a possible civil war,' Harper says with typical frankness. 'Empire first, Blood Shrike.'

'You mean Commandant first.'

A hairline crack fractures Avitas's unruffled façade. But he leashes whatever emotion lurks within.

'*Empire* first, Blood Shrike. Always. We wait.'

I don't argue. Weeks on the road with him, riding for Antium as if wraiths were on our backs, have given me a new respect for Harper's skills as a Mask. At Blackcliff, he and I never crossed paths. He was four years ahead of me – a Fiver when I was a Yearling, a Cadet when I was a Fiver, a Skull when I was a Cadet. In all that time, he must never have distinguished himself, for I never heard anything about him.

But I see now why the Commandant made him an ally. Like her, he has iron-fisted control over his emotions.

A rumble of hooves beyond the garrison has me leaping upon my saddle in an instant. Moments after I do, a company of soldiers appears, the screaming shrikes on their breastplates marking them as my men.

Upon seeing me, most salute smartly. Others appear more reluctant.

I straighten my back and glower. These are my men, and their obedience should be immediate.

'Lieutenant Harper.' One man – a captain and the commanding officer of this company – kicks his horse forward. 'Blood Shrike.'

The fact that he addressed Harper before me is offensive enough. The disgusted look on his face as he gives me the once-over has my fist aching to connect with his jaw.

'Your name, soldier,' I say.

'Captain Gallus Sergius.'

Captain Gallus Sergius, sir, I want to say.

I know him. He has a son at Blackcliff two years younger than me. The boy was a good fighter. Big mouth, though. 'Captain,' I say, 'why are you looking at me like I just seduced your wife?'

222

The captain draws back his chin and stares down his nose. 'How dare—'

I backhand him. Blood flies from his mouth, and his eyes spark, but he holds his tongue. The men of his company shift, a mutinous whisper rippling through them.

'The next time you speak out of turn,' I say, 'I'll have you whipped. Fall in. We're late.'

As the rest of the Black Guard falls into formation, creating a shield against attack, Harper pulls his horse up beside mine. I examine the faces around me surreptitiously. They are Masks – and Black Guards to boot. The best of the best. Their expressions are flat and unfeeling. But I can sense the anger simmering beneath the surface. I have not won their respect.

I keep one hand on the scim at my waist as we approach the Emperor's palace, a monstrosity built of white limestone that abuts the northern border of the city, the foothills of the Nevennes Range at its back. Arrow slats and guard towers line the crenellated battlements. The red-and-gold flags of Gens Taia have been replaced with Marcus's banner: a sledgehammer on a black field.

Many Martials traversing the streets have stopped to watch us pass. They peer out from thick, furry hats and knitted mufflers, fear and curiosity mingling on their faces as they eye me, the new Blood Shrike.

'*Little sssinger . . .*'

I start, and my horse tosses his head in irritation. Avitas, riding beside me, cuts me a look, but I ignore him and search the crowd. A flash of white catches my eyes. Amid a gaggle of urchins and vagrants gathered around a bin fire, I spot the curve of a hideously scarred jaw with a wing of snowy hair swinging down to hide it. Dark eyes meet mine. Then she's gone, lost in the streets.

Why in the bleeding skies is Cook in Antium?

I've never seen the Scholars as enemies, exactly. An enemy is someone you fear. Someone who might destroy you. But the Scholars will never destroy the Martials. They can't read. They can't fight. They have no steelcraft. They are a slave class – a lesser class.

But Cook is different. She is something more.

I am forced to push the old bat from my mind when we arrive at the palace gate and I see who awaits us. The Commandant. Somehow she beat me here. By her calm demeanor and neat appearance, I'd guess it was by at least a day.

All the men of the Black Guard salute upon seeing her, instantly giving her more respect than they afforded me.

'Blood Shrike.' The words saunter off her tongue. 'The road has taken its toll on you. I'd offer you a chance to rest, but the Emperor insisted I bring you in immediately.'

'I don't need to rest, Keris,' I say. 'I thought you'd still be chasing Scholars all over the countryside.'

'The Emperor requested my counsel,' the Commandant says. 'I could not, of course, refuse. But be assured that I am not idle whilst here. The prisons of Antium are being cleansed of the Scholar disease as we speak, and my men carry out the purges farther south. Come, Shrike. The Emperor awaits.' She glances at my men. 'Your escort is unnecessary.'

Her insult is obvious: *Why do you need an escort, Blood Shrike? Are you scared?* I open my mouth to retort, but then hold my tongue. She probably *wants* me to engage so that she can embarrass me further.

I expect Keris to lead me to the courtier-packed throne room. In fact, I'd hoped to see my father there. But instead, Emperor Marcus waits for us in a long drawing room filled with plush seats and low-hanging lamps. I see why he's chosen the space the second I enter. No windows.

'About bleeding time.' His mouth twists in disgust when I enter. 'Ten hells, couldn't you have taken a bath before showing up?'

Not if it makes you want to get an inch closer to me. 'Civil war matters more than my hygiene, your Imperial Majesty. How may I be of service?'

'You mean beyond catching the Empire's top fugitive?' Marcus's sarcasm is undercut by the hatred in his piss-yellow eyes.

'I was close to catching him,' I say. 'But you called me back. I suggest you tell me what you need so that I can return to the hunt.'

I see his blow coming but still lose my breath when it lands on my jaw. A hot rush of blood fills my mouth. I make myself swallow it.

'Don't cross me.' Marcus's spit lands on my face. 'You are *my* Blood Shrike. The sword that executes *my* will.' He takes a sheet of parchment and slams it down on a table beside us.

'Ten Gens,' he says. 'All Illustrian. Four have banded together with Gens Rufia. They propose an Illustrian candidate to replace me as Emperor. The other five offer their own Paters for the throne. All have sent assassins after me. I want a public execution and their heads on pikes in front of the palace by tomorrow morning. Understood?'

'Do you have proof—'

'He doesn't need proof.' The Commandant, lurking silently near the door beside Harper, cuts me off. 'These Gens have attacked the imperial house, as well as Gens Veturia. They openly call for the Emperor to be ousted. They are traitors.'

'Are you an oath-breaker, too?' Marcus says to me. 'Shall I toss you off Cardium Rock and shame your name for five generations, Shrike? I hear the Rock thirsts for the blood of traitors. For the more it drinks, the stronger the Empire grows.'

Cardium Rock is a cliff near the palace with a pit of bones at its base. It's used to execute only one kind of criminal: traitors to the throne.

I make myself examine the list of names. Some of these Gens are as powerful as Gens Aquilla. A few even more so. 'Your Majesty, perhaps we can try to negotiate—'

Marcus closes the space between us. And though my mouth still bleeds from his last attack, I hold my ground. I will not let him cow me. I force myself to look up into his eyes, only to suppress a shudder at what I see within: a controlled sort of madness, a rage that needs only the smallest spark to ignite into a conflagration.

'Your father tried to negotiate.' Marcus crowds me until my back is against a wall. The Commandant watches, bored. Harper looks away. 'His unending blathering only gave the traitorous Gens time to find more allies, to attempt more assassinations. Do not speak to me of negotiation. I didn't survive the hell of Blackcliff to negotiate. I didn't go through those bleeding Trials so I could negotiate. I didn't kill—'

He stops. A powerful and unexpected grief suffuses his body, as if another person deep within is attempting to get out. A tendril of fear unfurls in my belly. This is, perhaps, more terrifying than anything I've seen from Marcus yet. Because it makes him human.

'I will hold the throne, Blood Shrike,' he says quietly. 'I've given up too much not to. Keep your vow to me, and I will bring order to this Empire. Betray me, and watch it burn.'

The Empire must come first – above your desires, your friendships, your wants. My father spoke so adamantly when I last saw him. I know what he'd say now. *We are Aquilla, daughter. Loyal to the end.*

I must do Marcus's bidding. I must stop this civil war. Or the Empire will crumble under the weight of Illustrian greed.

I bow my head to Marcus. 'Consider it done, your Majesty.'

CHAPTER TWENTY-SEVEN

Laia

Laia,

The Soul Catcher tells me I do not have enough time to get Darin out of Kauf if I remain with Afya's caravan. I'll move twice as fast if I go ahead on my own, and by the time you reach Kauf, I'll have found a way to break Darin out. We – or he, at least – will await you in the cave I told Afya about.

In case it doesn't go as planned, use the map of Kauf that I drew and make a plan of your own in the time you have. If I fail, you must succeed – for your brother and for your people.

Whatever happens, remember what you told me: There is hope in life.

I hope I see you again.

– EV

Seven sentences.

Seven *bleeding* sentences after weeks of traveling together, of saving each other, of fighting and surviving. Seven sentences and then he disappears like smoke in a north wind.

Even now, four weeks after he's gone, my anger flares and fury reddens my gaze. Forget that Elias did not say goodbye — he did not even give me a chance to object to his decision.

Instead he left a note. A pathetically short note.

I find that my jaw is tight, my hands in a white-knuckled grip on the bow I hold. Keenan sighs beside me, his arms crossed as he leans against a tree in the clearing we've taken over. He knows me by now. He knows what I'm thinking about that's making me so angry.

'Focus, Laia.'

I try to push Elias from my mind and do as Keenan asks. I sight my target – an old bucket hanging from a scarlet-leafed maple – and let my arrow fly.

It misses.

Beyond the clearing, the Tribal wagons creak as the wind howls around them, an eerie sound that frosts my blood. *Deep autumn already. And winter soon.* Winter means snow. Snow means blocked mountain passes. And blocked passes mean not reaching Kauf, Darin, or Elias until spring.

'Stop worrying.' Keenan pulls my right arm taut as I draw the bowstring again. Warmth emanates from him, beating back the icy air. His touch on my bow arm sends a tingle all the way up my neck, and I'm certain he must notice it. He clears his throat, his strong hand holding mine steady. 'Keep your shoulders back.'

'We shouldn't have stopped so early.' My muscles burn, but at least I haven't dropped the bow after ten minutes, like I did the first few times. We stand just outside the circle of wagons, making best use of the last scraps of daylight before the sun sinks into the forests to our west.

'It's not even dark yet,' I add. 'We could have crossed the river.'

I look west, beyond the forest, to a square tower – a Martial garrison. 'I'd like to put the river between us and them, anyway.' I put down the bow. 'I'm going to talk to Afya—'

'I wouldn't.' Izzi sticks her tongue out of the corner her mouth as she draws back her own bowstring a few yards away from me. 'She's in a mood.' Izzi's target is an old boot atop a low-hanging branch. She's graduated to using actual arrows. I'm still using blunted sticks so as not to accidentally murder anyone unfortunate enough to get in my way.

'She doesn't like being so deep in the Empire. Or being within sight of the Forest.' Gibran, lounging on a tree stump near Izzi, nods at the northeastern horizon, where low green hills stretch, thick with old-growth trees. The Forest of Dusk is the sentinel on Marinn's western border – one so effective that in five hundred years of Martial expansion, even the Empire hasn't been able to penetrate it.

'You'll see,' Gibran goes on. 'When we cross the east branch north of here, she'll be even grumpier than normal. Very superstitious, my sister.'

'Are you afraid of the Forest, Gibran?' Izzi surveys the distant trees curiously. 'Have you ever gotten close?'

'Once,' Gibran says, and his ever-present humor fades. 'All I remember is wanting to leave.'

'Gibran! Izzi!' Afya calls from across the camp. 'Firewood!'

Gibran groans and flops his head back. As he and Izzi are the youngest in the caravan, Afya assigns them – and usually me – the most menial tasks: gathering firewood, doing the dishes, scrubbing the laundry.

'She might as well put bleeding slaves' cuffs on us,' Gibran grumbles. Then a sly look crosses his face.

'Hit that shot' – Gibran flashes his lightning smile at Izzi, and a blush rises in her cheeks – 'and I'll gather firewood for a week. Miss, and it's on you.'

Izzi draws the bow, sights, and knocks the boot off the branch easily. Gibran curses.

'Don't be such a baby,' Izzi says. 'I'll still keep you company while you do all the work.' Izzi slings her bow on her back and gives Gibran a hand up. For all his blustering, he holds on to her a little longer than he needs to, his eyes lingering on her as she walks ahead of him. I hide a smile, thinking of what Izzi said to me a few nights ago as we fell into sleep. *It's nice to be admired, Laia, by someone who means well. It's nice to be thought beautiful.*

They pass Afya, who chivvies them along. I clench my jaw and look away from the Tribeswoman. A feeling of impotence seizes me. I *want* to tell her we should keep going, but I know she won't listen. I *want* to tell her she was wrong for letting Elias leave – for not even bothering to wake me until he was well away, but she won't care. And I want to rage at her for refusing to allow me or Keenan to take a horse and track Elias down, but she'll just roll her eyes and tell me again what she told me when I learned Elias left: *My duty is to get you safely to Kauf. And you haring off after him interferes.*

I must admit that she has carried out her duty with remarkable cleverness. Here in the heart of the Empire, the countryside is crawling with Martial soldiers. Afya's caravan has been searched a dozen times. Only her savvy as a smuggler has kept us alive.

I put the bow down, my focus shattered.

'Help me get dinner going?' Keenan gives me a rueful smile. He knows well the look on my face. He's patiently suffered my frustration since Elias left, and he's realized the only cure is distraction. 'It's my turn to cook,' he says. I fall into step beside him, preoccupied enough that I do not notice Izzi running toward us until she calls out.

'Come quickly,' she says. 'Scholars – a family – on the run from the Empire.'

Keenan and I follow Izzi back to camp to find Afya speaking rapidly in Sadhese with Riz and Vana. A small group of anxious Scholars looks on, their clothing torn, faces streaked with dirt and tears. Two dark-eyed women who appear to be sisters stand together. One of them has her arm around a girl of perhaps six. The man with them carries a little boy no more than two.

Afya turns away from Riz and Vana, both of whom have similar, glowering expressions. Zehr keeps his distance, but he doesn't look happy either.

'We can't help you,' Afya says to the Scholars. 'I will not bring down the Martials' wrath upon my Tribe.'

'They're killing everyone,' one of the women says. 'No survivors, miss. They're even killing Scholar prisoners, massacring them in their cells—'

It is as if the earth at my feet has dropped away. 'What?' I push past Keenan and Afya. 'What did you say about Scholar prisoners?'

'The Martials are butchering them.' The woman turns to me. 'Every single prisoner. From Serra to Silas to our city, Estium, fifty miles west of here. Antium is next, we hear, and after that, Kauf. That woman – the Mask, the one they call the Commandant – she's killing them all.'

CHAPTER TWENTY-EIGHT

Helene

'What are you going to do about Captain Sergius?' Harper asks as we make for Antium's Black Guard barracks. 'Some of the Gens on Marcus's list are allied with Gens Sergia. He has heavy support within the Black Guard.'

'It's nothing a few whippings won't fix.'

'You can't whip them all. What will you do if there is open dissent?'

'They can bend to my will, Harper, or I can break them. It's not complicated.'

'Don't be stupid, Shrike.' The anger in his voice surprises me, and when I glance at him, his green eyes flash. 'There are two hundred of them and two of us. If they turn on us en masse, we're dead. Why else wouldn't Marcus just order them to take out his enemies himself? He knows he might not be able to control the Black Guard. He can't risk them directly defying him. But he *can* risk them defying you. The Commandant must have put him up to it. If *you* fail, then you're dead. Which is exactly what she wants.'

'And what you want too.'

'Why would I tell you any of this if I wanted you dead?'

'Bleeding skies, I don't know, Harper. Why do you do anything? You don't make sense. You never have.' I frown in irritation. 'I don't have time for this. I need to figure out how I'm going to get to the Paters of ten of the best-guarded Gens in the Empire.'

Harper is about to retort, but we've reached the barracks, a great, square building built around a training field. Most of the men within play dice or cards, cups of ale beside them. I clench my teeth in disgust. The old Blood Shrike is gone for a few weeks and discipline has already gone to the hells.

As I pass through the field, some of the men eye me curiously. Others give me blatant once-overs that make me want to rip their eyes out. Most just seem angry.

'We take out Sergius,' I say quietly. 'And his closest allies.'

'Force won't work,' Harper murmurs. 'You need to outwit them. You need secrets.'

'Secrets are a snake's way of doing business.'

'And snakes survive,' Harper says. 'The old Blood Shrike traded in secrets – it's why he was so valuable to Gens Taia.'

'I don't know any secrets, Harper.' But even as I say it, I realize it's not true. Sergius, for instance. His son talked about many things that he probably shouldn't have. Rumors at Blackcliff spread quickly. If anything that Sergius the younger said was true . . .

'I can deal with his allies,' Harper says. 'I'll get help from the other Plebeians in the Guard. But we need to move swiftly.'

'Get it done,' I say. 'I'll speak with Sergius.'

I find the captain with his feet up in the barracks mess hall, his cronies gathered around him.

'Sergius.' I don't comment on the fact that he doesn't stand. 'I must solicit your opinion on something. Privately.' I turn my back and make for the Blood Shrike's quarters, seething when he doesn't follow immediately.

'Captain,' I begin when he finally walks into my quarters, but he interrupts.

'Miss Aquilla,' he says, and I practically choke on my own saliva. I haven't been addressed as Miss Aquilla since I was about six.

'Before you ask for advice or favors,' he goes on, 'let me explain something. You'll never control the Black Guard. At best, you'll be a pretty figurehead. So whatever orders that Plebeian dog of an Emperor gave you—'

'How's your wife?' I hadn't planned to be so direct, but if he's going to be a dog, then I'll have to crawl down to his level until I get him on a leash.

'My wife knows her place,' Sergius says warily.

'Unlike you,' I say, 'sleeping with her sister. And her cousin. How many bastards do you have running around now? Six? Seven?'

'If you're trying to blackmail me' – the sneer on Sergius's face is practiced – 'it won't work. My wife knows of my women *and* my bastards. She smiles and does her duty. You should do the same: Put on a dress, marry for the good of your Gens, and produce heirs. In fact, I have a son—'

Yes, you cretin. I know your son. Cadet Sergius hates his father. *I wish someone would just tell her,* the boy once said of his mother. *She could tell Grandfather. He'd kick my ass of a father out into the cold.*

'Maybe your wife does know.' I smile at Sergius. 'Or *maybe* you've kept your dalliances a secret and learning of them would devastate her. Maybe she would tell her father, who, in rage at the insult, would offer her shelter and withdraw the money that funds your crumbling Illustrian estate. You can't very well be Pater of Gens Sergia with no money, can you, Lieutenant Sergius?'

'That's *Captain* Sergius!'

'You've just been demoted.'

Sergius first turns white, then an unusual shade of purple. When the shock drains from his face, it's replaced by a helpless rage that I find quite satisfying.

He straightens his back, salutes, and, in a tone suitable to addressing a superior officer, speaks. 'Blood Shrike,' he says. 'How may I serve you?'

Once Sergius is barking my orders to his toadies, the rest of the Black Guard fall into line, albeit reluctantly. An hour after walking into the commander's quarters, I am in the Black Guard war room, planning the attack.

'Five teams with thirty men each.' I point to five Gens on the list. 'I want Paters, Maters, and children older than thirteen in chains and waiting at Cardium Rock by dawn. Younger children are to remain under armed guard. Get in and out quietly, and keep it clean.'

'What about the other five Gens?' Lieutenant Sergius says. 'Gens Rufia and its allies?'

I know Pater Rufius. He's a typical Illustrian with typical prejudices. And he was once a friend to my father. According to Father's missives, Pater Rufius has attempted to pull Gens Aquilla into his traitorous coalition a dozen times already.

'Leave them to me.'

* * *

The dress I wear is white, gold, and supremely uncomfortable – probably because I haven't worn one since I was a four-year-old forced to participate in a wedding. I should have put one on sooner – the expression on Hannah's face alone, like she's swallowed a live snake – would have been worth it.

'You look beautiful,' Livvy whispers as we file into the dining room. 'Those idiots will never see it coming. But only' – she gives me a warning look, her blue eyes wide – 'if you rein yourself in. Pater Rufius is smart, even if he is foul. He'll be suspicious.'

'Pinch me if you see me doing anything stupid.' I finally notice the room, and my jaw drops. My mother has outdone herself, laying the table with snow-white china and long, clear vases of winter roses. Creamy tapers bathe the room in a welcoming glow, and a white whistling thrush sings sweetly from a cage in the corner.

Hannah follows Livvy and me into the room. Her dress is similar to mine, and her hair is done up in a mass of icy curls. She wears a small gold circlet atop – a not-so-subtle nod to her approaching nuptials.

'This won't work,' she says. 'I don't understand why you don't just take your guards, sneak into the traitors' houses, and kill them all. Isn't that what you're good at?'

'I didn't want to get blood on my dress,' I say dryly.

To my surprise, Hannah cracks a smile and then quickly raises a hand to her face to hide it.

My heart lifts, and I find that I am grinning back at her, just like when we shared a joke as girls. But a second later, she scowls. 'Skies only know what everyone will say when they learn we invited them here only to trap them.'

She steps away from me, and my temper snaps. Does she think I want to do this?

'You can't marry Marcus and expect to avoid getting blood on your hands, sister,' I hiss at her. 'Might as well get into the habit of it.'

'Stop it, both of you.' Livvy looks between us as, outside the dining room, the front door opens and Father greets our guests. 'Remember who the actual enemy is.'

Seconds later, Father enters, trailing a group of Illustrian men, each flanked by a dozen bodyguards. They secure every inch, from the windows to the table to the drapes – before allowing their Paters to file in.

The head of Gens Rufia leads, his yellow-and-purple silk robes straining against his paunch. A portly man, gone to seed after leaving the military, but still sly as a hyena. When he spots me, his hand goes to the sword at his waist – a sword I doubt he remembers how to use, judging from those flaccid arms.

'Pater Aquillus,' he brays. 'What is the meaning of this?'

My father glances at me with an expression of surprise. He is so sincere that for a second, even I'm fooled.

'This is my eldest,' Father says. 'Helene Aquilla.' He uses my name purposefully. 'Though I suppose we must call her Blood Shrike now, right, darling?' He pats my cheek patronizingly. 'I thought it would be good for her to learn a bit from our discussions.'

'She is the Emperor's Blood Shrike.' Pater Rufius doesn't remove his hands from his sword. 'Is this an ambush, Aquillus? Is that what we've come to?'

'She *is* the Emperor's Blood Shrike,' Father says. 'And as such, she is useful to us, even if she doesn't have a whit of sense about how to use her position. We'll teach her, of course. Come, Rufius, you've known me for years. Have your men search the premises if you must. If you see anything alarming, you and the others can depart.'

I smile openly at Pater Rufius, making my voice warm and winsome, the way I've seen Livvy do when she's charming someone into giving her information. 'Do stay, Pater,' I say. 'I wish to honor the new title bestowed upon me, and it is only through watching experienced men such as yourself work that I will be able to do so.'

'Blackcliff isn't for mice, girl.' He doesn't take his brick of a hand off his sword. 'What game are you playing?'

I look at Father as if bewildered. 'No game, sir,' I say. 'I am a daughter of Gens Aquilla, above all else. As for Blackcliff, there are . . . *ways* to survive there, if one is a woman.'

Even as surprise registers in his eyes, a look of mingled disgust and interest passes across his face. The look makes my skin crawl, but I steel myself. *Go on, you half-wit. Underestimate me.*

He grunts and sits. The other four Paters – Rufius's allies – follow suit, and Mother sweeps in shortly after, followed by a taster and a row of slaves bearing trays groaning with food.

Mother seats me across from Rufius, as I requested. Throughout the meal, I let my laugh go high. I toy with my hair. I act bored during key parts of the conversation. I giggle with Livvy. When I glance at Hannah, she's chattering with another of the Paters, distracting him utterly.

When the meal is over, Father stands. 'Let us retire to my study, gentlemen,' he says. 'Hel, my dear, bring the wine.'

Father doesn't wait for my response as he leads the men out, their bodyguards following.

'Go to your rooms, both of you,' I whisper to Livvy and Hannah. 'No matter what you hear, stay there until Father comes for you.'

When I approach the study a few minutes later with a tray of wine and tumblers, the Paters' many bodyguards are arrayed outside. The space is too small for them to fit within. I smile at the two men flanking the door, and they grin back. *Idiots.*

After I enter the room, Father closes the door behind me and puts a hand on my shoulder. 'Helene is a good girl, and loyal to her Gens.' He brings me into the conversation seamlessly. 'She'll do as we ask – and that will get us closer to the Emperor.'

As they discuss a potential alliance, I carry the tray around the table and past the window, where I pause for an indiscernible moment – a signal to the Black Guard waiting on the grounds. Slowly, I serve the wine. My father takes a leisurely sip of each glass before I hand them off to the Paters.

I pass the last glass to Pater Rufius. His piggish eyes fix on mine, his finger brushing against my palm deliberately. It is easy enough to hide my disgust, especially when I hear the faintest thud outside the study.

Don't kill them, Helene, I remind myself. *You need them alive for a public execution.*

With a small, secret smile just for Pater Rufius, I slowly pull my hand away from his.

Then, from the slits cut into my dress, I draw out my scims.

* * *

By dawn, the Black Guard have rounded up Illustrian traitors and their families. City criers have announced the impending executions at Cardium Rock. Thousands of people surround the square that stretches around the bone pit at the base of the Rock. The Illustrians and Mercators in the crowd have been ordered to voice their disapproval of the traitors – lest they face a similar fate. The Plebeians need no encouragement.

The top of the Rock slopes down in three terraces. Illustrian courtiers, including my family, stand upon the closest terrace. Leaders from less powerful Gens stand on the top tier.

Near the edge of the cliff, Marcus surveys the crowd. He wears full battle regalia, an iron circlet upon his head. The Commandant stands beside him, murmuring something into his ear. He nods and, as the sun rises, addresses those gathered, his words carried through the crowd by the criers.

'Ten Illustrian Gens chose to defy your Augur-chosen Emperor,' he roars. 'Ten Illustrian Paters believed that they knew better than the holy seers who have guided us for centuries. These Paters bring shame to their Gens through their treasonous actions. They are traitors to the Empire. There is only one punishment for traitors.'

He nods, and Harper and I, standing on either side of a writhing, gagged Pater Rufius, drag the man to his feet. Without ceremony, Marcus takes Rufius by his garish robes and casts him over the side of the cliff.

The sound of his body hitting the pit below is lost in the cheers of the crowd.

The next nine Paters follow swiftly, and when they are nothing but a mass of broken bones and shattered skulls at the base of the cliff, Marcus turns to their heirs – kneeling, chained, and lined up for all of Antium to see. The flags of their Gens fly behind them.

'You will swear your fealty,' he says, 'upon the lives of your wives and sons and daughters. Or I swear by the skies that my Blood Shrike will wipe out each of your Gens one by one, Illustrian or not.'

They trip all over each other to swear. Of course they do, what with the screams of their now-dead Paters echoing in their heads. With each oath proclaimed, the crowd cheers again.

When it is done, Marcus turns again to the masses. 'I am your Emperor,' his voice booms out across the square. 'Foretold by the Augurs. I *will* have order. I *will* have loyalty. Those who defy me will pay with their lives.'

The crowd cheers again, and, almost lost within the cacophony, the new Pater of Gens Rufia speaks to one of the other Paters beside him.

'What of Elias Veturius?' he hisses. 'The Emperor casts the finest men in the land to their deaths, while that bastard eludes him.'

The crowd does not hear the words – but Marcus does. The Snake turns to the new Pater slowly, and the man shrinks away, his eyes straying fearfully to the edge of the cliff.

'A fair point, Pater Rufius,' Marcus says. 'To which I say: Elias Veturius will be publicly executed by *Rathana*. My Blood Shrike has men closing on him. Don't you, Shrike?'

Rathana? That's only a few weeks away. 'I—'

'I hope,' the Commandant says, 'that you will not bore his Majesty with more excuses. We would not wish to learn that your loyalties are as suspect as those of the traitors we just executed.'

'How dare—'

'You were given a mission,' Marcus says. 'You have not succeeded. Cardium Rock is thirsty for the blood of traitors. If we do not slake that thirst with the blood of Elias Veturius, perhaps we will slake it with the blood of Gens Aquilla. Traitors are traitors, after all.'

'You can't kill me,' I say. 'Cain said doing so would bring your own doom upon you.'

'You are not the only member of Gens Aquilla.'

My family. As the import of his words washes over me, Marcus's eyes light with that unholy joy he only seems to feel when he's got someone by the gut.

'You're engaged to Hannah.' *Appeal to his lust for power,* I think frantically. *Make him see that this will hurt him more than you, Helene.* 'Gens Aquilla is the only ally you have.'

'He has Gens Veturia,' the Commandant says.

'And I can think of, oh'　Marcus glances at the new Illustrian Paters just yards away – 'about ten other Gens that will adamantly back me. Thank you for that gift, by the way. As for your sister' – he shrugs – 'I can find another highborn whore to marry. It's not as if there's a shortage.'

'Your throne is not secure enough—'

His voice drops to a hiss. 'You dare to challenge me about my throne – my allies – here, in front of the court? Never presume to think you know more than me, Blood Shrike. Never. Nothing angers me more.'

My body turns to lead at the cunning calculation in his eyes. He steps toward me, his malice like a poison that saps my ability to move, much less think.

'Ah.' He tilts my chin up and searches my face. 'Panic, fear, and desperation. I prefer you like this, Blood Shrike.' He bites my lip, sudden and painful, his eyes open the whole time. I taste my own blood.

'Now, Shrike,' he breathes into my mouth. 'Go fetch.'

CHAPTER TWENTY-NINE

Laia

That woman – the Mask – the one they call the Commandant.
She's killing them all.

All the Scholars. All the Scholar *prisoners*.

'Skies, Keenan,' I say. The rebel understands immediately, just like me. 'Darin.'

'The Martials are moving north,' Keenan whispers. The Scholars don't hear him, their attention fixed on Afya, who has yet to decide their fates. 'They likely haven't even reached Kauf yet. The Commandant is methodical. If she's going south to north, she won't change the plan now. She still has to get through Antium before she gets to Kauf.'

'Afya,' Zehr calls from the edge of the camp, spyglass in hand. 'Martials incoming. Can't tell how many, but they're close.'

Afya curses, and the Scholar man grabs her. 'Please. Just take the children.' His jaw is clenched, but his eyes fill. 'Ayan is two. Sena is six. The Martials won't spare them. Keep them safe. My sisters and I will run – we'll lead the soldiers off.'

'Afya.' Izzi looks at the Tribeswoman aghast. 'You cannot refuse them—'

The man turns to us. 'Please, miss,' he says to me. 'My name is Miladh. I'm a rope maker. I'm nothing. I don't care about myself. But my boy – he's smart, so smart—'

Gibran appears behind us and grabs Izzi's hand. 'Quickly,' he says. 'Get into the wagon. The Martials were tracking them, but they're killing every Scholar they see. We need to get you hidden.'

'Afya, please.' Izzi looks at the children, but Gibran pulls her toward his wagon, terror filling his eyes.

'Laia,' Keenan says. 'We should hide—'

'You have to take them in.' I turn to Afya. 'All of them. I've been inside your smuggler's compartments. You have the space for it.' I turn to Miladh. 'Did the Martials see you and your family? Are they hunting *you* specifically?'

'No,' Miladh says. 'We ran with a dozen others. We got separated only hours ago.'

'Afya, you must have slaver's cuffs somewhere,' I say. 'Why not do what we did in Nur—'

'Absolutely not.' Afya's voice is a hiss, and her dark eyes are daggers. 'I'm already putting my Tribe at risk with you lot,' she says. 'Now shut up and get to your spot in the wagon.'

'Laia,' Keenan says, 'come on—'

'*Zaldara.*' Zehr's voice is sharp. 'One dozen men. Two minutes out. There's a Mask with them.'

'Bleeding, burning skies.' Afya grabs my arm and shoves me bodily toward her wagon. 'Get. Into. That. Wagon,' she snarls. '*Now.*'

'Hide them.' I dart forward, and Miladh deposits his son into my arms. 'Or I'm not going anywhere. I'll stand here until the Martials come, they'll figure out who I am, and you'll die for harboring a fugitive.'

'Lies,' Afya hisses. 'You wouldn't risk your precious brother's neck.'

I step forward, my nose an inch from hers, and refuse to back down. I think of Mother. I think of Nan. I think of Darin. I think of all the Scholars who have perished beneath the blades of the Martials.

'Try me.'

Afya holds my gaze for a moment before uttering something between a snarl and a shout. 'If we die for this,' she says, 'see if I don't hunt you through the hells until you pay.'

'Vana,' she calls to her cousin. 'Take the sisters and the girl. Use Riz's wagon and the rug wagon.' She turns to Miladh. 'You're with Laia.'

Keenan grabs my shoulder. 'Are you sure?'

'We can't let them die,' I say. 'Go – before the Martials get here.' He darts away toward his hiding spot in Zehr's wagon, and seconds later, Miladh, Ayan, and I are inside Afya's wagon. I shove back the rug that hides a trapdoor in the floor. It is steel-reinforced and heavy as an elephant. Miladh grunts as he helps me lift it.

It opens to reveal a shallow, wide space full of ghas and fire-powder. Afya's trick compartment. In the past few weeks, many of the Martials who have searched the caravan have found it and, satisfied that they've discovered her illegal stash, get lazy about hunting further.

I pull on a hidden lever and hear a click. The compartment rolls back horizontally to reveal a space below the first. It's just big enough for three people. I drop in on one side, Miladh on the other, and Ayan, wide-eyed, lies between us.

Afya appears in the door of the wagon. Her face is still furious, and she is pointedly silent as she rolls the decoy compartment over us. The trapdoor thuds above that. The rug rustles as she straightens it. Then her footsteps recede.

Through the slats in the compartment, horses snort and metal clinks. I smell pitch. The clipped tones of a Martial are clearly audible, but I can't make out what he's saying. A shadow passes over the compartment, and I force myself not to move, not to make a sound. I've done this exact thing a dozen times already. Sometimes I've waited in here for a half an hour, once for nearly half a day.

Steady, Laia. Calm. Beside me, Ayan fidgets but keeps quiet, perhaps sensing the danger outside the compartment.

'—a group of Scholar rebels, running this way,' a flat voice speaks. The Mask. 'Have you seen them?'

'I've seen a slave or two,' Afya says. 'No rebels.'

'We'll be searching your wagon anyway, Tribeswoman. Where is your *Zaldar?*'

'I am *Zaldara.*'

The Mask pauses. 'Intriguing,' he says in a way that makes me shudder. I can practically imagine Riz's hackles going up. 'Perhaps you and I can discuss it later, Tribeswoman.'

'Perhaps.' Afya's voice is a purr, so smooth that I would not have caught the thin thread of rage deep beneath the surface if I hadn't spent the last few weeks in close quarters with her.

'Start with the green one.' The Mask's voice recedes. I turn my head, close one eye, and press the other to a space between the planks. I can just make out Gibran's mirror-encrusted wagon and the supply wagon beside it where Keenan hides.

I thought the rebel would want to hide with me, but the first time the Martials came, he took one look at Afya's compartment and shook his head.

If we remain separate, he'd said, *then even if the Martials discover one of us, the others can still remain hidden.*

Too soon, a horse snorts from nearby, and a soldier drops down from it. I catch a glimmer of a silver face and try to keep breathing. Beside me, Miladh holds a hand to his son's chest.

The stairs at the foot of Afya's wagon come down, and the heavy gait of the soldier's boots thunk above us. The footsteps stop.

Doesn't mean anything. He might not see the seams in the floor. The trapdoor is designed so cleverly that even the decoy compartment is almost impossible to detect.

The soldier paces back and forth. He leaves the wagon, but I cannot relax, for seconds later, he circles it.

'Zaldara,' he calls to Afya. 'Your wagon is built rather strangely.' He sounds almost amused. 'From the outside, the bottom of this wagon drops to a foot or so off the ground. But the inside is considerably higher.'

'Tribespeople like our wagons solid, my lord,' Afya says. 'Otherwise they break apart at the first pothole in the road.'

'Aux,' the Mask calls out to another soldier. 'Come here. *Zaldara,* you too.' Boots thud up Afya's stairs, followed by her lighter footsteps.

Breathe, Laia. Breathe. We're going to be fine. This has happened before.

'Pull back the rug, *Zaldara.*'

The rug shifts. A second later, I hear the telltale click of the trapdoor. *Skies, no.*

'You like your wagons solid, eh?' the Mask says. 'Not that solid, apparently.'

'Perhaps we can discuss this,' Afya says smoothly. 'I'm happy to offer a small tribute if you'll simply overlook—'

'I'm not an Empire toll collector you can bribe with a brick of ghas, Tribeswoman.' The Mask's voice is no longer amused. 'This substance is outlawed, and it will be confiscated and destroyed, as will the firepowder. Soldier, remove the contraband.'

All right, you've found it. Now keep going.

The soldier lifts the ghas out brick by brick. This too has happened before, though until now, Afya has managed to dissuade the Martials from looking further with only a few bricks of ghas. This Mask doesn't move until everything in the compartment is gone.

'Well,' Afya says when the aux soldier is finished. 'Happy?'

'Not remotely,' the Mask says. A second later, Afya swears. I hear a heavy thump, a gasp, and what sounds like the Tribeswoman choking back a scream.

Disappear, Laia, I think to myself. *You're invisible. Gone. Small. Smaller than a scratch. Smaller than dust. No one can see you. No one knows you're here.* My body tingles, like too much blood rushing to my skin all at once.

A moment later, the second portion of the compartment rolls back. Afya is slumped against the side of her cabin, one hand at her swiftly bruising neck. The Mask stands inches away, and as I stare up into his face, I find that I am paralyzed with fear.

I expect him to recognize me. But he has eyes only for Miladh and Ayan. The boy erupts into wails at the sight of the monster before him. He claws at his father, who desperately tries to shush him.

'Scholar trash,' the Mask says. 'Can't even hide properly. Get up, rat. And shut your brat up.'

Miladh's eyes cut to where I lie, and then widen. Swiftly, he looks away, saying nothing. He ignores me. They all ignore me. As if I'm not there. As if they can't see me.

Just like when you snuck up on the Commandant in Serra, like when you hid from the Tribesman at Raider's Roost. Like when Elias lost you in the crowd in Nur. You wish to disappear, and you do.

Impossible. I think it must be some strange trick by the Mask.

But he makes his way out of the wagon, shoving Afya, Miladh, and Ayan before him, and I am left alone. I look down at myself and gasp. I can see my own body, but I can also see the grain of the wood through it. Tentatively, I reach out for the edges of the smuggler's compartment, expecting that my hand will go through, the way ghosts' hands do in the stories. But my body is as solid as ever; it's simply more translucent to my eye – and invisible to others'.

How? How? How? Did the efrit in Serra do this? These are questions I must answer – but later. For now, I grab Darin's scim, and my dagger and pack, and tiptoe from the wagon. I stick to the shadows, but I might as well walk in front of the torches, because no one sees me. Zehr, Riz, Vana, and Gibran all kneel on the ground, their hands bound behind their backs.

'Search the wagons,' the Mask snarls. 'If there are two Scholar scum here, there are bound to be more.'

A moment later, one of the soldiers approaches. 'Sir,' he says. 'There's no one else.'

'Then you haven't looked hard enough.' The Mask grabs one of the torches and lights Gibran's wagon on fire. *Izzi!*

'No,' Gibran shouts, trying to break free from his bonds. '*NO!*'

A moment later, Izzi staggers out of the wagon, coughing at the smoke. The Mask smiles.

'See?' he says to his fellow soldiers. 'Like rats. All you need is to smoke them out. Burn the wagons. Where this lot is going, they won't need them.'

Oh skies. I need to move. I count the Martials. There are a dozen of them. The Mask, six legionnaires, and five auxes. Seconds after they light the fires, Miladh's sisters emerge from their hiding spots, carrying little Sena with them. The girl is unable to rip her terrified gaze from the Mask.

'I found another!' one of the auxes calls from the other side of the camp, and, to my horror, he drags Keenan out.

The Mask looks Keenan over, grinning. 'Look at that hair,' he says. 'I've a few friends who fancy redheads, boy. Pity my orders are to kill all Scholars. I'd have made a good bit of gold off you.'

Keenan clenches his jaw, searching for me in the clearing. When he doesn't find me, he relaxes and puts up no fight as the Martials tie him up.

They've found everyone. The wagons burn. In moments, they'll execute all of the Scholars and likely drag Afya and her Tribe to prison.

I have no plan, but I move anyway, reaching for Darin's scim. Is it visible? It can't be. My clothes clearly aren't, and neither is my pack. I make my way to Keenan.

'Don't move,' I whisper into his ear. Keenan stops breathing for a second. But he doesn't so much as twitch beyond that. 'I'm going to cut the bonds on your hands first,' I say. 'Then your feet. I'm going to hand you a scim.'

There's no indication that Keenan has heard. As I saw through the leather binding his hands, one of the legionnaires approaches the Mask.

'The wagons are destroyed,' he says. 'We have six Tribespeople, five Scholar adults, and two Scholar children.'

'Good,' the Mask says. 'We'll – aah—'

Blood fountains from the Mask's neck as Keenan flies to his feet and whips Darin's scim up and across the Martial's throat. It should be a killing blow, but this is a Mask, after all, and he backs away quickly. He presses his hand to the wound, his features twisting into a snarl of rage.

I run to Afya and cut through her ropes. Zehr is next. By the time I've gotten to Riz, Vana, and the Scholars, all hell has broken loose in the clearing. Keenan grapples with the Mask, who is attempting to wrestle him to the ground. Zehr dances around the blades of three legionnaires, shooting arrows so fast that I don't see him draw the bow. At the sound of a scream, I whirl and find Vana clutching her bloody arm as her father fights off two auxes with a cudgel.

'Izzi! Back!' Gibran shoves my friend behind him as he brandishes a sword against another legionnaire.

'Kill them!' the Mask bellows to his men. 'Kill them all!'

Miladh shoves Ayan at one of his sisters and takes up a burning piece of wood that has popped off one of the wagons. He waves it at an approaching aux, who jumps back warily. On his other side, an aux soldier moves for the Scholars, scim out, but I leap forward. I bring my dagger into the small of the soldier's back and yank it upward, the way Keenan taught me. The man drops, twitching, to the dirt.

One of Miladh's sisters engages the other aux, and when the soldier is distracted, Miladh stabs at him with the firebrand, setting his clothes alight. The soldier screams and rolls wildly on the ground, trying to get the fire out.

'You – you were gone.' Miladh stutters, staring at me, but there's no time to explain. I kneel down, tearing the aux's daggers from his body. I toss one to Miladh and another to his sister. 'Hide,' I scream at them. 'In the woods! Take the children!'

One of the sisters goes, but the other remains beside Miladh, and together they attack a legionnaire bearing down on them.

Across the camp, Keenan holds his own against the Mask, helped, no doubt, by the blood pouring down the bigger man's neck. Afya's short scim flashes wickedly in the firelight as she takes down an aux and turns immediately to do battle with a legionnaire. Zehr has taken out two of his attackers and battles the last ferociously. The last legionnaire circles Izzi and Gibran.

My friend has a bow in her hand, and she notches it, aims at the legionnaire fighting Zehr, and puts an arrow straight into the Martial's throat.

A few yards away from her, Riz and Vana still battle the auxes. Riz's brow is furrowed as he tries to fend off one of the soldiers. The man punches Riz in the belly. The silver-haired Tribesman doubles over, and to my horror, a blade is sticking out of his back a moment later.

'Father!' Vana screams. 'Skies, Father!'

'Riz?' Gibran throws off one of the legionnaires with a blow and lurches toward his cousin.

'Gibran!' I shriek. The legionnaire who's been circling him leaps forward. Gibran lifts his blade, but it shatters.

Then a flash of steel – a sickening crunch.

The color drains from Gibran's face as Izzi staggers back, an impossible amount of blood geysering from her chest. *She's not dead. She can survive that. She's strong.* I run for them, my mouth open in a rabid scream as the legionnaire who stabbed Izzi now lunges for Gibran.

The Tribal boy's neck is open for the kill, and all I can think as I fly forward is that if he dies, Izzi will be heartbroken, yet again. She deserves more than that.

'Gib!' Afya's scream of terror is hair-raising, echoing in my ears as my dagger clangs against the legionnaire's scim inches from Gibran's neck. I use a sudden, adrenaline-fueled burst of strength to throw the soldier back. He is off balance for a moment before he grabs me by the throat and disarms me with a twist of his hand. I kick at him, trying to knee him in the groin, but he slams me to the ground. I see stars, then a flash of red. Suddenly, a spray of hot blood hits my face, and the legionnaire collapses atop me, dead.

'Laia!' Keenan shoves the man off me and pulls me to my feet. Behind him, the Mask lies dead – as do the other Martials.

Vana sobs beside her fallen father, Afya at her side. Ayan clings to Miladh, while Sena tries to shake her dead mother awake. Zehr limps to the Scholars, blood leaking from a dozen slashes.

'Laia.' Keenan's voice is choked, and I turn. *No. No, Izzi.* I want to close my eyes, to run from what I see. But my feet take me forward, and I drop beside Izzi, cradled in Gibran's arms.

My friend's eye is open, and she seeks out mine. I force myself to pull my gaze from the gaping wound in her chest. *Damn the Empire. I will burn it down for this. I will destroy it.*

I scrabble at my pack. *She'll need stitches is all – a witch hazel poultice – tea, some sort of tea.* But even as I rifle through the bottles I know that there is no vial, no extract strong enough to counter this. She has moments – if that.

I take my friend's hand, small and cold. I try to say her name, but my voice is gone. Gibran sobs, begs her to stay.

Keenan stands behind me, and I feel his hands drop to my shoulders and squeeze.

'L-Laia—' A bubble of blood forms at the corner of Izzi's mouth and bursts.

'Iz.' I find my voice. 'Stay with me. Don't leave me. Don't you dare. Think of all the things you have to tell Cook.'

'Laia,' she whispers. 'I'm afraid—'

'Izzi.' I shake her gently, not wanting to hurt her. 'Izzi!'

Her warm brown eye meets mine, and for a moment, I think she's going to be fine. There is so much life there – so much *Izzi*. For a single heartbeat, she looks at me – into me, like she can see down into my soul.

And then she's gone.

CHAPTER THIRTY

Elias

The kennels outside Kauf reek of dog droppings and rancid fur. Even the scarf pulled across my face can't mask it. I gag at the stench.

From where I sidle in the snow along the building's southern wall, the cacophony of the dogs is deafening. But when I peer into the entrance, the Fiver on guard duty is fast asleep beside the kennel fire – as he has been the past three mornings.

I inch the kennel door open and stick to the walls, still swathed in predawn shadows. Three days of planning – of waiting and watching – have led to this. If all goes well, I'll have broken Darin out of Kauf by this time tomorrow.

Kennels first.

The Kennel Master visits his domain once a day, at second bell. Three Fivers trade shifts around the clock, but there is only one on duty at a time. Every few hours, one of a series of aux soldiers emerges from the prison to muck out the stalls, feed and exercise the animals, and tend to repairs on the sleds and reins.

At the shadowy end of the structure, I stop beside a pen, where three dogs bark at me as if I'm the Nightbringer himself. The legs of my fatigues and the back of my cloak shred easily – they are already worn through. I hold my breath and use a stick to soil my other pant leg with dung.

I pull up the hood on my cloak. 'Oi!' I bellow, hoping the shadows are deep enough to hide my clothing, which is clearly not a Kauf uniform. The Fiver jerks awake and spins, his eyes wild. He spots me and gibbers a defense, dropping his eyes out of respect and fear. I cut him off.

'You're asleep on the bleeding job,' I roar at him. Auxes, particularly Plebeians, are spat on by everyone else at Kauf. Most tend to be extra nasty to the Fivers and the prisoners – the only people at Kauf they can boss. 'I should report you to the Kennel Master.'

'Sir, please—'

'Stop yipping. Had enough of that from the dogs. One of the bitches attacked when I tried to take her out. Ripped my clothes straight through. Bring me another uniform. A cloak and boots too – mine are covered with dog scat. I'm twice your size, so make sure it fits. And don't bleeding tell the Kennel Master. Last thing I need is that bastard cutting my rations.'

'Yes, sir, right away, sir!'

He darts out of the kennel, so frightened that I'll turn him in for sleeping on duty that he doesn't look twice at me. While he's gone, I feed the dogs and muck out the pens. An aux showing up earlier than usual is strange but not noteworthy, considering the Kennel Master's lack of organization. An aux showing up and then not performing his assigned task would set off alarm bells.

When the Fiver returns, I'm stripped to my breeches, and I order him to leave the uniform and wait outside. I toss my old clothes and shoes in the fire, shout at the poor boy again for good measure, and turn north, to Kauf.

Half of the prison is rooted inside the darkness of the mountain behind it. The other half erupts from the rock like a diseased growth. A wide road snakes down from the enormous front gate, running like a rivulet of black blood along the River Dusk.

The prison walls, twice as high as Blackcliff's, are almost ornate, with friezes, columns, and gargoyles hewn from the pale gray rock. Aux archers patrol the crenellated ramparts, and legionnaires man four lookout towers, making the prison difficult to break into and impossible to break out of.

Unless one is a Mask who has spent weeks planning it.

Above, the cold sky is lit green and purple by undulating ribbons of light. The Northern Dancers, they're called – the spirits of the dead battling for eternity in the skies – at least according to Martial lore.

I wonder what Shaeva would say about it. *Maybe you can ask her in a fortnight, when you're dead.* I feel for the store of Tellis in my pocket – a two-week supply. Just enough to get me to *Rathana*.

Other than the Tellis, a lock pick, and the throwing knives across my chest, my belongings, including my Teluman scims, are hidden in the cave where I plan to stow Darin. The place was smaller than I remembered, half-collapsed and covered in debris from mudslides. But no predators had claimed it, and it is large enough to camp in. Darin and I should be able to lie low there until Laia arrives.

I narrow my focus to Kauf's yawning portcullis. Supply wagons snake up the road leading to the prison, bringing winter foodstuffs before the passes are snowed in. But with the sun not yet up and a guard change imminent, the deliveries are chaotic and the guard sergeant isn't paying attention to who is coming and going from the kennels.

I approach the caravan from the main road and sidle in among the other gate guards searching the wagons for contraband.

As I peer into a crate of gourds, a truncheon slams into my arm. 'Already checked this one, you dolt,' a voice says behind me, and I turn to face a surly, bearded legionnaire.

'Apologies, sir,' I bark out, quickly bolting to the next wagon. *Don't follow. Don't ask my name. Don't ask my squad number.*

'What's your name, soldier? I haven't seen you before—'

BOOM-boom-BOOM-BOOM-boom.

For once, I'm bleeding thrilled to hear the drums, which signal the guard change. The legionnaire turns, distracted for a moment, and I dart into the crowd of auxes heading into the prison. When I look back, the legionnaire has turned to the next wagon.

Too close, Elias.

I keep slightly behind the aux squad, my hood up and scarf wrapped close. If the men notice an extra soldier among them, I'm dead.

I fight to ease the tension in my body, to keep my gait steady and exhausted. *You're one of them, Elias. Bone tired after the grave-yard shift, ready for grog and bed.* I pass through the snow-dusted prison yard, twice the size of Blackcliff's training field. Torches – blue-fire and pitch – illuminate every inch of the space. The prison's innards, I know, are similarly lit; the Warden employs two dozen auxes whose sole job is to make sure those torches never go out. No prisoner of Kauf can ever claim the shadows as allies.

Though I risk being called out by the men I'm with, I work my way to the middle of the group as we approach the main prison entrance and the two Masks flanking it.

The Masks cast their eyes over the men entering, and my fingers twitch toward my weapons. I force myself to listen to the low conversation of the auxes.

'—double shifts because half the pit platoon got food poisoning—'

'—new prisoners arrived yesterday, a dozen of them—'

'—don't see why we bothered processing them. Commandant's on her way, captain said. New Emperor has ordered her to kill every last Scholar here—'

I stiffen at the words, trying to control the anger flooding every pore. I knew the Commandant was scouring the countryside for Scholars to kill. I didn't realize she was attempting to exterminate them entirely.

There are more than a thousand Scholars in this prison, and they will all die under her command. *Ten hells.* I wish I could free them. Storm the pits, kill the guards, incite a revolt.

Wishful thinking. Right now, the best thing I can do for the Scholars is get Darin out of here. His knowledge will at least give his people a chance to fight back.

That is, if the Warden hasn't destroyed his body or mind. Darin is young, strong, and obviously intelligent: the exact type of prisoner the Warden likes to experiment on.

I pass into the prison, the Masks none the wiser, and head with the other guards down the main corridor. The prison is arranged in an enormous pinwheel, with six long halls as spokes. Martials, Tribesmen, Mariners, and those from beyond the Empire's borders occupy two blocks of the prison on the east side. Scholars occupy two blocks on the west. The last two blocks house the barracks, mess hall, kitchens, and storage.

At the very center of the pinwheel sit two sets of stairs. One leads up to the Warden's office and Masks' quarters. Another leads down, down, down to the interrogation cells. I shudder, pushing the thought of that foul little hell from my mind.

The auxes around me drop their hoods and scarves, so I fall back. The scruffy beard I've grown in the past few weeks is an adequate disguise as long as no one looks too closely. But these men will know I wasn't on duty with them at the gate.

Move, Elias. Find Darin.

Laia's brother is a high-value prisoner. The Warden will have heard the rumors that Spiro Teluman spread about the boy's smithing prowess. He'll want to keep him separate from the rest of Kauf's population. Darin won't be in the Scholar pits or the other major prison blocks. Prisoners stay in the interrogation cells for no more than a day – any longer and they come out in a coffin. Which leaves solitary confinement.

I move quickly past the other guards on their way to their varied postings. As I pass the entrance to the Scholar pits, a blast of stinking heat hits me. Most of Kauf is so frigid you can see your breath cloud the air. But to keep the pits hellishly hot, the Warden uses enormous furnaces. Clothing disintegrates in weeks in the pits, sores fester, wounds rot. Weaker prisoners die days after getting here.

When I was a Fiver stationed here, I asked a Mask why the Warden didn't let the cold kill off the prisoners. *Because heat makes them suffer more*, he said.

I hear proof of that suffering in the wails that echo through the prison like a demon's chorus. I try to block them out, but they punch through my mind anyway.

Go, damn it.

As I approach Kauf's main rotunda, an uptick in activity catches my attention: soldiers moving swiftly away from the center staircase. A lean, black-clad figure descends the steps, his masked face gleaming.

Damn it. The Warden. The one man in this prison who will know me on sight. He prides himself on remembering the details of everything and everyone. I curse quietly. It's a quarter after sixth bell, and he always enters the interrogation cells at this time. I should have remembered.

The old man is yards from me, speaking with a Mask at his side. A case dangles from his long, thin fingers. Tools for his experiments. I force down the disgust rising in my throat and keep walking. I'm passing the stairs now, just yards from him.

Behind me, a scream pierces the air. Two legionnaires march past, escorting a prisoner from the pits.

The Scholar wears a filthy loincloth, and his emaciated body is covered with sores. When he catches sight of the iron door that leads to the interrogation block, his cries grow frantic and I think he's going to break an arm attempting to escape. I feel like a Fiver again, listening to the misery of the prisoners, unable to do anything but seethe with useless hate.

One of the legionnaires, sick of the man's howls, lifts a fist to knock him unconscious.

'No,' the Warden calls from the stairs in his eerie, reedy voice. *'The scream is the purest song of the soul,'* he quotes. *'The barbarous keen yokes us to the low beasts, to the unutterable violence of the earth.'* The Warden pauses. 'From Tiberius Antonius, philosopher to Taius the Tenth. Let the prisoner sing,' he clarifies, 'so his brethren hear.'

The legionnaires drag the man through the iron door. The Warden moves to follow but then slows. I am nearly across the rotunda now, close to the hallway that leads to solitary confinement. The Warden turns, scanning the corridors on five sides before his eyes land on the one I'm about to enter. My heart nearly drops out of my chest.

Keep walking. Try to look grumpy. He hasn't seen you for six years. You have a beard. He won't recognize you.

Waiting for the old man's gaze to pass is like waiting for the executioner's ax to fall. But after long seconds, he finally turns away. The door to the interrogation cells clangs shut behind him, and I breathe again.

The corridor I enter is emptier than the rotunda, and the stone stairway leading to solitary confinement is emptier still. A lone legionnaire stands guard at the block's entry door, one of three that lead to the prison cells.

I salute, and the man grunts a response, not bothering to look up from the knife he's sharpening. 'Sir,' I say. 'I'm here to see about a prisoner transfer—'

He lifts his head just in time for his eyes to widen fractionally at the fist flying into his temple. I stop his fall, relieve him of his keys and uniform jacket, and ease him to the ground. Minutes later, he is gagged, bound, and stuffed into a supply closet nearby.

Hopefully, no one opens it.

The day's transfer sheet is nailed to the wall beside the door, and I scan it quickly. Then I unlock the first door, the second, and the last, to find myself in a long, dank hallway lit by a single blue-fire torch.

The bored legionnaire manning the entry station glances up from his desk in surprise.

'Where's Corporal Libran?' he asks.

'Ate something that turned his stomach,' I say. 'I'm new. Came in on the frigate yesterday.' Surreptitiously, I drop my eyes to his tags. *Cpl. Cultar.* A Plebeian then. I offer a hand. 'Corporal Scribor,' I say. Upon hearing a Plebeian name, Cultar relaxes.

'You should get back to your post,' he says. At my hesitation, he grins knowingly. 'I don't know about your old posting, but the Warden here doesn't allow the men to touch the solitary prisoners. If you want jollies, you'll have wait until you're assigned to the pits.'

I bite back my disgust. 'Warden told me to bring him a prisoner at seventh bell,' I say. 'But he's not on the transfer sheet. You know anything about it? Scholar lad. Young. Blond hair, blue eyes.' I force myself not to say more. *One step at a time, Elias.*

Cultar grabs his own transfer sheet. 'Nothing on here.'

I let a touch of irritation enter my voice. 'You sure? Warden was insistent. The boy's high-value. Whole countryside is talking about him. They say he can make Serric steel.'

'Ah, him.'

I still my features into a semblance of boredom. *Bleeding hells.* Cultar knows who Darin is. Which means the boy *is* in solitary.

'Why in the bleeding hells would the Warden ask for him?' Cultar scratches his head. 'Boy's dead. Has been for weeks.'

My euphoria vanishes. *'Dead?'* Cultar looks at me askance, and I flatten my voice. 'How'd he die?'

'Went down to the interrogation cells and never came out. Served him right. Jumped-up little rat. Refused to give his number during lineup. Always had to announce his filthy Scholar name. *Darin.* Like he was proud of it.'

I sag against Cultar's desk. His words sink in slowly. Darin can't be dead. He *can't* be. What will I say to Laia?

You should have gotten here faster, Elias. You should have found a way. The enormity of my failure is staggering, and though Blackcliff trained me to show no emotion, I forget it all in this moment.

'Bleeding Scholars moaned about it for weeks when they heard,' Cultar, utterly oblivious, chuckles to himself. 'Their great savior, gone—'

'*Jumped-up*, you called him.' I yank the legionnaire toward me by his collar. 'Much like you, down here doing a job any idiot

Fiver could, yammering about things you don't *bleeding* under-stand.' I headbutt him hard and shove, my rage and frustration exploding through my body and pushing my good sense aside. He flies back and hits the wall with a sick thud, his eyes rolling up into his head. He slithers to the floor, and I give him a last kick. He won't be waking up any time soon. If ever.

Get out of here, Elias. Get to Laia. Tell her what's happened. Still enraged from the news that Darin is dead, I drag Cultar to one of the empty cells, toss him inside, and turn the lock.

But when I head to the door leading out of the block, the latch rattles.

Doorknob. Key in lock. Lock turning. Hide. My mind screams the words at me. *Hide!*

But there's no place to do so other than behind Cultar's desk. I dive down, pulling my body into a ball, heart thumping and knives at the ready.

I hope it's a Scholar slave coming in to bring the meals. Or a Fiver delivering an order. Someone I can silence. Sweat beads on my forehead as the door opens, as I hear a light step on the stones.

'Elias.' I go utterly still at the Warden's thin voice. *No, damn it. No.* 'Come out of there. I've been waiting for you.'

CHAPTER THIRTY-ONE

Helene

My family or Elias.

My family. Or Elias.

Avitas follows me as I leave Cardium Rock. My body feels numb with disbelief. I do not notice him dogging my heels until I'm halfway to Antium's northern gate.

'Leave me.' I wave a hand at him. 'I don't need you.'

'I'm tasked with—'

I whirl on him, a knife to his throat. He puts his hands up slowly, but without the wariness he'd have if he thought I was actually going to kill him. Something about it makes me even angrier.

'I don't care. I need to be alone. So stay away from me, or your body will soon find itself looking for a new head.'

'With respect, Shrike, please tell me where you're going and when you'll return. If something happens—'

I'm already walking away from him. 'Then your mistress will be pleased,' I call back. 'Leave me be, Harper. That's an order.'

Minutes later, I'm departing Antium. *Not enough men manning the north gate*, I find myself thinking, a desperate attempt to keep my mind off what Marcus has just told me. *I should chat with the captain of the city guard about that.*

When I look up, I realize where it is I am headed. My body knew before my mind. Antium is built in the shadow of Mount Videnns, where the Augurs lurk in their rocky lair. The path to their caves is well trod; pilgrims set out before dawn every day, climbing high into the Nevennes to pay homage to the red-eyed seers. I used to think I understood why. I used to think Elias's frustration with the Augurs smacked of cynicism. Blasphemy, even.

Conniving tricksters, he'd said. *Cave-dwelling charlatans.* Perhaps, all this time, he was right.

I pass the few pilgrims making their way up the mountain, and I am fueled by rage and something I don't care to identify. Something I last felt when I swore fealty to Marcus.

Helene, you are such a fool. I realize now that some part of me hoped Elias would escape – no matter what happened to the Empire as a result. Such weakness. I loathe that part of myself.

Now I can have no such hope. My family are blood, kin, Gens. And yet I didn't spend eleven months of every year with them. I didn't make my first kill with them at my side or walk Blackcliff's haunted, deadly halls with them.

The trail winds up two thousand feet before flattening out into a pebble-strewn bowl. Pilgrims mill in a crowd at the far end beside an unobtrusive cave.

Many approach the cave, but some unknown force stops them a few yards from its entrance.

Just try and stop me, I scream in my mind at the Augurs. *See what happens.*

My anger propels me past the knot of pilgrims and straight to the entrance of the cave. An Augur waits there in the darkness, her hands folded before her.

'Blood Shrike.' Her red eyes glimmer from beneath the hood, and I strain to hear her. 'Come.'

I follow her into a corridor lit with blue-fire lamps. Their glow tinges the glittering stalactites above us a startling cobalt.

We emerge from the long corridor into a high, perfectly square cave. A large pool of still water sits at its very center, lit by an opening in the cave rock directly above. A solitary form stands beside the pool, gazing into its depths.

My escort slows. 'He awaits you.' She nods to the figure. *Cain.* 'Temper your anger, Blood Shrike. We feel your rage in our blood the way you feel the bite of steel on your skin.'

I stride toward Cain, my hand tight on my scim. *I will crush you with my anger. I will flatten you.* I stop short before him, a vile curse upon my lips. Then I meet his sober gaze, and shudder. Strength fails me.

'Tell me he'll be all right.' I know I sound like a child. But I can't stop myself. 'Like before. Tell me that if I hold to my oath of fealty, he won't die.'

'I cannot do that, Blood Shrike.'

'You told me that if I held true to my heart, the Empire would be well served. You told me to have faith. How do you expect me to have faith if he's going to die? I have to *kill* him – or my family is lost. I have to *choose.* Do you – can you – comprehend—'

'Blood Shrike,' Cain says. 'How is a Mask made?'

A question for a question. Father did this when we argued philosophy. It always irritated me.

'A Mask is made through training and discipline.'

'No. How is a Mask made?'

Cain circles me, his hands in his robes, watching from beneath his heavy black cowl.

'Through rigorous instruction at Blackcliff.'

Cain shakes his head and takes a step toward me. The rocks beneath me quaver. 'No, Shrike. How is a Mask *made*?'

My anger sparks, and I yank it back like I would the reins of an impatient horse.

'I don't understand what you want,' I say. 'We're made through pain. Suffering. Through torment, blood, and tears.'

Cain sighs.

'It's a trick question, Aquilla. A Mask is not made. She is remade. First, she is destroyed. Stripped down to the trembling child that lives at her core. It doesn't matter how strong she thinks she is. Blackcliff diminishes, humiliates, and humbles her.

'But if she survives, she is reborn. She rises from the shadow world of failure and despair so that she might become as fearful as that which destroyed her. So that she might know darkness and use it as her scim and shield in her mission to serve the Empire.'

Cain lifts a hand to my face like a father caressing a newborn, his papery fingers cold against my skin. 'You are a Mask, yes,' he whispers. 'But you are not finished. You are my masterpiece, Helene Aquilla, but I have just begun. If you survive, you shall be a force to be reckoned with in this world. But first you will be unmade. First, you will be broken.'

'I'll have to kill him, then?' What else could this mean? The best way to break me is Elias. He has always been the best way to break me. 'The Trials, the vow I made to you. It was all for nothing.'

'There is more to this life than love, Helene Aquilla. There is duty. Empire. Family. Gens. The men you lead. The promises you make. Your father knows this. So will you, before the end.'

His eyes are unfathomably sad as he lifts my chin. 'Most people,' Cain says, 'are nothing but glimmers in the great darkness of time. But you, Helene Aquilla, are no swift-burning spark.

You are a torch against the night – if you dare to let yourself burn.'

'Just *tell* me—'

'You seek assurances,' the Augur says. 'I can offer you none. Breaking your fealty will have its cost, as will keeping it. Only you can weigh those costs.'

'What will happen?' I don't know why I ask. It's futile. 'You see the future, Cain. Tell me. Better that I know.'

'You think knowing will make it easier, Blood Shrike,' he says. 'But knowing makes it worse.' A millennia-old sadness weighs upon him, so consuming that I have to look away. His whisper is faint, and his body fades. 'Knowing is a curse.'

I watch him until he's gone. My heart is a vast chasm, empty of everything but Cain's warning and a staggering fear.

But first you will be unmade.

Killing Elias will destroy me. I sense that truth in my bones. Killing Elias is my unmaking.

CHAPTER THIRTY-TWO

Laia

Afya gave me no time to say goodbye, to mourn. I slipped Izzi's eye-patch off, threw a cloak over her face, and fled. At least I escaped with my pack and Darin's scim. Everyone else has only their clothes and the goods stowed in the horses' saddlebags.

The horses themselves are long gone, stripped of any sigils and sent galloping west the moment we reached the River Taius. Afya's only words of farewell to the beasts were wrathful mutters about their expense.

The boat she stole off a fisherman's pier will soon be gone too. Through the sagging door of a mold-fuzzed barn in which we have taken refuge, I can see Keenan standing at the riverside, sinking the boat.

Thunder rumbles. A drop of sleet shoots through the hole in the barn's roof and lands on my nose. Hours remain until dawn.

I look to Afya, who holds a dim lamp to the ground as she draws a map in the dirt while speaking to Vana in a low voice.

'—and tell him I'm calling in this favor.' The *Zaldara* hands

Vana a favor coin. 'He's to get you to Aish and get these Scholars to the Free Lands.'

One of the Scholars – Miladh – approaches Afya, standing firm against her blazing anger.

'I am sorry,' he says. 'If one day I can repay you for what you've done, I will, a hundredfold.'

'Stay alive.' Afya's eyes soften – just a touch – and she nods to the children. 'Protect them. Help any others you can. That's the only payment I expect I'll get.'

When she's out of earshot, I approach Miladh, who is now attempting to fashion a sling from a length of cloth. As I show him how to drape the cloth, he eyes me with nervous curiosity. He must be wondering about what he saw in Afya's wagon.

'I don't know how I disappeared,' I finally say. 'That was the first time I even realized I had done it.'

'A good trick for a Scholar girl to have,' Miladh says. He looks at Afya and Gibran, speaking quietly on the other side of the barn. 'In the boat, the boy said something about saving a Scholar who knows the secrets of Serric steel.'

I scuff my foot against the ground. 'My brother,' I say.

'This isn't the first time I've heard about him.' Miladh tucks his son into the sling. 'But it is the first time I've had cause to hope. Save him, Laia of Serra. Our people need him. And you.'

I look to the little boy in his arms. Ayan. Tiny dark crescents curve beneath his lower lashes. His eyes meet mine, and I touch his cheek, soft and round. He should be innocent. But he's seen things no child should. Who will he be when he grows up? What will all this violence make him? Will he survive? *Not another forgotten child with a forgotten name*, I plead. *Not another lost Scholar.*

Vana calls out and, with Zehr, leads Miladh, his sister, and the children into the night. Ayan twists about to look at me. I make myself smile at him – Pop always said you could never smile too much at a baby. The last thing I see before they are lost in darkness is his eyes, so dark, watching me still.

I turn to Afya, locked in conversation with her brother. From the look on her face, interrupting them would result in a fist to the jaw.

Before I decide what to do, Keenan ducks into the barn. The sleet falls steady now, and his red hair is plastered to his head, almost black in the darkness.

He halts when he sees the eyepatch in my hand. Then he takes two steps and pulls me to his chest without hesitation, wrapping his arms around me. This is the first time we've had a moment to even look at each other since we escaped the Martials. But I am numb as he holds me close, unable to relax into him or to allow his warmth to drive away a chill that set into my bones the moment I saw Izzi's chest torn open.

'We just left her there,' I say into his shoulder. 'Left her to—' *To rot. To have her bones picked clean by scavengers or tossed into some unmarked grave.* The words are too horrible to speak.

'I know.' Keenan's voice cracks, and his face is chalk-white. 'Skies, I know—'

'—can't bleeding make me!'

I jerk my head around to the other end of the barn, where Afya looks as if she's about to crush the lamp in her hand. Gibran, meanwhile, seems as if he's more like his sister than is currently convenient for her.

'It's your duty, you fool. Someone must take control of the Tribe if I don't come back, and I won't have it be one of our idiot cousins.'

'You should have thought of that before you brought me along.'

Gibran stands nose to nose with Afya. 'If Laia's brother can make the steel that brings the Martials down, then we owe it to Riz – and Izzi – to save him.'

'We've dealt with the Martials' cruelty before—'

'Not like this,' he says. 'They've disrespected us, robbed us, yes. But they've never butchered us. They've been killing Scholars, and it's making them bold. We're next. For where will they find slaves if they've killed all the Scholars off?'

Afya's nostrils flare. 'In that case,' she says, 'fight them from the Tribal lands. You certainly can't do it from Kauf Prison.'

'Listen,' I say, 'I don't think—'

The Tribeswoman whirls, as if the sound of my voice has triggered an explosion that's been building for hours. 'You,' she hisses. 'You're the reason we're in this mess. The rest of us bled while you – you *disappeared*.' She twitches with fury. 'You went into that smugglers' compartment, and when the Mask opened it, you were *gone*. Didn't realize I was transporting a witch—'

'Afya.' Keenan's voice holds a note of warning. He's said nothing about my invisibility. There hasn't been time until now.

'I didn't know I could do it,' I say. 'It was the first time. I was desperate. Maybe that's why it worked.'

'Well, it's very convenient for you,' Afya says. 'But the rest of us don't have any black magic.'

'Then you need to leave.' I hold up a hand as she tries to protest. 'Keenan knows the safe houses we can stay in. He suggested it before, but I didn't listen.' Skies, how I wish I had. 'He and I can get to Kauf alone. Without wagons, we can move even faster.'

'The wagons protected you,' Afya says. 'I made a vow—'

'To a man who's long gone.' The frost in Keenan's voice reminds me of the first time I met him. 'I can get her to Kauf safely. We don't need your help.'

Afya rises to her full height. 'As a Scholar and a rebel, *you* don't understand honor.'

'What honor is there in a useless death?' I ask her. 'Darin would hate that so many died to save him. I can't order you to leave me. All I can do is ask.' I turn to Gibran. 'I think the Martials *will* turn on the Tribesmen eventually. I vow that if Darin and I make it to Marinn, I will get you word.'

'Izzi was willing to die for this.'

'Sh-she had nowhere else to go.' The stark truth of my friend's loneliness in this world hits me. I swallow back the grief. 'I shouldn't have brought her along. It was my decision, and it was the wrong one.' Saying it makes me feel hollow inside. 'And I won't make that decision again. Please, go. You can still catch up with Vana.'

'I don't like this.' The Tribeswoman casts Keenan a look of distrust that surprises me. 'I don't like it at all.'

Keenan's eyes narrow. 'You'll like being dead even less.'

'My honor demands that I escort you, girl.' Afya puts out the lamp. The barn seems darker than it should be. 'But my honor also demands that I not take a woman's decision about her own fate away from her. Skies knows there's enough of that in this blasted world.' She pauses. 'When you see Elias, you tell him that from me.'

That is all the goodbye I get. Gibran storms out of the barn. Afya rolls her eyes and follows.

Keenan and I stand alone, the sleet drumming the earth in a steady tattoo around us. When I look into his eyes, a thought enters my head: *This is right. This is how it should be. This is how it always should have been.*

'There's a safe house a half dozen miles from here.' Keenan touches my hand to pull me from my thoughts. 'If we're swift, we can get there before dawn.'

273

Part of me wants to ask him if I have made the right decision. After so many mistakes, I yearn for the reassurance that I haven't ruined everything yet again.

He will say yes, of course. He will comfort me and tell me this is the best way. But doing the right thing now does not undo every mistake I have already made.

So I do not ask. I simply nod and follow as he leads the way. Because after all that has happened, I do not deserve comfort.

PART THREE

THE DARK PRISON

CHAPTER THIRTY-THREE

Elias

The Warden's rail-thin shadow falls over me. His long, triangular head and thin fingers bring to mind a praying mantis. I have a clear shot, but my knives do not leave my hands. All thoughts of murder flee my mind when I see what he is holding.

It's a Scholar child, nine or ten years old. Malnourished, filthy, and as silent as a corpse. The cuffs on his wrists mark him not as a prisoner but as a slave. The Warden digs a blade into his throat. Rivulets of blood trickle down the child's neck and onto a filthy shift.

Six Masks follow the Warden into the block. Each wears the sigil of Gens Sisellia, the Warden's family. Each has a notched arrow pointed at my heart.

I could take them, even with the arrows. If I drop fast enough, use the table as a shield –

But then the old man runs his pale hand through the child's lank, shoulder-length hair with chilling tenderness.

'*No star more fair than the bright-eyed child; for him I would lay down my life.*' The Warden delivers the quote in a clear tenor that matches his neat appearance. 'He's small' – the Warden nods to the boy – 'but wonderfully resilient, I've discovered. I can make him bleed for hours if you wish.'

I drop the knife.

'Fascinating,' the Warden breathes. 'See, Drusius, how Veturius's pupils widen, how his pulse accelerates, how, even when faced with certain death, his eyes dart, seeking a way out? It is only the presence of the child that stays his hand.'

'Yes, Warden.' One of the Masks – Drusius, I assume – responds with flat disinterest.

'Elias,' the Warden says. 'Drusius and the others will divest you of your weaponry. I suggest you not fight. I wouldn't want to hurt the child. He's one of my favorite specimens.'

Ten hells. The Masks surround me, and in seconds I am stripped of weapons, boots, lock pick, the Tellis, and most of my clothes. I do not resist. If I want to break out of this place, I need to conserve my strength.

And I will break out. The very fact that the Warden didn't kill me indicates that he wants something from me. He'll keep me alive until he gets it.

The Warden watches as the Masks manacle me and shove me against a wall, his pupils pitch-black pinpricks in the white-blue of his eyes.

'Your punctuality pleases me, Elias.' The old man keeps the knife loose in his hand, about an inch from the boy's neck. 'A noble trait, and one that I respect. Though I confess, I don't understand *why* you're here. A wise young man would be well away to the Southern Lands by now.' He looks at me expectantly.

'You don't actually expect me to tell you, do you?'

The boy whimpers, and I find the Warden pushing the knife

slowly into the side of his neck. But then the old man smiles, revealing small, yellowing teeth. He releases the child.

'Of course I don't,' he says. 'In fact, I hoped you wouldn't. I have a feeling you'd just lie until you convinced even yourself, and lies bore me. I'd much rather pull the truth from you. I haven't had a Mask as a subject for quite a while. I fear my research is quite outdated.'

My skin prickles. *Where there's life*, I hear Laia in my head, *there's hope*. He might experiment on me. Use me. But as long as I live, I still have a chance of getting out of here.

'You said you've been waiting for me.'

'Indeed. A little bird informed me of your arrival.'

'The Commandant,' I say. Damn her. She's the only one who might have figured out where I was going. But why would she tell the Warden about it? She hates him.

The Warden smiles again. 'Perhaps.'

'Where do you want him, Warden?' Drusius says. 'Not with the rest, I assume.'

'Of course not,' the Warden says. 'The bounty would tempt the lesser guards to turn him in, and I'd like a chance to study him first.'

'Clear out a cell,' Drusius barks at one of the other Masks, nodding to the row of solitary cells behind us. But the Warden shakes his head.

'No,' he says. 'I have somewhere else in mind for our newest prisoner. I've never studied the long-term effects of *that* place on a subject. Particularly one who demonstrates such' – he looks down at the Scholar boy – 'empathy.'

My blood chills. I know exactly the part of the prison he's talking about. Those long, dark hallways with air curdled from the smell of death. The moans and whispers, the scratches on the walls, the way you can't do anything even when you hear people screaming for someone, anyone to help them . . .

'You always hated it in there,' the Warden murmurs. 'I remember. I remember your face that time you brought me a message from the Emperor. I was mid-experiment. You went pale as the underbelly of a fish, and when you ran back out into the hallway, I heard you retching in a slop bucket.'

Ten bleeding hells.

'Yes.' The Warden nods, his expression pleased. 'Yes, I think the interrogation block will do very nicely for you.'

CHAPTER THIRTY-FOUR

Helene

Avitas awaits me when I return to the Black Guard barracks. Midnight approaches, and my mind slumps in exhaustion. The Northman says nothing of my haggard appearance, though I'm certain he can read the devastation in my eyes.

'Urgent message for you, Shrike.' His sallow cheeks tell me he hasn't slept. I don't like that he stayed awake until I returned. *He's a spy. That's what spies do.* He hands me an envelope, the seal of which is untouched. Either he's getting better at espionage or for once he didn't open it.

'New orders from the Commandant?' I ask. 'Gain my trust by *not* reading my mail?'

Avitas's lips tighten as I tear open the letter. 'It arrived at dusk with a runner. He said it left Nur six days ago.'

Blood Shrike,
  Mamie refuses to crack despite the deaths of several Tribesmen. I've held her son in reserve – she thinks he's dead.

She did let one thing slip. I think Elias went north, not south or east, and I think the girl is still with him

The Tribes know of the interrogations and have rioted twice in response. I need a half legion at least. I've put in requests at every garrison within a hundred miles, but everyone is short.
Duty Unto Death,
Lieutenant Dex Atrius

'North?' I hand the letter to Avitas, who reads it through. 'Why in the bleeding skies would Veturius head north?'

'His grandfather?'

'Gens Veturia's lands are west of Antium. If he cut straight north from Serra, he'd have gotten there faster. If he was headed for the Free Lands, he could have just taken a ship from Navium.'

Damn it, Elias, why couldn't you have just left the bleeding Empire? If he'd used his training to get as far away from here as fast as possible, I'd never have caught his trail, and my choice would have been made for me.

And your family would die. Bleeding skies, what's wrong with me? He *chose* this.

What did he do that was so wrong? He wished to be free. He wished to stop killing.

'Don't try to puzzle it out now.' Avitas follows me into my room and sets Dex's message on my desk. 'You need food. Sleep. We'll start on it in the morning.'

I hang up my weapons and go to the window. The stars are obscured, the purple-black sky promising snow. 'I should go to my parents.' They heard what Marcus said – everyone on top of that damned rock did, and there's no bigger bunch of gossips than Illustrians. The entire city must know of Marcus's threat to my family.

'Your father came by.' Avitas hovers by the door, his Masked face suddenly uncomfortable. I suppress a wince. 'He suggested you keep your distance for now. Apparently your sister Hannah is . . . upset.'

'You mean she wants to drink my blood.' I close my eyes. Poor Hannah. Her future rests in the hands of the one person she trusts the least. Mother will try to soothe her, as will Livia. Father will coax, then coerce, then order her to stop her hysterics. But in the end, they'll all be wondering the same thing: Will I choose my family and the Empire? Or will I choose Elias?

I turn my mind to the mission. North, Dex had said. *And the girl is still with him.* Why would he take her deeper into the Empire? Even if he had some pressing reason to remain in Martial territory, why put the girl at risk?

It's like he's not making the decisions. But who else would be? The girl? Why would he let her? What could she possibly know about escaping the Empire?

'Blood Shrike.' I jump. I'd forgotten that Avitas was in the room – he's so quiet. 'Shall I bring you some food? You need to eat. I asked the kitchen slaves to keep some warm for you.'

Food – eat – slaves – Cook.

The Cook.

The girl – Laia, the old woman said. *Don't touch her.*

They must have grown close while enslaved. Maybe the Cook knows something. After all, she figured out how Laia and Elias escaped Serra.

All I have to do is find her.

But if I start looking, someone will inevitably blab that the Blood Shrike is searching for a white-haired, scar-faced woman. The Commandant will hear, and that will be the end of Cook. Not that I care about the old hag's fate. But if she knows anything about Laia, I need her alive.

'Avitas,' I say. 'Does the Black Guard have contacts in Antium's underground?'

'The Black Market? Of course—'

I shake my head. 'The city's unseen. Urchins, beggars, transients.'

Avitas frowns. 'They're mostly Scholars, and the Commandant's been herding them for enslavement or execution. But I know a few people. What are you thinking?'

'I need to get a message out.' I speak carefully. Avitas doesn't know Cook helped me – he'd go straight to the Commandant with such information.

'Singer seeks meal,' I finally say.

'Singer seeks meal,' Avitas repeats. 'That's . . . it?'

Cook seems a bit crazy, but hopefully she'll understand.

'That's it. Get it to as many people as you can, and swiftly,' I say. Avitas looks at me quizzically.

'Did I not say I wanted this done quickly?'

A ghost of a frown on his face. Then he's gone.

After he leaves, I pick up Dex's message. Harper didn't read it. But why? I have never sensed malice in him, true. I've never sensed anything at all. And since leaving the Tribal lands, he's been . . . not friendly, exactly, but slightly less opaque. What game is he playing now, I wonder?

I file Dex's message away and drop into my cot, boots still on. Still, I cannot sleep. It will take Avitas hours to get the message out and hours more for Cook to hear it – if she hears it at all. I know this, yet I jump at every sound, expecting the old woman to materialize as suddenly as a wraith. Finally, I drag myself over to my desk, where I read through the old Blood Shrike's files – information he's gathered about some of the highest-ranking men in the Empire.

Many of the reports are straightforward. Others less so. I did not, for instance, know that Gens Cassia had hushed up the murder of a Plebeian servant on their premises. Or that the Mater of Gens Aurelia had four lovers, all Paters of noted Illustrian houses.

The old Shrike kept files about the men of the Black Guard too, and when I spot Avitas's file, my fingers are moving before I can think twice. It's as lean as he is, with just one piece of parchment within.

Avitas Harper: Plebeian
Father: Combat Centurion Arius Harper (Plebeian). Killed in service, age twenty-eight. Avitas age four at time of death. Remained with mother, Renatia Harper (Plebeian), in Jeilum until selection for Blackcliff.

Jeilum is a city west of here, deep in the Nevennes tundra. Isolated as the ten hells.

Mother: Renatia Harper. Died age thirty-two. Avitas age ten at time of death. Subsequently kept by paternal grandparents during school leaves.
Spent four years under Blackcliff Commandant Horatio Laurentius. Remaining Blackcliff training carried out by Commandant Keris Veturia.
Showed great potential as Yearling. Remained average during tenure of Commandant Keris Veturia. Multiple sources report Veturia's interest in Harper from early age.

I turn the paper over, but there is nothing more.

Hours later, just before dawn, I wake with a jerk – I've fallen asleep at my desk. I scan the room for the scraping noise that disturbed me, dagger in hand.

A hooded figure hunches at the window, her glittering eyes hard as sapphires. I throw back my shoulders and lift the blade Her scarred mouth twists into a nasty smirk.

'That window is thirty feet off the ground, and I locked it,' I say. A Mask could get through, certainly. But a Scholar granny?

She ignores my unspoken question. 'You should have found him by now,' she says. 'Unless you don't *want* to find him.'

'He's a bleeding Mask,' I say. 'He's trained to throw people off his scent. I need you to tell me about the girl.'

'Forget the girl,' Cook snarls, dropping heavily into my room. 'Find *him*. You should have done it weeks ago, so that you could be back here, keeping an eye on *her*. Or are you too stupid to see that the Bitch of Blackcliff is planning something? It's big this time, girl. Bigger than her going after Taius.'

'The Commandant?' I snort. 'Went after the Emperor?'

'Don't tell me you think the Resistance thought of that on their own?'

'They're *working* with her?'

'They don't know it's her, now do they?' The derision in the Cook's voice slices as sharply as any scim. 'Tell me why you want to know about the girl.'

'Elias isn't making rational decisions, and the only thing I can think is that she—'

'You don't want to know more about her.' Cook almost sounds relieved. 'You just want to know where he's going.'

'Yes, but—'

'I can tell you where he's going. For a price.'

I raise my blade. 'How's this for a trade: You tell me, and I don't gut you.'

A sharp bark from the Cook makes me thinks she's having some sort of fit – until I realize this is her version of a laugh.

'Someone beat you to it.' She pulls up her shirt. Her skin, disfigured from some long-ago torment, is further marred by an enormous, rotting wound. The smell of it hits like a fist, and I gag.

'Bleeding hells.'

'Certainly smells like it, doesn't it? Got it from an old friend – just before I killed him. Never tended to it. Heal me, Little Singer, and I'll tell you what you want to know.'

'When did this happen?'

'Do you want to catch Elias before you sisters go splat, or do you want a bedtime story? Hurry. Sun's almost up.'

'I haven't healed anyone since Laia,' I say. 'I don't know how I'll—'

'Then I'm wasting my time.' She reaches the window with one step and pulls herself up with a grunt.

I step forward and grab her shoulder. Slowly, she comes back down.

'All your weapons on the desk,' I say. 'And don't you dare hide anything, because I will search you.'

She does as I ask, and when I've ensured that she's doesn't have any nasty surprises tucked away, I reach for her hand. She snatches it away.

'I have to touch you, you mad old bat,' I snap. 'It won't work otherwise.'

She curls her lip in a snarl and offers me her hand reluctantly. To my surprise, it trembles.

'It won't hurt too much.' My voice is kinder than I expected. Bleeding skies, why am I reassuring her? She's a murderess and a blackmailer. Brusquely, I hold her steady and close my eyes.

Fear curls up in my belly. I want this to work – and I don't want it to work. It's the same feeling I had when I healed Laia.

Now that I've seen the wound and Cook's asked for help, it feels *necessary* to fix it, like a tic I can't stop. The lack of control, the way my whole body yearns toward this, frightens me. It is *not* me. It is nothing I've ever trained for or wanted.

If you wish to find Elias, do it.

A sound fills my ears: humming – my own. I don't know when it began.

I look into Cook's eyes and dive into that blue darkness. I have to understand her all the way through to her core if I wish to remake bones and skin and flesh.

Elias felt like silver, a bolt of adrenaline beneath a cold, clear dawn. Laia was different. She made me think of sorrow and a green-gold sweetness.

But the Cook . . . her insides slither like eels. I flinch away from them. Somewhere behind the roiling blackness, I catch a glimpse of what she once was, and I reach for it. But in doing so, my hum becomes suddenly discordant. That goodness within her – it's a memory. Now the eels take the place of her heart, writhing with mad vengeance.

I change the melody to catch hold of this truth at her core. A door springs open inside her. I go through, walk down a long corridor that is strangely familiar. The floor sucks at my feet, and when I look down, I half expect to see the tentacles of a squid wrapped around me.

But there is only darkness.

I cannot bear to sing Cook's truth out loud, so instead I scream the words in my head, looking into her eyes all the while. To her credit, she doesn't look away. When the healing begins, when I've captured her essence and her body begins to knit itself back to health, she doesn't even twitch.

Pain grows in my side. Blood drips down into the waist of my fatigues. I ignore it until I'm gasping, when I finally force myself to release Cook. I feel the injury I've taken on from her. It's much smaller than the old woman's, but it still hurts like hell.

Cook's wound is a bit bloodied and raw, but the only sign of infection is the lingering smell of death.

'Take care of that,' I gasp. 'If you can get into my room, you can thieve yourself herbs to make a poultice.'

She peers down at the wound and then at me. 'The girl has a brother linked to the – the – the Resistance,' she stutters for a moment, then goes on. 'The Martials sent him to Kauf months ago. She's trying to get him out. Your boy is helping her.'

He's not my boy is my first thought.

He's bleeding insane is my second.

A Martial or Mariner or Tribesman sent to Kauf might emerge eventually, chastened, purged, and unlikely to defy the Empire again. But Scholars have no way out that doesn't involve a hole in the ground.

'If you're lying to me—'

She climbs up into the window, this time with the spryness I last saw in Serra. 'Remember: Hurt the girl and you'll regret it.'

'Who is she to you?' I ask. I saw something inside Cook during the healing – an aura, or shadow, some ancient music that made me think of Laia. I frown, trying to remember. It's like dredging up a decade-old dream.

'She's *nothing* to me.' The Cook bites out the words as if even the thought of Laia is repugnant. 'Just a foolish child on a hopeless mission.'

When I stare at her uncertainly, she shakes her head.

'Don't just stand there gawping at me like a stunned cow,' she says. 'Go save your family, you stupid girl.'

CHAPTER THIRTY-FIVE

Laia

'Slow down.' Keenan, panting as he runs beside me, reaches for my hand. The brush of his skin is a welcome shot of warmth in the freezing night.

'In the cold, you don't realize how much you're pushing yourself. You'll collapse if you're not careful. And it's too bright out, Laia – someone could see us.'

We're nearly to our destination – a safe house in a stretch of farmland far north of where we parted from Afya a week ago. There are even more patrols up here than farther south, all hunting the Scholars fleeing the Commandant's merciless attacks in cities north and west of here. Most of the patrols, however, hunt Scholars during the day.

Keenan's knowledge of the land has allowed us to travel at night and make good time, especially since we've been able to steal horses more than once. Kauf is now only three hundred miles away. But three hundred miles might as well be three thousand if the damned weather doesn't cooperate. I kick at the thin layer of snow on the ground.

I grab Keenan's hand and urge him forward. 'We need to reach that safe house tonight if we want to make for the mountain passes tomorrow.'

'We won't get anywhere if we're dead,' Keenan says. Frost beads on his dark lashes, and patches of his face are purplish blue. All of our cold-weather gear was burned with Afya's wagon. I have the cloak Elias gave me weeks ago, but it was meant for a Serran winter, not this biting cold, which gets under the skin and clings like a lamprey.

'If you exhaust yourself into illness,' Keenan says, 'one night of rest isn't going to fix it. Besides, we're not being careful. That last patrol was yards away – we nearly walked right into it.'

'Bad luck.' I'm already moving on. 'We've been fine since then. I hope this safe house has a lamp. We need to look at the map Elias gave us and work out how we're going to get to that cave if the storms get bad.'

The snow swirls down in thick patches, and nearby, a rooster caws. The landowner's mansion is just visible a quarter mile away, but we veer away from it and head for an outbuilding near the slaves' quarters. In the distance, two hunched figures trudge to a barn, buckets in hand. The place will be swarming with slaves and their overseers soon. We need to take cover.

We finally make it to the cellar door behind a squat granary. The door's latch is stiff from cold, and Keenan groans as he tries to pry it up.

'Hurry.' I crouch beside him. In the slaves' hovels a few dozen yards away, smoke rises and a door creaks. A Scholar woman, her head wrapped in cloth, emerges.

Again, Keenan digs his dagger into the latch. 'Bleeding thing won't – ah.' He sits back, the latch having finally come loose.

The sound echoes, and the Scholar woman spins around.

Keenan and I both freeze – there's no chance that she hasn't seen us. But she simply waves us into the cellar.

'Quick,' she hisses. 'Before the overseers wake!'

We drop into the cellar's dimly lit interior, our breath clouding above us. Keenan bars the door as I inspect the space. It is a dozen feet wide, a half dozen feet long, and cramped with barrels and wine racks.

But a lamp hangs from the roof on a chain, and below it, a table boasts fruit, a paper-wrapped loaf of bread, and a tin tureen.

'The man who runs this farm is a Mercator,' Keenan says. 'Scholar mother, Martial father. He was the only heir, so they passed him off as a full-blooded Martial. But he must have been closer to his mother, because last year, when his father died, he started helping runaway slaves.' Keenan nods at the food. 'Looks like he's still at it.'

I pull Elias's map from my pack, unroll it carefully, and clear a space on the ground. My stomach rumbles with hunger, but I ignore it. Safe houses usually have little room to move, let alone light enough to see. Keenan and I spend every hour of the day sleeping or running. This is a rare chance to discuss what's to come.

'Tell me more about Kauf.' My hands shake with cold – I can hardly feel the parchment between my fingers. 'Elias drew a rough layout, but if he fails and we have to go inside, it won't be—'

'You haven't said her name since she died.' Keenan cuts through the torrent of words spilling from my mouth. 'Do you know that?'

My hands shake more violently. I fight to still them as he sits in front of me.

'You only talk about the next safe house. About how we'll make our way out of the Empire. About Kauf. But you won't talk about her or what happened. You won't talk about this strange power of yours—'

'Power.' I want to scoff. 'A power that I can't even tap into.' Though skies know I've tried. Every free moment, I've attempted to will myself into invisibility until I feel like I'll go mad thinking the word disappear. Every time, I fail.

'Perhaps if you talked about it, it would help,' Keenan suggests. 'Or if you ate more than a bite or two. Or slept more than a few hours.'

'I don't feel hungry. And I can't sleep.'

His gaze falls upon my shaking fingers. 'Skies, look at you.' He shoves the parchment away and envelops my hands in his own. His warmth fills up an emptiness inside. I sigh, wanting to fall into that warmth – to let it wrap around me so that I forget all that's to come – even for a few minutes.

But that's selfish. And stupid, considering that at any moment, we might be caught by Martial soldiers. I try to take my hands away, but as if Keenan knows what I'm thinking, he pulls me near, pressing my fingers against the heat of his stomach and throwing his cloak around us both. Beneath the rough weave of his shirt, I can feel the ridges of muscle, hard and smooth. His head is bent as he looks at our hands, red hair hiding his eyes. I swallow and look away from him. We've traveled together for weeks, but we've never been this close before.

'Tell me something about her,' he whispers. 'Something good.'

'I didn't know anything.' My voice cracks, and I clear my throat. 'I knew her for weeks? Months? And I never even asked her anything worthwhile about her family or what it was like when she was young or – or what she wanted or what she hoped for. Because I thought we had time.'

A tear snakes down my face, and I pull a hand from him and dash it away. 'I don't want to talk about this,' I say. 'We should—'

'She deserves better than you pretending she didn't exist,'

Keenan says. I look up, shocked, expecting anger, but his dark eyes are sympathetic. It makes it worse somehow. 'I know it hurts. Of all people, I know. But pain is how you know you loved her.'

'She loved stories,' I whisper. 'Her eyes would fix on me, and I could see when I told them that she'd lose herself in whatever I was saying. That she could see it all in her head. And later, sometimes days later, she'd ask me questions about them, like that whole time she was living in those worlds.'

'After we left Serra,' Keenan says, 'we'd been walking – running, really, for hours. When we finally stopped and settled into our rolls for the night, she looked up and said, "The stars are so different when you're free."' Keenan shakes his head. 'After running all day, eating hardly anything, and being so tired she couldn't take another step, she fell asleep smiling at the sky.'

'I wish I didn't remember,' I whisper. 'I wish I didn't love her.'

He takes a breath, his eyes still on our hands. The cellar is no longer frigid, warmed by our body heat and the sun hitting the door above.

'I know what it is to lose those you love. I taught myself not to feel anything at all. For so long that it wasn't until I met you that . . .' He holds tight to my hands but doesn't look at me. I can't bring myself to look at him either. Something fierce kindles between us, something that has perhaps been quietly burning for a long time.

'Don't lock yourself away from those who care about you because you think you'll hurt them or – or they'll hurt you. What point is there in being human if you don't let yourself feel anything?'

His hands trace a path over mine, moving like a slow flame to my waist. Ever so slowly, he tugs me closer. The emptiness inside, the guilt and failure and well of hurt, it fades in the ache of desire that throbs low in my body and propels me forward. As I slide onto his lap, his hands tighten on my waist, sending fire up my spine. He lifts his fingers to my hair, and the pins within drop to the cellar floor. His heart thuds against my chest, and he breathes against my mouth, a hair's breadth between our lips.

I stare down at him, hypnotized. For a fleeting second, something dark passes across his face, some shadow unknown but not, perhaps, unexpected. Keenan has always had a darkness about him. I feel a flicker of unease in my stomach, swift as a beat of a hummingbird's wings. It is forgotten a moment later as his eyes shut and he closes the distance between us.

His lips are gentle against mine, his hands less so as they roam across my back. My hands are equally hungry, flitting across the muscles of his arms, his shoulders. When I tighten my legs around his waist, his lips drop to my jaw, his teeth scrape my neck. I gasp when he tugs on my shirt to trace a torturously slow trail of heat down my bare shoulder.

'Keenan—' I breathe. The cold of the cellar is nothing against the fire between us. I pull his shirt off and drink in the sight of his skin, tawny in the lamplight. I trace a finger along the freckles that dust his shoulders, down the hard, precise muscles of his chest and stomach, before dropping to his hip. He catches my hand, his eyes searching my face.

'Laia.' The word changes utterly when he says it in that voice, no longer a name but a plea, a prayer. 'If you want me to stop—'

If you want to keep your distance . . . if you want to remember your pain . . .

Keenan. Keenan. Keenan. My mind is filled with him. He has guided me, fought for me, stayed with me. And in doing so, his aloofness has given way to a potent, unspoken love I feel whenever he looks at me. I silence the voice within and take his hand. Every other thought grows distant as calm settles over me, a peace I haven't felt in months. Without looking away from him, I guide his fingers to the buttons of my shirt, pulling open one, then another, leaning forward as I do so.

'No,' I whisper against his ear. 'I don't want you to stop.'

CHAPTER THIRTY-SIX

Elias

The unceasing whispers and moans from the cells around me burrow into my head like carnivorous worms. After only a few minutes in the interrogation block, I cannot remove my hands from my ears, and I consider ripping them off altogether.

Torchlight from the block's hallway leaks in through three slits positioned high on the door. I have just enough light to see that the cold stone floor of my cell is bare of anything I could use to pick the locks on my manacles. I test the chains, hoping for a weak link. But they are Serric steel.

Ten hells. My seizures will begin anew in a half day at the most. When they do, my ability to think – to move – will be severely hindered.

A tortured keen sounds from one of the nearby cells, followed by the gibbering of some poor bastard who can barely form words.

At least I'll put the Commandant's interrogation training to use. Nice to know all that suffering at her hands wasn't for nothing.

After a time, I hear scuffling at the door, and the lock turns. *The Warden?* I tense, but it is only the Scholar boy the Warden used as leverage. The child holds a cup of water in one hand and a bowl of hard bread and mold-encrusted jerky in the other. A patchy blanket hangs from his shoulder.

'Thank you.' I swig the water in one gulp. The boy stares at the floor as he sets the food and blanket down within my reach. He is limping – something he wasn't doing before.

'Wait,' I call out. He stops but doesn't look at me. 'Did the Warden punish you more after . . .' *After he used you to control me.*

The Scholar might as well be a statue. He just stands there, like he's waiting for me to say something that isn't obvious.

Or maybe, I think, *he's waiting for me to stop blathering long enough to respond.* Though I want to ask his name, I force myself not to speak. I count the seconds. Fifteen. Thirty. A minute passes.

'You're not afraid,' he finally whispers. 'Why aren't you afraid?'

'Fear gives him power,' I say. 'Like feeding oil to a lamp. It makes him burn brighter. It makes him strong.'

I wonder if Darin was afraid before he died. I only hope it was quick.

'He hurts me.' The boy's knuckles are white as he digs his hands into his legs. I wince. I know well how the Warden hurts people – and how he hurts Scholars in particular. His experiments in pain are only part of it. Scholar children handle the lowest tasks in the prison: cleaning rooms and prisoners after torture sessions, burying bodies with their bare hands, emptying slop buckets. Most of the children here are dead-eyed drudges wishing for death before they're ten.

I cannot even imagine what this boy has experienced. What he's seen.

Another wretched scream echoes from same cell as before. Both the boy and I jump. Our eyes meet in shared disquiet, and

I think he's going to speak. But the cell door opens again, and the Warden's loathsome shadow falls across him. The boy scurries out, squeezing against the door like a mouse trying to escape the notice of a cat, before disappearing amid the flickering torches of the block.

The Warden doesn't spare him a glance. He's empty-handed. Or at least it looks that way. I'm certain he has some torture device tucked out of sight.

For now, he closes the door and takes out a small ceramic bottle. The Tellis extract. It's all I can do not to lunge for it.

'About time.' I ignore the bottle. 'I thought you might have lost interest in me.'

'Ah, Elias.' The Warden clucks his tongue. 'You served here. You know my methods. *True suffering lies in the expectation of pain as much as in the pain itself.*'

'Who said that?' I snort. 'You?'

'Oprian Dominicus.' He paces back and forth, just out of my reach. 'He was Warden here during the reign of Taius the Fourth. Required reading at Blackcliff in my day.'

The Warden holds up the Tellis extract. 'Why don't we start with this?' At my silence, he sighs. 'Why were you carrying it, Elias?'

Use the truths your interrogators want, the Commandant's voice hisses in my ear. *But use them sparingly.*

'A wound went bad.' I tap the scar on my arm. 'The blood cleanser was the only thing I could find to treat it.'

'Your right forefinger twitches ever so slightly when you lie,' the Warden informs me. 'Go on, try to stop doing it. You won't be able to. *The body does not lie, even if the mind does.*'

'I'm telling the truth.' A version of it, anyway.

The Warden shrugs and pulls on a lever beside the door. A

mechanism in the wall behind me grinds, and the chains attached to my hands and feet pull tighter and tighter, until I am flush against the wall, my body yanked into a taut X.

'Did you know,' the Warden says, 'that a single set of pliers can be used to break every bone in the human hand if pressure is applied in the correct manner?'

It takes four hours, ten mangled fingernails, and skies know how many broken bones for the Warden to get the truth about the Tellis out of me. Though I know I could last longer, I eventually let him have the information. Better that he think me weak.

'Most strange,' he says when I confess that the Commandant poisoned me. 'But, ah' – understanding lights his face – 'Keris wanted the little Shrike out of the way so she could whisper what she liked to whomever she liked without interference. But she didn't want to risk leaving you alive. Clever. A bit too risky for my taste, but . . .' He shrugs.

I twist my face in pain so that he doesn't see my surprise. I've wondered for weeks why the Commandant poisoned me instead of killing me outright. I'd finally decided she simply wanted me to suffer.

The Warden opens the cell door and pulls on the lever to loosen my chains. I thud gratefully to the floor. Moments later, the Scholar boy enters.

'Clean the prisoner,' the Warden says to the child. 'I don't want infection.' The old man cocks his head. 'This time, Elias, I let you play your games. I found them fascinating. This invincibility syndrome you seem to have: How long will it take to break it? Under what circumstances? Will it require more physical pain, or will I be forced to delve into the weaknesses of your mind? So much to discover. I look forward to it.'

He disappears, and the boy approaches, weighed down by a

clay pitcher and a crate of clinking jars. His eyes flicker to my hand and widen. He crouches beside me, his fingers as light as a butterfly as he applies various pastes to clean the wounds.

'It's true what they say then,' he whispers. 'Masks don't feel pain.'

'We feel pain,' I say. 'We're just trained to withstand it.'

'But he – he had you for hours.' The boy's brow furrows. He reminds me of a lost starling, alone in the darkness, searching for something familiar, something that makes sense. 'I always cry.' He dips a cloth in water and wipes away the blood on my hands. 'Even when I try not to.'

Damn you, Sisellius. I think of Darin, suffering down here, tormented like this boy, like me. What horror did the Warden unleash upon Laia's brother before he finally died? My hands burn for a scim so I can separate the old man's insectile head from his body.

'You're young,' I say gruffly. 'I cried too when I was your age.' I offer him my good hand to shake. 'My name is Elias, by the way.'

His hand is strong, if small. He lets go of me quickly.

'The Warden says names have power.' The boy's eyes flit to mine. 'All of us children are *Slave*. Because we are all the same. Though my friend Bee – she named herself.'

'I won't call you *Slave*,' I say. 'Do – do you want your own name? In the Tribal lands, families sometimes don't name children until years after they are born. Or maybe you already have a name?'

'I don't have a name.'

I lean against the wall, biting back a grimace as the boy splints my hand. 'You're smart,' I say. 'Fast. What about *Tas*? In Sadhese, it means *swift*.'

'Tas.' He tries the name out. There is the hint of a smile on his face. 'Tas.' He nods 'And you – you are not just Elias. You are Elias *Veturius*. The guards talk about you when they think no one is listening. They say you were a Mask once.'

'I took the mask off.'

Tas wants to ask a question – I can see him working himself up to it. But whatever it is, he chokes it back when voices sound outside the cell and Drusius enters.

The child rises quickly, gathering his things, but he's not fast enough.

'Hurry up, filth.' Drusius closes the distance in two strides, aiming a vicious kick at Tas's stomach. The boy yelps. Drusius laughs and kicks him again.

A roaring fills my mind, like water rushing up against a dam. I think of Blackcliff's Centurions, their casual, daily beatings that ate away at us when we were Yearlings. I think of the Skulls who terrorized us, who never saw us as human, only as victims for the sadism bred into them, layer by layer, year by year, like complexity builds so slowly into wine.

And suddenly, I am leaping for Drusius, who has, to his detriment, gotten too close. I snarl liked a crazed animal.

'He's a *child*.' I use my right hand to punch the Mask in the jaw, and he drops. The rage within breaks free, and I don't even feel the chains as I rain down blows. *He's a child who you treat like garbage, and you think he doesn't feel it, but he does. And he'll feel it until he's dead, all because you're too sick to see what it is you do.*

Hands tear at my back. Boots thunder, and two Masks veer into the cell. I hear the whistle of a truncheon and dodge it. But a punch to the gut takes the wind out of me, and I know that any moment I'll be knocked into unconsciousness.

'*Enough.*' The dispassionate tone of the Warden cuts through the chaos. Immediately, the Masks back away from me. Drusius snarls and rises to his feet. My breath comes heavy, and I glare at the Warden, letting all my hate for him, for the Empire, fill my gaze.

'The poor little boy getting vengeance for his lost youth. Pathetic, Elias.' The Warden shakes his head, disappointed. 'Do you not understand how irrational such thoughts are? How useless? I shall have to punish the boy now, of course. Drusius,' he says crisply, 'bring a parchment and a quill. I will take the child next door. You will record Veturius's responses.'

Drusius wipes the blood from his mouth, jackal eyes shining. 'With pleasure, sir.'

The Warden grabs the Scholar child – Tas – cowering in the corner and pitches him out of the cell. The boy lands with a sickening thump.

'You're a monster,' I snarl at the old man.

'*Nature weeds out those who are lesser,*' the Warden says. 'Dominicus again. A great man. Perhaps it is good that he did not live to see how sometimes the weak are left alive to totter about, sniveling and puling. I am no monster, Elias. I am Nature's assistant. A gardener of sorts. And I'm very handy with shears.'

I strain against my chains, though I know it will do no good. 'Damn you to the hells!'

But the Warden is already gone. Drusius takes his place, leering. He records my every expression while beyond the locked door, Tas screams.

CHAPTER THIRTY-SEVEN

Laia

The feeling in my bones when I awake in the cellar safe house cannot be regret. But it is not happiness either. I wish I could understand it. I know it will only eat at me until I do, and with so many miles yet to travel, I cannot afford for my focus to erode. Distraction leads to mistakes. And I've made enough of those.

Though I don't want to think that what happened earlier between Keenan and me is one of those mistakes. It was heady. Intoxicating. And filled with a depth of emotion that I did not expect. *Love. I love him.*

Don't I?

When Keenan's back is turned, I swallow the concotion of herbs that Pop taught me about – one that slows a girl's moon cycle so that she cannot get with child.

I look to Keenan, quietly changing into warmer clothing in preparation for the next leg of our journey. He senses my regard and comes over to where I'm lacing my boots. With a shy affection that's so very unlike him, he caresses my cheek. An uncertain smile lights his face.

Are we fools? I want to ask. *For finding comfort in the midst of such madness?* I can't bring myself to say the words. And there's no one else to ask.

A desire to speak to my brother sweeps over me, and I bite my lip angrily to keep my tears at bay. I'm certain Darin had sweethearts before he began apprenticing with Spiro. He would know if this unease, this confusion, was normal.

'What's bothering you?' Keenan pulls me to my feet, holding tight to my hands. 'You don't wish that we didn't—'

'No,' I say quickly. 'I just . . . with everything going on, was it . . . wrong?'

'To find an hour or two of bliss in such dark times?' Keenan says. 'That's not wrong. What is there to live for if not the moments of joy? What is there to fight for?'

'I want to believe in that,' I say. 'But I feel so guilty.' After weeks of keeping my emotions bottled and corked, they explode forth. 'You and I are here, alive, and Izzi is dead, Darin is in prison, Elias is dying—'

Keenan wraps an arm around me and tucks my head beneath his chin. His warmth, his wood-smoke-and-lemon scent soothe me immediately.

'Give me your guilt. I'll hold on to it for you, all right? Because you shouldn't feel this way.' He pulls back just a bit and tips my face up. 'Try to forget the anxiety for a bit.'

It's not that simple! 'Just this morning,' I say, 'you asked me what the point was in being human if I didn't let myself feel.'

'I meant attraction. Desire.' His cheeks go a bit red, and he looks away. 'Not guilt and fear. Those you should try to forget. I could help you forget' – he cocks his head, and heat flashes through me – 'but we should get moving.'

I muster a weak smile, and he releases me. I cast around for Darin's scim, and by the time I buckle it on, I'm frowning again. I don't need a distraction. I need to work out what in the skies is going on in my own head.

Your emotions make you human, Elias said to me weeks ago in the Serran Range. *Even the unpleasant ones have a purpose. If you ignore them, they just get louder and angrier.*

'Keenan.' We start up the cellar stairs, and Keenan unhooks the lock. 'I don't regret what happened. But I can't just will away the guilt.'

'Why not?' he turns back to me. 'Listen—'

We both jump when the cellar door opens with a blistering squeal. Keenan draws, notches, and aims his bow in one motion.

'Hold,' a voice says. The figure raises a lamp. It's a young, curly-haired Scholar. He curses when he sees us.

'I knew I saw someone down here,' he says. 'You need to leave. Master says there's a Martial patrol on the way and they're killing every free Scholar they find—'

We do not hear the rest. Keenan grabs my hand and drags me up the steps and out into the night. 'That way.' He nods at tree line to the east of us, beyond the slaves' quarters, and I fall into a jog as I follow him, my pulse frantic.

We pass through the woods and turn north again, cutting through long, fallow fields. When Keenan spots a stable, he leaves me and disappears. A dog barks, but the sound is suddenly cut off. A few minutes later, Keenan returns, a horse in tow.

I'm about to ask about the dog, but at the grim look on his face, I keep silent.

'There's a trail through those woods up ahead,' he says. 'Doesn't look heavily traveled, and the snow's falling hard enough that our tracks will be covered within an hour or two.'

He pulls me in front of him, and when I keep my body apart, he sighs.

'I don't know what's wrong with me,' I whisper. 'I feel like – like I can't find an equilibrium.'

'You've been carrying too much weight for too long. All this time, Laia, you've led, you've made difficult decisions – and perhaps you weren't ready to. There's no shame in that, and I'll gut anyone who tells me different. You did the best you could. But let go now. Let me carry that weight for you. Let me *help* you. Trust that I'll do the right thing. Have I steered you wrong yet?'

I shake my head. My disquiet returns. *You should believe in yourself more than this, Laia*, a voice within says. *Not every decision you've made has been a bad one.*

But the ones that mattered – the ones where lives hung in the balance – those decisions were wrong. The weight of it *is* crushing.

'Close your eyes,' Keenan says. 'Rest now. I'll get us to Kauf. We'll get Darin out. And all will be well.'

*   *   *

Three nights after we leave the cellar safe house, we stumble upon a half-dug mass grave of Scholars. Men. Women. Children. All tossed carelessly within, like offal. Ahead of us, the snow-capped peaks of the Nevennes Range blot out half the sky. How cruel their beauty seems. Do they not know the evil that has taken place in their shadow?

Keenan quickly urges us past, moving even after the sun is up. When we're well away from the grave and traversing a high, forested bluff, I catch a glimpse of something to the west, in the low hills that lie between us and Antium. Tents, it looks like, and men, campfires. Hundreds of them.

'Skies.' I stop Keenan. 'Do you see that? Aren't those the Argent Hills? It looks like an entire damned army out there.'

'Come on.' Keenan pulls me onward, worry driving his impatience and igniting my own. 'We need to take cover until nightfall.'

But the night only brings more horrors. Hours into our journey, we come so suddenly upon a group of soldiers that I gasp, nearly giving away our position.

Keenan pulls me back with a hiss of breath. The soldiers guard four ghost wagons – so called because once you disappear inside, you might as well be dead. The wagons' high, black sides prevent me from seeing how many Scholars are within. But hands clutch at the bars on the back window, some large and others far too small. More prisoners are loaded into the last wagon as we watch. I think of the grave we passed earlier. I know what will happen to these people. Keenan tries to pull me onward, but I find I am unable to move.

'Laia!'

'We can't just leave them.'

'There are a dozen soldiers and four Masks guarding those wagons,' Keenan says. 'We'd be slaughtered.'

'What if I disappeared?' I look back toward the wagons. I can't stop thinking of those hands. 'The way I did in the Tribal camp. I could—'

'But you can't. Not since . . .' Keenan's reaches out and squeezes my shoulder in sympathy. *Not since Izzi died.*

At the sound of a shout, I turn back to the wagons. A Scholar boy claws at the face of the Mask who drags him forward.

'You can't keep doing this to us!' the boy screams as the Mask tosses him in the wagon. 'We're not animals! One day, we'll fight back!'

'With what?' The Mask chuckles. 'Sticks and rocks?'

'We know your secrets now.' The boy throws himself against the bars. 'You can't stop it. One of your own smiths turned against you, and *we know*.'

The sneer drops off the Mask's face, and he looks almost thoughtful. 'Ah yes,' he says quietly. 'The rats' great hope. The Scholar who stole the secret of Serric steel. He is dead, boy.'

I gasp, and Keenan puts a hand over my mouth, holding me steady as I flail, whispering that I cannot make a sound, that our lives depend on it.

'He died in prison,' the Mask says. 'After we extracted every bit of useful information from his weak, miserable mind. You *are* animals, boy. Less than that, even.'

'He's lying,' Keenan whispers, pulling me bodily from the trees. 'He's doing it to torment that boy. There's no way the Mask could know if Darin was dead.'

'What if he's not lying?' I say. 'What if Darin is dead? You've heard the rumors about him. They're spreading further and further. Maybe by killing him, the Empire thinks they can crush those rumors. Maybe—'

'It doesn't matter,' Keenan says. 'As long as there's a chance that he's alive, then we have to try. Do you hear me? We must keep going. Come on. A lot of ground to cover.'

* * *

Nearly a week after leaving the cellar safe house, Keenan comes trudging back to camp – this one beneath the gnarled, leafless boughs of an oak tree. 'The Commandant has gotten as far as Delphinium,' he says. 'She slaughtered every free Scholar.'

'What about slaves? Prisoners?'

'Slaves were left alone – their masters no doubt protested the loss of property.' He looks ill as he says it. 'She cleared out the prison. Held a mass execution in the city square.'

Skies. The darkness of the night feels deeper and quieter somehow, as if the Reaper walks these trees and every living thing knows it but us. 'Soon,' I say, 'there will be no Scholars left.'

'Laia,' Keenan says. 'She's heading to Kauf next.'

My head jerks up. 'Skies, what if Elias hasn't gotten Darin out? If the Commandant starts killing the Scholars up there —'

'Elias left six weeks ago,' Keenan says. 'And he seemed damned confident. Perhaps he's already broken Darin out. They might be waiting for us in the cave.'

Keenan reaches into his bulging pack. He pulls out a loaf of bread, still steaming, and half a chicken. Skies know what he did to get it. Still, I can't bring myself to eat.

'Do you ever think about those people in the wagons?' I whisper. 'Do you ever wonder what happened to them? Do – do you care?'

'I joined the Resistance, did I not? But I can't dwell, Laia. It accomplishes nothing.'

But it's not dwelling, I think. *It's remembering. And remembering is not nothing.*

A week ago, I'd have said the words out loud. But since Keenan took the yoke of leadership from me, I've felt weaker. Diminished. As if I grow smaller by the day.

I should be thankful to him. Despite the Martial-infested countryside, Keenan has safely avoided every patrol and scouting party, every outpost and watchtower.

'You must be freezing.' His words are soft, but they pull me from my thoughts. I look down in surprise. I still wear the thick black cloak that Elias gave me a lifetime ago in Serra.

I pull the cloak closer. 'I'm all right.'

The rebel rummages around in his bag and eventually pulls

out a heavy, fur-lined winter cloak. He leans forward and gently unhooks my cloak, letting it fall. Then he drapes the other over my shoulders and secures it.

He doesn't mean ill. I know that. Though I've pulled away from him over the past few days, he's been solicitous as ever.

But a part of me wants to fling the cloak off and put Elias's back on. I know I'm acting the fool, but somehow Elias's cloak made me feel good. Perhaps because more than reminding me of him, it reminded me of who I was around him. Braver. Stronger. Flawed, certainly, but unafraid.

I miss that girl. That Laia. That version of myself that burned brightest when Elias Veturius was near.

The Laia who made mistakes. The Laia whose mistakes led to needless death.

How could I forget? I thank Keenan quietly and stuff the old cloak in my bag. Then I pull the new one closer and tell myself that it's warmer.

CHAPTER THIRTY-EIGHT

Elias

The night silence of Kauf Prison is chilling. For it is not a silence of sleep, but of death, of men giving up, letting their lives slip away, of finally allowing the pain to wash over them until they fade to nothingness. At dawn, the children of Kauf will lug out the bodies of those who haven't lasted the night.

In the quiet, I find myself thinking of Darin. He was always a ghost to me, a figure we strained toward for so long that though I never met him, I feel tied to him. Now that he's dead, his absence is palpable, like a phantom limb. When I remember that he's gone, hopelessness washes over me anew.

My wrists bleed from my manacles, and I cannot feel my shoulders; my arms have been outstretched all night. But the pain is a sear, not a conflagration. I've dealt with worse. Still, when the blackness of a seizure falls over me like a shroud, it is a relief.

But it is short-lived, for when I wake in the Waiting Place, my ears are filled with the panicked whispers of spirits – hundreds – thousands – too many.

The Soul Catcher offers me a hand up, her face drawn.

'I told you what would happen in that place.' My wounds aren't visible here, but she winces when she looks at me, as if she can see them anyway. 'Why didn't you listen to me? Look at you.'

'I didn't expect to get caught.' Spirits whirl around us, like flotsam spinning about in a gale. 'Shaeva, what in the ten hells is going on?'

'You shouldn't be here.' Her words are not hostile, as they would have been weeks ago. But they are firm. 'I thought I wouldn't see you until your death. Go back, Elias.'

I feel the familiar pull in my belly but fight it. 'Are the spirits restless?'

'More than usual.' She slumps. 'There are too many. Scholars, mostly.'

It takes me a moment to understand. I feel sick when I do. The whispers I hear – thousands upon thousands – are Scholars murdered by Martials.

'Many move on without my aid. But some are so anguished. Their cries upset the jinn.' Shaeva puts her hand to her head. 'I have never felt so old, Elias. So helpless. In a thousand years as Soul Catcher, I have seen war before. I watched the fall of the Scholars, the rise of the Martials. Still, I have not seen anything like this. Look.' She points to the sky, visible through a space in the Forest canopy.

'The archer and the shield maiden fade.' She points out the constellations. 'The executioner and the traitor arise. The stars always know, Elias. Of late, they whisper only of the approaching darkness.'

Shadows gather, Elias, and their gathering cannot be stopped. Cain spoke those words – and worse – to me just months ago, in Blackcliff.

'What darkness?'

'The Nightbringer,' Shaeva whispers. Fear rolls over her, and the strong, seemingly impervious creature I've become accustomed to vanishes. In her place is a frightened child.

In the distance, the trees glow red. The jinn grove.

'He seeks a way to free his brethren,' Shaeva says. 'He seeks the scattered pieces of the weapon that locked them away here so long ago. Every day he gets closer. I – I sense it, but I cannot *see* him. I can only feel his malice, like the chill shadow of a Nevennes gale.'

'Why do you fear him?' I ask. 'If you're both jinn?'

'His power is a hundred times my own,' she says. 'Some jinn can ride the winds or disappear. Others can manipulate minds, bodies, the weather. But the Nightbringer – he possesses all of these powers. More. He was our teacher, our father, our leader, our king. But . . .' She looks away. 'I betrayed him. I betrayed our people. When he learned of it – skies, in centuries of life, I have never known fear like that.'

'What happened?' I ask softly. 'How did you betray—'

A snarl ripples through the air from the grove. *Ssshhhaeva* . . .

'Elias,' she says, anguished. 'I—'

Shaeva! The snarl is a whipcrack, and Shaeva jumps. 'You've upset them. Go!'

I back away from her, and the spirits jostle and teem around me. One separates from the rest, small and wide-eyed, her eyepatch still part of her, even in death.

'Izzi?' I say in horror. 'What—'

'Be*gone!*' Shaeva shoves me, knocking me back into burning, painful consciousness.

My chains are loose, and I'm curled on the floor, aching and freezing. I feel a fluttering on my arms, and a pair of large, dark eyes regards me, wide and worried. The Scholar boy.

'Tas?'

'The Warden ordered the soldiers to loosen the chains so I could clean your wounds, Elias,' Tas whispers. 'You must stop thrashing.'

Gingerly, I sit up. *Izzi*. It was her. I'm certain of it. But she can't be dead. What happened to the caravan? To Laia? Afya? For once, I want another seizure to take me. I want answers.

'Nightmares, Elias?' Tas's voice is soft, and at my nod, his brow furrows.

'Always.'

'I also have bad dreams.' His gaze skitters briefly to mine before breaking away.

I don't doubt it. The Commandant manifests in my memory, standing outside my jail cell months ago, just before I was set to be beheaded. She caught me in the middle of a nightmare. *I have them too*, she said.

And now, miles and months from that day, I find that a Scholar child condemned to Kauf Prison is no different. So disturbing that the three of us should be linked by this one experience: the monsters crawling through our heads. All the darkness and evil that others perpetrate upon us, all the things we cannot control because we are too young to stop them – they have all stayed with us through the years, waiting in the wings for us to sink to our lowest. Then they leap, ghuls on a dying victim.

The Commandant, I know, is consumed by the darkness. Whatever her nightmares were, she has made herself a thousand times worse.

'Don't let the fear take you, Tas,' I say. 'You're as strong as any Mask as long as you don't let it control you. As long as you fight.'

From the hallway, I hear that familiar cry, the same one I've heard since I was thrown into this cell. It starts as a moan before disintegrating into sobs.

'He is young.' Tas nods in the direction of the tormented prisoner. 'The Warden spends much of his time with him.'

Poor bastard. No wonder he sounds mad half the time.

Tas pours spirits onto my wounded fingernails, and they burn like the hells. I stifle a groan.

'The soldiers,' Tas says. 'They have a name for the prisoner.'

'The Screamer?' I mutter through gritted teeth.

'The Artist.'

My eyes snap to Tas's, the pain forgotten.

'Why,' I ask quietly, 'do they call him that?'

'I have never seen anything like it.' Tas looks away, unnerved. 'Even with blood as his ink, the pictures he draws on the walls – they are so real, I thought they'd – they'd come to life.'

Bleeding, burning hells. It can't be. The legionnaire in the solitary block said he was dead. And I believed him, fool that I am. I let myself forget about Darin.

'Why are you telling me this?' A sudden, horrible suspicion grips me. Is Tas a spy? 'Does the Warden know? Did he put you put to it?'

Tas shakes his head rapidly. 'No – please listen.' He glances at my fist, which, I realized, is clenched. I feel sick that this child would think I'd strike him, and I unfurl it.

'Even here, the soldiers speak of the hunt for the Empire's greatest traitor. And they speak of the girl you travel with: Laia of Serra. And – and the Artist . . . sometimes in his nightmares, he speaks too.'

'What does he say?'

'Her name,' Tas whispers. '*Laia.* He cries out her name – and he tells her to run.'

CHAPTER THIRTY-NINE

Helene

The voices on the wind wrap around me, sending jolts of unease down to my core. Kauf Prison, still two miles distant, makes its presence known through the pain of its inmates.

'About bleeding time.' Faris, waiting at the supply outpost outside the valley, emerges from within. He pulls his fur-lined cloak close, gritting his teeth at the freezing wind. 'I've been here three days, Shrike.'

'There was flooding in the Argent Hills.' A trip that should have taken seven days instead took more than a fortnight. *Rathana* is little more than a week away. *No bleeding time.* I hope my trust in the Cook was not misplaced.

'The soldiers at the garrison there insisted we go around,' I explain to Faris. 'Ten hells of a delay.'

Faris takes the reins of my horse as I swing down. 'Strange,' he said. 'The Hills were blocked off on the east side too, but they told me mudslide.'

'Mudslide because of the flooding, likely. Let's eat, stock up, and start tracking Veturius.'

A blast of warm air from the roaring hearth hits us as we enter the outpost, and I take a seat beside the fire as Faris speaks quietly to the four auxes hovering. As one, they nod vigorously at whatever he's saying, casting nervous glances in my direction. Two disappear into the kitchens while the other two tend to the horses.

'What did you tell them?' I ask Faris.

'That you'd purge their families if they spoke of our presence to anyone.' Faris grins at me. 'I assume you don't want the Warden to know we're here.'

'Good thinking.' I hope we do not need the Warden's aid in tracking Elias. I shudder to think what he'd want in trade.

'We need to scout the area,' I say. 'If Elias is here, he might not have gone in yet.'

Faris's breathing hitches and then continues as before. I glance at him, and he appears suddenly and deeply interested in his meal.

'What is it?'

'Nothing.' Faris speaks far too quickly and mutters a curse when he realizes that I've noticed. He sets down his plate.

'I hate this,' he says. 'And I don't care if the Commandant's spy knows.' He gives Avitas a dark look. 'I hate that we're like dogs hunting a kill, with Marcus cracking his whip at our backs. Elias saved my life during the Trials. And Dex's too. He knew what it felt like . . . after . . .' Faris looks at me accusingly. 'You've never even spoken of the Third Trial.'

With Avitas watching my every move, the wise path would be to give a speech about loyalty to the Empire right now.

But I am too tired. And too sick at heart.

'I hate it too.' I look down at my half-eaten food, my appetite gone. 'Bleeding skies, I hate everything about it. But this isn't about Marcus. It's about the survival of the Empire. If you can't bring yourself to help, then pack your things and go back to Antium. I can assign you to another mission.'

Faris looks away, jaw clenched. 'I'll stay.'

Quietly, I release a sigh. 'In that case' – I pick up my fork again – 'maybe you can tell me why you clammed up when I said we should scout the area for Elias.'

Faris groans. 'Damn it, Hel.'

'You were stationed at Kauf at the same time as him, Lieutenant Candelan,' Avitas says to Faris. 'You, Shrike, were not.'

True – Elias and I ended up at Kauf at different times when we were Fivers.

'Did he go somewhere when things in the prison were too much?' There's an intensity to Avitas that I've rarely seen. 'An . . . escape?'

'A cave,' Faris says after a moment. 'I followed him once when he left Kauf. I thought – skies, I don't know what I thought. Probably something stupid: that he'd found a hidden stash of ale in the woods. But he just sat inside and stared at the walls. I think . . . I think he was trying to forget the prison.'

A great emptiness opens up inside me when Faris says it. Of course Elias would find such a place. He wouldn't be able to bear Kauf without it. It's so like him that I want to laugh and break something at the same time.

Not now. Not when you're so close.

'Take us there.'

*   *   *

At first, I think the cave is a dead end. It looks as if it's been abandoned for years. But we light torches anyway and search every inch of it. Just as I'm about to order us to move out, I catch a glimpse of something glimmering deep within a crack in the wall. When I go to pull it out, I nearly drop it.

'Ten hells.' Faris grabs the bound, crossed scabbards from me. 'Elias's scims.'

'He's here.' I ignore the dread pooling in my stomach – *you'll have to kill him!* – and pretend it is the adrenaline rush of a hunt. 'And recently. The spiders have covered everything else.' I hold up a torch to the webs in the crack.

I look about for signs of the girl. Nothing. 'If he's here, then Laia should be too.'

'And,' Avitas adds, 'if he left all of this here, he can't have believed he'd be gone for long.'

'You're on watch,' I say to Faris. 'Remember, this is Veturius we're dealing with. Keep your distance. Don't engage. I need to go down to the prison.' I turn to Avitas. 'I suppose you'll insist on coming with me?'

'I know the Warden better than you,' he says. 'It is unwise to go barging into the prison. There are far too many of the Commandant's spies inside. If she knows you're here, she'll try to sabotage you.'

I lift my eyebrows. 'You mean she doesn't know I'm here? I assumed you'd told her.'

Avitas says nothing, and as his silence grows longer, Faris shifts uncomfortably beside me. I see the faintest of cracks in Harper's cold façade.

'I'm not her spy anymore,' he finally says. 'If I were, you'd be dead by now. Because you're too close to capturing Elias, and her orders were to kill you quietly when you got this close – to make it look like an accident.'

Faris draws his scim. 'You filthy, traitorous—'

I hold up a hand to stop him and nod for Avitas to continue.

He pulls a thin paper envelope from his fatigues. 'Nightweed,' he says. 'Outlawed in the Empire. Skies only know where Keris got it. A little bit kills you slowly. A little more and your heart expires. The Commandant planned to say that the pressure of the mission was too much for you.'

'You think I'm so easy to kill.'

'No, actually.' The torchlight throws Avitas's masked face into shadow, and for a second, he reminds me of someone I cannot place. 'I've spent weeks figuring out how I'd do it without anyone the wiser.'

'And?'

'I decided I wouldn't do it. As soon as that happened, I began misinforming her about what we were doing and where we were going.'

'Why change your mind? You must have known what the mission would entail.'

'I asked for the mission.' He puts the Nightweed away. 'I told her she needed someone in close proximity to you if she wanted to take you down quietly.'

Faris doesn't sheathe his scim. He's edged forward, his huge body seeming to take up half the cave. 'Why in the bleeding hells would you ask for *this* mission? You've got something against Elias?'

Avitas shakes his head. 'I had . . . a question that needed an answer. Coming with you was the best way to get it.'

I open my mouth to ask him what question, but he shakes his head.

'The question doesn't matter.'

'Of course it bleeding matters,' I snap. 'What could possibly have made you change your alliance? And how am I to know that you won't change it back?'

'I may have been her spy, Blood Shrike.' He meets my eyes, and the crack in his façade grows wider. 'But I have *never* been her ally. I needed her. I needed answers. That is all I will tell you. If you cannot abide that, then send me away – or punish me. Whichever suits you. Just—' He pauses. Is that *anxiety* in his face? 'Don't go into Kauf to speak to the Warden. Send him a message. Get him out of his domain, where he's strongest. Then do what you wish.'

I knew I couldn't trust Harper. I never *have* trusted him. Yet he's come clean now – here, where he has no allies and I have one at my back.

Still, I pinion him with my gaze. He doesn't breathe.

'Double-cross me,' I say, 'and I'll rip your heart out with my bare hands.'

Avitas nods. 'I'd expect no less, Blood Shrike.'

'Right,' I say. 'Regarding the Warden, I'm not a Yearling still wetting the bed, Harper. I know what that monster trades in: secrets and pain disguised as science and reason.'

But he loves his foul little kingdom. He won't want it taken away. I can use that against him.

'Get the old man a message,' I say. 'Tell him I wish to meet in the boathouse tonight. He's to come alone.'

Harper leaves immediately, and when we're sure he's gone, Faris turns to me.

'Please don't tell me you believe he's suddenly on our side.'

'I don't have time to puzzle it out.' I grab Elias's things and shove them back in the crack in the wall. 'If the Warden knows anything about Veturius, he won't share that knowledge for free. He'll want information in return. I have to figure out what I'm going to give him.'

*   *   *

At midnight, Avitas and I slip into Kauf's boathouse. The broad cross-beams of the roof gleam dully in the blue torchlight. The only sound is the occasional slap of the river against the sides of the boats.

Though Avitas asked the Warden to come alone, I still expect him to bring guards. As I peer into the shadows, I loosen my scim and roll my shoulders. The wooden hulls of canoes clank against each other, and outside, the prisoner transports anchored to the boathouse cast long shadows across the windows. A stiff wind rattles the glass.

'You're *sure* he's coming?'

The Northman nods. 'He's very interested in meeting you, Shrike. But—'

'Now, now, Lieutenant Harper, no need to coach our Shrike. She's not a child.'

The Warden, as spindly and pale as an overgrown catacomb spider, slinks out of the darkness on the far side of the boathouse. How long was he skulking there? I force myself not to reach for my scim.

'I have questions, Warden.' *You're a worm. A twisted, pathetic parasite.* I want him to hear the indifference in my voice. I want him to know that he is beneath me.

He stops a few feet away from me, his hands clasped behind his back. 'How may I serve?'

'Have any of your prisoners escaped in the past few weeks? Have you had any break-ins or thefts?'

'No on all counts, Shrike.' Though I watch him carefully, I see no indication that he is lying.

'What about strange activity? Any guards seen where they shouldn't be? Unexpected prisoners coming in?'

'The frigates bring new prisoners all the time.' The Warden

taps his long fingers together thoughtfully. 'I processed one myself quite recently. None, however, have been unexpected.'

My skin tingles. The Warden is telling the truth. But he's hiding something at the same time. I feel it. Beside me, Avitas shifts his weight, as if he too senses something off.

'Blood Shrike,' the Warden says. 'Forgive me, but why are you here, in Kauf, looking for such information? I thought you had rather an urgent mission to find Elias Veturius?'

I draw myself up. 'Do you always ask questions of your superior officers?'

'Do not take offense. I am merely wondering if something might have brought Veturius here.'

I notice how he watches my face for a reaction, and I steel myself for whatever he's going to say next.

'Because if you were willing to tell me why you suspect he is here, then perhaps I might be able to share something . . . useful.'

Avitas glances at me. A warning. *The game begins.*

'For instance,' the Warden says, 'the girl he's traveling with – who is she?'

'Her brother is in your prison.' I offer the information freely – a show of good faith. *You help me, I'll help you.* 'I believe Veturius is attempting to free him.'

The light in the Warden's eyes means I've given him something he wants. For a second, guilt floods me. If the boy *is* in the prison, I've made it far more difficult for Elias to get him out.

'What is she to him, Blood Shrike? What hold does she have over him?'

I take a step toward the old man so he can see the truth in my eyes. 'I don't know.'

Outside the boathouse, the wind picks up. It sighs in the eaves, eerie as a death rattle. The Warden tilts his head, his lashless eyes unblinking.

'Say her name, Helene Aquilla, and I'll tell you something worth your while.'

I exchange a glance with Avitas. He shakes his head. I grip my scim to find that my palms are slick on the hilt. As a Fiver, I spoke to the Warden no more than twice. But I knew – all of the Fivers knew – that he was watching. What did he learn about me in that time? I was a child, only twelve. What *could* he have learned about me?

'Laia.' I allow no inflection in my voice. But the Warden cocks his head in cold assessment.

'Jealousy and anger,' he says. 'And . . . ownership? A connection. Something deeply irrational, I believe. Strange . . .'

A *connection*. The healing – the protectiveness I don't wish to feel. Bleeding skies. He got all of that from one word? I school my face, refusing to let him know what I feel. Still, he smiles.

'Ah,' he says softly. 'I see that I'm correct. Thank you, Blood Shrike. You have given me much. But now I must depart. I don't like to be away from the prison for too long.'

As if Kauf is a new bride he pines for. 'You promised me information, old man,' I say.

'I've already told you what you need to know, Blood Shrike. Perhaps you weren't listening. I thought you would be' – the Warden looks vaguely disappointed – 'smarter.'

The Warden's bootsteps echo in the empty boathouse as he walks away. When I reach for my scim, fully intending to *make* him talk, Avitas grabs my arm.

'No, Shrike,' he whispers. 'He never says anything without reason. Think – he must have given us a hint.'

I don't need bleeding hints! I throw off Avitas's hand, unsheathe my blade, and stride toward the Warden. And as I do, it hits me – the one thing he said that raised the hairs on my neck. *I processed one myself quite recently. Not unexpected, however.*

'Veturius,' I say. 'You have him.'

The Warden stops. I cannot quite see the old man's face as he half turns toward me, but I hear the smile in his voice. 'Excellent, Shrike. Not so disappointing after all.'

CHAPTER FORTY

Laia

Keenan and I crouch behind a fallen log and survey the cave. It doesn't look like much.

'A half mile from the river, surrounded by hemlock trees, east-facing, with a creek to the north and a granite slab turned on its side a hundred yards south.' Keenan nods to each landmark. 'It can't be anyplace else.'

The rebel pulls his hood lower. A small mountain of snow grows on each of his shoulders. The wind whistles around us, flinging bits of ice into our eyes. Despite the fleece-lined boots Keenan stole for me from Delphinium, I cannot feel my feet. But at least the storm covered our approach and muted the prison's haunting moans.

'We haven't seen any movement.' I pull my cloak tight. 'And this storm is getting worse. We're wasting time.'

'I know you think I'm mad,' Keenan says. 'But I don't want us to walk into a trap.'

'There's no one here,' I say. 'We've seen no tracks, no signs of anyone in these woods other than us. And what if Darin and Elias are in there and they're hurt or starving?'

Keenan watches the cave for a second more, then stands. 'All right Let's go.'

When we get close, my body will no longer allow me any caution. I draw my dagger, stride past Keenan, and step warily inside.

'Darin?' I whisper to the darkness. 'Elias?' The cave feels abandoned. But then, Elias would make sure it didn't look like the place was occupied.

A light flares from behind me – Keenan holds up a lamp, illuminating the cobwebbed walls, the leaf-strewn floor. The cave is not large, but I wish it were. Then the sight of its emptiness would not be so crushingly definitive.

'Keenan,' I whisper. 'It doesn't look like anyone's been here in years. Elias might not have even reached here.'

'Look.' Keenan reaches into a deep crack at the back of the cave and pulls out a pack. I grab the lamp from him, my hope flaring. Keenan drops the pack, reaches in deeper, and digs out a familiar set of scims.

'Elias,' I breathe. 'He was here.'

Keenan opens the pack, pulling out what looks like week-old bread and moldering fruit. 'He hasn't been back recently, or he'd have eaten this. And' – Keenan takes the lamp from me and illuminates the rest of the cave – 'there's no sign of your brother. *Rathana* is in a week. Elias should have gotten Darin out by now.'

The wind wails like an angry spirit desperate for release. 'We can shelter here for now.' Keenan drops his own pack. 'The storm is too bad for us to find another camp anyway.'

'But we have to *do* something,' I say. 'We don't know if Elias went in, if he got Darin out, if Darin is alive—'

Keenan takes my shoulders. 'We made it here, Laia. We made it to Kauf. As soon as the storm blows over, we'll find out what happened. We'll find Elias and—'

'No,' a voice speaks from the entrance to the cave. 'You won't. Because he's not here.'

My heart plunges, and I clutch the hilt of my dagger. But when I see the three masked figures standing at the entrance of the cave, I know it will do me little good.

One of the figures steps forward, a half head taller than me, her mask a quicksilver glimmer beneath her furred hood.

'Laia of Serra,' Helene Aquilla says. If the storm outside had a voice, it would be hers, gelid, deathly, and utterly unfeeling.

CHAPTER FORTY-ONE

Elias

Darin is alive. He's in a cell yards from me.

And he's being tortured. Into insanity.

'I need to find a way into that cell,' I muse out loud. Which means I need schedules for guard shifts and interrogations. I need keys for my manacles and Darin's door. Drusius runs this part of the interrogation block; he holds the keys. But he never gets close enough for me to get a good hold on him.

No key. Pins to pick the locks, then. I'd need two —

'I can help you.' Tas's quiet voice cuts into my scheming. 'And — there are others, Elias. The Scholars in the pits have a rebel movement. The Skiritae — dozens of them.'

Tas's words take a long moment to sink in, but once they do, I stare at him, aghast.

'The Warden would skin you — and anyone who helped you. Absolutely not.'

Tas shies like a struck animal at my vehemence. 'You — you said that my fear gives him power. If I help you . . .'

Ten hells. I have enough death on my hands without adding a child to the list.

'Thank you.' I meet his gaze squarely. 'For telling me about the Artist. But I don't need your help.'

Tas gathers up his things and slips toward the door. He pauses there for a moment, looking back at me. 'Elias—'

'So many have suffered,' I say to him, 'because of me. No more. Please go. If the guards hear you and me talking, you'll be punished.'

After he leaves, I stagger to my feet, jerking at the lancing pain in my hands and feet. I force myself to pace, a once thoughtless movement that has, in the absence of the Tellis, transformed into a feat of near-impossible proportions.

A dozen ideas race through my head, each more outlandish than the last. Every single one requires the help of at least one other person.

The boy, a practical voice inside says. *The boy can help you.*

Might as well kill him myself, then, I hiss back at that voice. *It would be a faster death, at least.*

I must do this alone. I only need time. But time is one of the many things I just don't have. Only an hour after Tas leaves, and with no solution in sight, my head spins and my body jerks. *Damn it, not now.* But all my cursing and stern words to myself are for nothing. The seizure drops me – first to my knees and then straight into the Waiting Place.

* * *

'I should just build a bleeding house here,' I mutter as I pick myself up from the snow-covered ground. 'Maybe get a few chickens. Plant a garden.'

'Elias?'

Izzi peers at me from behind a tree, a wasted version of herself. My heart aches at the sight of her. 'I – I hoped you'd come back.'

I look around for Shaeva, wondering why she hasn't helped Izzi move on. When I grasp my friend's hands, she looks down in surprise at my warmth.

'You're alive,' she says dully. 'One of the other spirits told me. A Mask. He said that you walk the worlds of the living and the dead. But I didn't believe him.'

Tristas.

'I'm not dead yet,' I say. 'But it won't be long now. How did you . . .' Is it indelicate to ask a ghost how they died? I am about to apologize, but Izzi shrugs.

'Martial raid,' she says. 'A month after you left. One second I was trying to save Gibran. The next I was here and that woman was standing in front of me . . . the Soul Catcher, welcoming me to the realm of ghosts.'

'What of the others?'

'Alive,' Izzi says. 'I'm not sure how I know, but I'm certain of it.'

'I'm sorry,' I say to her. 'If I had been there, maybe I could have—'

'Stop.' Izzi's eyes flash. 'You always think everyone is your responsibility, Elias. But we're not. We're our own people, and we deserve to make our own decisions.' Her voice trembles with an uncharacteristic anger. 'I didn't die because of you. I died because I wanted to save someone else. Don't you dare take that away from me.'

Immediately after she is done speaking, her wrath dissipates. She looks stunned.

'I'm sorry,' she squeaks. 'This place – it gets inside you. I don't feel

right, Elias. These other ghosts – all they do is cry and wail and—'
Her eye goes dark, and she spins around, snarling at the trees.

'Don't apologize.' Something is holding her back, making her stay here, making her suffer. I feel an almost uncontrollable need to help her. 'You . . . can't move on?'

The branches rustle in the wind, and the whispering of the ghosts in the trees hushes, as if they too wish to hear what Izzi will say.

'I don't want to move on,' she whispers. 'I'm afraid.'

I take her hand in mine and walk, shooting a dark look at the trees. Just because Izzi is dead doesn't mean her thoughts should be eavesdropped upon. To my surprise, the whispers cease, as if the ghosts wish to give us our privacy.

'Are you scared that it will hurt?' I say.

She looks down at her booted feet. 'I don't have family, Elias. I only had Cook. And she's not dead. What if there's no one waiting for me? What if I'm alone?'

'I don't think it's like that,' I say. Through the trees, I see the sparkle of sun on water. 'There's no alone or together on that side. I think it's different.'

'How do you know?'

'I don't,' I say. 'But the spirits can't move on until they've dealt with whatever ties them to the living world. Love or anger, fear or family. So maybe those emotions don't exist on that side. In any case, it will be better than this place, Izzi. This place is haunted. You don't deserve to be stuck here.'

I spy a path ahead, and my body moves to it instinctively. I think of a pale-feathered hummingbird that once hatched in Quin's courtyard, how it would disappear in winter and return in the spring, guided home by some unknowable compass within.

But why do you know this path, Elias, when you've never been to this part of the Forest before?

I brush away the question. Now is not the time for it.

Izzi leans on me as the path leads down to an embankment padded with dried leaves. The trail drops suddenly, and we step down. A slow river whispers at our feet.

'Is this it?' She gazes out at the clear water. The strange, muted sun of the Waiting Place shines in her blonde hair, making it appear almost white. 'Is this where I go on?'

I nod, the answer coming to me as if I've always known it. 'I won't leave until you're ready,' I say. 'I'll stay with you.'

She lifts her dark eye to my face, looking a bit more like her old self again. 'What becomes of you, Elias?'

I shrug. 'I'm' – *fine, good, alive* – 'alone,' I blurt out. Immediately, I feel like a fool.

Izzi tilts her head and puts a ghostly hand to my face. 'Sometimes, Elias,' she says, 'loneliness is a choice.' She fades at the edges, bits of her disappearing as delicately as dandelion fluff. 'Tell Laia I wasn't afraid. She was worried.'

She releases me and steps into the river. One moment she is there, the next she is not, gone before I even raise a hand in farewell. Something lightens within me at her departure, as if a bit of the guilt that plagues me has melted away.

Behind me, I sense another presence. Memories on the air: the clash of practice scims, footraces in the dunes, his laughter at the endless teasing about Aelia.

'You could let go, too.' I don't turn. 'You could be free, like her. I'll help you. You don't have to do it alone.'

I wait. I hope. But Tristas's only response is silence.

* * *

The next three days are the worst in my life. If my seizures take me to the Waiting Place, I am unaware of it. All I know is pain and the Warden's white-blue eyes as he bombards me with questions. *Do tell me about your mother – such a fascinating woman. You were dear friends with the Blood Shrike. Does she feel others' pain as keenly as you do?*

Tas, his little face worried, tries to keep my wounds clean. *I can help you, Elias. The Skiritae can help.*

Drusius softens me up every morning for the Warden – *will never let you get the best of me again, you bastard –*

In whatever bits of lucidity I have left, I gather what information I can. *Don't give up, Elias. Don't fall into the dark.* I listen to the guards' footsteps, the timbre of their voices. I learn to identify them by the little bits of shadow that pass by my door. I figure out their rotations and identify a pattern in the interrogations. Then I search for an opportunity.

None appears. Instead, Death circles, a patient vulture. I feel his crooked shadow approaching, chilling the air I breathe. *Not yet.*

Then one morning, footsteps thud outside my door and keys rattle. Drusius enters my cell to give me my daily beating. Right on schedule. I let my head loll and my mouth hang open. He chuckles to himself and saunters forward. When he's inches away from me, he grabs me by my hair and makes me look at him.

'Pathetic,' he spits in my face. *Swine.* 'I thought you were supposed to be strong. The all-mighty Elias Veturius. You're nothi—'

Stupid man, you forgot to tighten my chains. I drive my knee up, straight between his legs. He squeaks and doubles over, and I chase the blow with a brain-jarring head butt. His eyes go glassy, and he doesn't notice that I've wrapped one of my chains around his neck until his face is already turning blue.

'You,' I snarl at him when he finally passes out, 'talk too damn much.'

I let him down and search his body for keys. I find them and clap my manacles on him in case he wakes up before I want him to. Then I gag him.

I peer out the slats of the door. The other Mask on duty hasn't yet come looking for Drusius. But he will soon enough. I count the sound of that Mask's bootsteps until I'm certain he's well away from me. Then I slip out the door.

The light of the torches stings my eyes, and I squint. My cell is at the end of a short hallway that branches out from the main hallway of the block. This hall has only three cells, and I'm certain that the one next to me is empty. Which leaves only one other cell to check.

My fingers are useless from the torture, and I grit my teeth at the long seconds it takes to paw through the keys. *Hurry, Elias, hurry.*

Finally I find the right key, and moments later, I unlock the door. It squeals wildly, and I turn sideways to squeeze through. It squeals again when I close it, and I curse softly.

Though I was only in the torchlight for a moment, it takes my eyes a bit to adjust to the darkness. At first, I cannot see the drawings. When I do, my breath catches. Tas was right. They do look as if they'll come to life.

The cell is silent. Darin must be sleeping – or unconscious. I take a step toward the emaciated form in the corner. Then I hear the rattle of chains, the pant of harsh breath. A ravaged specter leaps from the darkness, his face inches from my own, bony fingers around my neck. His light hair is missing in chunks from his head, his bruised face is criss-crossed with scars. Two of his fingers are stubs, and his torso is covered in burns. *Ten hells.*

'Who in the *bleeding* skies,' the specter says, 'are you?'

I remove his hands easily from my neck, but for a second, I can't speak. It's him. I know it instantly. Not because he resembles Laia. Even in the dim cell, I can see his eyes are blue, his skin pale. But the fire in his gaze – I've only ever seen that in one other person. And though I expect his eyes to be mad, judging from the sounds I've heard, they appear completely sane.

'Darin of Serra,' I say. 'I'm a friend.'

He responds with a dark chuckle. 'A Martial as a friend? I think not.'

I look over my shoulder at the door. We have no time. 'I know your sister, Laia,' I say. 'I'm here to break you out at her request. We need to go – *now*—'

'You're a liar,' he hisses.

The echo of a footstep outside, then silence. We don't have time for this. 'I can prove it to you,' I say. 'Ask me about her. I can tell you—'

'You can tell me what I told the Warden, which is bleeding *everything* about her. *No stone unturned*, he said.' Darin glares at me with a searing hatred. He must be exaggerating his pain during interrogations so that the Warden believes he is weak, because from that look, it's obvious he's no pushover. Normally I'd approve. But right now, it's damned inconvenient.

'Listen to me.' I keep my voice low but sharp enough to cut through his suspicion. 'I'm not one of them, or else I wouldn't be dressed like this and with wounds of my own.' I bare my arms, marked with cuts from the Warden's latest interrogation. 'I'm a prisoner. I broke in to get you out, but I was caught. Now I have to break us both out.'

'What does he want with her?' Darin snarls at me. 'Tell me what he wants with my sister and maybe I'll believe you.'

'I don't know,' I say. 'Likely he wants to get into your head. Get to know you by asking about her. If you're not answering his questions about the weapons—'

'He hasn't *asked* any questions about the bleeding weapons.' Darin runs a claw across his scalp. 'All he's asked about is *her*.'

'That doesn't make any sense,' I say. 'You were captured because of the weapons. Because of what Spiro taught you about Serric steel.'

Darin goes still. 'How the hells do you know that?'

'I *told* you—'

'I've never told any of them that,' he says. 'As far as they know, I'm a Resistance spy. Skies, do you have Spiro too?'

'Wait.' I hold up a hand, baffled. 'He's *never* questioned you about the weapons? Only about Laia?'

Darin juts his chin out and snorts. 'He must be even more desperate for information than I thought. Did he really think you could convince me that you were a friend of Laia's? Tell him one other thing about her, from me. Laia would *never* ask a Martial for help.'

Footsteps pass in the main hallway. We need to get the hell out of here.

'Did you tell them how your sister sleeps with her hand on your mother's armlet?' I ask. 'Or that up close, her eyes are gold and brown and green and silver. Or that since the day you told her to run, all she has felt is guilt, and all she has thought about is somehow getting to you? Or that she has a fire inside her that's more than a match for any Mask, if only she's willing to believe in it?'

Darin's mouth gapes open. 'Who *are* you?'

'I told you,' I say. 'I'm a friend. And right now, I need to get us out of here. Can you stand?'

Darin nods, limping forward. I put his arm around my shoulders. We shuffle to the door, and I hear the approaching footsteps of a guard. I can tell from the gait that it's a legionnaire – they're always louder than the Masks. I wait impatiently for him to pass.

'What did the Warden ask about your sister?' I say as we wait.

'He wanted to know everything,' Darin says darkly. 'But he felt around for the information. He was frustrated. It was as if he wasn't quite sure what to ask. As if the questions weren't his to begin with. I tried to lie at first. But he always knew.'

'What did you tell him?' The guard is well away now. I reach for the door handle and pull it open with painful slowness, lest it creak.

'Whatever I could to make the pain stop. Stupid things: That she loves the Moon Festival. That she could watch kites fly for hours. That she likes her tea with enough honey in it to choke a bear.'

The pit of my stomach drops away. Those words are familiar. *Why are they familiar?* I turn my attention to Darin in full, and he looks at me uncertainly.

'I didn't think it would help him,' he says. 'He never seemed satisfied, no matter what I told him. Anything I said, he'd demand more.'

It's a coincidence, I tell myself. Then I remember something Grandfather Quin used to say: *Only a jackass believes in coincidence*. Darin's words swirl in my head, linking to things I don't want them to, drawing lines where there should not be any.

'Did you tell the Warden that Laia loves lentil stew in the winter?' I ask. 'That it made her feel safe? Or – or that she didn't want to die without seeing the Great Library of Adisa?'

'I used to tell her about the library all the time,' Darin says. 'She loved hearing about it.'

Words float through my head, snippets of conversation between Laia and Keenan overheard as we traveled. *I've been flying kites*

since I was a boy, he'd once said. *I could watch them for hours. . . .
I would love to see the Great Library one day.* And Laia, that night
before I left, smiling as she drank the too-sweet tea that Keenan
handed her. *Good tea is sweet enough to choke a bear*, he'd said.

No, *bleeding hells*, no. All that time, lurking among us.
Pretending to care about her. Trying to get in good with Izzi.
Acting like a friend when he was really a tool of the Warden.

And his face before I left. That hardness that he never showed
to Laia but that I sensed was there from the beginning. *I know
what it is to do things for the people you love.* Damn it all, *he* must
have told the Warden of my arrival, though how he could have
gotten a message to the old man without using the drums is
beyond me.

'I tried not to tell him anything important,' Darin says. 'I
thought—'

Darin falls silent at the sharp voices of approaching soldiers. I
close the door, and we back up into Darin's cell until they pass.

Only they don't pass.

Instead they turn down the hallway leading to this cell. As I
cast about for some way to defend myself, the door flies open and
four Masks pour in, truncheons raised.

It's not a fight. They are too fast, and I am injured, poisoned,
and starved. I drop – I know when I'm outnumbered, and I can't
withstand any more serious injuries. The Masks desperately want
to use those truncheons to pound my head in, but they don't,
instead cuffing me roughly and yanking me to my feet.

The Warden strolls in, hands behind his back. When he sees
Darin and me confined next to each other, he doesn't appear
surprised.

'Excellent, Elias,' he murmurs. 'Finally, you and I have something worthwhile to discuss.'

CHAPTER FORTY-TWO

Helene

The red-headed Scholar reaches for his scim but halts at the simultaneous hiss of two blades leaving their scabbards. With a slight shift of weight, he eases himself in front of Laia.

She sidesteps him, her glare formidable. She is not the same, frightened child I healed in Blackcliff's slaves' quarters. That bizarre protectiveness grips me, the same emotion I felt for Elias in Nur. I reach out and touch her face. She starts, and Avitas and Faris exchange a glance. Immediately I pull away. But not before I discern from the touch that she is well. Relief sweeps through me – and anger.

Did my healing mean nothing to you?

She had a strange song, this girl, with a fey beauty that raised the hair on the back of my neck. So different from Elias's song. But not discordant. Livia and Hannah took singing lessons – what would they call it? *Countermelody.* Laia and Elias are each other's countermelodies. I am just a dissonant note.

'I know you're here for your brother,' I say. 'Darin of Serra, Resistance spy—'

'He's *not* a—'

I wave off her protestations. 'I don't bleeding care. You'll probably end up dead.'

'I assure you, I won't.' The girl's gold eyes spark, and her jaw is set. 'I made it here despite the fact that you were hunting us.' She takes a step forward, but I give no ground. 'I survived the Commandant's genocide—'

'A few patrols to round up rebels is not—'

'Patrols?' Her face twists in horror. 'You're killing *thousands*. Women. Children. You bastards have an entire skies-forsaken army parked in the Argent Hills—'

'Enough,' the redhead says sharply, but I ignore him, my mind is fixed on what Laia just said.

– *an entire bleeding army* –

– *the Bitch of Blackcliff is planning something.* . . . *It's big this time, girl* –

I need to get out of here. A hunch has taken root in my mind, and I need to consider it.

'I am here for Veturius. Any attempt to rescue him will result in your death.'

'Rescue,' Laia says flatly. 'From – from the prison.'

'Yes,' I say impatiently. 'I don't want to kill you, girl. So stay out of my way.'

I stride from the cave into the heavy snowdrifts, mind churning.

'Shrike,' Faris says when we've nearly reached our camp. 'Don't take off my head, but we can't just leave them alive to carry out an illegal prison break.'

'Every garrison we went to in the Tribal lands was short on soldiers,' I say. 'Even Antium didn't have a full complement of guards for the walls. Why do you think that is?'

Faris shrugs, bewildered. 'The men were sent to the borderlands. Dex heard the same.'

'But my father told me in his letters that the border garrisons needed reinforcements. He said the Commandant requested soldiers too. Everyone is short. Dozens of garrisons, thousands of soldiers. An *army* of soldiers.'

'You mean what the girl said about the Argent Hills?' Faris scoffs. 'She's a Scholar – she doesn't know what she's talking about.'

'The Hills have a dozen valleys big enough to hide an army in,' I say. 'And only one pass in and one pass out. Both of those passes—'

Avitas swears. 'Blocked,' he says. 'By the weather. But those passes are never blocked so early in winter.'

'We were in such a hurry, we didn't think twice about it,' Faris says. 'If there is an army, what is it for?'

'Marcus might be planning to attack the Tribal lands,' I say. 'Or Marinn.' Both options are disastrous. The Empire has enough to deal with without a full-scale war. We reach our camp, and I hand Faris the reins to his horse. 'Find out what's going on. Scout the Argent Hills. I ordered Dex back to Antium. Have him keep the Black Guard at the ready.'

Faris's eyes shift to Avitas, and he tilts his head at me. *You trust him?*

'I'll be all right,' I say. 'Go.'

Moments after he leaves, a shadow steps out from the woods. My scim is half-drawn when I realize it's a Fiver, trembling and half-frozen. He silently hands me a note.

The Commandant arrives this evening to oversee the cleansing of Kauf Prison's Scholar population. She and I will meet at midnight, in her pavilion.

Avitas grimaces at the look on my face. 'What is it?'

'The Warden,' I say. 'Coming out to play.'

*   *   *

By midnight, I ghost along the base of Kauf's high outer wall toward the Commandant's camp, eyeing the friezes and gargoyles that make Kauf almost ornate when compared to Blackcliff. Avitas follows, covering our tracks.

Keris Veturia has erected her tents in the shadow of Kauf's southeast wall. Her men walk the perimeter, and her pavilion sits at the center of the camp, with five yards of clear space on three sides. The tent backs to Kauf's ice-slick wall. No woodpiles, no wagons, not even a bleeding horse to use as cover.

I stop along the far edge of the camp and nod to Avitas. He takes out a grappling hook and heaves it at a pinnacle atop a buttress about forty feet up. The hook catches. He hands me the rope and silently backtracks through the snow.

When I'm ten feet up, I hear the crunch of boots on snow. I turn, expecting to whisper-shout at Avitas for being so damned loud. Instead, a soldier lumbers out from between the tents, unbuttoning his pants to relieve himself.

I scramble for a knife, but my boots, slick with snow, slip on the rope, and I drop the blade. The soldier whirls at the sound. His eyes widen, and he gathers his breath to shout. *Damn it!* I prepare to drop, but an arm wraps around the soldier's throat, choking off his air. Avitas glares up at me as he grapples with the man. *Go!* he mouths.

Swiftly, I snake the rope between my boots and pull myself up hand over hand. Once at the top, I take aim at a second pinnacle thirty feet away, directly over the Commandant's tent. I let the

344

grappling hook fly. When I'm certain it's secure, I tie the rope around my waist and take a deep breath, preparing to drop.

Then I look down.

The stupidest bleeding thing you could have done, Aquilla. Freezing wind whips at me, but sweat rolls down my back anyway. *Don't retch. Commandant wouldn't thank you for spewing sick all over the top of her tent.* My mind flashes to the Second Trial. To Elias's ever-smiling mouth and silver eyes as he roped himself to me. *I won't let you fall. I promise.*

But he's not here. I'm alone, perched like a spider over an abyss. I grab the rope, test it one last time, and jump.

Weightlessness. Terror. My body slams into the wall. I swing wildly – *you're dead, Aquilla.* Then I center myself, hoping the Commandant didn't hear my scrabbling from her tent. I rappel down, slipping easily into the narrow, dark space between the tent and Kauf's wall.

'—and I both serve the same master, Warden. His time has come. Give me your influence.'

'If our master wanted my aid, he would have asked for it. This is your plot, Keris, not his.' The Warden's voice is flat, but its toneless boredom hides a deep wariness. He was not nearly so careful when he and I spoke.

'Poor Warden,' the Commandant says. 'So loyal and yet always the last to know of our master's plans. How it must rankle you that he chose *me* as the instrument of his will.'

'It will rankle me more if your plan jeopardizes all we have worked for. Do not take this risk, Keris. He will not thank you for it.'

'I am speeding the pace at which we carry out his will.'

'You are furthering your own will.'

'The Nightbringer has been gone for months.' The Commandant's chair scrapes back. 'Perhaps he wishes for us to do something useful instead of awaiting his orders like Fivers facing their first battle. We're running out of time, Sisellius. Marcus has garnered fear, if not respect, from the Gens after the Shrike's display on Cardium Rock.'

'You mean after she foiled your plot to foment dissent.'

'The plot would have succeeded,' Keris says, 'if you had helped me. Don't make the same mistake this time. With the Shrike out of the way' – *not yet, you hag* – 'Marcus is still vulnerable. If you would simply—'

'Secrets are not slaves, Keris. They are not meant to be used and cast aside. I will deploy them with patience and precision, or I will not deploy them at all. I must consider your request.'

'Consider quickly.' The Commandant's voice takes on the soft edge known to send men scurrying away in fear. 'My men will march on Antium in three days and arrive on *Rathana*. I must leave by morning. I cannot claim my throne if I'm not leading my own army.'

I put my fist in my mouth to keep from gasping. *My men . . . my throne . . . my army.*

Finally, the pieces fall into place. The soldiers ordered to report elsewhere, leaving garrisons empty. The lack of men in the countryside. The troop shortage on the embattled borders of the Empire. It all leads back to her.

That army in the Argent Hills doesn't belong to Marcus. It belongs to the Commandant. And in less than a week she's going to use it to murder him and declare herself Empress.

CHAPTER FORTY-THREE

Laia

The moment the Blood Shrike is out of earshot, I turn to Keenan. 'I'm not leaving Elias,' I say. 'If Helene gets her hands on him, he'll go straight to Antium for execution.'

Keenan grimaces. 'Laia,' he says. 'It might be too late for that. There is nothing stopping her from walking in and taking custody of him.' He lowers his voice. 'Perhaps we should focus on Darin.'

'I will not leave Elias to die at her hands,' I say. 'Not when I'm the only reason he's in Kauf in the first place.'

'Forgive me,' Keenan says, 'but the poison will take Elias soon, in any case.'

'So you'd leave him to torture and public execution?' I know Keenan has never liked Elias, but I did not think the animosity ran this deep.

The lamplight flickers, and Keenan runs a hand through his hair, brow furrowed. He kicks a few damp leaves out of the way and gestures for me to sit.

'We can get him out too,' I argue. 'We just have to move fast and find a way in. I don't think Aquilla can just walk in and take him out. She would have already done it if that were the case. She wouldn't have bothered to talk to us.'

I roll out Elias's map – dirt-stained and faded now. 'This cave.' I point to a spot Elias marked on the map. 'It's north of the prison, but perhaps we could get inside—'

'We'd need firepowder for that,' Keenan says. 'We have none.'

Fair enough. I point to another path marked on the north side of the prison, but Keenan shakes his head. 'That route is blocked, according to the information I have, which is from six months ago. Elias was last here six *years* ago.'

We stare at the parchment, and I point to the west side of the prison, where Elias marked a path. 'What about this? There are sewers here. And it's exposed, yes, but if I could make myself invisible, like I did during the raid—'

Keenan looks at me sharply. 'Have you been working at that again? When you should have been resting?' When I don't answer, he groans. 'Skies, Laia, we need all of our wits to pull this off. You're exhausting yourself trying to harness something you don't understand – something *unreliable*—'

'Sorry,' I mumble. If all my practice actually amounted to something, then perhaps I could argue that the risk of exhaustion was worth it. And yes, a few times, while Keenan was on watch or off scouting, I felt like I almost grasped that strange, tingling feeling that meant no one could see me. But as soon as I'd open my eyes and look down, I'd see that I'd failed again.

We eat in silence, and when we're done, Keenan stands. I scramble to my feet.

'I'm going to go scout the prison,' he says. 'I'll be gone for a few hours. Let me see what I can come up with.'

'I'll go with—'

'Easier for me to scout alone, Laia,' he says. At the irritated look on my face, he takes my hand and draws me close.

'Trust me,' he says against my hair. His warmth eases away the cold that seems to have taken up residence in my bones. 'It'll be better this way. And don't worry.' He pulls away, his dark eyes searing. 'I'll find us a way in. I promise. Try to rest while I'm gone. We'll need all our strength in the next few days.'

After he leaves, I organize our limited belongings, sharpen all of my weapons, and practice the little that Keenan had a chance to teach me. The desire to try again to discover my power pulls at me. But Keenan's warning echoes in my head. *Unreliable.*

As I unfurl my bedroll, the hilt of one of Elias's scims catches my eye. I gingerly pull the weapons from their hiding spot. As I examine the scims, a chill runs through me. So many souls sundered from the earth at the edges of these blades – some on my behalf.

It's eerie to think of it, and yet I find the scims offer a strange sort of comfort. They *feel* like Elias. Perhaps because I am so used to seeing them poking up behind his head in that familiar V. How long since I saw him reaching back for those scims at the first hint of a threat? How long since I heard his baritone urging me on or drawing a laugh from me? Only six weeks. But it feels like much longer.

I miss him. When I think of what will happen to him at Helene's hands, my blood boils in rage. If I were the one dying of Nightweed poisoning, the one chained in a prison, the one facing torture and death, Elias would not acquiesce. He would find a way to save me.

The scims go back into their scabbards, the scabbards back into their hiding place. I drop into my bedroll with no intention of sleeping. *One more time*, I think to myself. *If it doesn't work, I'll leave it, like Keenan asked. But I owe Elias at least this.*

As I close my eyes and try to forget myself, I think about Izzi. About how she would blend into the Commandant's house like a chameleon, unseen, unheard. She was soft-footed and soft-spoken and she heard and saw everything. Perhaps this is not just about a state of mind but about my body. About finding the quiet version of myself. The Izzi-like version of myself.

Disappear. Smoke into cold air and Izzi with her hair in front of her eyes and a Mask moving stealthily through the night. Quiet mind, quiet body. I keep each word distinct, even when my mind begins to tire.

And then I feel it, a tingling, first at the tip of my finger. *Inhale. Exhale. Don't let it go.* The tingling spreads to my arms, my torso, my legs, my head.

I open my eyes, look down and nearly whoop for joy. Because it's worked. I've done it. I've disappeared.

When Keenan returns to the cave hours later, a bundle tucked under his arm, I jump to my feet and he sighs. 'No rest then, I assume,' he says. 'I have good news and bad.'

'Bad first.'

'I knew you'd say that.' He sets his bundle down and begins to unwrap it. 'Bad news: The Commandant has arrived. Kauf's auxes have started digging graves. From what I heard, not a single Scholar prisoner will be spared.'

My elation at being able to disappear evaporates. 'Skies,' I say. 'All of those people . . .' *We should try to save them.* It's such a mad idea that I know better than to speak it aloud to Keenan.

'They'll begin tomorrow evening,' he says. 'At sundown.'

'Darin—'

'Is going to be fine. Because we're going to get him out before then. I know a way in. *And* I stole these.' He lifts a pile of black cloth from the bundle. Kauf uniforms.

350

'Burgled them from a storage outbuilding. We won't fool anyone up close,' he says. 'But if we can keep far enough away from prying eyes, we can use them to get in.'

'How will we know where Darin is?' I ask. 'The prison is enormous. And once we're inside, how will we move around?'

He pulls another pile of cloth from the bundle. This one dingier. I hear the clink of slaves' cuffs. 'We change,' he says.

'My face is all over the Empire,' I say. 'What if I'm recognized? Or what if—'

'Laia,' Keenan says patiently. 'You have to trust me.'

'Maybe . . .' I hesitate, wondering if he'll be upset. *Don't be stupid, Laia.* 'Maybe we won't need the uniforms. I know you said not to, but I tried the disappearing again. And I've got it.' I pause for his reaction, but he only waits for me to go on. 'I figured it out,' I clarify. 'I can disappear. I can hold it.'

'Show me.'

I frown, having expected . . . *something* from him. Perhaps anger or excitement. But then, he hasn't seen what I can do – he's only seen my failure. I close my eyes and keep my inner voice clear and calm.

But yet again, I fail.

Ten minutes after I begin, I open my eyes. Keenan, waiting calmly, simply shrugs.

'I don't doubt that it works some of the time.' The kindness in his voice only frustrates me. 'But it's not reliable. We can't stake Darin's life on it. Once Darin is free, toy with it all you want. For now, leave it alone.'

'But—'

'Think about the past few weeks.' Keenan fidgets but doesn't pull his gaze away. Whatever he's about to say, he's steeled himself for it. 'If we'd broken away from Elias and Izzi, like I'd suggested,

Elias's Tribe would have been safe. And just before the raid on Afya's camp – it's not that I didn't want to help the Scholars. I *did*. But we should have thought about what would happen as a result. We didn't, and Izzi *died*.'

He says *we*. I know he means *you*. My face feels hot. How dare he throw my failures in my face as if I'm a schoolchild to be reprimanded?

But he's not wrong, is he? Every time I needed to make a decision, I chose wrong. Disaster after disaster. My hand goes to my armlet, but it feels cold – hollow.

'Laia, I haven't cared about anyone in a very long time.' Keenan puts his hands on my arms. 'I don't have family like you do. I don't have anyone or anything.' He traces a finger along my armlet, and a sudden weariness suffuses his movements. 'You're *all* I have. Please, my intent is not to be cruel. I simply don't want anything to happen to you, or to the people who care for you.'

He *must* be wrong. The disappearing is at my fingertips – I can feel it. If only I could figure out what's blocking me. If I could remove that one obstacle, it would change everything.

I force myself to nod and repeat the words he's said to me before, when he's given in.

'Your will, then.' I look at the uniforms he's brought, at the resolve in his eyes. 'Dawn?' I ask.

He nods. 'Dawn.'

CHAPTER FORTY-FOUR

Elias

When the Warden enters my cell, his mouth is turned downward, his brow furrowed, as if he's encountered a problem that none of his experiments can solve.

After pacing back and forth a few times, he speaks. 'You will answer my questions completely and in detail.' He lifts his white-blue eyes to me. 'Or I will cut off your fingers one by one.'

His threats are usually far less blunt – one of the reasons he enjoys extracting secrets is the games he plays as he does so. Whatever he wants of me, he must want it badly.

'I know that Darin's sister and Laia of Serra are one and the same. Tell me: Why did you travel with her? Who is she to you? Why do you care for her?'

I keep the emotion from my face, but my heart thuds uncomfortably fast. *Why do you want to know?* I want to scream. *What do you want with her?*

When I don't immediately answer, the Warden takes a knife from his fatigues and spreads my fingers flat against the wall.

'I have an offer for you,' I say quickly.

He raises his eyebrows, the knife inches from my forefinger. 'If you examine the facts, Elias, you'll see that you are in no position to make offers.'

'I won't need fingers or toes or anything else for much longer,' I say. 'I'm dying. So a deal: I'll answer any question you put to me honestly if you do the same.'

The Warden appears genuinely mystified. 'What information could you possibly use at death's door, Elias? Oh.' He grimaces. 'Skies, don't tell me. You want to know who your father is?'

'I don't care who my father is,' I say. 'In any case, I'm certain you don't know.'

The Warden shakes his head. 'How little faith you have in me. Very well, Elias. Let us play your game. A slight adjustment to the rules, however: I ask all my questions first, and if I'm satisfied with your answers, you may ask me one – and only one – question.'

It's a terrible deal, but I have no other options. If Keenan plans to double-cross Laia on the Warden's behalf, I must know why.

The Warden leans out the cell door and barks at a slave to bring him a chair. A Scholar child carries it in, her gaze flitting to me with brief curiosity. I wonder if it's Bee, Tas's friend.

At the Warden's prompting, I tell him about how Laia saved me from execution and about how I vowed to help her. When he presses, I tell him that I came to care for her after seeing her at Blackcliff.

'But *why*? Does she possess some peculiar knowledge? Is she, perhaps, gifted with power that is beyond human ken? What specifically makes you value her?'

I'd filed away Darin's observations about the Warden, but now they come back to me: *He was frustrated. It was as if he wasn't quite sure what to ask. As if the questions weren't his to begin with.*

Or, I realize, as if the Warden has no idea why he's even asking the questions.

'I've only known the girl for a few months,' I say. 'She's smart, brave—'

The Warden sighs and waves a dismissive hand at me. 'I do not care for moon-eyed blathering,' he says. 'Think with your *rational* mind, Elias. Is there anything unusual about her?'

'She's survived the Commandant,' I say, impatient now. 'For a Scholar, that's quite unusual.'

The Warden leans back, stroking his chin, gaze far away. 'Indeed,' he says. 'How *did* she survive? Marcus was supposed to have killed her.' He fixes me with an appraising stare. The freezing cell suddenly feels colder. 'Tell me about the Trial. Exactly what happened in the amphitheater?'

It's not the question I expected, but I relate what happened. When I describe Marcus's attack on Laia, he stops me.

'But she survived,' he says. 'How? Hundreds of people saw her die.'

'The Augurs tricked us,' I say. 'One of them took the hit meant for Laia. Cain named Marcus victor. In the chaos, his brethren took Laia away.'

'And then?' the Warden says. 'Tell me the rest. Leave nothing out.'

I hesitate, because something about this seems wrong. The Warden stands, flings open the cell door, and calls for Tas. Footsteps patter, and a second later, he yanks Tas in by the scruff of his neck and puts his knife to the boy's throat.

'You are correct when you say that you will soon die,' the Warden says. 'This boy, however, is young and relatively healthy.

Lie to me, Elias, and I show you his insides while he still lives. Now, I'll say it again: Tell me everything that happened with the girl after the Fourth Trial.'

Forgive me, Laia, if I give away your secrets. I swear it's not for nothing. I watch the Warden carefully as I speak about Laia's destruction of Blackcliff, our escape from Serra, and all that happened after.

I wait to see if he reacts to my mention of Keenan, but the old man gives no sign that he knows any more about the rebel than what I'm telling him. My gut tells me his disinterest is genuine. *What the bleeding hells?* Perhaps Keenan isn't working for the Warden. And yet from what Darin told me, it's obvious that they are somehow communicating. Could they both be reporting to someone else?

The old man shoves Tas away, and the child cowers on the floor, waiting to be dismissed. But the Warden is deep in thought, methodically filing away relevant facts from the information I've given him. Sensing my gaze, he pulls himself from his musings.

'You had a question, Elias?'

An interrogator can learn as much from a statement as from a question. My mother's words coming to aid me when I least expect it.

'The questions you asked Darin about Laia,' I say. 'You don't know their purpose. Someone else is pulling your strings.' I watch the Warden's mouth, for that is where he hides his truths, in twitches of those dry, too-thin lips. As I speak, his mouth tightens almost imperceptibly. *Got you.* 'Who is it, Warden?'

The Warden stands so quickly that he knocks his chair over. Tas quickly lugs it out of the cell. My chains loosen when the Warden yanks down the lever on the wall.

'I answered everything you asked of me,' I say. Ten hells, why am I even trying? I was a fool to think he'd honor his vow. 'You're not upholding your end of the bargain.'

The Warden pauses at the cell's threshold, his face half-turned toward me, unsmiling. The torchlight in the hallway deepens the grooves in his cheeks and jaw. For a moment, it's as if I can see the stark outline of his skull beneath.

'That's because you asked *who* it is, Elias,' the Warden says. 'Instead of *what*.'

CHAPTER FORTY-FIVE

Laia

Like so many nights before this one, rest is elusive. Keenan sleeps beside me, arm thrown across my hip, his forehead tipped down against my shoulder. His quiet breathing almost lulls me into dreams, but every time I get close, I jerk awake and fret anew.

Does Darin live? If so, and if I *can* save him, how will we make it to Marinn? Will Spiro be waiting there, as he promised? Will Darin even *want* to make weapons for the Scholars?

What of Elias? Helene might already have him. Or he might be dead, destroyed by the poison coursing through his body. If he does live, I do not know if Keenan will help me save him.

But I *must* save him. And I cannot leave the other Scholars either. I cannot abandon them to be executed in the Commandant's purge.

They'll begin tomorrow evening. At sundown, Keenan said of the executions. A bloody gloaming then, and bloodier still as twilight fades to night.

I ease Keenan's arm away and roll to my feet, pulling on my cloak and boots and slipping out into the cold night.

A nagging dread steals over me. Keenan's plan is as unknowable as the inside of Kauf itself. His confidence offers some reassurance, but not enough to make me feel like we will succeed. Something about all of this just feels wrong. Rushed.

'Laia?' Keenan emerges from the cave, his red hair mussed, making him look younger. He offers his hand, and I wind my fingers through his, taking comfort from his touch. What a change a few months has wrought in him. I could not have imagined such a smile from the dark-visaged fighter I first met in Serra.

Keenan looks at me and frowns.

'You're nervous?'

I sigh. 'I cannot leave Elias.' Skies, I hope I'm not wrong again. I hope that pushing this, fighting for it, doesn't lead to some other disaster. An image of Keenan lying dead floats through my mind, and I fight back a shudder. *Elias would do it for you. And going into Kauf is a terrible risk no matter what.* 'I *will not* leave him.'

The rebel tilts his head, his eyes on the snow. I hold my breath.

'Then we must find a way to get him out,' he says. 'Though it will take longer—'

'Thank you.' I lean into him, breathing in wind and fire and warmth. 'It's the right thing to do. I know it is.'

I feel the familiar pattern of my armlet against my palm and realize that, as ever, my hand has drifted to it for comfort.

Keenan watches me, his eyes strange. Lonely.

'What is it like to have something of your family's?'

'It makes me feel close to them,' I say. 'It gives me strength.'

He reaches out, almost touching the armlet but then self-consciously dropping his hand. 'It's good to remember those who are lost. To have a reminder in the dark times.' His voice is soft. 'It's good to know that you were . . . are . . . loved.'

My eyes fill. Keenan has never spoken of his family other than to tell me that they are gone. At least I had a family. He has had nothing and no one.

My fingers tighten on my armlet, and on impulse, I pull it off. At first, it is as if it doesn't *want* to come off, but I give it a good yank, and it releases.

'I'll be your family now,' I whisper, opening Keenan's hands and placing the armlet on his palm. I close his fingers around it. 'Not a mother, father, brother, or sister, perhaps, but family nonetheless.'

He breathes in sharply, staring down at the armlet. His brown eyes are opaque, and I wish I knew what he felt. But I allow him his silence. He pulls the armlet onto his wrist with slow reverence.

A chasm opens up inside me, as if the last bit of my family is gone. But I take comfort from the way Keenan looks at the armlet, as if it's the most precious thing he's ever been given. He turns to me and rests his hands on my waist, closing his eyes, leaning his head against mine.

'Why?' he whispers. 'Why did you give it to me?'

'Because you are loved,' I say. 'You're not alone. And you deserve to know that.'

'Look at me,' he murmurs.

When I do, I flinch, pained to see his eyes so anguished – haunted – like he's seeing something he doesn't wish to accept. But a moment later, his expression changes. Hardens. His hands, gentle a moment ago, tighten and grow warm.

Too warm.

The irises of his eyes brighten. I see myself reflected within, and then I feel as if I'm falling into a nightmare. A scream claws its way out of my throat, for in Keenan's eyes I see ruin, failure, death: Darin's mangled body; Elias turning away from me, impassive as he disappears into an ancient forest; an army of fiery, enraged faces advancing; the Commandant standing over me, drawing her blade across my throat in one clean, deadly stroke.

'Keenan,' I gasp. 'What—'

'My name' – his voice changes as he speaks, his warmth souring, twisting into something foul and grating – 'is not Keenan.'

He jerks his fingers away, and his head is flung back as if by an otherworldly fist. His mouth opens in a silent howl, the muscles of his forearms and neck bulging.

A cloud of darkness breaks over us both, knocking me back. 'Keenan!'

I cannot make out the crisp whiteness of the snow or the undulating lights in the sky. I lash out blindly at whatever attacks us. I can't *see* anything. All is obscured until the blackness curls back from the edges of my vision, slowly resolving into a hooded figure with malevolent suns for eyes. I take hold of a nearby tree trunk and grab for my knife.

I know this figure. The last I saw him, he was hissing orders at the woman who frightens me most in this world.

Nightbringer. My body trembles – I feel as though some hand has taken me by my core and now squeezes, waiting to see when I will break.

'What in the bleeding skies did you do with Keenan, you monster?' I must be mad to scream at him so. But the creature only laughs, impossibly low, like boulders grinding beneath a black sea.

'There was no Keenan, Laia of Serra,' the Nightbringer says. 'There was only ever me.'

'*Lies.*' I clutch my knife, but the hilt burns hot as fresh-forged steel, and I drop it with a yelp. 'Keenan has been with the Resistance for years.'

'What are years when one has lived for millennia?' At the look

361

of dumb shock on my face, the thing – the jinn – lets out a strange sound. It might be a sigh.

Then it turns, whispering something into the air, slowly rising up, as if to depart. *No!* I lunge forward and grab on to him, desperate to understand what in the skies is happening.

Beneath the robe, the creature's body is burning hot, powerful, with the warped musculature of a demon instead of a man. The Nightbringer tilts his head. He has no face, only those damned fiery eyes. Still, I can sense him sneering.

'Ah, the little girl has fight in her after all,' he says. 'Just like her stone-hearted bitch of a mother.'

He shakes me, attempting to free himself, but I hold tight, even while squelching my revulsion at touching him. An unknown darkness rises within me, some atavistic part of myself that I did not know existed.

The Nightbringer, I sense, is no longer amused. He jerks away hard. I make myself hold on.

What did you do to Keenan – the Keenan I knew? The Keenan I loved? I scream in my mind. *And why?* I glare into his eyes, the darkness rising, taking over. I sense alarm from the Nightbringer, and surprise. *Tell me! Now!* Quite suddenly, I am weightless as I fly into the chaos of the Nightbringer's mind. Into his memories.

At first, I see nothing. I only feel . . . sadness. An ache that he's buried beneath centuries of life. It permeates every part of him, and though I am bodiless, my mind nearly collapses from the weight of it.

I force myself through it, and I stand in a cold alley in Serra's Scholar quarter. Wind bites through my clothing, and I hear a strangled cry. I turn to find the Nightbringer changing, screaming in pain as he uses all his power to morph into a redheaded child of five. He staggers out of the alley and into the street beyond, collapsing on the stoop of a dilapidated house. Many seek to help him, but he does not speak to anyone. Not until an achingly familiar dark-haired man stops and kneels beside him.

My father.

He scoops up the child. The memory shifts to an encampment deep in a canyon. Resistance fighters eat, chatter, train with weapons. Two figures sit at a table, and my heart drops when I see them: my mother and Lis. They welcome my father and the redheaded child. They offer him a plate of stew and tend his wounds. Lis gives him a wooden cat that Father carved for her, and she sits beside him so he is not afraid.

Even as the memory shifts again, I think back to a cold and rainy day in the Commandant's kitchen months ago, when Cook told Izzi and me a story about the Nightbringer. *'He infiltrated the Resistance. Took human form and posed as a fighter. Got close to your mother. Manipulated and used her. Your father caught on. Nightbringer had help. A traitor.'*

The Nightbringer didn't have help, and he didn't pose as a fighter. He *was* the traitor, and he posed as a child. For no one would think a young, starving orphan could be a spy.

A snarl echoes in my mind, and the Nightbringer tries to fling me from his thoughts. I feel myself returning to my body, but the darkness within roars and fights, and I do not let myself release him.

No. You will show me more. I need to understand.

Back in the creature's memories, I see him befriend my lonely sister. I grow uneasy at their friendship – it seems so real. As if he truly cares about her. At the same time, he wheedles information from her about my parents: where they are, what they are doing. He stalks my mother, his covetous eyes fixed on her armlet. His hunger for it is like that of a starving animal in its potency. He doesn't want it. He *needs* it. He must get her to give it to him.

But one day, my mother arrives at the Resistance encampment without the armlet. The Nightbringer has failed. I feel his fury, overlaid by that yawning sadness. He arrives in a torch-lit barracks and speaks to a familiar silver-faced woman. Keris Veturia.

He tells Keris where she can find my parents. He tells her what they will be doing.

Traitor! You led them to their deaths! I rage at him, forcing myself further into his mind. *Why? Why the armlet?*

I fly with him deep into the past, streaming along the winds to the far-flung Forest of Dusk. I feel his desperation and panic for his people. They face a grave danger at the hands of a Scholar coven bent on stealing their power, and he cannot get to them fast enough. *Too late*, he howls in the memory. *I am too late.* He cries out the names of his kin as a shock wave ripples out from the center of the Forest, throwing him into darkness.

An explosion of pure silver – a Star, the Scholars' weapon – used to imprison the jinn. I expect it to disintegrate – I know the story. But it does not. Instead, it shatters into hundreds of shards flung across the land. Shards that are picked up by Mariners and Scholars, Martials and Tribesmen. Fashioned into necklaces and armlets, spearheads and blades.

The Nightbringer's rage steals my breath. For he cannot simply take back these pieces. Each time he finds one, he must ensure that it is offered freely, in absolute love and trust. For that is the only way he can reassemble the weapon that imprisoned his people, so he might set them free again.

My stomach churns as I hurtle through his memories, watching as he transforms himself into husband or lover, son or brother, friend or confidant – whatever is necessary to get the lost shards.

He *becomes* whomever he transforms into. He creates them – he *is* them. He feels what a human would feel. Including love.

And then I watch as he discovers me.

I see myself through his eyes: a nobody, a naïve little girl come to beg the Resistance for aid. I watch as he realizes who I am and what I possess.

It is torture to witness how he deceived me. How he used information stolen from my brother to win me over, to get me to trust him, to care for him. In Serra, he'd been close – so close – to getting me to fall for him. But then I gave Izzi the freedom he'd offered me, and I disappeared with Elias. And his carefully wrought plan fell to pieces.

And all the while, he had to keep his cover among the Resistance in order to carry out a plan months in the making: persuading the rebels to kill the Emperor and rise up in the Scholar revolution.

Two actions that allowed the Commandant to unleash an unchecked genocide upon my people. It was the Nightbringer's revenge for what the Scholars did to his kin centuries before.

Bleeding skies.

A hundred little things suddenly make sense: How cold he was when he first met me. How well he seemed to know me, even when I hadn't told him about myself. How he used his voice to soothe me. How strange the weather was when Elias and I first set out from Serra. How the attacks on us by supernatural creatures stopped after he arrived with Izzi.

No, no, you liar, you monster –

As soon as I think it, I sense something deep within him that underlies every memory and shakes me to my core: a sea of regret he strives to hide, stirred into madness as if by some great tempest. I see my own face, then Lis's face. I see a child with brown braids and an ancient silver necklace. I see a smiling, crook-backed Mariner holding a silver-topped cane.

Haunted. It is the only word to describe what I see. The Nightbringer is haunted.

As the full weight of what this creature is rolls over me, I gasp, and he casts me from his mind – and his body. I fly back a dozen feet, slamming into a tree and sinking to the ground, breathless.

My armlet glimmers on his tenebrous wrist. The silver – tarnished black for most of my life – gleams now, as if made of starlight.

'What in the skies are you?' he hisses. The words trigger a memory: the efrit back in Serra, asking me the same thing. *You say what am I, but what are you?*

A frosty night wind blows into the clearing, and the Nightbringer rises up on it. His eyes are still fixed on me, hostile and curious. Then the wind whooshes past, taking him with it.

The woods are silent. The skies above are still. My heart thuds as madly as a Martial war drum. I close my eyes and open them, waiting to wake up from this nightmare. I reach for my armlet, needing the comfort it offers, the reminder of who I am, what I am.

But it is gone. I am alone.

PART FOUR

UNMADE

CHAPTER FORTY-SIX

Elias

'You're getting close, Elias.'

When I fall into the Waiting Place, Shaeva stares at me. There is a crispness to her – to the trees and the sky – that makes it seem as if this is my reality and the waking world is the dream.

I look around curiously – I have only ever woken up amid the thick trunks of the Forest. But this time, I stand atop a rocky bluff that overlooks the trees. The River Dusk surges below, blue and white beneath the bright winter sky.

'The poison is nearly to your heart,' Shaeva says.

Death so soon. 'Not yet,' I make myself say through numb lips, squelching the fear that threatens. 'I need to ask you something. I beg you, Shaeva, hear me out.' *Pull it together, Elias. Make her understand how important this is.* 'Because if I die before I'm ready, I will haunt these damn trees forever. You'll never be rid of me.'

Something crosses her face, a flicker of disquiet that fades in less than a second.

'Very well,' she says. 'Ask.'

I consider all that the Warden told me. *Who*, he'd said. *Not what.*

No human controls the Warden. It must be one of the fey. But I cannot imagine a wraith or efrit manipulating the Warden. Such weak creatures could not best him in a battle of wits – and he spits upon those he perceives to have a weaker intellect than him.

But then, not all fey creatures are wraiths or efrits.

'Why would the Nightbringer be interested in a seventeen-year-old girl traveling to Kauf to break her brother out of prison?'

The color drains from the Soul Catcher's face. Her hand flutters at her side, as if she is trying to catch herself on a bulwark that doesn't exist.

'Why would you ask such a thing?'

'Just answer.'

'Because – because she has something he wants,' the Soul Catcher sputters. 'But he cannot possibly *know* she has it. It has been hidden for years. And he has been dormant.'

'Not as dormant as you'd like. He's in league with my mother,' I say. 'And the Warden. The old man has been passing information about Laia to someone traveling with us. A Scholar rebel.'

Shaeva's eyes widen fearfully, and she steps forward, reaching out.

'Take my hands, Elias,' she says. 'And close your eyes.'

Despite the urgency of her tone, I hesitate. At my obvious wariness, the Soul Catcher's mouth hardens, and she springs forward to grab me. I yank my hands back, but her fey reflexes are swifter.

When she takes hold, the earth beneath me twitches. I stumble as a thousand doors in my mind fly open: Laia telling me her story in the desert outside Serra; Darin speaking of the Warden; Keenan's oddities, the fact that he tracked me when he shouldn't have been able to; the rope between Laia and me that came apart in the desert . . .

The Soul Catcher fixes her black eyes on me and opens her own mind. Her thoughts pour into my head in a white-water rush, and when she is done, she takes my memories and her knowledge and lays the fruit of that union at my feet.

'Bleeding, burning hells.' I stumble back from her and catch myself on a boulder, finally understanding. *Laia's armlet – the Star.* 'It's him – Keenan. He's the Nightbringer.'

'Do you see it, Elias?' the Soul Catcher asks. 'Do you see the web he spun to ensure his revenge?'

'Why the games?' I push up from the boulder and pace across the bluff. 'Why not just kill Laia and take the armlet?'

'The Star is bound by unbreakable laws. The knowledge that led to its creation was given in love – in trust.' She looks away, shame in her eyes. 'It is an old magic meant to limit any evil the Star might be used for.' She sighs. 'Much good it has done.'

'The jinn living within your grove of trees,' I say. 'He wants to free them.'

Shaeva's eyes are troubled as she stares down into the river below. 'They should not be free, Elias. The jinn were creatures of light once. But as with any living thing that is jailed for too long, their imprisonment has driven them mad. I have tried to tell this to the Nightbringer. Of all the jinn, he and I are the only two who still walk this land. But he does not listen to me.'

'We have to do something,' I say. 'When he gets the armlet, he'll kill Laia—'

'He cannot kill her. All who have been given the Star, even if only for a few moments, are protected from him by its power. He can't kill you either.'

'But I never . . .' *Touched it*, I was going to say, until I realize that I asked Laia if I could see it months ago, in the Serran Range.

'The Nightbringer must have ordered the Warden to kill you,' Shaeva says. 'But his human slaves are not as obedient, perhaps, as he would like.'

'The Warden didn't care about Laia,' I realize. 'He wanted to understand the Nightbringer better. '

'My king confides in no one.' The Soul Catcher shivers at the crisp air. For a moment, she looks barely older than me. 'The Commandant and the Warden are likely his only allies – he does not trust humans. He will have told them nothing of the armlet or the Star, lest they find a way to turn the knowledge against him.'

'What if Laia had died some other way?' I ask. 'What would have happened to her armlet?'

'Those who bear pieces of the Star do not die easily,' Shaeva says. 'It protects them, and he knows that. But if she had, the armlet would have evanesced into nothingness. The Star's power would have weakened. It has happened before.'

She puts her head in her hands. 'No one understands how deep his hatred for humans runs, Elias. If he frees our brethren, they will search out the Scholars and annihilate them. They will turn on the rest of humanity. Their bloodlust will know no reason.'

'Then we stop him,' I say. 'We get Laia away before he can take the armlet.'

'I cannot stop him.' Shaeva's voice rises in impatience. 'He will not *let* me. I cannot leave my lands—'

'SHAEVA.'

A tremor rolls through the Forest, and Shaeva twists around. 'They know,' she hisses. 'They'll punish me.'

'You can't just leave. I have to find out if Laia's all right. You could help me—'

'No!' Shaeva rears back. 'I can have nothing to do with this. *Nothing*. Don't you see? He—' She reaches for her throat and grimaces. 'The last time I crossed him, he killed me, Elias. He forced me to suffer the torture of a slow death, and then he *brought me back*. He released the sorry creature that had ruled the land of death before me, and he chained me to this place as punishment for what I did. I live, yes, but I am a slave to the Waiting Place. That is *his* doing. If I cross him again, skies know what he will inflict upon me. I am sorry – more sorry than you can know. But I have *no* power over him.'

I lunge for her, desperate to *make* her help me, but she spins out of my grasp and darts down the bluff, disappearing within seconds into the trees.

'Shaeva, damn it!' I start after her, swearing when I realize how futile it is.

'Aren't you dead yet?' Tristas emerges from the trees as the Soul Catcher disappears. 'How much longer are you planning to cling to your miserable existence?'

I should ask you the same. But I do not, for instead of the malice I've come to expect from Tristas's ghost, his shoulders slump, as if an invisible boulder rests on his back. Distracted as I am, I order myself to turn my full attention to my friend. He looks drawn and desperately unhappy.

'I'll be here soon enough,' I say. 'I have until *Rathana*. That's six days away.'

'*Rathana*.' Tristas wrinkles his forehead in thought. 'I remember last year. Aelia proposed to me that night. I sang all the way home, and you and Hel gagged me so the Centurions wouldn't hear. Faris and Leander teased me for weeks.'

'They were just jealous that you'd met a girl who truly loved you.'

'You defended me,' Tristas says. Behind him, the Forest is still, as if the Waiting Place holds its breath. 'You always did.'

I shrug and look away. 'That doesn't undo the evil I've done.'

'Never said it did.' Tristas's ire returns. 'But you're not the judge, are you? It's *my* life you took. It's *my* choice whether I wish to forgive you or not.'

I open my mouth, about to tell him that he shouldn't forgive me. Instead I think of Izzi's reprimand. *You always think everyone is your responsibility. . . . We're our own people, and we deserve to make our own decisions.*

'You're right.' Hells, it's hard to say. Harder to make myself believe. But as I speak, the anger clears from Tristas's eyes. 'All your choices have been taken from you. Except this one. I'm sorry.'

Tristas cocks his head. 'Was that so hard?' He walks to the edge of the bluff and peers down at the River Dusk. 'You said I didn't have to do it alone.'

'You *don't* have to do it alone.'

'I could say the same to you.' Tristas puts a hand on my shoulder. 'I forgive you, Elias. Forgive yourself. You still have time left among the living. Don't waste it.'

He turns and leaps off the bluff in a perfect dive, his body fading. The only sign of his passing is a slight ripple in the river.

I could say the same to you. The words kindle a flame within me, and the thought that first flickered to life with Izzi's words now grows into a blaze.

Afya's strident assertion sounds in my head: *You shouldn't just leave, Elias. You should ask Laia what she wants.* Laia's angry pleadings: *You close yourself up. You shut me out because you don't want me to get close. What about what I want?*

Sometimes, Izzi had said, *loneliness is a choice.*

374

The Waiting Place fades. When cold seeps into my bones, I know I am back in Kauf.

I also know exactly how I can get Darin out of this damned place. But I can't do it alone. I wait – planning, plotting – and when Tas enters my cell the morning after I learn the truth about Keenan, I am ready.

The boy keeps his head down, shuffling toward me as timid as a mouse. His skinny legs are marked with a fresh whipping. A dirty bandage encircles his frail wrist.

'Tas,' I whisper. The boy's dark eyes snap up. 'I'm getting out of here,' I say. 'I'm taking the Artist with me. And you too, if you wish. But I need help.'

Tas bends over his crate of bandages and ointments, his hands shaking as he changes a poultice on my knee. For the first time since I've met him, his eyes shine.

'What do you need me to do, Elias Veturius?'

CHAPTER FORTY-SEVEN

Helene

I do not recall hauling myself back up Kauf's outer wall or making my way to the boathouse. I only know that it takes longer than it should because of the anger and disbelief clouding my sight. When I arrive within the cavernous structure, dazed by what I've just learned about the Commandant, the Warden awaits me.

This time, he's not alone. I sense his men lurking in the corners of the boathouse. Glints of silver catch the blue torchlight – Masks, with arrows pointed at me.

Avitas stands beside our boat, one wary eye turned toward the old man. His clenched jaw is the only sign that he's upset. His anger calms me – at least I am not alone in my frustration. As I approach, Avitas meets my gaze and nods curtly. The Warden has filled him in.

'Don't help the Commandant, Warden,' I say without preamble. 'Don't give her the influence she wants.'

'You surprise me,' the Warden says. 'Are you so loyal to Marcus that you would reject Keris Veturia as Empress? It's foolish to do so. The transition would not be seamless, but in time the populace would accept her. She did, after all, crush the Scholar revolution.'

'If the Commandant was meant to be Empress,' I say, 'the Augurs would have chosen her instead of Marcus. She does not know how to negotiate, Warden. The second she takes power, she'll punish every Gens who has ever crossed her, and the Empire will fall to civil war, as it nearly did just weeks ago. Besides, she wants to kill you. She said as much in front of me.'

'I am well aware of Keris Veturia's dislike,' he says. 'Irrational, when one considers that we serve the same master, but she is, I believe, threatened by my presence.' The Warden shrugs. 'Whether I aid her or not makes no difference. She will still launch the coup. And it is very possible that it will succeed.'

'Then I must stop her.' And now we've come to it: the crux of our discussion. I decide to forgo subtlety. If the Commandant intends to launch a coup, I have no time. 'Give me Elias Veturius, Warden. I cannot return to Antium without him.'

'Ah yes.' The Warden taps his fingers together. 'That might be a problem, Shrike.'

'What do you want, Warden?'

The Warden gestures for me to walk with him down one of the docks, away from his men and Harper. The Northman shakes his head sharply when I follow, but I have no choice. When we are out of earshot, the old man turns to me.

'I hear, Blood Shrike, that you have a specific . . . skill.' He fixes his eyes on me hungrily, and a chill rolls up my spine.

'Warden, I don't know what you've heard, but—'

'Do not insult my intelligence. Blackcliff's physician, Titinius, is an old friend. He shared with me recently the most remarkable story of recovery he's witnessed in his time at the school. Elias Veturius was hovering on the edge of death when a southern poultice saved him. But when Titinius tried the poultice on

377

another patient, it didn't work. He suspects that Elias's recovery was due to something – someone – else.'

'What,' I say again, my hand straying to my weapon, 'do you want?'

'I want to study your power,' the Warden says. 'I want to understand it.'

'I don't have time for your experiments,' I snap. 'Give me Elias and we'll talk.'

'If I give you Veturius, you will simply abscond with him,' the Warden says. 'No, you must remain. A few days, no more, and then I'll release you both.'

'Warden,' I say. 'There's a bleeding coup that's going to take down the Empire. I *must* return to Antium to warn the Emperor. And I cannot return without Elias. Give him to me and I vow by blood and by bone that I will come back here for your . . . *observation* as soon as the situation is under control.'

'A pretty vow,' the Warden says. 'But unreliable.' He strokes his chin thoughtfully, an eerie light in his eyes. 'Such a fascinating philosophical quandary you face, Blood Shrike. Stay here, submit to experimentation, and risk that, in your absence, the Empire will fall to Keris Veturia? Or go back, stop the coup, and save the Empire, but risk forfeiting your family?'

'This isn't a game,' I say. 'My family's lives are at stake. Bleeding hells, the *Empire* is at stake. And if neither of those things matter to you, then think of yourself, Warden. Do you think Keris will just let you lurk up here after she becomes Empress? She'll kill you the first chance she gets.'

'Oh, I think our new Empress will find my knowledge of the Empire's secrets . . . compelling.'

My blood seethes in hatred as I glare at the old man. Could I perhaps break into Kauf? Avitas knows the prison well. He spent years here. But there are only two of us and a fortress of the Warden's men.

I remember, then, what Cain said to me when all this began, just after Marcus ordered me to bring him Elias.

You will hunt Elias. You will find him. For what you learn on that journey – about yourself, your land, your enemies – that knowledge is essential to the Empire's survival. And to your destiny.

This. This is what he meant. I do not yet know what I have learned about myself, but I understand now what is happening within my land, within the Empire. I understand what my enemy is planning.

I was going to bring Elias to Marcus for execution to show the Emperor's strength. To give him a victory. But killing Elias isn't the only way to do that. Crushing a coup led by one of the Empire's most feared soldiers would work just as well. If Marcus and I take down the Commandant, the Illustrian Gens will be loath to cross him. Civil war will be averted. The Empire will be safe.

As for Elias, my gut twists when I think of him in the hands of the Warden. But I cannot concern myself with his welfare any longer. Besides which, I know my friend. The Warden won't be able to keep him locked up for long.

'Empire first, old man,' I say. 'You can keep Veturius – and your experiments.'

The Warden regards me without expression.

'*Callow is the hope of our youth,*' he murmurs. '*They are fools. They know no better.* From *Recollections*, by Rajin of Serra – one of the only Scholars worth quoting. I believe he wrote that a few moments before Taius the First lopped his head off. If you do not want your Emperor's fate to be similar, then you'd best be on your way.'

He signals to his men, and moments later the door of the boathouse thuds shut behind them. Avitas pads silently to my side.

'No Veturius, and a coup to stop,' Avitas says. 'Do you want to explain your thinking now,' he asks, 'or on the way?'

'On the way.' I step into the canoe and grab an oar. 'We're already out of time.'

CHAPTER FORTY-EIGHT

Laia

Keenan is the Nightbringer. A jinn. A demon.

Though I repeat the words in my head, they do not penetrate. Cold seeps into my bones, and I look down, surprised to find I've fallen to my knees in the snow. *Get up, Laia.* I cannot move.

I hate him. Skies, I hate him. *But I loved him. Didn't I?* I reach for my armlet, as if pawing at myself will make it reappear. Keenan's transformation flashes through my mind – then the mockery in his warped voice.

He's gone, I tell myself. *You're still alive. Elias and Darin are in the prison, and they have no way out. You have to save them. Get up.*

Perhaps grief is like battle: After experiencing enough of it, your body's instincts take over. When you see it closing in like a Martial death squad, you harden your insides. You prepare for the agony of a shredded heart. And when it hits, it hurts, but not as badly, because you have locked away your weakness, and all that's left is anger and strength.

Part of me wants to mull over every moment spent with that

thing. Did he oppose my mission with Mazen because he wanted me alone and weak? Did he save Izzi because he knew I'd never forgive him if he left her behind?

No thinking. No considering. You must act. Move. Get. Up.

I stand. Though I am at first unsure of where I am going, I make myself walk away from the cave. The snowdrifts reach my knees, and I plow through, shivering, until I find the trail Helene Aquilla and her men must have left. I follow it to a trickle of a stream and walk along the waterway.

I don't realize where I am walking until a figure steps out from the trees in front of me. The sight of the silver mask threatens to make my stomach plunge, but I harden myself and draw my dagger. The Mask puts up his hands.

'Peace, Laia of Serra.'

It is one of Aquilla's Masks. Not the fair-haired one or the handsome one. This one reminds me of the freshly sharpened edge of an ax. This is the one who walked right past Elias and me in Nur.

'I have to speak to the Blood Shrike,' I say. 'Please.'

'Where is your redheaded friend?'

'Gone.'

The Mask blinks. I find his lack of cold implacability unnatural. His pale green eyes are almost sympathetic. 'And your brother?'

'Still in Kauf,' I say warily. 'Will you take me to her?'

He nods. 'We're breaking camp,' he says. 'I was scouting for the Commandant's spies.'

I halt. 'You – you have Elias—'

'No,' the Mask says. 'Elias is still inside. We have something pressing to attend to.'

More pressing than catching the Empire's top fugitive? A slow ember of hope kindles in my belly. I thought I'd have to lie to

382

Helene Aquilla and tell her I wouldn't interfere with her extraction of Elias. But she's not planning on leaving Kauf with him anyway.

'Why did you trust Elias, Laia of Serra?' The Mask's question is too unexpected for me to hide my surprise. 'Why did you save him from execution?'

I consider lying, but he'd know. He's a Mask.

'Elias saved my life so many times,' I say. 'He broods and makes questionable choices that put his own life at risk, but he's a good person.' I glance over at the Mask, who stares impassively ahead. 'One – one of the best.'

'But he killed his friends during the Trials.'

'He didn't want to,' I say. 'He thinks about it all the time. He'll never forgive himself, I think.'

The Mask is silent, and the wind carries the moans and sighs of Kauf to our ears. I clench my jaw. *You're going to have to go in there*, I tell myself. *So get used to it.*

'My father was like Elias,' the Mask says after a moment. 'My mother said he always saw the good when no one else did.'

'Was – was he a Mask too?'

'He was. Strange trait for a Mask, I suppose. The Empire tried to train it out of him. Perhaps they failed. Perhaps that's why he died.'

I do not know what to say, and the Mask remains silent also, until Kauf's ominous black bulk appears in the distance.

'I lived there for two years.' He nods at the prison. 'Spent most of my time in the interrogation cells. Hated it at first. Twelve-hour guard shifts, seven days a week. I became numb to the things I heard. It helped that I had a friend.'

'Not the Warden.' I inch a bit away from him. 'Elias told me about him.'

'No,' the Mask says. 'Not the Warden, nor any of the soldiers. My friend was a Scholar slave. A little girl who called herself Bee, because she had a scar shaped like a ziberry fruit on her cheek.'

I stare at him, nonplussed. He doesn't seem like the type of man to befriend a child.

'She was so thin,' the Mask says. 'I used to sneak her food. At first, she feared me, but when she realized I didn't mean her harm she started talking to me.' He shrugs. 'After leaving Kauf I wondered about her. A few days ago, when I took a message to the Warden from the Shrike, I went looking for Bee. Found her, too.'

'Did she remember you?'

'She did. In fact, she told me a very peculiar story of a pale-eyed Martial locked in the interrogation block of the prison. He refuses to fear the Warden, she said. He befriended one of her companions. Gave him a Tribal name: Tas. The children whisper of this Martial – carefully, of course, so the Warden doesn't hear. They're good at keeping secrets. They've taken word of this Martial to the Scholar movement within the prison – to those men and women who still hold out hope that they'll one day escape.'

Bleeding skies.

'Why are you telling me this?' I look around, nervous. A *trap*? A *trick*? It's obvious that the Mask is speaking of Elias. But what is his purpose?

'I can't tell you why.' He sounds almost sad. 'But strange as it sounds, I think that one day you, of all people, will understand best.'

He shakes himself and meets my eyes. 'Save him, Laia of Serra,' he says. 'From all that you and the Blood Shrike have told me, I think that he is worth saving.'

The Mask watches me, and I nod at him, not understanding

but relieved that he is, at least, more human and less Mask. 'I'll do my best.'

We reach the Blood Shrike's clearing. She fastens a saddle onto her horse, and when she hears our footsteps and turns, her silver face tightens. The Mask quickly makes himself scarce.

'I know you don't like me,' I say before she can tell me to get lost. 'But I'm here for two reasons.' I open my mouth, trying to find the right words, and decide that simplest is best. 'First, I need to thank you. For saving me. I should have said it before.'

'You're welcome,' she grunts. 'What do you want?'

'Your help.'

'Why in the bleeding skies would I help you?'

'Because you're leaving Elias behind,' I say. 'You don't want him dead. I know that. So help me save him.'

The Blood Shrike turns back to her horse, yanking a cloak from one of her saddlebags and pulling it on.

'Elias won't die. He's probably trying to break your brother out right now.'

'No,' I say. 'Something went wrong in there.' I step closer to her. Her stare cuts like a scim. 'You owe me nothing. I know that. But I heard what he said to you at Blackcliff. *Don't forget us.*' The devastation in her eyes at the memory is sudden and raw, and guilt twists in my stomach.

'I won't leave him,' I say. 'Listen to that place.' Helene Aquilla looks away from me. 'He deserves better than to die in there.'

'What do you want to know?'

'A few things about layout, locations, and supplies.'

She scoffs. 'How in the hells are you going to get in? You can't pose as a slave. Kauf's guards know the faces of their Scholar slaves, and a girl who looks like you won't be quickly forgotten. You won't last five minutes.'

'I have a way in,' I say. 'And I'm not afraid.'

A violent gust of wind sends blonde strands fluttering like birds around her silver face. As she sizes me up, her expression is unreadable. What does she feel? She is more than just a Mask – I learned that the night she brought me back from the brink of death.

'Come here,' she sighs. She kneels down and begins to draw in the snow.

* * *

I'm tempted to pile Keenan's things outside and light a fire, but the smoke would only attract attention. Instead, I hold his bag away from myself, as if it's diseased, and walk a few hundred yards from the cave, until I find a stream running swiftly down to the River Dusk. His pack lands with a splash in the water, and his weapons soon follow. I could do with a few more knives, but I don't want anything that belonged to him.

When I return to the cave, I sit down, cross my legs, and decide that I will not move until I have mastered my invisibility.

I realize that each time I succeeded, Keenan was out of sight and often far away. All that self-doubt I felt when he was around – could he have planted it on purpose, to suppress my power?

Disappear! I scream the word in my mind, queen of the desolate landscape therein ordering her ragged troops to a last stand. Elias, Darin, and all the rest I must save depend on this one thing, this power, this magic that I *know* lives within.

A rush pours through my body, and I steady myself, looking down to see that my limbs shimmer, translucent, as they did during the raid on Afya's caravan.

I whoop, loud enough that the echo in the cave startles me, and the invisibility falls away. *Right. Work on that, Laia.*

All that day, I practice, first in the cave and then out in the snow. I learn my limits: A branch I hold while invisible is also invisible. But anything living or anchored to the earth appears to float in midair.

I am so deep within my own head that at first, I don't hear the footsteps. Someone speaks, and I spin around, scrambling for a weapon.

'Oh, calm down, girl.' I recognize the haughty tone even before she lowers her hood. Afya Ara-Nur.

'Skies, you're jumpy,' she says. 'Though I can't say I blame you. Not when you have to listen to that racket.' She waves her hand in the general direction of the prison. 'No Elias, I see. No brother either. And . . . no redhead?'

She raises her eyebrows, waiting for an explanation, but I just stare at her, wondering if she's real. Her riding clothes are stained and filthy, her boots wet with snow. Her braids are tucked beneath a scarf, and it doesn't look like she has slept in days. I could kiss her, I'm so happy to see her.

She sighs and rolls her eyes. 'I made a promise, girl, all right? I vowed to Elias Veturius that I would see this through. A Tribeswoman breaking a sacred vow is foul enough. But to do it when another woman's life is at stake? That is unforgiveable – as my little brother reminded me every hour of every day for three days straight, until I finally agreed to follow you.'

'Where is he?'

'Almost to the Tribal Lands.' She sits on a nearby rock and massages her legs. 'At least, he better be. Last thing he said to me was that your friend Izzi didn't trust the redhead.' She looks at me expectantly. 'Was she right?'

'Skies,' I say. 'Where do I even begin?'

Night has fallen by the time I finish filling Afya in on the past few weeks. I leave out a few things – in particular the night in the cellar safe house.

'I know I failed,' I say. She and I sit in the cave now, sharing a meal of flatbread and fruit that she has brought. 'I made stupid decisions—'

'When I was sixteen,' Afya interrupts, 'I left Nur to carry out my first trade. I was the oldest, and my father spoiled me. Instead of forcing me to spend interminable hours learning to cook and weave and other boring rubbish, he kept me close and taught me about the business.

'Most of our Tribe thought he indulged me. But I knew I wanted to be *Zaldara* of Tribe Nur after my father. I didn't care that there hadn't been a female chieftain for more than two hundred years. I only knew that I was my father's heir and that if I wasn't chosen, the role of *Zaldar* would go to one of my greedy uncles or useless cousins. They'd marry me off to some other Tribe, and that would be that.'

'You pulled it off beautifully,' I guess with a smile. 'And now look at you.'

'Wrong,' she says. 'The trade was a disaster. A travesty. A humiliation for both myself and my father. The Martial I planned to sell to seemed honest enough – until he manipulated me and tricked me out of my goods for a fraction of what they were worth. I returned from the trade a thousand marks poorer, with my head low and my tail between my legs. I was convinced my father would have me married off within a fortnight.

'Instead, he smacked the back of my head and barked at me to stand up straight. *Do you know what he said? Failure doesn't define you. It's what you do after you fail that determines whether you are a leader or a waste of perfectly good air.*'

Afya stares hard at me. 'So you've made a few bad decisions.

So have I. So has Elias. So has everyone attempting to do something difficult. That doesn't mean that you give up, you fool. Do you understand?'

I mull over her words and recall the past few months. It takes only a split second for life to go horribly wrong. To fix the mess, I need a thousand things to go right. The distance from one bit of luck to the next feels as great as the distance across oceans. But, I decide in this moment, I will bridge that distance, again and again, until I win. I will not fail.

I nod at Afya. Immediately she claps me on the shoulder.

'Good,' she says. 'Now that that's out of the way, what's your plan?'

'It's—' I search for a word that will make my idea not look like complete lunacy, but realize that Afya would see right through me. 'It's insane,' I finally say. 'So insane that I can't imagine how it will work.'

Afya lets out a peal of high laughter that rings through the cave. She is not mocking me – there is genuine amusement on her face as she shakes her head.

'Skies,' Afya says. 'I thought you told me you loved stories. Have you *ever* heard a story of an adventurer with a sane plan?'

'Well . . . no.'

'And why do you think that is?'

I am at a loss. 'Because . . . ah, because—'

She chuckles again. 'Because sane plans *never* work, girl,' she says. 'Only the mad ones do.'

CHAPTER FORTY-NINE

Elias

A whole night and day pass before Tas returns. He says nothing, looking pointedly at my cell door. There's a slight shift in the flickering torchlight beyond my cell – one of the Warden's Masks watches us. Finally, the Mask outside the cell leaves. I bend my head in case he decides to return, keeping my voice quieter than a whisper.

'Tell me you have good news, Tas.'

'The soldiers moved the Artist to another cell.' Tas looks over his shoulder at the door, then draws swiftly in the grime on the cell floor. 'But I found him. The block is arranged in a circle, yes? With the guard quarters in the center and' – he marks an X at the top of the circle – 'the Artist is here,' he says. Then he marks an X at the bottom. 'You are here. The stairs are in between.'

'Excellent,' I whisper. 'The uniforms?'

'Bee can get one for you,' he says. 'She has access to the laundry.'

'You're certain you trust her?'

'She hates the Warden.' Tas shudders. 'More than me, even. She will not betray us. But, Elias, I have not spoken to the Skiritae leader, Araj. And . . .' Tas looks apologetic. 'Bee said there's no Tellis to be found anywhere in the prison.'

Ten burning hells.

'Also,' Tas says, 'the Scholar cleansing has begun. The Martials have built a pen in the prison yard where they are being herded. The cold has killed off many, but' – his voice trembles in anticipation and I sense he's been working himself up to this – 'something else has happened – something wonderful.'

'The Warden has erupted in boils that will kill him slowly?'

Tas grins. 'Almost as good,' he says. 'I have a message, Elias, from a girl with golden eyes.'

My heart practically falls out of my chest. It can't be. *Can it be?*

'Tell me everything.' I glance toward the door. If Tas is in my cell for longer than ten minutes, one of the Masks will come to check on us. The boy's hands work swiftly as he cleans my wounds and replaces my bandages.

'She found Bee first.' I strain to hear him. A few cells over, the guards have begun an interrogation, and the prisoner's screams echo across the block.

'Bee thought it was a ghost, because the voice came out of nowhere. The voice led her to an empty barracks room, and the girl appeared out of thin air. She asked Bee about you, so Bee came to get me.'

'And she – she was invisible?' At Tas's nod, I sit back, stunned. But then I begin to think back to the times she seemed to almost fade out of view. When did it begin? *After Serra*, I realize. After the efrit touched her. The creature only laid hands on Laia for a second. But perhaps that second was enough to awaken something within her.

'What was her message?'

Tas takes a deep breath. '*I found your scims*,' he recites. '*I was happy to see them. I have a way in and can keep out of sight. Afya can steal horses. What of the Scholars? Executions have begun. The boy says there's a Scholar leader who can help. If you see my brother, tell him I'm here. Tell him I love him.*'

'She said she'd return at nightfall for your answer.'

'All right,' I say to Tas. 'This is what I want you to tell her.'

For three days, Tas carries messages back and forth between Laia and me. I'd have thought her presence here was a sick trick of the Warden's if it wasn't for the fact that I trust Tas and that the messages he brings back are so eminently Laia – sweet, slightly formal, but with a strength behind the words that speaks of her determination. *Tread carefully, Elias. I do not wish to see you injured further.*

Slowly, painstakingly, we pull together a plan that is part her, part me, part Tas, and complete madness. It's also heavily dependent on the competency of Araj, the man who leads the Skiritae. A man I've never met.

The morning of *Rathana* dawns like all other mornings in Kauf: without any indication that it is morning, other than the sounds of the guards changing shifts and a vague internal sense that my body is waking up.

Tas arrives with a bowl of watery gruel, which he drops quickly in front of me before streaking out. He is pale, terrified, but when I meet his eyes, he gives me the briefest of nods.

After he leaves, I force myself to my feet. It takes most of my breath to stand, and my chains seem heavier than they did just last night. Everything hurts, and beneath the pain, weariness seems to have penetrated my very marrow. This is not the tiredness of interrogation or a long journey. It is the exhaustion of a body that's nearly done fighting.

Just get through today, I tell myself. *Then you can die in peace.*

The next few minutes are nearly as torturous as one of the Warden's interrogation sessions. I *hate* waiting. But soon enough, a promising smell wafts into my cell.

Smoke.

A second later, urgent voices. A shout. The ringing of alarm bells. The echoing, frantic boom of drums.

Well done, Tas. Boots pound past the door, and the already bright torchlight outside intensifies. The minutes pass, and I rattle my chains impatiently. Fire spreads quickly, especially if Tas has been dribbling as much fuel in the soldiers' section as I told him to. Already, smoke pours into my cell.

A shadow passes by my door and looks in – no doubt to make sure I'm still securely chained – then moves on. Seconds later, I hear the key in the lock, and it opens to reveal Tas's small form.

'I could only find the cell keys, Elias.' Tas scurries in and shoves a thin blade and a bent pin at me. 'Can you pick the locks with this?'

I curse. My left hand is still clumsy from the damage the Warden did with his pliers, but I take the picks. The smoke grows thicker, my hands clumsier.

'Hurry, Elias.' Tas eyes the door. 'We must still get Darin out.'

The locks on my manacles finally creak open, and a minute later I unlock the ankle shackles. The smoke in my cell is thick enough that Tas and I must crouch to breathe, but still, I force myself to pull on the guard uniform he's brought me. The uniform cannot hide the stink of the interrogation cells or my filthy hair or wounds, but it's enough of a disguise to get through Kauf's hallways and into the prison yard.

We pull wet kerchiefs around our faces, easing the sting of the smoke. Then we open the door and dart out of my cell. I try to move swiftly, but every step is pain, and Tas quickly darts out of sight. The smoky stone hallways are not yet aflame, though their wooden beams will catch soon enough. But the soldiers' quarters in the middle of the block, filled with wood furniture and littered with pools of fuel, courtesy of Tas, are fast turning into a solid wall of fire. Shadows move through the smoke, and shouts echo. I lurch past the stairwell, and moments later I look back to see a Mask waving away the smoke and heading up and out of the block. *Excellent.* The guards are bolting, as I expected them to.

'Elias!' Tas appears out of the smoke ahead of me. 'Hurry! I heard the Masks say that the fires upstairs are spreading!'

All the damn torches the Warden uses to light this place are finally coming to good use. 'Are you sure we're the only prisoners down here?'

'I checked twice!' A minute later, we make for the last cell at the north end of the block. Tas unlocks the door, and we enter in a cloud of smoke.

'It's me,' I rasp to Darin, my throat already raw. 'Elias.'

'Thank the bleeding skies.' Darin scrambles to his feet and holds out his manacled hands. 'I thought you were dead. I wasn't sure whether to believe Tas or not.'

I set to picking the locks. I can feel the air growing hotter and more poisonous by the second, but I make myself work methodically. *Come on, come on.* The familiar *snick* sounds, the shackles fall away, and we bolt from the cell, keeping low to the ground. We're nearly to the staircase when a silver face suddenly looms out of the smoke ahead of us. *Drusius.*

'You sly, conniving little mongrel.' Drusius grabs Tas by the neck. 'I *knew* you had something to do with this.'

Begging the skies for enough strength to at least knock Drusius off his feet, I spring forward. He sidesteps and shoves me into a wall. Just a month ago, I'd have been able to use his brutish attack to get the best of him. But the poison and the interrogations have stripped me of my swiftness. Before I can stop him, Drusius wraps his hands around my neck and presses. A streak of filthy blond hair flashes past. Darin dives into Drusius's stomach, and the Mask stumbles.

I cough for breath and drop to one knee. Even during the Commandant's whippings or the Centurions' harsh training, I sensed my own resilience, buried deep where it could not be touched. But now, as I watch Drusius flip Darin onto his back and knock him senseless with a blow to the temple, I cannot harness that strength. I cannot find it.

'Elias!' Tas is beside me, shoving a knife into my hand. I make myself lunge at Drusius. My leap is more like a crawl, but I have enough fighter's instinct left to drive the dagger into the Mask's thigh and twist. He howls and grabs me by the hair, but I stab his leg and stomach again and again, until his hands stop moving.

'Get up, Elias.' Tas is frantic. 'The fire is spreading too swiftly!'

'C-can't—'

'You can – you must.' Tas pulls at me now, using all of his weight. 'Pick up Darin! Drusius has knocked him out!'

My body is frail and slow, so slow. It is worn out by the seizures, the beatings, the interrogation, the poison, the endless punishment of the past few months.

'Rise, Elias Veturius.' Tas smacks my face, and I blink at him in surprise. His eyes are fierce. 'You gave me a name,' he says. 'I want to live to hear it on the lips of others. *Rise.*'

I growl as I drag myself to my feet, as I move to Darin, kneel, and lift him over my shoulders. I stagger at his weight, though Kauf has left him far lighter than a man of his height should be.

Desperately hoping that no other Masks emerge, I lurch toward the stairs. The interrogation block is fully engulfed now, the beams of the roof aflame, the smoke so thick that I can hardly see. I stumble up the stone steps, Tas steadfast at my side.

Break it down to what you can do. One foot. One inch. The words are a garbled chant in my head, fainter and fainter when faced with the screaming panic of my failing body. What will happen at the top of the stairwell? We'll open the door to chaos or order, and either way, I don't know if I'll be able to carry Darin out of the prison.

The field of battle is my temple. The swordpoint is my priest. The dance of death is my prayer. The killing blow is my release. I'm not ready for my release. Not yet. *Not yet.*

Darin's body grows heavier by the second, but I can see the door that leads out into the prison now. I reach for the handle, pull it down, push.

It does not open.

'No!' Tas leaps up, clawing at the door handle, pushing with all of his might.

Open it, Elias. I drop Darin and yank at the enormous handle, peering at the locking mechanism. I fumble for makeshift lock picks, but when I shove one into the lock, it breaks.

There must be another way out. I spin around and drag Darin halfway down the stairwell. The wood beams that hold up the weight of the stone have caught fire. Flame races overhead, and I am convinced that the world has dropped away but for Darin, Tas, and me.

The shudders of a seizure take me, and I sense the approach of an inexorable darkness that dwarfs everything I've endured until now. I fall, my body worse than useless. I can only sputter and choke as Tas leans over me, shouting something I cannot hear.

Is this what my friends felt in the moment of death? Were they also consumed by this futile rage, made more insulting because it meant nothing? Because, in the end, Death would take his due, and nothing could stop him?

Elias, Tas mouths at me, his face streaked with tears and soot. *Elias!*

His face and voice fade.

Silence. Darkness.

Then a familiar presence. A quiet voice.

'Arise.' The world comes back into focus, and I find the Soul Catcher leaning over me. The stark, empty boughs of the Forest of Dusk stretch like fingers overhead.

'Welcome, Elias Veturius.' Her voice is infinitely gentle and kind, as if she's talking to an injured child, but her eyes are the same empty black they've been since I've known her. She takes my arm like an old friend would. 'Welcome to the Waiting Place, the realm of ghosts. I am the Soul Catcher, and I am here to help you cross to the other side.'

CHAPTER FIFTY

Helene

Avitas and I arrive in Antium just as *Rathana* dawns. As our horses clatter through the city gates, stars still glint above and sunrise has not yet graced the jagged mountains to the east of the city.

Though Avitas and I scoped out the land around the capital, we saw no sign of an army. But the Commandant is clever. She might have slipped her forces into the city and hidden them in multiple places. Or she might be waiting until nightfall to unleash her attack.

Faris and Dex join up with us as we enter the city, having spotted our approach from one of the watchtowers.

'Hail, Shrike.' Dex clasps my hand as he steers his horse to fall in with mine. He looks like he hasn't slept in a year. 'The Masks of the Black Guard are deployed and await your orders. I had three squads secure the Emperor. Another squad is out scouting for the army. The rest have taken over the city guard.'

'Thank you, Dex.' I am relieved he doesn't question me about Elias. 'Faris,' I say. 'Report.'

'The girl was right,' my big friend says. We weave through the

398

wagons, men, and animals entering Antium at this early hour. 'There is an army. At least four thousand men—'

'It's the Commandant's,' I say. 'Harper can explain.' When we clear the traffic, I kick my horse into a gallop. 'Think carefully about what you saw,' I call to Faris. 'I need you to bear witness before the Emperor.'

The streets are starting to fill with Mercators out early to stake out the best spots for the festivities of *Rathana*. A Plebeian ale merchant trundles through the city with extra barrels of his goods to supply to the taverns. Children hang up blue and green lanterns that symbolize the day. Everyone seems so normal. Happy. Still, they clear the way when they see four Black Guards galloping through the streets. When we reach the palace, I leap off my horse, nearly mowing down the groom who comes to take the reins.

'Where is the Emperor?' I snap at a legionnaire on gate duty.

'In the throne room, Shrike, with the rest of the court.'

As I hoped. The leaders of the Empire's Illustrian Gens are early risers, particularly when they want something. They'll have begun lining up to petition the Emperor hours ago. The throne room will be packed with powerful men, men who can bear witness to the fact that I saved the throne from the Commandant's predations.

I have spent days planning my speech, and as we approach the throne room, I go over it again in my head. The two legionnaires guarding the throne room doors attempt to announce me, but Dex and Faris step ahead of me, shove them out of the way, and open the doors for me. It's like having two walking battering rams at my side.

Black Guard soldiers line the room at intervals, most standing between the colossal tapestries that depict the deeds of past

Emperors. As I make for the throne, I spot Lieutenant Sergius, the Black Guard who was stupid enough to address me as *Miss Aquilla* the last time I was here. He salutes respectfully as I pass.

Faces turn toward me. I recognize the Paters of a few dozen Mercator and Illustrian Gens. Through the enormous glass ceiling, the last stars give way to daylight.

Marcus sits on the ornately carved ebony throne, his usual sneer replaced by a look of cold wrath as he listens to a report from a courier who looks fresh from the road. A circlet of sharp points, patterned with Blackcliff's four-sided diamond, adorns his head.

'—pushed past the border and are harassing the villages outside Tiborum. The city will be overrun if we do not get men out there immediately, my lord.'

'Blood Shrike.' Marcus notices me and waves off the legionnaire giving his report. 'It is good to lay eyes upon you again.' He flicks his glance up and down my form but then grimaces and puts a finger to his temple. I am relieved when he looks away.

'Pater Aquillus,' he says through gritted teeth. 'Come and greet your daughter.'

My father emerges from the rows of courtiers, my mother and sisters trailing. Hannah wrinkles her nose when she sees me, as if she's smelled something foul. My mother nods a greeting, her knuckles white as she clasps her hands in front of her. She looks too afraid to speak. Livvy manages a smile when she sees me, but I'd have to be a fool not to notice that she's been crying.

'Greetings, Blood Shrike.' Father's pained glance takes in Avitas, Faris, and Dex before returning to me. *No Elias*, he seems to say. I give him a reassuring nod, trying to communicate with my eyes. *Do not fear, Father.*

'Your family has been kind enough to grace me with their presence daily since you left.' Marcus's mouth curves into a smile before he pointedly looks behind me. 'You've returned empty-handed, Shrike.'

'Not empty-handed, Emperor,' I say. 'I come bearing something far more important than Elias Veturius. As we speak, an army marches on Antium, lead by Keris Veturia. For months, she has siphoned off soldiers from the Tribal lands and the border regions to create this treasonous army. That is why you're getting reports of Wildmen and Barbarians attacking our outlying cities.' I nod to the courier. He backs away, not wanting to get involved in any discussion between the Blood Shrike and the Emperor. 'The Commandant means to launch a coup.'

Marcus cocks his head. 'And you have proof of this supposed army?'

'I saw it, my lord,' Faris rumbles from beside me. 'Not two days ago, in the Argent Hills. Couldn't get close enough to recognize the Gens represented, but there were at least twenty standards flying.' The Empire supports 250 Illustrian Gens. That the Commandant could muster the support of so many gets Marcus's attention. He tightens a big fist on his throne.

'Your Majesty,' I say. 'I dispatched the Black Guard to take control of Antium's walls and to scout beyond the city. The Commandant will likely attack tonight, so we still have a full day to prepare the city. But we must get you to a safe loca—'

'So you did not bring me Elias Veturius?'

Here goes. 'My lord, it was either bring Veturius back or report this coup. Time did not allow both. I thought the security of the Empire mattered more than one man.'

Marcus regards me for a long moment before his gaze shifts to something behind me. I hear a familiar, hated gait, the *thunk-thunk* of steel-bottomed boots.

Impossible. I left before she did. I rode without stopping. She might have reached her army before us, but we would have seen her if she was headed to Antium. There are only so many roads that lead here from Kauf.

A slice of darkness in the recesses of the throne room catches my attention: a hood with suns glaring out from within. A swish of a cloak and he's gone. *The Nightbringer. The jinn. He brought her here.*

'I told you, Emperor.' The Commandant's voice is smooth as a snake's coils. 'The girl is deluded by her obsession with Elias Veturius. Her inability – or unwillingness – to catch him has led her to concoct this ridiculous story – and to deploy valuable members of the Black Guard in a haphazard and senseless way. An ostentatious move. No doubt she's hoping that it will support her claim. She must think us fools.'

The Commandant circles me to stand beside Marcus. Her body is calm, her features unruffled, but when she meets my eyes, my throat goes dry at her fury. If I were at Blackcliff I'd be sagging from the whipping post right about now, breathing my last.

What in the bleeding skies is she doing here? She should be with her army right now. I eye the room again, expecting to see her men pour in through the doors at any moment. But though I see Gens Veturia soldiers throughout the throne room, they don't look as if they're readying themselves for battle.

'According to the Commandant, Blood Shrike,' Marcus says, 'Elias Veturius managed to get stuck in Kauf Prison. But you knew that, didn't you?'

He'll know if I lie. I bow my head. 'I did, Your Majesty. But—'

'Yet you didn't bring him with you. Though he likely would have been dead by now anyway. Is that correct, Keris?'

'It is, Your Majesty. The boy was poisoned somewhere on his journey,' the Commandant says. 'The Warden reports that he has been having seizures for weeks. The last I heard, Elias Veturius was a few hours from death.'

Seizures? When I saw Elias in Nur, he looked ill, but I assumed it was because of a hard march from Serra.

Then I remember what he said – words that made no sense at the time but that now send a knife through my gut: *We both know I'm not long for this world.*

And the Warden, after I told him I'd see Elias again: *Callow is the hope of our youth.* Behind me, Avitas takes a sharp breath.

'The Nightweed she gave me, Shrike,' he whispers. 'She must have had enough to use it on him.'

'You' – I turn to the Commandant, and everything falls together – 'you poisoned him. But you must have done it weeks ago, when I found your tracks in Serra. When you fought him.' Is my friend dead, then? Truly dead? *No. He can't be.* My mind will not accept it.

'You used Nightweed because you *knew* it would take him a long time to die. You knew I'd hunt him. And as long as I was out of your way, I wouldn't be able to stop your coup.' *Bleeding skies.* She killed her own son – and she's been playing me for months.

'Nightweed is illegal in the Empire, as everyone here knows.' The Commandant looks at me like I'm covered in dung. 'Listen to yourself, Shrike. To think that you trained at my school. I must have been blind to let a novice like you graduate.'

The throne room buzzes, going silent when I step toward her. 'If I'm such a fool,' I say, 'then explain why every garrison in the Empire is undermanned. Why didn't you ever have enough soldiers? Why aren't there enough on the borders?'

'I needed men to quell the revolution, of course,' she says. 'The Emperor himself gave those transfer orders.'

'But you kept asking for more —'

'This is embarrassing to watch.' The Commandant turns to Marcus. 'I am ashamed, my lord, that Blackcliff produced someone so weak-minded.'

'She's *lying*,' I say to Marcus, but I can well imagine how I must sound — tense and shrill against the Commandant's cool defense. 'Your Majesty, you must believe me —'

'Enough.' Marcus speaks in a voice that silences the entire room. 'I gave you an order to bring in Elias Veturius, alive, by *Rathana*, Blood Shrike. You failed to carry out that order. Everyone in this room heard what the punishment for your failure would be.' He nods to the Commandant, and she signals her troops.

In seconds, the men of Gens Veturia step forward and seize my parents, my sisters.

I find that my hands and feet have gone numb. *It's not supposed to be like this. I'm being true to the Empire. I'm holding my fealty.*

'I promised the Paters of our great families an execution,' Marcus says. 'And unlike you, Blood Shrike, I mean to keep my vow.'

CHAPTER FIFTY-ONE

Laia

THE MORNING OF RATHANA

When it is still dark outside, Afya and I leave the warmth of the cave and head out toward Kauf in the frigid morning. The Tribeswoman carries Darin's sword for me, and I've strapped on Elias's scims. Skies know he'll need them when we're fighting our way out of the prison.

'Eight guards,' I say to Afya. 'And then you *must* sink the spare boats. Do you understand? If you—'

'Skies, shut it, would you?' Afya waves an impatient hand at me. 'You're like a Tibbi bird from the south that chirps the same few words over and over until you want to strangle its pretty neck. Eight guards, ten barges to secure, and twenty boats to sabotage. I'm not an idiot, girl. I can handle it. You just make sure you get that fire inside the prison nice and hot. The more Martials we barbecue, the fewer to hunt us down.'

We reach the River Dusk, where we must part ways. Afya digs her booted toes into the dirt.

'Girl.' She adjusts her scarf and clears her throat quietly. 'Your brother. He . . . might not be what he was. I had a cousin sent to Kauf once,' she adds. 'When he came back, he was different. Be prepared.'

The Tribeswoman edges to the shore of the river and flits away into the darkness. *Don't die*, I think, before turning my attention to the monstrous building behind me.

The invisibility still feels strange, like a new cloak that doesn't quite fit. Though I've practiced for days, I do not understand how the magic works, and the Scholar in me itches to learn more, to find books about it, to speak to others who know how to control it. *Later, Laia. If you survive.*

When I'm certain I'm not going to reappear at the first sign of trouble, I find a path leading up to Kauf and carefully step in footprints larger than mine. My invisibility doesn't guarantee silence, nor does it hide signs of my passage.

Kauf's studded, spiked portcullis is flung wide open. I see no wagons making their way into the prison – it is too late in the season for traders. When I hear a whip crack, I finally understand why the gates aren't shut. A cry breaks the quiet of the morning, and I see several bent, gaunt figures shuffling out of the gate under the unforgiving eye of a Mask. My hands go for my dagger, though I know I can do nothing with it. Afya and I watched from the woods as pits were dug outside the prison. We watched as the Martials filled those pits with dead Scholars.

If I want the rest of the Scholars in the prison to escape, I cannot reveal my position. But still, I force myself to watch. To bear witness. To remember this image so that these lives are not forgotten.

When the Scholars disappear around the eastern edge of Kauf's wall, I slide through the gates. This path is not unfamiliar to me.

Elias and I have exchanged messages for days through Tas, and I've come this way every time. Still, I stiffen as I pass the eight legionnaires who stand watch at the base of Kauf's entry gate. The space between my shoulder blades twinges, and I look up at the battlements, where archers patrol.

As I cross the garishly lit prison yard, I try to avoid looking to the right at the two giant wooden pens where the Martials keep the Scholar prisoners.

But in the end, I cannot help but stare. Two wagons, each half-filled with the dead, are parked beside the closest pen. A group of younger, maskless Martials – Fivers – load in more dead Scholars, those who haven't survived the cold.

Bee and many of the others can get them weapons, Tas had said. *Hidden in slop buckets and rags. Not knives or scims, but spear heads, broken arrows, brass beaters.*

Though the Martials have already killed hundreds of my people, a thousand Scholars still sit in those pens, awaiting death. They are ill, starved, and half-frozen from the cold. Even if everything goes as planned, I do not know if they have enough strength to take on the prison guards when the time comes, especially with such crude weaponry.

Then again, it's not as if we have many other choices.

At this hour, there are few soldiers wandering the blindingly bright halls of Kauf. Still, I sneak along the walls and steer clear of the few guards on duty. My eyes flit briefly to the entrances that lead to the Scholar pits. I passed them the first day I came here, when they were still occupied. Moments after, I had to run to find a place to retch.

I make my way down the entry hall, through the rotunda and past the staircase that, according to Helene Aquilla, leads up to Masks' quarters and the Warden's office. *Time for you soon enough.*

A great steel door looms ominously on one side of the rotunda wall. The interrogation block. *Darin is down there. Right now. Yards away.*

Kauf's drums thud out the time: half past five in the morning. The hallway that leads to the Martial barracks, kitchen, and storage closets is far busier than the rest of the prison. Talk and laughter drifts from the mess hall. I smell eggs, grease, and burned bread. A legionnaire veers out of a room just ahead of me, and I stifle a gasp as he passes within a hair's breadth. He must hear me, because his hand falls to his scim and he looks around.

I don't dare to breathe until he moves on. *Too close, Laia.*

Go past the kitchens, Helene Aquilla told me. *The oil storage is at the very end of the hall. The torch-lighters are always coming and going, so whatever you're planning, you'll have to move quickly.*

When I find the closet, I am forced to wait as a sullen-faced aux wrestles out a barrel of pitch and rolls it down the hall. He leaves the door cracked open, and I eye the closet's contents. Drums of pitch line its base like a row of stout soldiers. Above them sit cans the length of my forearm and the width of my hand. Blue-fire oil, the translucent yellow substance the Empire imports from Marinn. It reeks of rotted leaves and sulfur, but it will be more difficult to spot than pitch when I dribble it all over the prison.

It takes me nearly a half hour to empty out a dozen canisters in the back hallways and the rotunda. I stuff each can back in the closet when it is empty, hoping no one notices until it's too late. Then I pack three more cans into my now bulging bag and enter the kitchen. A Plebeian lords over the stoves, bellowing orders at Scholar slave children. The children whiz around, their speed driven by fear. They are, presumably, exempt from the culling going on outside. My mouth twists in disgust. The Warden needs at least a few drudges to continue doing the chores around here.

I spot Bee, her thin arms shaking beneath a tray of dirty dishes from the mess hall. I sidle toward her, stopping often to avoid the scurrying bodies around me. She jumps when I speak in her ear, but covers her surprise swiftly.

'Bee,' I say. 'In fifteen minutes, light the fire.'

She nods imperceptibly, and I move out of the kitchen and to the rotunda. The drum tower thuds six times. According to Helene, the Warden will head to the interrogation cells in a quarter-hour. *No time, Laia. Move.*

I bolt up the rotunda's narrow stone staircase. It ends in a wood-beamed hallway lined with dozens of doors. Masks' quarters. Even as I get to work, the silver-faced monsters exit their quarters and head down the stairs. Every time one passes, my stomach clenches and I look down at myself, making sure my invisibility is still intact.

'Do you smell something?' A short, bearded Mask stumps down the hall with a leaner companion, only to stop a few feet from me. He takes a deep sniff of the air. The other Mask shrugs, grunts, and moves on. But the bearded Mask continues to look about, sniffing along the walls like a hound that's caught a scent. He stops short at one of the beams I've anointed with oil, his eyes dropping to the pool gleaming at its base.

'What in the hells . . .' As he kneels down, I slip behind him, to the end of the hallway. He spins at the sound of my footsteps, his ears keen. I feel my invisibility falter at the rasp of his scim leaving its scabbard. I grab a torch off the wall. The Mask gapes at it. Too late, I realize that my invisibility extends to the wood and pitch, but not the flame itself.

He swings his sword, and startled, I back away. My invisibility drops entirely, a strange rippling that starts at my forehead and cascades down to my feet.

The Mask's eyes widen, and he lunges. *'Witch!'*

I throw myself out of his path, hurling the torch at the nearest pool of oil. It flares with a roar, distracting the Mask, and I use the moment to tear away from him.

Disappear, I tell myself. *Disappear!* But I'm going too fast – it's not working.

But it *must* work, or I'm dead. *Now*, I scream in my mind. The familiar ripple runs back over me just as a tall, thin figure steps out of a hallway and swivels his triangular head toward me.

Though I wasn't sure I'd recognize him based on Helene's description, I know him immediately. The Warden.

The Warden blinks, and I cannot tell if he saw me wink out of sight or not. I don't wait to find out. I hurl another can of blue-fire oil at his feet, rip two torches off the wall, and throw one down. When he shouts and jumps back, I swerve around him and hurtle down the stairs two by two, dropping the last can of oil as I do and pitching the final torch over my shoulder. I hear the *whoosh* of flame as the stair railing catches fire.

I have no time to look back. Soldiers rush through the rotunda, and smoke pours from the hallway near the kitchens. *Yes, Bee!* I pivot around to the back of the staircase, the spot where Elias said he would meet me.

A heavy thud sounds on the staircase. The Warden has leaped over the fire and stands in the rotunda. He grabs a nearby aux by the collar and snarls at him: 'Have the drum tower deliver the evacuation message. Auxes are to herd the prisoners in the yard and muster a cordon of spearmen to prevent escape. Double the perimeter guard. The rest of you' – his crisp roar brings every soldier in earshot to attention – 'proceed with the evacuation in an orderly fashion. The prison is under attack from within. Our enemy seeks to sow chaos. Do not let them succeed.'

The Warden turns to the interrogation cells, pulling open the door just as three Masks spill out.

'Bleeding inferno down there, Warden,' one of them says.

'And the prisoners?'

'Only the two, both still in their cells.'

'My medical equipment?'

'We believe Drusius got it out, sir,' another of the Masks says. 'I'm certain one of the Scholar brats set the fire, acting in league with Veturius.'

'Those children are subhuman,' the Warden says. 'I doubt they are capable of speech, much less a plot to burn down the prison. Go – ensure the cooperation of the remaining prisoners. I will not allow my domain to descend into insanity over a bit of flame.'

'What about the prisoners down there, sir?' The first Mask nods to the stairs leading to the interrogation block.

The Warden shakes his head as smoke billows from the doorway. 'If they're not dead already,' he says, 'they will be in seconds. And we need every man in the yard, controlling the prisoners. Lock that door,' he says. 'Let them burn.'

With that, the man clears a path through the stream of black-clad soldiers, delivering orders in his high, crisp voice as he goes. The Mask he spoke to slams the interrogation door shut, throws a bolt, and secures it with a padlock. I sneak up behind him – I need his keys. But when I reach for the ring, he senses my tampering and swings his elbow back, connecting with my stomach. As I double over, gasping for air and fighting to maintain my invisibility, he peers over his shoulder but is pulled away by the rush of soldiers pouring out of the prison.

Right. Brute force. I yank one of Elias's scims from my back

411

and hack at the padlock, not caring about the racket. It's hardly noticeable above the roar of the approaching fire. Sparks fly, but the lock holds. Again and again I swing Elias's blade, screaming in impatience. My invisibility flickers in and out, but I don't care. I *must* get this lock open. My brother and Elias are down there, burning.

We made it this far. We survived Blackcliff and the attacks in Serra, the Commandant, the journey here. It cannot end like this. I will not be done in by a bleeding, burning lock.

'Come on!' I scream. The lock cracks, and I put all of my rage into the next blow. Sparks explode, and it finally opens. I sheathe the sword, and fling the door wide.

Almost immediately, I drop, choking on the foul smoke pouring out. Through squinted, tear-filled eyes, I stare at what should be a staircase.

There is nothing but a wall of flame.

CHAPTER FIFTY-TWO

Elias

Even if the Soul Catcher hadn't welcomed me to the realm of death, an emptiness yawns at my core. I *feel* dead.

'I died choking in a prison stairwell, steps from salvation?' *Damn it!* 'I need more time,' I say to the Soul Catcher. 'A few hours.'

'I do not choose when you die, Elias.' She helps me up, her face pained, as if she genuinely mourns my death. Behind her, other spirits jostle in the trees, watching.

'I'm not ready, Shaeva,' I say. 'Laia is up there waiting for me. Her brother is beside me, dying. What did we fight for if it was just going to end like this?'

'Few are ready for death,' Shaeva sighs. She's given this speech before. 'Sometimes even the very old, who have lived full lives, fight against its cold grasp. You must accept—'

'No.' I look around for some way to get back. A portal or weapon or tool I can use to change my fate. *Stupid, Elias. There is no way back. Death is death.*

Nothing is impossible. My mother's words. If she were here,

413

she'd bully, threaten, or trick the Soul Catcher into giving her the time she wanted.

'Shaeva,' I say, 'you've ruled these lands for a thousand years. You know everything about death. There must be some way to go back, just for a little while.'

She turns away, her back stiff and unyielding. I pivot around her, my ghost form so swift that I see the shadow that passes across her eyes.

'When the seizures began,' I say, 'you told me you were watching me. Why?'

'It was a mistake, Elias.' Shaeva's eyelashes glint with moisture. 'I saw you as I saw all humans: lesser, weak. But I was *wrong*. I – I should never have brought you here. I opened a door that should have remained shut.'

'But *why*?' She's dancing around the truth. 'Why did I catch your attention in the first place? It's not as if you spend all your time making moon-eyes at the human world. You're too busy with the spirits.'

I reach for her hands, startled when they pass through her. *Ghost, Elias, remember?*

'After the Third Trial,' she says, 'you sent many to their deaths. But they were not angry. I found it strange, since murder usually results in restless spirits. But these spirits didn't rage about you. Other than Tristas, they moved on quickly.

'I didn't understand why. I used my power to see into the human world.' She laces her fingers together and fixes her black gaze upon me. 'In the catacombs of Serra, you ran into an cave efrit. *Murderer*, it called you.'

'*If your sins were blood, child, you would drown in a river of your own making*,' I say. 'I remember.'

'What it said mattered less than your reaction, Elias. You

were . . .' She frowns, contemplating. 'Horrified. The spirits you sent to their deaths were at peace because you *mourned* them. You bring pain and suffering to those you love. But you do not wish to. It is as if your very fate is to leave a trail of destruction. You are like me. Or rather, like I was.'

The Waiting Place suddenly feels colder. 'Like you,' I say flatly.

'You are not the only living creature to have wandered my woods, Elias. Shamans come here sometimes. Healers too. To the living or the dead, the wailing is unbearable. Yet you didn't mind it. It took me decades to learn to communicate with the spirits. But you picked it up after a few visits.'

A hiss cuts through the air, and I spot the all too familiar glow of the jinn grove getting brighter. For once, Shaeva ignores it.

'I tried to keep you from Laia,' she says. 'I wanted you to feel isolated. I wanted something from you, and so I wished you to be fearful. But after I waylaid you on your journey to Kauf, after you spoke my name, something awoke inside me. Some remnant of my better self. I realized how wrong I was to ask anything of you. Forgive me. I was so tired of this place. I only wished for release.'

The glow grows brighter. The trees seem to tremble.

'I don't understand.'

'I wanted you to take my place,' she says. 'To become Soul Catcher.'

At first I think I've misheard her. 'Is that why you asked me to help Tristas move on?'

She nods. 'You are human,' she says. 'Thus you have limits the jinn do not. I had to see if you could do it. To be Soul Catcher, you must know death intimately, but you cannot worship it. You must have lived a life in which you wished to protect others but found that all you could do was destroy. Such a life instills remorse.

That remorse is a doorway through which the power of the Waiting Place can enter you.'

Shaaeeva . . .

She swallows. I'm certain she hears the call of her kindred. 'The Waiting Place is sentient, Elias. The oldest magic there is. And' – she grimaces apologetically – 'it likes you. Already, it has begun to whisper its secrets to you.'

I grasp at something she told me before. 'You said that when you became Soul Catcher, the Nightbringer killed you,' I say, 'but that he brought you back and chained you here. And now, you live.'

'This is no life, Elias!' Shaeva says. 'It is living death. Always I am surrounded by the spirits. I am *bound* to this place—'

'Not entirely,' I say. 'You left the Forest. You came all the way to get me.'

'Only because you were near my lands. Leaving for more than a few days is torture. The further afield I go, the more I suffer. And the jinn, Elias – you do not understand what it is to deal with my trapped brethren.'

SHAEVA! They cry out to her now, and she turns toward them.

No! I shout the word in my head, and the ground beneath me shudders. The jinn fall silent. And I know, suddenly, what I must ask of her.

'Shaeva,' I say. 'Make me your successor. Bring me back to life, the way the Nightbringer did for you.'

'You are a fool,' she whispers, unsurprised at my request. 'Accept death, Elias. You would be free of want, worry, pain. I will help you pass on, and all will be quiet and peaceful. If you become Soul Catcher, your life will be one of repentance and loneliness, for the living cannot enter the Forest. The ghosts cannot abide them.'

I cross my arms. 'Maybe you're too soft on the bleeding ghosts.'

'You may not even be capable—'

'I am capable. I helped Izzi and Tristas pass through. Do this for me, Shaeva. I'll live, save Darin, finish what I started. Then I will tend to the dead and have a chance to redeem myself in full for all that I've done.' I step toward her. 'You've repented long enough,' I say. 'Let me take over.'

'I would still have to teach you,' she says, 'as I was taught.' A great part of her wants this, I can see it. But she is frightened.

'Do you fear death?'

'No,' she whispers. 'I fear that you do not understand the burden you ask for.'

'How long have you been waiting to find someone like me?' I wheedle. I *have* to get back. I *have* to get Darin out of Kauf. 'A thousand years, right? Do you *really* want to stick around here for a thousand more years, Shaeva? Give me this gift. Take the one I'm offering you.'

For a second, her pain and suffering, the truth of her existence for the last millennium, is writ in her expression as clearly as if she'd screamed it out. I see the moment she decides, the moment the fear is replaced by resignation.

'Hurry,' I say. 'Skies know how much time has already passed in Kauf. I don't want to get back to my body just in time for it to burn to a crisp.'

'This is old magic, Elias. It is not of jinn or man or efrit but of the earth itself. It will take you back to the moment of death. And it will hurt.'

When she takes my hands, her touch burns hotter than a Serran forge. She clenches her jaw and releases a shrill keen that shakes me to my core. Her body glows, filled with a fire that consumes her, until she is no longer Shaeva but a creature of writhing black flame. She releases my hands and spins around me so rapidly that it's as if I'm enveloped by a cloud of darkness. Though I am a ghost, I feel my essence draining away. I fall to my knees, and her voice fills my head. A deeper voice rumbles beneath it, an ancient voice, the Waiting Place itself, taking possession of her jinn body and speaking through it.

'Son of shadow, heir of death, hear me: To rule the Waiting Place is to light the way for the weak, the weary, the fallen, and the forgotten in the darkness that follows death. You will be bound to me until another is worthy enough to release you. To leave is to forsake your duty – and I will punish you for it. Do you submit?'

'I submit.'

A vibration in the air – the taut silence of the earth before a land tremor. Then a sound as if the sky is being torn in half. Pain – *ten hells, pain* – the agony of a thousand deaths, a spike through my soul. Every heartbreak, every lost opportunity, every life cut short, the torment of those left to mourn – it tears through me endlessly. This is beyond pain, the pinprick heart of pain, a dying star exploding in my chest.

Long after I'm certain I can handle no more, the pain fades. I am left shaking on the Forest floor, filled with a rightness and a terror, like twin rivers of light and dark joining to become something else altogether.

'It's done, Elias.'

Shaeva kneels beside me in her human form once more. Her face is streaked with tears.

'Why so sad, Shaeva?' I wipe her tears with a thumb, feeling an ache when I see them. 'You're not alone anymore. We're comrades in arms now. Brother and sister.'

She does not smile. 'Only until you are ready,' she says. 'Go, brother. Return to the human world and finish what you have begun. But know you do not have much time. The Waiting Place will call you back. The magic is your master now, and it does not like its servants to be away for long.'

I will myself back to my body, and when I open my eyes I see Tas's frantic face. My limbs are free of the exhaustion I've felt for ages.

'Elias!' Tas sobs with relief. 'The fire – it is everywhere! I cannot carry Darin!'

'You don't have to.' I still ache from the interrogations and the beatings, but with the poison gone from my blood, I understand, for the first time, how it stole away my life bit by bit until it seemed to me that I had always been a shadow of myself.

The fire blasts up the stairwell and races along the beams above, creating a wall of flames behind and ahead.

Light flares above, visible through the fire. Shouts, voices, and for the briefest moment, a familiar figure beyond the flames.

'The door, Tas!' I shout. 'It's open!' At least, I think it's open. Tas staggers to his feet, dark eyes filled with hope. *Go, Elias!* I throw Darin over one shoulder, sweep the Scholar child up in my arm, and fly up the stairs, through the wall of flame, and into the light beyond.

CHAPTER FIFTY-THREE

Helene

The men of Gens Veturia surround my parents and sisters. The courtiers look away, embarrassed and frightened by the sight of my family having their arms twisted around their backs, marched to the throne, and forced to their knees like common criminals.

Mother and Father submit to the manhandling silently, and Livvy only casts me an imploring look, as if I can somehow fix this.

Hannah fights – scratching, kicking at the soldiers, her intricate blonde coiffure collapsing about her shoulders. 'Don't punish me for her betrayal, Your Majesty!' she screams. 'She's no sister of mine, my lord. *She's no kin of mine.*'

'Quiet,' he roars at her, 'or I'll kill you first.' She falls silent. The soldiers turn my family to face me. The silk-and-fur-clad courtiers on either side of me shift and whisper, some horror-struck, others barely restraining their glee. I spot the new Pater of Gens Rufia. At the sight of his cruel smile, I remember his father's scream as Marcus cast him over Cardium Rock.

Marcus paces behind my family. 'I did think we would have the executions at Cardium Rock,' he says. 'But as so many of the

420

Gens are represented here, I don't see why we shouldn't just get this over with.'

The Commandant steps forward, her eyes fixed on my father. He saved me from torture, against her wishes. He calmed angry Gens when she attempted to sow dissent, and he aided me when his negotiations failed. Now she will have her vengeance. A raw, animal hunger lurks in her eyes. She wants to tear my father's throat out. She wants to dance in his blood.

'Your Majesty,' she croons. 'I'd be happy to assist in the execution—'

'No need, Commandant,' Marcus says levelly. 'You've done enough already.' The words carry a strange weight, and the Commandant eyes the Emperor, suddenly wary.

I thought you would be safe, I want to say to my family. *The Augurs told me* –

But the Augurs, I realize, promised me nothing.

I force myself to meet my father's eyes. I have never seen him so defeated.

Beside him, Mother's white-blonde hair shines as if lit from within, her fur-lined gown draped gracefully even as she kneels for death. Her pale face is fierce. 'Strength, my girl,' she whispers to me. Beside her, Livvy breathes in short, panicked gusts. She whispers rapidly to a violently trembling Hannah.

I try to grasp the scim at my waist to steady myself, but I can hardly feel it beneath my palm.

'Your Majesty,' I say. 'Please. The Commandant *is* planning a coup. You heard Lieutenant Faris. You must listen to me.'

Marcus lifts his eyes to me, their flat yellow chilling my blood. Slowly, he draws a dagger from his belt. It is thin and razor-sharp with a Blackcliff diamond as its hilt. His prize for winning the First Trial, so long ago.

'I can make it quick, Shrike,' he says quietly. 'Or I can make it very, very slow. Speak out of turn again and see which one I choose. Lieutenant Sergius,' he calls out. The Black Guard I cowed through blackmail and coercion just weeks ago slinks forward.

'Secure the Shrike and her allies,' Marcus says. 'We wouldn't want their emotions to get the better of them.'

Sergius hesitates for just a second before signaling the other Black Guards.

Hannah sobs quietly, turning imploring eyes to Marcus. 'Please,' she whispers. 'Your Majesty. We are engaged – I am your betrothed.' But Marcus doesn't spare her any more attention than he would a beggar.

Marcus turns to the Paters in the throne room, and power exudes from him. He is no embattled Emperor now but one who has survived a Scholar rebellion, assassination attempts, and the betrayal of the strongest families in the land.

He twirls his dagger in his hand, and the silver catches the light of the sun now rising overhead. Dawn illuminates the room with gentle beauty that sickens me when I think of what is about to happen. Marcus paces back and forth behind my family, a brutal predator deciding whom to kill first.

My mother whispers something to my father and sisters. *I love you.*

'Men and women of the Empire.' Marcus slows behind Mother. Her eyes burn into mine, and she straightens her spine and throws back her shoulders. Marcus stills the movement of the dagger. 'Observe what happens when you fail your Emperor.'

The throne room falls silent. I hear the silver blade dip into my mother's throat, the gurgling tear it makes as he draws it across her neck and into her artery. She sways. Her gaze slides to the floor, her body soon following.

'No!' Hannah shrieks, giving voice to the despair that has gripped my body. My mouth is salty with blood – I've bitten through my lip. While the courtiers watch, Hannah keens like a wounded animal, rocking over my mother's body, not caring about anything but her wretched, all-consuming grief. Livia's face is empty, her eyes confused as she peers down at the blood pooling, soaking the knees of her pale blue dress.

I cannot feel the pain in my lip. My feet, my legs seem so far away. That is not my mother's blood. That is not her body. Those are not her hands, lifeless and white. No.

Hannah's scream yanks me from my daze. Marcus has grabbed her by her ruined hair. 'No, please.' Her frantic eyes seek me out. 'Hel, help me!'

I strain against Sergius, a strange wounded snarl coming from my throat. I can barely hear her as she chokes out the words. My baby sister. She had the softest hair when we were girls. 'Helly, I'm sorry—'

Marcus draws the knife across her throat swiftly. His face is blank as he does so, as if the task requires all of his concentration. He releases her, and she thuds down beside my mother. The pale strands of their hair mingle.

Behind me, the door to the throne room opens. Marcus sneers at the interruption.

'Y-your Majesty.' I cannot see the soldier who enters, but the crack in his voice suggests that he wasn't expecting to walk into a bloodbath. 'A message from Kauf . . .'

'I'm in the middle of something. Keris,' Marcus barks at the Commandant without looking at her, 'deal with it.'

The Commandant bows and turns to leave, slowing as she passes me. She leans forward, putting a cold hand on my shoulder. I am too numb to flinch away from her. Her gray eyes are remorseless.

'It is glorious to witness your unmaking, Blood Shrike,' she whispers. 'To watch as you break.'

My whole body shakes as she throws Cain's words back at my face. *First you will be unmade. First, you will be broken.* Bleeding skies, I thought he meant when I killed Elias. But he knew. All that time while I agonized over my friend, he and his brethren *knew* what it was that would truly break me.

But how could the Commandant possibly know what Cain said to me? She releases me and saunters out of the room, and I have no more time to wonder, for Marcus is before me.

'Take a moment to say goodbye to your father, Shrike. Sergius, release her.'

I take three steps to my father and fall to my knees. I cannot look away from my mother and sister.

'Blood Shrike,' my father whispers. 'Look at me.'

I want to beg him to call me by my name. *I'm not the Shrike. I'm Helene, your Helene. Your little girl.*

'Look at me, daughter.' I lift my eyes, expecting to see defeat in his gaze. Instead, he is my calm, collected father, though his whisper is ragged with grief. 'And listen. You cannot save me. You could not save your mother, or your sister, or Elias. But you can still save the Empire, for it is in far graver danger than Marcus realizes. Tiborum will soon be surrounded by hordes of Wildmen, and I hear tell of a fleet out of Karkaus, heading north to Navium. The Commandant is blind to it – she is too fixated on the destruction of the Scholars and on securing her own power.'

'Father.' I glance at Marcus, who is watching from a few yards away. 'Damn the Empire—'

'Listen to me.' The sudden desperation in his voice terrifies me. My father fears nothing. 'Gens Aquilla must remain powerful. Our alliances must remain powerful. *You* must remain powerful. When war comes to this land from without, which it inevitably will, we cannot falter. How many Martials in this Empire?'

'M-millions.'

'More than six million,' my father says. 'Six million men, women, and children whose futures rest in your hands. Six million who will depend on your strength so that they may remain untouched by the torment of war. You are all that holds back the darkness. Take my necklace.'

With shaking hands, I pull off the chain I used to bat at as a child. One of my first memories is Father leaning over me, the Aquilla ring dangling from his collar, the embossed falcon in full flight catching the lamplight.

'You are Mater of Gens Aquilla now,' Father whispers. 'You are Blood Shrike of the Empire. And you are my daughter. Do not fail me.'

The moment my father eases back, Marcus strikes. It takes my father longer to die – he has more blood, perhaps. When his eyes darken, I think I cannot hurt any more. Marcus has wrung me dry of all my pain. Then my eyes fall upon my littlest sister. *You fool, Helene. When you love, there is always more pain.*

'Men and women of the Empire.' Marcus's voice echoes from the rafters of the throne room. *What in the bleeding hells is he doing?*

'I am but a Plebeian, given the burden of rulership by our esteemed holy men, the Augurs.' He sounds almost humble, and I gape at him as he looks around at the assembly of the Empire's finest. 'But even a Plebeian knows that sometimes an Emperor must show mercy.

'The bond between Shrike and Emperor is one ordained by the Augurs.' He goes to Livia and lifts her to her feet. She looks between Marcus and me, mouth parted, skin blanched to gray.

'It is a bond that must weather the darkest of tempests,' the

Emperor says. 'My Shrike's first failure is one such tempest. But I am not unmerciful. Nor do I wish to begin my reign with broken promises. I signed a marriage agreement with Gens Aquilla.' He glances at me, stone-faced. 'And so I shall honor it – by marrying Mater Aquilla's youngest sister, Livia Aquilla, immediately. By joining my line to one of the oldest Gens in the land, I seek to establish my dynasty and bring glory to the Empire once more. We shall put this' – he looks distastefully at the bodies on the ground – 'behind us. If, of course, Mater Aquilla accepts.'

'Livia.' I can only mouth my sister's name. I clear my throat. 'Livia would be spared?' At Marcus's nod, I stand. I force myself to look at my sister, because if she would rather die, then I cannot deny her that, even if it unravels my last bit of sanity. But the reality of what is happening finally hits her. I see my own torment mirrored in her eyes – but I see something else too. My parents' strength. She nods.

'I – I accept,' I whisper.

'Good,' Marcus says. 'We will marry at sunset. The rest of you – get out,' he barks at the courtiers, who watch in horrified fascination. 'Sergius.' The Black Guard steps forward. 'Take my . . . *bride* to the east wing of the palace. Make sure she is comfortable. And safe.'

Sergius escorts Livia away. The courtiers file out silently. As I stare at the ground in front of me, at the spreading pool of blood, Marcus approaches.

He stands behind me and runs one finger along the back of my neck. I shudder in disgust, but a second later, Marcus jerks his body away.

'Shut up,' he hisses, and when I glance up, I find he's not addressing me. Instead, he's looking over his shoulder – at empty air. '*Stop.*'

I watch with a dull sort of fascination as he growls and shakes his shoulders, like he's shaking off someone's grasp. A moment later, he turns back to me – but keeps his hands to himself.

'You stupid girl.' His voice is a soft hiss. 'I told you: Never presume that you know more than me. I was well aware of Keris's little plot. I warned you not to defy me pubicly, and still you barged in, screaming of a coup, making me look *weak*. If you'd kept your damned mouth shut, this wouldn't have happened.'

Bleeding skies. 'You – you knew—'

'I always know.' He digs his hand into my hair, yanking my head up and away from the sight of the blood. 'I will *always* win. And now I possess the last living member of your family. If you *ever* disobey an order again, if you fail me, speak against me, or double-cross me, I swear to the skies that I will make her suffer more than you can possibly imagine.'

He releases me violently. His boots are silent as he leaves the throne room.

I am alone, but for ghosts.

CHAPTER FIFTY-FOUR

Laia

I stumble away from the flames, my invisibility gone. *No! Skies, no!*

Darin, Elias, little Tas – they cannot be dead in the inferno. Not after everything. I find that I am sobbing, that my invisibility has fallen. And I don't care.

'You there! Scholar!' Bootsteps thunder toward me, and I slide back across the polished stone of the rotunda, trying to avoid the grasping hand of a legionnaire who clearly thinks I'm an escaped prisoner. His eyes narrow, and he lunges forward, his fingers fastening onto my cloak, ripping it off. He casts it to the ground as I scramble away, then he hurtles his big body into mine.

'Oof!' The breath leaves my lungs as I hit the bottom steps of the staircase. The soldier tries to flip me on my stomach, to capture my hands.

'Get off!'

'Did you escape the pens? Arrrg!' He jerks when I knee him in the groin. I unsheathe my dagger, drive it into his thigh, and twist. He bellows, and a second later, his weight is yanked off me and he goes flying into the staircase, my blade still embedded in his leg.

A shadow fills the space where he stood, familiar and utterly changed at the same time. 'E-Elias?'

'I'm here.' He hauls me to my feet. He is lean as a rail, and his eyes appear to almost glow in the thickening smoke. 'Your brother is here. Tas is here. We're alive. We're all right. And that was beautifully done.' He nods to the soldier, who has ripped the dagger out of his thigh and is now crawling away. 'He'll be limping for months.'

I leap up and pull him into a hug, something between a sob and a cry erupting from my chest. We are both injured and exhausted and heart-sore, but when I feel his arms around me, when I realize that he is *real* and here and alive, I believe, for the first time, that we have a chance at surviving.

'Where's Darin?' I pull away from Elias, looking around, expecting my brother to appear out of the smoke. Soldiers rush past us, desperate to escape the fire engulfing the Martial section of the prison. 'Here, take your scims.' I shrug out of the cross-body scabbard, and Elias pulls them on. Darin does not appear.

'Elias?' I say, worried now. 'Where —' As I speak, Elias kneels, pulling something from the floor onto his shoulder. I think, at first, that it is a filthy bag of sticks.

Then I see the hands. *Darin's* hands. His skin is scarred, and he's missing a pinky and a middle finger. Still, I'd know those hands anywhere.

'Skies.' I try to see Darin's face, but it's obscured by hanks of long, filthy hair. My brother was never particularly heavy, but he seems so small suddenly – a depleted, nightmare version of himself. *He might not be what he was*, Afya had warned.

429

'He's alive,' Elias reminds me when he sees my face. 'He got a knock on the head is all. He's going to be all right.'

A small figure appears behind Elias, my bloody dagger in hand. He gives it to me, then takes my fingers. 'You must not be seen, Laia,' he says. 'Hide yourself!'

Tas pulls me down the hall, and I let my invisibility fall over me. Elias starts at my sudden disappearance. I squeeze his hand so he knows I am close. Ahead of us, the prison doors are flung open. A knot of soldiers teems outside.

'You have to open the Scholar pens,' Elias says. 'I can't do it while carrying Darin. The guards would be on me in a second.'

Skies! I was to set more fires in the prison yard to add to the mayhem.

'We'll have to do without the extra distraction,' Elias says. 'I'll pretend I'm delivering Darin to the pens. I'll be right behind you. Tas, stay with Laia – watch her back. I'll find you.'

'One thing, Elias.' I don't want to worry him, but he should know. 'The Warden might know I'm here. I lost my invisibility upstairs for a moment. I got it back, but he could have seen the change.'

'Then stay away from him,' Elias says. 'He's wily, and from the way he interrogated Darin and me, I'm certain he'd love to get his hands on you.'

Seconds later, we burst out of the prison and into the yard. The cold is like a knife in the face after the stifling heat of the prison.

The yard, though crowded, is devoid of chaos. Prisoners emerging from Kauf are immediately escorted away. Kauf's guards, many of them coughing, ash-faced, or burned, are ushered into a line, where another soldier assesses them for injuries before assigning them to a task. One of the legionnaires in charge spots Elias and calls out to him.

'You!' he says. 'You there!'

'Let me dump this body,' Elias grumbles, the perfect impression of a sullen aux. He pulls his cloak closer and edges away as another group of soldiers tumbles out of Kauf's inferno.

'Go, Laia,' he whispers under his breath. 'Quickly!'

Tas and I bolt toward the Scholar pens, far to our left. Behind us echo the voices of thousands of prisoners: Martials, Tribesmen, Mariners – even Wildmen and Barbarians. The Martials have gathered them into one enormous circle and formed a cordon of spearmen two guards thick around them.

'There, Laia.' Tas shoves the keys he stole into my hands and nods to the north side of the pen. 'I will warn the Skiritae!' He veers away, staying close to the edges of the pen and whispering through the wide spaces between its wooden slats.

I spot the door – which is guarded by six legionnaires. The racket of the prison yard is loud enough that they could not possibly hear me approach, but I tread carefully anyway. When I am within three feet of the door, and just inches from the closest legionnaire, he shifts, putting a hand on his sword, and I freeze. I can smell the leather of his armor, the steel tips of the arrows across his back. *Just one more step, Laia. He can't see you. He has no idea you're here.*

As if handling an angry snake, I remove the key ring from my pocket, holding on to it tightly so it doesn't jangle. I wait until one of the legionnaires turns to say something to the rest before I put the key in the lock.

It jams.

I wiggle the key, first gently and then a bit harder. One of the soldiers turns toward the door. I look at him, right at his eyes, but he shrugs and turns back.

Patience, Laia. I take a deep breath and lift the lock. Because it's attached to something that is grounded in the earth, it does not disappear. I hope no one is looking at this door right now – they'd see a lock floating inches from where it should be, and even the most dimwitted aux would know that's unnatural. Again, I twist the key. *Almost* –

Just then, something fastens on to my arm – a long hand that curls like a feeler around my bicep.

'Ah, Laia of Serra,' someone breathes into my ear. 'What a talented girl you are. I am *very* interested in examining your skill further.'

My invisibility falters, and the keys fall to the icy stones with a clatter. I look up to find myself staring into a pointed face with large, watery eyes.

The Warden.

CHAPTER FIFTY-FIVE

Elias

Shaeva warned me that the Waiting Place would pull at me. As I make my way across the freezing prison yard to the pens, I feel it, a yank in my chest, like an invisible hook.

I'm coming, I shout in my head. *The more you bully me, the slower I'll be, so stop it.*

The pull lessens slightly, as if the Waiting Place has heard. Fifteen yards to the pens . . . thirteen . . . ten . . .

Then I hear footsteps. The soldier from Kauf's entrance has caught up with me. From his cautious gait, I can tell that my uniform and the scims across my back haven't fooled him. *Ten hells.* Ah well. This was always a stretch, as far as disguises go.

He attacks. I try to sidestep him, but Darin's body has me off balance, and the soldier clips me, knocking me down and sending Darin rolling away.

The legionnaire's eyes widen when my hood falls back. 'Prisoner loose,' he bellows. 'Pris—' I snatch a knife from his belt and plunge it into his side.

Too late. The legionnaires at Kauf's entrance have heard his cry. Four of the spearmen guarding the prisoners break away. Auxes.

I smile. *Not enough to take me down.*

I draw my scims as the first soldier approaches, duck under his spear, and slice his wrist. He screams and releases the weapon. I drop him with a blow across the temple, then pivot and halve the spear of the next soldier, felling him with a blade through the stomach.

My blood rises now, my warrior's instincts at full tilt. I sweep up the fallen soldier's spear and send it flying into the shoulder of the third aux. The fourth hesitates, and I take him down with a shoulder to his gut. His head cracks against the cobblestones, and he does not move again.

A spear whizzes by my ear, and pain explodes in my head. It's not enough to stop me.

A dozen spearmen break from the prisoners. They know now that I am more than just an escaped prisoner.

'Run!' I roar at the gaping prisoners, pointing at the gap in the cordon. 'Escape! Run!'

Two Martials bolt through the cordon and make for Kauf's portcullis. For a moment, it seems as if the entire yard watches them, holding its breath. Then a guard shouts, the spell is broken, and all at once, dozens of inmates surge out, not caring if they are impaling their fellows on spears. The Martial spearmen attempt to fill the gap, but there are thousands of prisoners, and they've caught the scent of freedom.

The soldiers running toward me slow at the shouts of their comrades. I heave Darin up and race for the Scholar pens. Why in the ten hells aren't they open yet? There should be Scholars flooding the yard.

'Elias!' Tas darts toward me. 'The lock is stuck. And Laia – the Warden—'

I spot the Warden scuttling across the yard with Laia in a chokehold. She kicks at him desperately, but he's lifted her off the ground, and her face turns red from lack of air. *No! Laia!* I'm already moving for her, but I grit my teeth and force myself to stop. We need those pens open if we want to get the Scholars out and loaded onto the boats.

'Get to her, Tas,' I say. 'Distract the Warden. I'll deal with the lock.'

Tas runs, and I drop Darin beside the Scholar pen. The legionnaires guarding its entrance have bolted toward Kauf's in an attempt to stop the mass exodus of prisoners, and I turn my attention to the lock. It's jammed good and tight, and no matter how I twist, it does not open. Within the pens, a man shoves his way forward, only his dark eyes visible through the slats. His face is so filthy that I cannot tell if he is old or young.

'Elias Veturius?' he says in a harsh whisper.

As I unsheathe my scim to break the lock, I venture a guess. 'Araj?'

The man nods. 'What's taking so long? We've – Behind you!'

His warning saves me a spear through the gut, and I barely dodge the next. A dozen soldiers close on me, undistracted by the chaos at the gate.

'The lock, Veturius!' Araj says. 'Quickly.'

'Either give me a minute,' I hiss through gritted teeth, flicking my scims to divert two more spears, 'or make yourself useful.'

Araj barks an order to the Scholars within the pen. Seconds later, a barrage of rocks flies over the top and rains down upon the spearmen.

Watching this tactic is like witnessing a pack of mice flinging pebbles at a horde of ravening cats. Fortunately for me, these mice have good aim. Two of the closest spearmen falter, giving me enough time to spin and break the lock with a swipe of my scim.

The door bursts open, and with a roar, the Scholars explode from the pen.

I swipe up a Serric steel dagger from one of the fallen spearmen and hand it to Araj, who barrels out with the rest. 'Open the other pen!' I shout. 'I have to get to Laia!'

A sea of Scholar prisoners now crowds the yard, but the Warden's form pokes out above them. A small group of Scholar children, Tas among them, attack the old man. He lashes out with his scim to keep them at bay, but he's loosened his hold on Laia, and she thrashes in an attempt to break free.

'Warden!' I bellow. He turns at my voice, and Laia kicks her heel straight back into his shin while biting the flesh of his arm. The Warden jerks up his scim, and one of the Scholar children slips close and bashes his knee with a heavy skillet. The Warden roars, and Laia tumbles away from him, reaching for the dagger at her waist.

But it's not there. It gleams now in Tas's hands. His small face twists with rage as he lunges for the Warden. His friends swarm all over the old man, biting, clawing, bringing him down, taking their revenge on the monster who has abused them since the day they were born.

Tas plunges the dagger into the Warden's throat, flinching from the geyser of blood that erupts. The other children scurry away, surrounding Laia, who pulls Tas to her chest. I am beside them moments later.

'Elias,' Tas whispers. He cannot take his eyes off the Warden. 'I—'

'You slew a demon, Tas of the north.' I kneel beside him. 'I am proud to fight by your side. Get the other children out. We're not free yet.' I look up at the gate, where the guards now battle a horde of crazed prisoners. 'Meet us at the boats.'

'Darin!' Laia looks at me. 'Where—'

'By the pens,' I say. 'I can't wait until he wakes up and I can give him hell. I've had to drag him all around this bleeding prison.'

The drums thud frenziedly, and over the chaos, I can just barely hear the answering drums of a distant garrison. 'Even if we escape onto the boats,' Laia says as we race for the pens, 'we'll have to get out before we reach the Forest of Dusk. And the Martials will be waiting, won't they?'

'They will,' I say. 'But I have a plan.' Well, not exactly a *plan*. More like a hunch – and a possibly delusional hope that I can use my new occupation to do something quite mad. It's a gamble that will depend on the Waiting Place and Shaeva and my power of persuasion.

With Darin slung over my shoulder, we head for Kauf's entry gate, inundated with prisoners. The crowd is rabid – there are too many people fighting to get out, and too many Martials fighting to keep us in.

I hear a metallic groaning. 'Elias!' Laia points at the portcullis. Slowly, ponderously, it begins to drop. The sound gives new heart to the Martials beating back the prisoners, and Laia and I are driven farther from the gate.

'Torches, Laia!' I shout. She snatches two off a nearby wall, and we wield them like scims. Those around us instinctively cringe from the fire, allowing us to force a path through.

The portcullis drops another few feet, almost at eye level now. Laia grabs my arm. 'One push,' she shouts. 'Together – now!'

We lock arms, lower the torches, and ram our way through the crowd. I shove her beneath the portcullis ahead of me, but she resists and whips around, forcing me to come with her

And then we are beneath, through, running past the soldiers battling prisoners, making straight for the boathouse, where I see two barges already a quarter mile down the river and two more launching from the docks, Scholars hanging off the sides.

'She did it!' Laia shouts. 'Afya did it!'

'Bowmen!' A line of soldiers appears atop Kauf's wall. 'Run!'

A hail of arrows rains down around us, and half the Scholars racing for the boathouse with us go down. *Almost there. Almost.*

'Elias! Laia!' I spot Afya's red-black braids at the boathouse door. She waves us into the structure, her eyes on the bowmen. Her face is slashed, her hands covered in blood, but she quickly leads us to a small canoe.

'As much as I'd enjoy a boating adventure with the unwashed masses,' she says, 'I think this will be faster. Hurry.'

I lay Darin down between two benches, grab an oar, and push off from the boathouse. Behind us, Araj pulls Tas and Bee onto the final Scholar barge and launches it. His people pole it forward with panicked speed. Swiftly, the current pulls us away from the ruin of Kauf – and toward the Forest of Dusk.

'You said you had a plan.' Laia nods to the soft green line of the Forest to the south. Darin lies between us, still unconscious, his head resting on his sister's pack. 'Might be a good time to share it.'

What do I say to her of the trade I made with Shaeva? Where do I even begin?

With the truth.

'I'll share it,' I say quietly enough that only she can hear. 'But first, there's something else I need to tell you. About how I survived the poison. And about what I've become.'

438

CHAPTER FIFTY-SIX

Helene

ONE MONTH LATER

Deep winter roars into Antium on the back of a three-day blizzard. Snow blankets the city so thickly that the Scholar sweepers work around the clock to keep the thoroughfares clear. Midwinter candles glow all night in windows across the city, from the finest mansions to the poorest hovels.

Emperor Marcus will celebrate the holiday at the imperial palace with the Paters and Maters of a few dozen important Gens. My spies tell me that many deals will be struck – trade agreements and government postings that will further cement Marcus's power.

I know it to be true, because I helped arrange most of those deals.

Within the Black Guard barracks, I sit at my desk, signing an order to send a contingent of my men to Tiborum. We have wrested the port back from the Wildmen who nearly took it, but they have not given up. Now that they've smelled blood in the water, they will return – with more men.

I gaze out the window at the white city. A thought flits through my mind, a memory of Hannah and me throwing snowballs at each other long ago, when Father brought us to Antium as girls. I smile. Remember. Then I lock the memory away in a dark place – where I will not see it again – and turn back to my work.

'Learn to lock your damned window, girl.'

The raspy voice is instantly recognizable. Still, I jump. The Cook's eyes glint beneath a hood that hides her scars. She keeps her distance, ready to slip back out the window at the first sign of a threat.

'You could just use the front door.' I keep a hand on a dagger strapped to the underside of my desk. 'I'll make certain no one stops you.'

'Friends now, are we?' The Cook tilts her scarred face and shows her teeth in an approximation of a smile. 'How sweet.'

'Your wound – has it healed fully?'

'I'm still here.' The Cook peers out the window and fidgets. 'I heard about your family,' she says gruffly. 'I'm sorry.'

I raise my eyebrows. 'You went through the trouble of sneaking in here to pay your condolences?'

'That,' the Cook says, 'and to tell you that when you're ready to take on the Bitch of Blackcliff, I can help. You know how to find me.'

I consider the sealed letter from Marcus on my desk. 'Come back tomorrow,' I say. 'We'll talk.'

She nods and, without so much as a whisper, slips back out the window. Curiosity pulls at me, and I walk over and peer out, scanning the sheer walls above and below for a hook, scratches, any indication as to how she scaled an unscaleable wall. Nothing. I'll have to ask her about that trick.

I turn my attention to Marcus's letter:

Tiborum is under control, and Gens Serca and Gens Aroman have fallen in line. No more excuses. It is time to deal with her.

There is only one *her* he could be talking about. I read on.

Be quiet and careful. I do not want a quick assassination, Shrike. I want utter destruction. I want her to feel it. I want the Empire to know my strength.

Your sister was a delight at the dinner with the Mariner ambassador last night. She quite put him at ease about the shift in power here. Such a useful girl. I pray she remains healthy and serves her Empire for a long time to come.

– Emperor Marcus Farrar

The Fiver on message duty jumps when I open my office door. After I give him his task, I reread Marcus's letter and wait impatiently. Moments later, a knock sounds.

'Blood Shrike,' Captain Harper says when he enters. 'You called?'

I hand him the letter. 'We need a plan,' I say. 'She disbanded her army when she realized I was going to tell Marcus of the coup, but that doesn't mean she can't muster it again. Keris won't go down easily.'

'Or at all,' Harper mutters. 'This will take months. Even if she doesn't expect an attack from Marcus, she will expect an attack from you. She'll be prepared.'

'I know that,' I say. 'Which is why we need a plan that actually works. That starts with finding Quin Veturius.'

'No one has heard from him since his escape in Serra.'

'I know where to find him,' I say. 'Pull a team together. Make sure Dex is on it. We'll leave in two days. Dismissed.'

Harper nods, and I turn back to my work. When he doesn't leave, I raise my eyebrows. 'Do you require something, Harper?'

'No, Shrike. Only . . .' He looks more uncomfortable than I've ever seen him – enough to actually alarm me. Since the execution, he and Dex have been invaluable. They supported my reshuffling of the Black Guard – Lieutenant Sergius is now posted on Isle South – and unwaveringly backed me when some of the Black Guard attempted to rebel.

'If we're going after the Commandant, Shrike, then I know something that might be of use.'

'Go on.'

'Back in Nur, the day before the riot, I saw Elias. But I never told you.'

I lean back in my seat, sensing that I'm about to learn more about Avitas Harper than the previous Blood Shrike ever did.

'What I have to say,' Avitas goes on, 'is about *why* I never told you. It's about why the Commandant kept an eye out for me in Blackcliff and got me into the Black Guard. It's about Elias. And' – he takes a deep breath – 'about our father.'

Our father.

Our father. *His and Elias's.*

It takes a moment for the words to sink in. Then I order him to sit, and I lean forward.

'I'm listening.'

* * *

After Harper leaves, I brave the slush and muck of the streets to head to the courier's office, where two packages have arrived from the Aquilla villa in Serra. The first is my midwinter gift for Livia. After checking to make sure it's intact, I open the second package.

I catch my breath at the glimmer of Elias's mask in my hand. According to a Kauf courier, Elias and a few hundred Scholar fugitives disappeared into the Forest of Dusk shortly after breaking out of the prison. A dozen Empire soldiers tried to follow, but their mangled bodies were found on the Forest's borders the next morning.

No one has seen or heard from the fugitives since.

Perhaps the Nightweed killed my friend, or perhaps the Forest did. Or perhaps, somehow, he found some other way to evade death. Like his grandfather and mother, Elias has always had an uncanny skill at surviving what would kill anyone else.

It doesn't matter. He's gone, and the part of my heart where he lived is dead now. I tuck the mask in my pocket – I'll find a place for it in my quarters.

I head for the palace, Livvy's gift nestled under my arm, mulling over what Avitas told me: *The Commandant kept an eye on me in Blackcliff because it was my father's last request. At least, that's my suspicion. She's never acknowledged it.*

I asked the Commandant to give me the mission to shadow you because I wanted to learn about Elias through you. I didn't know any more about our father than what my mother told me. Her name was Renatia, and she said my father never fit the mold that Blackcliff tried to force him into. She said he was kind. Good. For a long time, I thought she was lying. I've never been those things, so it couldn't be true. But perhaps I just didn't inherit my father's better traits. Perhaps they went to a different son.

I berated him, of course – he should have said something long ago – but after my anger and incredulity settled, I understood the information for what it was: a crack in the Commandant's armor. A weapon I can use against her.

The guards of the palace let me pass into the imperial wing

with only nervous glances at each other. I have begun rooting out the enemies of the Empire – and I started here. Marcus can burn in the hells for all I care, but Livvy's marriage to him puts her in danger. His enemies will be hers, and I will not lose her.

Laia of Serra had the same type of love for her sibling. For the first time since meeting her, I understand her.

I find my sister sitting out on a balcony that overlooks her private garden. Faris and another Black Guard stand in the shadows a dozen feet away. I told my friend that he didn't need to take the posting. Guarding an eighteen-year-old girl is certainly not a coveted position for a member of the Blood Shrike's force.

If I'm going to kill, he'd said, *I'd rather do it while protecting someone.*

He nods a greeting to me, and my sister looks up.

'Blood Shrike.' She stands but doesn't hug me or kiss me the way she once would have, though I can tell she wants to. I nod to her room curtly. *I want privacy.*

My sister turns to the six girls who sit near her, three of whom are dark-skinned and yellow-eyed. When she first wrote to Marcus's mother, requesting that the woman send three girls from Marcus's extended family to serve as her ladies-in-waiting, I was stunned, as was every Illustrian family that had been passed over. The Plebeians, however, still talk about it.

The girls and their Illustrian counterparts disappear at Livia's gently given order. Faris and the other Black Guard move to follow us, but I wave them off. My sister and I enter her bedchamber, and I lay her midwinter gift on the bed and watch as she tears it open.

She gasps when the light shines off the ornate silver edges of my old mirror.

'But this is yours,' Livia says. 'Mother—'

'—would want you to have it. There's no place for it in the Blood Shrike's quarters.'

'It is beautiful. Will you hang it up for me?'

I summon a servant to bring me a hammer and nails, and when he returns, I remove Livvy's old mirror and plug the spy hole behind it. Marcus will just have his spies cut a new one. But for now, at least, my sister and I can speak in private.

She sits on the vanity chair beside me as I hammer in a nail. When I speak, I keep my voice low.

'Are you all right?'

'If you're asking the same thing you've asked every day since the wedding,' Livvy lifts an eyebrow, 'then yes. He hasn't touched me since the first time. Besides, I approached *him* that night.' My sister lifts her chin. 'I will not have him thinking I fear him, no matter what he does.'

I suppress a shudder. Living with Marcus – being his wife – is Livvy's life now. My disgust and loathing of him will only make that more difficult. She did not speak to me of her wedding night, and I haven't asked.

'I walked in on him talking to himself the other day.' Livvy looks at me. 'It wasn't the first time.'

'Lovely.' I hammer in a nail. 'An Emperor who is sadistic *and* hears voices.'

'He's not crazy,' Livvy says thoughtfully. 'He's in control until he speaks about doing violence to you – just you. Then he gets twitchy. I think he sees his brother's ghost, Hel. I think that's why he hasn't touched you.'

'Well, if he *is* haunted by Zak's ghost,' I say, 'I hope it sticks around. At least until—'

We lock eyes. *Until we have our vengeance.* Livia and I haven't spoken of it. It was understood the first moment I saw her after that horrible day in the throne room.

My sister brushes out her hair. 'You've heard nothing more of Elias?'

I shrug.

'And what of Harper?' Livvy tries again. 'Stella Galerius has been angling to meet him.'

'You should introduce them.'

My sister furrows her brow as she watches me. 'How is Dex? You two are so—'

'Dex is a loyal soldier and an excellent lieutenant. Marriage might be a bit more complicated for him. Most of your acquaintances aren't his type. And' – I lift up the mirror – 'you can stop now.'

'I don't want you to be lonely,' Livvy says. 'If we had Mother or Father or even Hannah, it would be different. But, Hel—'

'With respect, Empress,' I say quietly. 'My name is Blood Shrike.'

She sighs, and I attach the mirror, straightening it with a touch. 'All done.'

I catch my reflection. I appear as I did just a few months ago, on the eve of my graduation. Same body. Same face. Only the eyes are different. I look into the pale gaze of the woman in front of me. For a moment, I see Helene Aquilla. The girl who hoped. The girl who thought the world was fair.

But Helene Aquilla is broken. Unmade. Helene Aquilla is dead.

The woman in the mirror is not Helene Aquilla. She is the Blood Shrike. The Blood Shrike is not lonely, for the Empire is her mother and her father, her lover and her best friend. She needs nothing else. She needs no one else.

She stands apart.

CHAPTER FIFTY-SEVEN

Laia

Marinn rolls out beyond the Forest of Dusk, a vast white carpet dotted with iced-over lakes and patches of forest. I've never seen a sky so clear and blue or breathed air that feels as if it's filling me with life every time I inhale.

The Free Lands. Finally.

Already, I love everything about this place. It is familiar in the way my parents would be familiar, I think, if I could see them again after all these years. For the first time in months, I do not feel the chokehold of the Empire around my throat.

I watch Araj give the final order to the Scholars to move out. Their relief is palpable. Despite Elias's assurances that no spirits would trouble us, the Forest of Dusk weighed heavier and heavier upon us the longer we spent within it. *Leave,* it seemed to hiss at us. *You don't belong here.*

Araj finds me beside the once-abandoned cabin I've reclaimed for Darin, myself, and Afya, a few hundred yards from the border of the Forest.

'Are you sure you don't wish to join us? I hear Adisa has healers that even the Empire cannot match.'

'Another month in the cold would do him in.' I nod to the cabin, sparkling clean within and glowing with the heat of a roaring fire. 'He needs rest and warmth. If he is still not well in a few weeks, I will find a healer to come to me.' I do not tell Araj my deepest secret fear: that I do not think Darin will wake up. That I think the blow was too much after all he had already suffered.

That I worry my brother is gone forever.

'I am in your debt, Laia of Serra.' Araj looks out at the Scholars trickling to a road about a quarter mile distant. Four hundred and twelve, in the end. So few. 'I hope I will see you in Adisa one day soon, with your brother at your side. Your people have need of someone like you.'

He takes his leave and calls to Tas, who bids goodbye to Elias. A month of food, baths, and clean – if too large – clothes has done wonders for the child. But he's been pensive since killing the Warden. I've heard him moaning and crying out in his sleep. The old man haunts Tas still.

I watch as Elias offers Tas one of the Serric steel blades he stole off a Kauf guard.

Tas throws his arms around Elias's neck, whispering something that makes him grin, and scampers off to join the rest of the Scholars.

As the last of the group moves out, Afya emerges from the cabin. She too is dressed for travel.

'I've already spent too long away from my Tribe,' the *Zaldara* says. 'Skies know what Gibran's been up to in my absence. Probably has a half dozen girls with child by now. I'll be paying bribes to silence their angry parents until I'm broke.'

'Something tells me Gibran is fine.' I smile at her. 'Did you say goodbye to Elias?'

She nods. 'He's hiding something from me.' I look away. I know very well what Elias is hiding. He has confided only to me about his deal with the Soul Catcher. And if the others have noticed that he's gone most of the night and for long stretches during the day, they've not seen fit to mention it.

'Best be sure he's not hiding anything from you,' Afya continues. 'Bad way to get into bed with someone.'

'Skies, Afya,' I sputter, looking behind me and hoping Elias hasn't heard. Thankfully, he's disappeared back into the Forest. 'I'm not *getting into bed* with him, nor do I have *any* interest—'

'Don't bother, girl.' Afya rolls her eyes. 'It's embarrassing to listen to.' She considers me for a second and then gives me a hug – swift and surprisingly warm.

'Thank you, Afya,' I say into her braids. 'For everything.'

She releases me with an arched brow. 'Speak of my honor far and wide, Laia of Serra,' she says. 'You owe me that. And take care of that brother of yours.'

I look in through the cabin's windows at Darin. His dark blond hair is clean and cropped short, his face youthful and handsome again. I've carefully tended all of his wounds, and most are now nothing but scars.

But still, he has not stirred. Perhaps he never will.

A few hours after Afya and the Scholars have disappeared over the horizon, Elias emerges from the Forest. The cabin, so quiet now that everyone has left, suddenly feels less lonely.

He knocks before entering, bringing a burst of cold in with him. Beardless now, and with his hair cropped short and some of his weight back, he looks more like his old self.

Except his eyes. They are different. More thoughtful, perhaps.

The weight of the burden he has taken on still astounds me. Though he has explained to me multiple times – that he accepted it with a whole heart, wanted it, even – I still feel angry at the Soul Catcher. There must be *some* way out of this vow. Some way Elias can live a normal life, travel to the Southern Lands he's always spoken of with such fondness. Some way he can visit his Tribe and be reunited with Mamie Rila.

For now, the Forest holds to him tightly. When he does emerge from the trees, it is never for long. Sometimes the ghosts even follow him out. More than once, I've heard the low timbre of his voice murmuring words of comfort to a wounded soul. Every now and then, he leaves the Forest frowning, his mind on some troublesome spirit. I know he's struggled with one in particular. I think it's a girl, but he doesn't speak about her.

'Dead chicken for your thoughts?'

He holds up the limp animal, and I nod to the basin. 'Only if you pluck it.'

I slide up onto the counter beside him as he works. 'I miss Tas and Afya and Araj,' I say. 'It's so quiet without them.'

'Tas worships you,' Elias says with a grin. 'I think he's in love, actually.'

'Only because I told him stories and fed him,' I say. 'If only every boy were so easy to win over.' I do not mean for the comment to sound so pointed, and I bite my lip as soon as I say it. Elias lifts a dark eyebrow and gives me a fleeting glance of curiosity before looking back down at the half-plucked chicken.

'You know he and all the other Scholars are going to talk about you in Adisa. You're the girl who razed Blackcliff and liberated Kauf. Laia of Serra. The ember waiting to burn down the Empire.'

'It's not like I didn't have help,' I say. 'They'll talk about you too.' But Elias shakes his head.

'Not in the same way,' he says. 'Even if they do, I'm the outsider. You're the Lioness's daughter. I think your people will expect much of you, Laia. Just remember, you don't have to do everything they ask.'

I snort. 'If they knew about Kee – the Nightbringer, they might change their minds about me.'

'He fooled all of us, Laia.' Elias gives the chicken a particularly violent chop. 'And one day, he'll pay.'

'Maybe he already is paying.' I think of the ocean of sadness inside the Nightbringer, the faces of all those he loved and destroyed in his quest to reconstruct the Star.

'I trusted him with my heart, and my brother, and my – my body.' I have not spoken much with Elias about what happened between Keenan and me. We never had the privacy to do so. But now, I want to get it out. 'The part of him that wasn't manipulating me – that wasn't using the Resistance, or planning the Emperor's death, or helping the Commandant sabotage the Trials – that part of him loved me, Elias. And some part of me, at least, loved him back. His betrayal can't be without cost. He must feel it.'

Elias stares out the window at the swiftly darkening sky. 'True enough,' he says. 'From what Shaeva told me, the armlet wouldn't pass to him unless he loved you truly. The magic isn't one-sided.'

'So a jinn is in love with me. I far prefer the ten-year-old.' I put my hand to the place my armlet once was. Even now, weeks later, I feel the ache of its absence. 'What will happen now? The Nightbringer has the armlet. How many more pieces of the Star does he need? What if he finds them and sets his brethren free? What if—'

Elias puts a finger to my lips. Does he let it linger a little longer than it needs to?

'We'll figure it out,' he says. 'We'll find a way to stop him. But not today. Today, we eat chicken stew and tell stories of our friends. We talk about what you and Darin will do after he wakes up, and about how enraged my bat-crazy mother will be when she learns she didn't kill me. We'll laugh and complain about the cold and enjoy the warmth of this fire. Today, we celebrate the fact that we're still alive.'

*　　*　　*

Sometime in the middle of the night, the wooden floor of the cabin creaks. I bolt up from my chair by Darin's bed, where I've fallen asleep wrapped in Elias's old cloak. My brother slumbers on soundly, his face unchanged. I sigh, wondering for the thousandth time if he will ever come back to me.

'Sorry,' Elias whispers from behind me. 'I didn't mean to wake you. I was at the edges of the Forest. Saw the fire went out and thought I'd bring in more wood.'

I wipe the sleep from my eyes and yawn. 'What time is it?'

'A few hours before dawn.'

Through the window by my bed, the sky is dark and clear. A star shoots across the sky. Then two more.

'We could watch from outside,' Elias says. 'It will only go on for an hour or so.'

I pull on my cloak and join him in the doorway of the little cabin. He stands slightly apart from me, his hands in his pockets. Falling stars streak overhead every few minutes. I catch my breath each time.

'It happens every year.' Elias's eyes are fixed on the sky. 'You can't see it from Serra. Too much dust.'

I shiver in the cold night, and he eyes my cloak critically. 'We should get you a new one,' he says. 'That can't be warm enough.'

'You gave this to me. It's my lucky cloak. I'm not giving it up – ever.' I pull it closer and catch his eyes as I say it.

I think of Afya's teasing when she left, and I flush. But I meant what I said to her. Elias is bound to the Waiting Place now. He does not have time for anything else in his life. Even if he did, I'm wary about incurring the wrath of the Forest.

At least, that is what I have resigned myself to thinking until this moment. Elias tilts his head, and for a second, the longing in his eyes is written as clearly as if he'd spelled it out in the stars.

I should say something, though, skies, what do I say, with the heat rising in my face and my skin so alive beneath his gaze? He too looks uncertain, and the tension between is as heavy as a rain-filled sky.

Then his uncertainty vanishes, replaced by a raw, unfettered desire that sends my pulse into a frenzy. He steps toward me, backing me into the smooth, worn wood of the cabin. His breath goes as ragged as mine, and he brushes his fingers against my wrist, his warm hand trailing sparks up my arm, my neck, and across my lips.

He cups my face in both of his hands, waiting to see what I want, even as his pale eyes burn with need.

I grab the collar of his shirt and pull him to me, exulting at the feel of his lips against mine, at the *rightness* of finally giving in to each other. I think briefly of our kiss months ago in his room – frantic, born of desperation, desire, and confusion.

This is different – the fire hotter, his hands more certain, his lips less hurried. I slide my arms around his neck and rise to my toes, pressing my body against his. His rain-and-spice scent intoxicates me, and he deepens the kiss. When I run my teeth across his lower lip, savoring its lushness, he growls low in his throat.

Beyond us, deep in the Forest, something stirs. He inhales sharply and pulls away, lifting a hand to his head.

I look to the Forest. Even in the dark, I can see the treetops rustling. 'The spirits,' I say quietly. 'They don't like it?'

'Not in the least. Jealous, probably.' He tries to grin but only grimaces, his eyes pained.

I sigh and trace his mouth, letting my fingers drop to his chest and then his hand. I pull him toward the cabin. 'Let's not upset them.'

We tiptoe into the cabin and settle down beside the fire, arms entwined. At first, I am certain he will leave, called back to his task. But he doesn't, and I soon relax against him, my lids heavier and heavier as sleep beckons. I close my eyes, and I think I dream of clear skies and free air, Izzi's smile, Elias's laughter.

'Laia?' says a voice behind me.

My eyes fly open. *It is a dream, Laia. You are dreaming.* I must be. For I have wanted to hear that voice for months, since the day he screamed at me to run. I have heard that voice in my head, spurring me on during my weakest moments and giving me strength in my darkest.

Elias rises to his feet, joy etched onto his features. My legs don't seem to work, so he takes my hands to pull me standing.

I turn to look into my brother's eyes. For a long moment, all we can do is take in each other's faces.

'Look at you, little sister,' Darin finally whispers. His smile is the sun rising after the longest, darkest night. 'Look at you.'

ACKNOWLEDGMENTS

To Emberlings everywhere: the book bloggers who unlock worlds for readers, the artists who spent hours on drawings that bring Ember to life, the fans who laugh, yell, and cry with Laia, Elias, and Helene, and who pass their story on to others – none of this would exist without you. Thank you, thank you, with all my heart.

To Kashi – thank you for unconditional love, midnight grilled cheeses, ice cream runs, and endless encouragement. For making me laugh every day and for all the times you calmly took the helm while I wrote. You are the finest of dragon caretakers.

To my beloved boys – thank you for your patience with Mama when she was working. You make me brave. All of this is for you.

Immense thanks to my father, whose steady presence is a balm when everything else is topsy-turvy, and to my mother, who recently climbed a mountain of her own and still cheered as I climbed mine. You are the bravest person I know.

Mer and Boon, thank you for the calls, the conversations in British accents, the advice, the inappropriate jokes, and all the support you give without even realizing it.

Ben Schrank, thank you for seeing from the beginning what I hoped this book would be and having the wisdom and patience to help me get it right. I am so very lucky to have you as a publisher and friend.

Alexandra Machinist – your advice, gentle humor, and honesty kept me sane and on track. I don't know what I'd do without you.

Cathy Yardley – you pulled me out of the dark, listened, laughed with me, and said the words I needed to hear: 'You can do this.' Thank you.

My great appreciation to Jen Loja, who leads all of us with grace and whose belief in this series has been such a gift. Major thanks to the bad-asses at Razorbill: Marissa Grossman, Anthony Elder, Casey McIntyre, and Vivian Kirklin. Thank you to Felicia Frazier and the incomparable Penguin sales team; Emily Romero, Erin Berger, Rachel Lodi, Rachel Cone-Gorham, and the marketing team; Shanta Newlin, Lindsay Boggs, and the publicity team; and Carmela Iaria, Alexis Watts, Venessa Carson, and the school and library team. I have no words for how fantastic you all are.

Renée Ahdieh, soul sister and fellow lover of 7s, bless you for the laughter, love, sob sessions, and the things I have no name for, all of which make you you. Adam Silvera, the trenches were less lonely because we were in them together – thank you for everything. Nicola Yoon – my thoughtful friend, I am so grateful for you. Lauren DeStefano, thank you for the all-hours chats, cat pictures, advice, and encouragement.

Much appreciation to Heelah S. for her wonderful sense of humor, Armo and Maani for their cuteness, and Auntie and Uncle for their unflagging support and belief in me.

Thank you to Abigail Wen (one day, we'll have our Sundays), Kathleen Miller, Stacey Lee, Kelly Loy Gilbert, Tala Abbasi, Marie Lu (we did it!), Margaret Stohl, Angela Mann, Roxane Edouard, Stephanie Koven, Josie Freedman, Rich Green, Kate Frentzel, Phyllis DeBlanche, Shari Beck, and Jonathan Roberts. A great big thank-you to all my foreign publishers, cover artists, editors, and translators for the incredible work you do.

Music is my home and that was made clear in the writing of this book. All my admiration to Lupe Fiasco for 'Prisoner 1 & 2',

Sia and The Weeknd for 'Elastic Heart,' Bring Me the Horizon for 'Sleepwalking,' George Ezra for 'Did You Hear the Rain?,' Julian Casablancas + the Voidz for 'Where No Eagles Fly,' Misterwives for 'Vagabond,' and M83 for 'Wait.' This book would not be what it is without these songs.

Final thanks to the one who is First and Last. I drifted this time. But you know my heart, and you know I'll return.

Turn over for an extract from book three of
the Ember Quartet:

A

REAPER

AT THE

GATES

CHAPTER ONE

The Nightbringer

You love too much, my king.

My queen spoke the words often across the centuries we spent together. At first, with a smile. But in later years, with a furrowed brow. Her gaze settled on our children as they tore about the palace, their bodies flickering from flame to flesh, tiny cyclones of impossible beauty.

"I fear for you, *Meherya*." Her voice trembled. "I fear what you will do if harm comes to those whom you love."

"No harm shall befall you. I vow it."

I spoke with the passion and folly of youth, though I was not, of course, young. Even then. That day, the breezes off the river ruffled her midnight hair and sunlight poured like liquid gold through the sheer curtains of the windows. It lit our children umber as they trailed scorch marks and laughter across the stone floor.

Her fears held her captive. I reached for her hands. "I would destroy any who dared hurt you," I said.

"*Meherya*, no." I have wondered in the years since then if she already feared what I would become. "Swear you would never. You are our *Meherya*. Your heart is made to love. To give. Not to take. That is why you are king of the jinn. Swear it."

I swore two vows that day: to protect, always. To love, always.

Within a year, I had broken both.

«»«

The Star hangs from the wall of the cavern far from human eyes. It is a four-pointed diamond, with a narrow gap at its apex. Thin striations spiderweb across it, a reminder of the day the Scholars shattered it after imprisoning my people. The metal gleams with impatience, potent as the glare of a jungle beast closing in on prey. Such vast power within this weapon—enough to destroy an ancient city, an ancient people. Enough to imprison the jinn for a thousand years.

Enough to set them free.

As if sensing the armlet clinging to my wrist, the Star rattles, yearning toward the missing piece. A wrench shudders through me as I offer the armlet up, and it oozes away like a silver eel to join with the Star. The gap shrinks.

The four points of the Star flare, lighting the far reaches of the speckled granite cavern, eliciting a wave of angry hisses from the creatures around me. Then the glow fades, leaving only pallid moonlight. Ghuls swish at my ankles. *Master. Master.*

Beyond them, the Wraith Lord awaits my orders, along with the efrit kings and queens—of wind and sea, sand and cave, air and snow.

As they watch, silent and wary, I consider the parchment in my hands. It is as unobtrusive as sand. The words within are not.

At my summons, the Wraith Lord approaches. He submits reluctantly, cowed by my magic, straining always to be free of me. But I have need of him yet. The wraiths are disparate scraps of lost souls, joined by ancient sorcery and undetectable when they wish to be. Even by the Empire's famed Masks.

As I offer him the parchment, I hear her. My queen's voice is a whisper, gentle as a candle on a chill night. *Once you do this, you can never come back. All hope for you is lost,* Meherya. *Consider.*

I do as she asks. I consider.

Then I remember she is dead and gone and has been for a millennium. Her presence is a delusion. Her voice is my weakness. I proffer the scroll to the Wraith Lord.

"See that it finds Blood Shrike Helene Aquilla," I tell him. "And no other." He bows, and the efrits sail forward. I order the efrits of air away; I have a separate task for them. The rest kneel.

"Long ago, you gave the Scholars knowledge that led to the destruction of my people and the fey world." A jolt of memory ripples through their ranks. "I offer you redemption. Go to our new allies in the south. Help them understand what they can call forth from the dark places. The Grain Moon will rise six months hence. See it done well before then. And you"—the ghuls press close—"glut yourselves. Do not fail me."

When they have all left me, I contemplate the Star and think of the treacherous jinn girl who helped bring it into being. Perhaps to a human, the weapon would shine with promise.

I feel only hatred.

A face drifts to the forefront of my mind. Laia of Serra. I recall the heat of her skin beneath my hands, how her wrists crossed behind my neck. The way she closed her eyes and the golden hollow of her throat. She felt like the threshold of my old home when the rushes were fresh-changed. She felt safe.

You loved her, my queen says. *And then you hurt her.*

My betrayal of the Scholar girl should not linger. I deceived hundreds before her.

Yet unease grips me. Something inexplicable occurred after Laia of Serra gifted me her armlet—after she realized that the boy she called Keenan was naught but a fabrication. Like all humans, she glimpsed in my eyes the darkest moments of her life. But when I looked into her soul, something—*someone*—peered back: my queen, gazing at me across the centuries.

I saw her horror. Her sadness at what I had become. I saw her pain at what our children and our people suffered at the hands of the Scholars.

I think of my queen with every betrayal. Going back a thousand years, to each human found, manipulated, and loved until they freely gave me their piece of the Star with love in their hearts. Again and again and again.

But never had I seen her in the gaze of another. Never had I felt the sharp blade of her disappointment so keenly.

Once more. Only once more.

My queen speaks. *Do not do this. Please.*

I crush her voice. I crush her memory. I think I will not hear her again.